Readers love ARIEL TACHNA's *Partnership in Blood* novels

"I absolutely love this series."

—Romance Junkies

"I've thoroughly enjoyed the premise for these books and the characters, and recommend them to any reader who enjoys paranormal fantasy; especially those involving vampires, wizards and magic."

— Literary Nymphs Reviews

"...an amazingly well written series that I know that paranormal romantics will enjoy."

—Night Owl Reviews

"[Reparation in Blood] is action packed and full of fascinating and amazing characters. A worthwhile read and fitting end to the series."

—Bitten by Books

"This series is definitely for anyone looking for a new twist on Vampires, and who likes a bit of angst and a bit of adventure mixed into their romance."

—Dark Diva Reviews

"Ariel Tachna has created a truly original version of the vampire archetype..."

—Steve Williams, Suite 101

http://www.dreamspinnerpress.com

By Ariel Tachna

All For One (with Nicki Bennett)
Best Ideas
Château d'Eternité
Checkmate (with Nicki Bennett)
Fallout
Her Two Dads
Highland Lover
In Search of Fireworks
The Inventor's Companion
The Matelot
Music of the Heart
Once in a Lifetime
Out of the Fire
Overdrive
The Path
Rediscovery
Revelations in the Dark
Riding Double (Dreamspinner Anthology)
Rose Among the Ruins
Seducing C.C.
Stolen Moments
A Summer Place
Sutcliffe Cove (with Madeleine Urban)
Testament to Love
Under the Skin (with Nicki Bennett)
Why Nileas Loved the Sea

The Exploring Limits Series (with Nicki Bennett)
Exploring Limits • Stretching Limits • Refining Limits
Breaking Limits • Transcending Limits • No Limits

Games Lovers Play
Amorous Liaison • Best Behavior • Ride 'em Cowboy

Hot Cargo
Hot Cargo (with Nicki Bennett) • Something About Harry (with Nicki Bennett)
Healing in His Wings

Lang Downs
Inherit the Sky • Chase the Stars • Outlast the Night • Conquer the Flames

Partnership in Blood
Alliance in Blood • Covenant in Blood • Conflict in Blood • Reparation in Blood
Perilous Partnership • Reluctant Partnerships • Lycan Partnership • Partnership Reborn

Available at Dreamspinner Press
http://www.dreamspinnerpress.com

Mark,
Wonderful to meet you!
The end is worth the adventure.
Ariel Tachna
RT 2016

Conflict in Blood

ARIEL TACHNA

Partnership in Blood:
Volume Three

Dreamspinner Press

Published by
DREAMSPINNER PRESS

5032 Capital Circle SW, Suite 2, PMB# 279, Tallahassee, FL 32305-7886 USA
http://www.dreamspinnerpress.com/

ISBN: 978-1-63216-664-7
Digital ISBN: 978-1-63216-665-4
Library of Congress Control Number: 2014950195
Second Edition October 2014
First Edition published by Dreamspinner Press, May 2009.

Printed in the United States of America
∞
This paper meets the requirements of
ANSI/NISO Z39.48-1992 (Permanence of Paper).

To my adopted sisters, Nancy, Holly, Connie,
Cat, Carol, Madeleine, Gwen, and Julianne,
who read and reread and edit and encourage.
Without you, this dream
would never have come to pass.

Chapter 1

"WHAT DOES he think to gain from this… farce?" Pascal Serrier spat, switching off the television in disgust. Chavinier's announcement of an alliance between the Milice wizards and the Parisian vampires turned his stomach, the thought of such creatures having any say in the ruling of the country more than he could stand. It was one more reason to overthrow the current government and replace it with one run by wizards—his wizards—who understood the value of magic and the appropriate place for such lesser beings. "He has to know this alliance won't avail him. What can a vampire do against our spells? And even if they can resist some of them, we can simply move our plans to daytime. Chavinier won't mess with the natural order enough to confuse night and day, if he's even powerful enough, which I doubt. He's put his reputation on the line for nothing."

"Then there's more to this than he's telling," Eric Simonet disagreed. "He might be a bleeding heart, but he wouldn't make claims about the war that he couldn't carry through on. He's not stupid. He knows what that would do to morale and to his reputation."

"So what's the angle?" Serrier demanded. "What can he gain from this?"

"If the vampires cover the night patrols, he can move more wizards to fight during the day," Simon Aguiraud pointed out.

"But that's fewer wizards to counter us if we attack at night," Simonet disagreed. "He spoke the truth when he mentioned the turning tides, a fact he laid firmly at the feet of the vampires. They have to have a weakness, though. Joëlle managed to defeat them before she was killed."

"Sunlight and fire," Serrier repeated slowly. "That's what Bellaiche said at the press conference. Sunlight and fire."

"What are you thinking?"

"A few minutes before dawn," Serrier declared. "If we engage a patrol just before dawn, they'll lose their numbers as the sun comes up, either to the vampires seeking shelter or to the sunlight itself."

"Is it instantaneous, though?"

"I don't know," Serrier admitted, "but our resident bloodsucker will. And he'll tell me the truth or I'll stop providing victims for him. Send Claude to get him."

Eric frowned, but did as the dark wizard asked. The very idea of the vampire made him uncomfortable, though he took pains not to show it. "What about the woman?"

"What about her?" Serrier demanded.

"You don't need her anymore, do you?"

Serrier shrugged. "You never know when she might prove useful. Even if she can't tell us what we need to know, I'm sure Claude would enjoy playing with her. It's been a while since I've given him a new toy."

Eric hid a flinch at the thought of the twisted wizard getting his hands on the slender woman he had helped bring in at Serrier's command. He had never been terribly hopeful where her fate was concerned, but he had allowed himself to believe Serrier would at least kill her mercifully once she had told them all she knew. He might have thrown his lot in with Serrier and his wizards after his wife was killed, but some of their methods made him question his judgment at times. He had burned his bridges, though, so he would just have to find other ways to preserve his humanity. His misdirection over a mercy killing had worked once. He doubted Claude—or Serrier—would buy it a second time.

"Sunlight and fire," Serrier repeated musingly. "We can't force the sun to rise early, but there are spells for fire. We'll need to work on refining those spells for battle. Simon?"

"I'm on it," Aguiraud declared, standing and heading toward the door. "The vampires will regret revealing their weakness."

As soon as he was gone, Serrier turned back to Eric. "Now more than ever, we need to know what's going on in Chavinier's head," he told his lieutenant. "Have you given any more thought to returning to him as my eyes and ears?"

"I have," Eric admitted, "and it's an appealing thought, being able to use his naïveté to undermine him, but I don't think I could convince him. I don't think I could pretend to work with my wife's murderer again, even to bring him down. And with that anger still in my heart and my magic, I don't think he'll take me back. You'd do better to find someone else, someone with less of a history with the Milice."

"Suggestions?" Serrier asked curiously.

"Monique," Eric replied after a moment's thought. "She's ruthless enough to do what needs to be done, but she can put on a pretty enough face that she should pass muster."

"YOU CAN never ask for anything simple, can you, General Chavinier?" Denise Cadoret demanded, looking at the draft of the law in front of her. "Equal rights for vampires under the constitution is no small matter in itself, and now you ask us to engage the responsibility of the full government on this issue?"

"As you are well aware, madame le ministre," Marcel said, suppressing a glare at the Ministre de la Justice, "the matter is of some urgency."

"Why?" madame Cadoret demanded. "For better or worse, the situation has existed for as long as there's been a government to grant rights to anyone. Why do we have to push this through now? I'm not saying we shouldn't grant them equal rights. I just don't understand why this can't go through a normal legislative process. You're asking us to do something incredibly controversial and risk the entire government being dissolved if the Assemblée decides to vote down your proposal."

"Because it's the right thing to do," André Guy, the Secrétaire des Droits de l'Homme, interrupted. "The vampires are risking life and limb to protect us. The least we can do is take a risk for them."

"Because since they started risking life and limb to protect us," Marcel added, "we've only lost one battle with Serrier's rebels. The stalemate is breaking and the tide is turning in our favor."

"That's all well and good," the Ministre de l'Economie, des Finances, et de l'Emploi protested before realizing how sarcastic he sounded. He turned to the chef de la Cour, sitting at Chavinier's right, looking quite imposing. "I mean that. It's a wonderful thing that we're making progress against the rebels, but creating an unknown number of new citizens all at once... it's an administrative nightmare. There are jobs to consider, health care, social security...."

"Yes, there are thousands of us," Jean agreed, "but we will not strain the system nearly as much as you imagine. We don't need health care. We only need to feed, something we manage quite well on our own. We don't age or grow infirm, so social security isn't necessary. The chefs des Cours each know their own cities. They could easily provide a list to the local préfecture of vampires there, in order to get them identity papers. We have all found ways to provide ourselves with the money we need for lodgings or else we don't survive past the dawn so housing isn't a problem."

"It isn't just those agencies who are unprepared for this," madame Cadoret countered. "Vampires have never been governed by our laws, but if we grant them legal protection, the courts will have to deal with them."

"We have not recognized mortal law because it does not recognize us," Jean acknowledged, "but that does not make us ungovernable. We have had our own laws, our own courts, and our own justice for far longer than this Republic has existed."

"All the more reason to take this slowly," madame Cadoret insisted. "We know nothing of your laws and how they would mesh with ours. This is asking for nothing but trouble." Seeing the vampire's scowl, she continued, "I'm not saying we should keep the law from going to the Assemblée. I just don't think General Chavinier's timeline is a reasonable one."

"Let me see if I can't put it in perspective for you," Jean bit out coldly. "My people and I have volunteered to help in this war to sustain a government that, at the moment, doesn't even acknowledge our right to exist, much less our right to anything else. Fortunately for you, we realize that more is at stake than simply which shortsighted mortals sit in these chairs. The one condition we placed on our assistance was this law."

"We've barely recovered from one imbalance in the elemental magic," Marcel spoke up. "Having the vampires on our side allows us to divert wizards to deal with that, both the clean up and the problem itself. You don't really want to explain to the French people why your recalcitrance caused the alliance to fail, the Milice to lose the war, and the Republic to fall, do you, madame le ministre?"

"WHAT A bitch," Jean muttered when Marcel had transported them back to his office from the Conseil des Ministres.

"She didn't get where she is by being nice," Marcel agreed, "but she isn't reactionary, just cautious. Once the Premier Ministre makes his decision, she'll support it and make sure it's the best law possible. We just have to wait now on monsieur Pequignot's decision."

Jean hesitated a moment and then gambled. "You know at this point we won't walk away even if he doesn't invoke l'alinéa 49-3, right? For better or worse, we're committed now."

"I know," Marcel replied, having already guessed that the vampires would not withdraw if the government did not support the up or down vote on the proposed equality legislation, "and more than likely, so does the Premier Ministre. By coming out publicly on our side, you've made yourselves as much targets for Serrier as the Milice wizards. You may want to warn those not directly involved to take extra care now. If Serrier's wizards find your people, they won't ask whether their victims are involved in the alliance or not. They'll just attack, and while the *Abbatoire* doesn't work on vampires, other spells certainly will. I know why you told the press that sunlight and fire were all vampires have to fear, and I know sunlight isn't an issue for those vampires with partners, but it was still a huge risk because it will narrow down the spells Serrier has his people direct at you."

"I've fought at the side of the wizards," Jean pointed out. "I've watched them neutralize spells before they can do any damage. They'll just have to neutralize those spells instead. And the bond that seems to be forming between partners will certainly give them plenty of motivation." He did not mention the more intimate dimension that many of the partnerships now encompassed, not wanting that issue to influence the old general's championing of the vampires. Nonetheless, he could not keep from remembering the intimate sounds he and Raymond had overheard as they checked the balance of the elemental magic while dealing with the aftermath of the magic-fuelled typhoon in La Réunion.

"They'll get that chance soon enough," Marcel informed him sadly. "We need Thierry in here, and probably Alain as well. Our young spy has sent us some information that we can't afford to ignore. The orders will be mine, but Thierry is far better at strategy than this old man."

Jean gritted his teeth against his instinctive reaction to the blond wizard's partner, stemming from his belief that the other vampire had stolen his lover, his potential Avoué, out from beneath his very nose five centuries ago, mere days after his arrival in Paris. Their recent conversation on the subject notwithstanding, he did not like Sebastien and was not entirely sure he trusted him. Unfortunately, Marcel trusted his wizard, which meant Jean had little choice but to tolerate the other vampire. He smiled at Orlando as he came in and kept the expression in place as he turned to face Sebastien, who answered with an amicable nod. Jean wanted to shake his head at the constant maneuvering, even putative allies playing le jeu des Cours at every turn. The game was too ingrained, though, to stop, even for this. He glanced again at Orlando and Alain, trying to decide if they had mended matters between them. His young friend certainly seemed outwardly calmer than the last time they had talked. He would watch and wait, but if he saw anything that concerned him, he would speak to the wizard before the day was over. He had been Orlando's protector too long to stop looking out for the youngling now. Instead, he leaned back against the wall, ready to listen to what Marcel had to say and the discussion that came out of it.

"What's going on?" Alain asked after they were all seated. He could feel the elder vampire's eyes on his back, but he did not know how to reassure him, particularly not in this forum. If Marcel had called them together, something was happening, and the war came first. It had to.

"Our young spy sent us some information this morning," Marcel told them, "that I think bears considering. According to him, Serrier has decided to use Samhain to demonstrate his continuing power. He has to know we were hoping to use the holy day to stabilize the elemental magic and so wouldn't be as able to counter his plans."

"That's no surprise," Thierry agreed, "although the news of the alliance may change his methods somewhat."

"The message arrived after the announcement was made," Marcel replied, "but you're right that he could still change his mind. For the moment, though, he intends to bring down the Tour Eiffel at noon."

"That alone suggests he's taken the alliance into consideration," Alain observed. "Historically, he's preferred to attack under cover of darkness rather than during the daylight hours."

"Yes, if the vampires were still limited by the cycle of the sun, we would have to choose between meeting him in battle to preserve one of our city's landmarks—not to mention the lives that would be lost in such an attack—and balancing the elemental magic," Marcel affirmed. "Fortunately, our allies don't suffer such limitations anymore."

"With the right assistance," Jean acknowledged immediately, painfully aware as he looked around the room of the man who was not there. Raymond's absence nagged at him like a sore tooth, not so distracting that he could not function but always there in the back of his mind.

"Did Raymond say when he thought he'd be back?" Marcel asked suddenly, turning to Jean. "His expertise would be invaluable."

"We can do it without him," Thierry grumbled.

"Yes, we can," Marcel agreed, "but that doesn't mean we should if he's here. None of us have studied the elemental powers to the extent he has, and why not use every resource at our disposal?"

Jean bristled a little, hearing his partner referred to so lightly, but he had dealt with vampires with attitudes like Thierry's before and knew that Marcel's approach would be the most effective. It still bothered him to hear Raymond's abilities denigrated. "How many wizards will be required to make the balancing ritual a success?"

"Raymond for his finesse, and Thierry has volunteered as well since he often helped in such matters before the war," Marcel enumerated. "We will ask for another fifty volunteers to lend their strength. It is not a dangerous ritual, but it is a demanding one. Most of the wizards involved will need to rest for several days afterwards. I will only take two volunteers from any patrol so we don't gut our resources any more than necessary."

"I'll lead the patrol at the Tour Eiffel," Alain volunteered. "If Thierry can't be there to coordinate, I'm the next best one to send."

At his side, Orlando hid a frown. He and Alain were only beginning to find their feet again after their fight, a stupid misunderstanding about Orlando's limits and Alain's subsequent fear that Orlando had lost all trust in him, and his lover was volunteering to walk into what could be a horrendous battle. He understood that the war was necessary and even understood Alain's participation, but his protective instincts kicked into overdrive at the thought of anything threatening his Avoué. He would stay at Alain's side the entire time, but he knew there was only so much he could do to protect his wizard—particularly if Serrier's wizards started tailoring spells to inflict damage on the vampires, a possibility he and Alain had discussed since the announcement of the alliance.

"Take my patrol with you at least, and maybe another one as well," Thierry advised. "Serrier wants this to be a victory. He isn't going to send just a few wizards. We'll be lucky if he doesn't send everyone he's got."

"And if the attack there is a diversion?" Jean asked. "That's what a vampire would do—let it be known he intended one thing while secretly planning another. I'm not saying we should ignore the threat, but it seems awfully straightforward for a man of Serrier's twisted darkness."

"He's got a point," Thierry admitted. "The boy didn't seem highly placed. This could be a trap, either for him or for us."

"It could be," Marcel agreed slowly, "but young Dominique is not my only source of information. *Je ne suis pas né de la dernière pluie*, as they say. I have enough corroboration to believe the threat is a credible one. The Tour Eiffel is hardly a strategic location, but it is a symbolic one. If they succeed in toppling it, they'll have dealt a serious blow to the Milice's and the government's image."

"Then we'll just have to make sure they don't bring it down," Thierry declared, voice hard.

Chapter 2

RAYMOND STUMBLED a little as he appeared at Milice headquarters, just as the sun was rising. The displacement from La Réunion had exhausted him, but he had not wanted to delay his return any longer. He was painfully aware of the time that had passed since Jean's departure, and the need to be at his partner's side again had grown nigh irresistible. Knowing it was magically inspired did nothing to mitigate the effect. He would check in with Marcel and give his report, and then he would find his partner and insist the vampire feed properly again. Raymond's heart lurched jealously at the thought that Jean might have resorted to drinking someone else's blood during his absence. He had pushed himself to the wall trying to stabilize the situation on the island enough to leave it in the hands of Lt. Raynaud de Lage and her partner, acutely cognizant that with each passing hour, the nourishment and protection his blood had provided to Jean would be wearing off. He had seen news clips of Jean and Marcel announcing the alliance two days before, drinking in the sight of his partner's understated elegance, and had finally admitted to himself that magically inspired or not, he was falling for the vampire. He would not act on it except to encourage Jean to feed as much and as often as he needed to. One small part of his mind feared to give in completely to the influence of the elemental magic, yet the realization was there now, to the depths of his being.

Wending his way through the quiet corridors, he leaned heavily on the wall as he knocked on the door to Marcel's office.

"Raymond?"

The wizard pushed away from the wall at the sound of his name, not wanting to show any weakness before the others, who barely tolerated his presence. It took a moment for him to realize who had spoken. "What are you still doing here, Jean?" he asked. "The sun's come up, and I'm sure my magic has worn off."

"It did," Jean agreed, "yesterday midafternoon. I came in last night after dark to help with a night patrol and stayed to talk with Marcel about the progress with the legislation. We got caught up and didn't watch the time until he had to leave for a meeting—after sunrise. I was going down to your office to rest since it has no windows. What are you doing here?"

"I came to let Marcel know I was back, and to see if he knew where you were," Raymond explained. "He's not here, but I've found you at least. You need to feed."

Jean chuckled. "It can wait until nightfall. You're exhausted. Go home and get some rest."

Slumping against the wall, Raymond smiled tiredly. "I don't think I can stay awake long enough to take the Métro, and I know I don't have the energy to get there magically. I'll just find a quiet corner here and crash after you've fed."

The vampire chef frowned, slipping his arm around his partner's waist and turning them toward his office. If he thrilled silently at the feeling of the wizard walking so close, he sublimated it for the moment beneath his concern at his partner's state. "You'll do no such thing. We'll go back to your office and you can transfigure a bed for yourself. I can read while you sleep—you have more than enough books in your office and I should learn as much as I can now that we're allies—and when you wake up, I'll feed and we'll decide what needs to be done then. Is there anything you need to tell Marcel that can't wait until you've slept for at least a few hours? You're dead on your feet."

"No, it can wait," Raymond mumbled as they crossed the threshold into his office. "I just wanted to let him know I was back."

"I'll make sure he's aware of it," Jean promised. "Make yourself a bed and get some rest."

Raymond nodded and muttered a transformation spell, the desk becoming a narrow cot. If he weren't so exhausted, he'd go home and sleep in his own bed, but even the simple spell had taken almost all his remaining strength. "A real bed," Jean scolded. "You can hardly rest well on that."

Raymond summoned a smile and spoke again, the cot disappearing and a small but proper bed taking its place. Exhausted, the two spells having used up what little energy he had left, he collapsed onto the soft mattress, asleep almost before his head hit the pillow. Jean shook his head as he lifted Raymond's feet onto the bed and covered him with the light blanket. The room felt comfortable to him, but he had been around enough mortals to realize that they preferred a warmer ambiance than he found necessary. His partner was already worn out. The last thing he wanted was for Raymond to get sick as well.

Settling down in the desk chair, Jean picked up a book on wizarding history. He imagined it would be dry reading, but monsieur Lombard, his mentor and the oldest vampire in Pars, had mentioned vampires being involved with wizards once before, and that had the chef curious. He wanted to see if he could find any references to vampires fighting alongside wizards. If he could, he might be able to figure out how to keep his people from being decimated again as monsieur Lombard had said they were before. Certainly, the existence of the partnerships would help this time—protecting paired vampires from sun exposure and giving the wizards someone specific to protect—but not every vampire had a partner, and now that Serrier knew about the alliance, the dark wizards would surely change the spells they were using to something more detrimental to the undead.

He managed to skim the first two chapters before his thoughts strayed from the material to the man sleeping nearby. He had not expected to miss Raymond. His blood and the protection it afforded him, yes, but not the man himself. More than once, though, in the past days, he had found himself wanting to share a thought with the wizard or wondering what Raymond's opinion on a subject would be. When he stopped to think about it, he had trouble believing he had not even known the wizard two weeks ago, but in that short time, proximity—and the magical connection between them—had rendered Raymond a part of his existence. He could still function without his partner at his side, but it felt as if he was missing something, like his senses were dulled. Now that Raymond was back in Paris again, everything had come back into focus as if a veil had been lifted from his eyes. He told himself such a reaction was ridiculous, but it did not lessen the feeling.

Setting aside the book, he crossed to the bed and perched on the edge, staring down intently at the dark-haired wizard. Raymond's eyes were closed, making it impossible to see the irises, but Jean could imagine them easily enough. Imagine them opening softly, the thin lips parting in a welcoming smile as Raymond reached up….

Jean's hand was reaching out to stroke Raymond's face before he could stop himself, the unexpected train of thought catching him off guard. His hand hovered an inch above his partner's short-cropped hair as he warred with himself, the knowledge that their bond was magically inspired fighting the compulsive desire to claim the handsome wizard as his own. He had not fed since before he left La Réunion. He should have been famished, barely able to control his need to hunt after so long. Forty-eight hours, he could handle with ease. Seventy-two hours was reasonable. But he had passed ninety hours now and his hunger should have been debilitating. He could certainly feel the need for blood, but not as acutely as he expected. Knowing Raymond would offer as soon as he awoke—he had offered before he slept, but that would have been an abuse of trust at the very least—he should have had to hold himself back through sheer force of will. Instead, he sat patiently at his partner's side, waiting for Raymond to wake.

Raymond's eyes fluttered open slowly as if summoned by Jean's intent gaze. He blinked a couple of times, not sure he believed what he saw. Each time he slept while he and Jean were apart, he dreamed of waking to find his partner there. Each time, it had been only a dream. "Am I still dreaming?" he asked groggily.

Jean shook his head. "No, this is real."

"I wasn't sure," Raymond explained, the uncensored words slipping out in his half-awake state. "I dreamed…," he trailed off as he realized what he had been about to reveal. Shaking his head to clear it, he offered Jean his arm. "You should feed."

Jean clasped Raymond's hand in his but did not immediately lift it to his mouth. His gaze was fixed on the pulse pounding in his partner's neck. He wanted to close his lips over that spot, sink his teeth into that portion of flesh, but to do so uninvited would surely shatter the détente that currently reigned between them. Not even for the intimate knowledge such a vampire's kiss would bring would Jean threaten that peace. Something in his expression must have given away his desire, because Raymond met his eyes boldly and then slowly, ever so slowly, tilted his head back. A millennium of experience as a vampire, a thousand years of sustaining himself on the lifeblood of others, had not prepared Jean for this moment. There should have been nothing special, nothing unusual about the offer Raymond made with such careful deliberation. Mortals had offered themselves knowingly and unknowingly to Jean more times than he could count in the years since he had been turned. Many of them had offered their necks. Perhaps it was knowing how hesitant—Jean suppressed a chuckle; *revolted* was the better word—Raymond had been the first time that made his new willingness so tempting. Perhaps it was the length of time since he had last fed that influenced his hunger now. Perhaps it was the magical bonds between them driving his possessive instincts. Whatever it was, his hand trembled as he braced himself to lean over his partner and feed from the offered vein.

The sensation of a body hovering over his, nearly brushing, sent tremors down Raymond's back. He fought the twin urges to fight or to flee as the feeling of being trapped grew in him. Then Jean's lips brushed his neck and all desire to move away left him. Instead, his head dropped farther back, giving the vampire better access to the skin of his neck.

Jean froze, the impulse growing to pinch himself in reassurance, as he had assured Raymond, that this was no dream. He breathed deeply, fighting for the control that had been so easy moments ago, before Raymond offered himself so willingly. Jean's senses were wreathed suddenly in the scents of sand and sweat and sandalwood. Conscientiously, he prepared his partner's throat, the pounding pulse beckoning urgently. He could taste the salt on the wizard's skin, but whether it came from his sweat or from the ocean, he could not tell. It mattered little either way, except to entice Jean further. The hiss and rasp of Raymond's breath feathered his hair, blowing the longish strands off his face as one of the wizard's hands lifted slowly to cradle his skull.

Jean cracked. His fangs dropped so quickly it was almost painful, his teeth closing over the patch of skin without conscious direction. He drove them deep into Raymond's neck, taking the offered nourishment and reveling in the implied intimacy.

The pain was as real as Raymond had always feared, but it disappeared as quickly as it came. It was replaced by a sense of connection far more immediate than what he felt each time Jean fed from his wrist. His eyes closed as the vampire's lips moved over his skin, sucking deeply. All the hunger Jean should have felt the past two days suddenly overtook him. Raymond's blood was rich and hot, a banquet of flavors as complex as the man himself. A part of Jean's mind catalogued the flavors for subsequent examination, but he was too caught up in the intense, intimate joining, to decorticate them now. Before long, one taste overpowered the rest. Distrustful of his senses given how opposed to the idea Raymond had been on the island, Jean did nothing to further the lust he could perceive, but he knew that emotion's signature far too well to misinterpret or misidentify it. It would be hard enough on his partner to deal with the suddenly changed landscape between them without bringing up the issues raised by the magical bond. Instead, Jean focused on keeping his own reactions under control, on doing nothing that would exacerbate the problems in their relationship. He needed to feed almost desperately, having stretched his reserves as far as he felt safe doing, but he did not want his voraciousness to scare Raymond. All other considerations aside, for him to participate effectively in the alliance, he needed the protection only his partner's blood could provide.

Jean's body pressed into Raymond's the way a lover's would, the arrangement bringing to mind sweaty dreams of tangled limbs and damp, fragrant skin. Raymond shivered beneath the sudden wash of subconscious cravings, his sleeping mind having come to terms during their separation with what his waking self continued to reject. His hand tightened in Jean's hair, urging the vampire to take all he needed. He shifted restlessly on the bed as the emotions evoked by Jean's fangs grew in him. His other hand moved blindly on the sheets, seeking its mate, fingers twining with his partner's as the vampire continued to draw from him.

If it had been anyone else beneath his fangs, Jean would have taken that gesture as a sign to move beyond simple sustenance and on to even more enjoyable interactions. The rising lust he could taste in Raymond's blood only added to that impulse, but he had not risen to his position as chef de la Cour by giving in to his impulses. Raymond was not some stranger he had picked up in a goth club or paid for at Sang Froid. He was Jean's partner, his protection against sunlight, and his ally in this war. Even more than that, though, Jean had come to respect him over the past two weeks, seeing the depth of knowledge and character that hid beneath the handsome exterior and occasionally sullen attitude. And so he did not let his hands wander as they wished, keeping them instead firmly where they were, one held by Raymond's hand, the other braced beside his head to support his weight so he did not press too intimately against the wizard. The knowledge that he was making the right choice did nothing to offset the temptation Raymond presented, though, especially with lust rushing hard through his veins. He had already taken enough to sustain him even after his fast of several days, but he wanted to know the taste of Raymond's completion. He might never know the thrill of making love with the wizard beneath him, might never have anything more than this moment and moments like it. That thought was enough to keep him selfishly feeding. Just this once, he would show Raymond all the pleasure a vampire could offer and hope it was enough to bring the wizard back for more, not because it benefited the alliance but because it benefited them.

Raymond could not have said what changed, but he knew the moment it did. Jean's fangs penetrated no less deeply, no less urgently, but their interaction suddenly took on a new dimension. Suddenly, his enjoyment seemed the point of their actions. He wanted to shake his head, to tell Jean not to make this anything more than it was, but he no longer knew what "this" was. Jean had not gone for four days without feeding simply for the alliance. While they had agreed he would be discreet if he went elsewhere for sustenance, no one would have blamed him with Raymond not even on the same continent. Least of all, Raymond. Nor was Jean now squeezing his hand so carefully because of the alliance. Perhaps part of it was the bond created between them by the elemental magic—but although they understood it better now than they had before, the bond itself was not new, having formed the first time Jean fed from him. Then the vampire's tongue lapped across his skin just below where his fangs penetrated and Raymond lost all sense of rational thought. Jean's body did not move any closer to his, his hands stayed where they were, but Raymond had one last realization before the lust swamping his senses took complete control: Jean was making love to him.

With a shuddering sigh, Raymond climaxed, his eyes rolling back in his head, his back arching as his fingers tightened their grip on Jean's hair and hand. His emotions rioting, he collapsed back on the bed, trying to make sense of what had just happened. With Jean's tongue gently soothing the marks left by his fangs, though, Raymond found his usual concentration difficult to attain.

"Delicious."

That one word, murmured almost tenderly against his skin, broke the sensual spell that surrounded Raymond, leaving him squirming with embarrassment, flushing as the movement drew his attention to the spreading wet spot beneath the fabric of his trousers. With an annoyed grimace, he sat up, muttering a cleansing spell to erase the evidence of his indiscretion. The contentment he read on Jean's face only unnerved him further, and he took refuge, as he always did, in the distance provided by academic examinations. "From everything I've read, I didn't think vampires could go four days without feeding."

Jean suppressed a sigh at the change of subject, but went along with the diversion. After all, he, too, had been surprised by his ability to wait for Raymond's return. He would not have been able to wait much longer; four days was pushing the limits even for a vampire of his strength and experience. "We generally can't," he agreed. "Two days, maybe three, is usually the limit. I can't really explain what happened unless Orlando was right. He told me the first time he fed from Alain that one sip left him feeling as strong as if he'd drained another man dry. At the time, I didn't think anything of it. Then later, I attributed it to the Aveu de Sang, which will one day allow him to go far longer without feeding than the rest of us, but perhaps it's the magical bond again. The Aveu de Sang protects Alain from overfeeding. Orlando could gorge himself every day and still not drain his Avoué. The same isn't true—at least, it shouldn't be true—with the other pairings. Then again, nothing else has been as we expected it where these partnerships are concerned, so maybe the magic that allows your blood to protect me from sunlight also gives me greater latitude in how often I feed."

Raymond pondered his words. "That isn't something we could afford to test," he decided after a few minutes. "I don't know what happens to a vampire who doesn't get the blood he needs, but I don't want to weaken anyone by trying to stretch the limits."

"You could liken it to a car running out of gas," Jean explained. "If he gets blood quickly enough, it's not a problem and any blood will reawaken him. If he waits too long, though, the vampire would go into a sort of hibernation. The problem is the only way to wake that vampire back up is with the blood of his or her line."

"Line?" Raymond inquired.

"Vampires don't have families the way mortals do, but we do have an ancestry of sorts through the vampires that made each of us and the ones who made them. I keep the genealogy, but I haven't taken the time to look into it more than that. I think monsieur Lombard has, though, if you want more details. It's so rarely an issue because we simply feed when we're hungry. Only a vampire like Orlando, who can only feed from one person, or a vampire who's been locked away for some reason, would ever need to worry about such things."

Raymond smiled. "The thought of having the time to pursue that kind of interest again is incredibly appealing. I'll make sure to add it to my list of things to study when the war is over and we can return to our normal lives."

Jean froze for a moment before daring to ask, "And will you still be interested in vampires when this is over?"

Raymond looked away, uncomfortable with the intimacy of the moment, but honesty compelled him to answer. "I rarely lose interest in something once it's piqued my curiosity."

Chapter 3

"YOU CAN'T tell me you trust her," Thierry protested.

"Not blindly," Marcel assured him, "but that doesn't mean she isn't telling the truth."

"You don't find it convenient that she showed up two days before the Rite d'équilibrage and two days after you announced the alliance?" Alain challenged.

"I find it most convenient," Marcel agreed, "but again, that doesn't mean she isn't telling the truth. You found it unbelievable when Raymond defected from Serrier's ranks, too, if you remember, and we wouldn't be anywhere near where we are now if it weren't for his help."

Neither Alain nor Thierry appeared happy with Marcel's point, but they could hardly argue it. "So what do we do?" Alain asked. "Let her in, try to find her a partner, and risk the details getting back to Serrier?"

"I'm optimistic, not naïve," Marcel reminded him. "We can assign her to a night patrol and make it clear to the other operatives not to reveal the details of the alliance. She'll see the vampires fighting, even working with us, but she won't know how."

"There are ways to find out if she's telling the truth," Jean reminded the assembled team. "If Antonio or Blair or one of the other unpaired vampires bites her, we'll know if she's sincere or not."

"And if she's not, she'll know more than we want Serrier to find out about the inner workings of the alliance," Thierry pointed out.

"So we don't tell her why he's biting her," Jean suggested. "You could even use a spell on her like we did on Dominique Cornet at the Gare de Lyon."

"At which point she knows we don't trust her. If she's sincere, it won't matter, but if she isn't, she'll know we're hiding something from her. If someone is going to bite her to test her sincerity, you'll have to give her an explanation of some kind," Raymond said. "She's not going to simply hold out her wrist for no reason."

Jean chuckled. "No, I don't imagine she would, but until the alliance formed, we all hunted for our prey, and since fear leaves a bitter taste in the blood, most of us prefer to find willing donors. Antonio can be quite persuasive when he wants to be."

"Get him," Marcel directed. "We'll see if he's willing, and if he is, we'll introduce him to Monique."

When Antonio joined them a few minutes later, Marcel brought him up to speed. "We have a wizard applying for sanctuary," the general explained. "She claims she's left Serrier because he's brought in a vampire who is killing people, which we already knew, and that the cruelty of it convinced her to leave him. The timing seems… coincidental, shall we say, and we need to know if she's telling the truth. Jean suggested you could help."

Antonio nodded. "I can certainly tell you what I taste in her blood if she'll let me bite her."

"It won't be quite that simple," Jean intervened. "We don't want to tell her anything more than necessary until we know for sure she's sincere, which means we can't tell her why we need you to bite her."

"We don't want her to see it as part of the alliance at all," Marcel added. "She needs to view it as completely unrelated."

Antonio nodded again. "I can do that. It may take some time, particularly if she truly is distrustful of our kind because of the rogue, but I'll find out what we need to know. So where is she?"

"In the basement," Alain replied. "We have rooms down there for people who need a place to sleep for whatever reason. Our argument to her is that she won't be safe returning home once Serrier realizes she's defected. I don't know if she believes it, but she can't refuse without negating her argument that she's left him and needs our protection."

"If someone will take me down there, I'll be full of sympathy for another trapped refugee. It will be light soon enough that I probably wouldn't be able to make it home anyway. It'll give me a reason to offer to keep her company."

"Good," Marcel declared. "Let us know what you've learned. In the meantime, we have preparations to make, both for the upcoming battle and for the Rite d'équilibrage."

"I'll let you get to it, then," Antonio agreed, rising and starting toward the door.

"I'll show you where she is," Sebastien volunteered, rising as well. "I won't be much help in either of the discussions anyway, and this way, it'll look like we stumbled across her accidentally. She hasn't seen me yet."

Thierry frowned, wondering jealously if Sebastien would appeal more to Monique than Antonio would. Before he could react more, though, his partner trailed his fingers across the back of Thierry's neck and smiled at him. "I'll be back as soon as Antonio sights his prey."

Thierry could not hide the relief that surged through him despite telling himself he and Sebastien had made no promises. He already knew he did not want to share the vampire with anyone else. He caught the smirk on Alain's face and shot his best friend a glower, but he could hardly deny what Alain had guessed.

"The partnerships seem incredibly… powerful," Antonio commented almost wistfully to Sebastien as they headed toward the bowels of the building where Monique waited for Marcel's decision.

"They are," Sebastien confirmed. "The only time I've ever felt anything close to this was with my Avoué."

"I'd hoped to find a partner myself, but it doesn't seem to have happened," Antonio remarked quietly. "I feel like I'm letting Jean down."

Sebastien shrugged. "I don't know about that, but I do know you wouldn't be able to do this now if you had a partner. The bond isn't exclusive like an Aveu de Sang is, but the idea of feeding elsewhere isn't one I'd entertain now except in dire circumstances. I can still drink someone else's blood, but I find I don't want to. Don't give up on finding a partner, though. I don't know if you heard, but the chef de la Cour amiénoise found his partner a few days ago with a wizard here in Paris. As the alliance expands, you may well find someone."

"I'd heard that," Antonio replied as they reached the basement. "So where's my target?"

Sebastien pointed down the hall. "Last room on the left."

Antonio's grin turned rakish. "I think I need a place to rest. I'll let you know what I find out."

"Watch yourself," Sebastien warned as he turned to climb the stairs again. "Even if she really has reformed, she fought for Serrier for at least two years."

"She won't get the drop on me," Antonio promised. He walked on down the hall to the room where the dark wizard waited and opened the door as if he had every expectation of finding the room empty. "Oh, I'm sorry," he apologized when he had flung the door open wide to reveal the curvaceous woman inside, her dark hair falling to her shoulders. "I didn't realize anyone else was down here. I was just looking for a place to sleep since I can't leave until after sunset."

Monique turned toward the door, hiding her nerves beneath an exterior polished in Serrier's cutthroat world. She knew well that physical appearance could be deceiving, but that did not stop her from appreciating the Latin beauty of the man at her door: dark hair, dark eyes, pale skin, and the slightest music of Spain still in his voice. Add to that his height and muscular build and he was everything a woman could ask for in a man.

"You must be one of the vampires," she observed, remembering Serrier's order to learn anything and everything she could about the alliance and the vampires, no matter what it took. She had no idea if vampires retained any interest in physical pleasures—other than blood—but she was not above finding out if it would sway him. Chavinier obviously did not trust her yet, not unexpectedly, but her information did not have to come exclusively from him. In fact, a vampire like this one who clearly did not expect to find her here might not know enough to be on his guard. "I'm so glad you've joined the fight against Serrier."

Antonio schooled himself not to react to the obvious attempt to gain his trust. He did not need to bite her to know she was fishing, but he would still see how everything played out and bite her if he could get the chance to make sure his reading of the situation was accurate. "It seemed in our best interest to make sure Serrier doesn't win," he informed her, for that was certainly true and not beyond anything Jean had stated on public record.

"You must be worried about the sunlight, though," she probed, gesturing for the vampire to come inside. "If you get caught outside…." She glanced down at the watch on her wrist, drawing his eyes to the long, elegant curve of her arm, the position of her forearm underscoring her generous bosom.

"None of us are newly made," Antonio countered, moving farther into the room. "We've been avoiding daylight for years, for centuries in many cases. We can handle ourselves."

Monique smiled, unaware of how revealing the cruelty of her expression was to one used to the subtlety of le jeu des Cours. Her thoughts focused instead on being able to tell Serrier that the vampires would indeed have to leave a battle at dawn. "And their magic?" she probed. "Aren't you worried about what their spells will do to you?"

"We don't fight alone," Antonio delayed, taking another step closer. "There are always wizards with us to help counter their spells." When the woman did not back away as he advanced, he smiled engagingly and held out his hand. "I'm Antonio, by the way."

"Monique Le Clerc," she replied, taking the offered hand. She could not stop the ridiculously feminine thrill that went through her when, instead of shaking her hand, he lifted it to his lips and kissed it with a courtly bow.

Not releasing her hand, Antonio moved toward the narrow couch against one wall, drawing her with him. "So what are you doing here?" he asked disingenuously. "I've never seen anyone but vampires down here before."

"Do you stay down here often?" Monique asked evasively, not ready to reveal her uncertain status to an unknown factor.

Antonio shrugged. "A few times," he replied, fingers stroking back and forth across her hand, beginning the kind of subtle seduction he used to persuade his victims to let him feed.

Monique jumped when she felt the unexpected touch, but Antonio crooned softly, soothing her back into relaxation. She reminded herself that she had to use whatever means necessary to get the information Serrier desired, or she would have far more important things to worry about than whether the vampire developed an interest in her.

Antonio would have been surprised had Monique not been a little startled when he came on to her. Certainly, as attractive as she was, she must have had her share of propositions—but here, in Milice headquarters while she was awaiting Marcel's decision concerning her future, was probably not where she expected to encounter one. He was shrewd enough to realize that part of her capitulation was probably self-interest, but given that he was not acting out of pure motives either, he could hardly blame her.

"So are you here every night then?" she pressed. "At Milice headquarters, I mean."

Antonio smiled and leaned a little closer. "I can be," he purred in her ear, "if you're offering to meet me here."

Monique stopped herself from pulling back in surprise. The vampire's offer could be the entrée she needed into the Milice, and more importantly, into the inner workings of the alliance. She had learned long ago to use her feminine wiles as a way of getting information. This would be no different. Summoning a welcoming smile, she rested a hand on his thigh. "I think that could probably be arranged."

Antonio almost shook his head. No vampire would ever be so obvious. She had handed him the opportunity he needed, though, so he leaned in closer, lips brushing against her hair. When she did not pull away, he moved lower, along the line of her neck. Her head tipped back as his tongue flicked out. Her slight intake of breath encouraged him, and he caught her with his fangs, barely even enough to scrape her skin, licking the blood off the tips of his teeth.

Two impressions assailed him immediately: her dissemblance and the blanketing sensation he had heard described by paired vampires. Pulling away swiftly, he summoned a smile. "I wouldn't be a very good host if I didn't offer you something to eat, maybe a bottle of wine. I'm here until sunset at the very least."

"I am a little hungry," Monique admitted coyly. "Do you want me to come with you?"

"No, it's fine," Antonio delayed. "I'll be back before you know I'm gone."

Monique pouted prettily, but the vampire seemed immune to the expression that had gotten her what she wanted from more men than she cared to count. "Hurry back."

"I will," he promised, slipping out the door and hearing it latch shut behind him. Indecision tore at him. He could hardly accept her as his partner knowing that everything they did, everything he revealed would be passed to Serrier, but unlikely as it appeared, she was his partner. Without her, he could not contribute fully to the alliance.

Despite his desire to walk in daylight again, he knew where his loyalties lay. With a last, longing look toward the doorway, he climbed the steps back up to where the others waited.

"That was fast," Marcel commented when Antonio came back in. "Were you able to find out what we needed to know?"

"Yes, she's a spy," Antonio reported dutifully. "I didn't even need to bite her to figure it out, but her emotions confirm it. Her disdain, her lies, her calculation all gave her away."

"Merci," Marcel said. "Now we just have to decide what to do with her."

"Do with her?" Antonio questioned, feeling ridiculously protective of a woman who would certainly try to destroy him if she could. Despite the ruthlessness he had tasted in her blood, a part of him acknowledged that she was his partner, a fact he chose not to mention. It had no bearing on the discussion at hand, and since nothing could come of it anyway—he was not about to switch sides for her, and he doubted he would have the opportunity to convince her to switch sides for him—no one else needed to know.

"We can throw her in jail for conspiring with Serrier, although I don't know what we can prove," Thierry explained, "or we can see what kind of wild goose chase we can send Serrier on with a little bit of misinformation."

"He's got to wonder where we're planning to perform the Rite d'équilibrage," Alain mused aloud. "Can we send him somewhere looking for us?"

"If he has any inkling I'm involved, he'll know it has to involve water," Raymond reminded them.

"So we find a subterranean lake outside of Paris," Thierry suggested. "We can explain it by citing security concerns and it'll send him out of the city, or at least distract him from our real choice of location."

"Where do you suggest?" Marcel asked.

"The lake in Saint-Léonard would be the most obvious choice," Thierry replied, "but Serrier isn't likely to believe that we went through all the diplomatic wrangling to get permission to go to Switzerland when there are sites in France that would be appropriate, the Grottes de Choranche, for example."

"Is there any reason not to use that one?" Jean asked curiously.

"It's open to the public," Thierry explained, "but we could probably close it for the day, under the circumstances."

"Why not use the Grotte de Thaïs?" Alain suggested. "I think it's closed already from the middle of October until sometime in the spring. That would guarantee us the privacy we need to concentrate."

"It's not as if you actually have to do the ritual there," Sebastien intervened.

"No," Raymond agreed, "but Serrier is hardly naïve. If the choice of decoy location isn't realistic, he isn't going to fall for it."

"Is it worth the energy it would take to make the decoy believable?" Jean queried. "Are you that worried he'll try to disrupt the ritual?"

"Honestly, I don't know that he will," Raymond replied. "It's the one side effect of this war he can't spin to his advantage. He'll use our distraction to his advantage if he can, but I don't think he'll actually try to stop the ritual."

"Then let's figure out something we can tell him that will truly put a wrench in his plans," Jean proposed, frustration obvious in his voice. No vampire would squander such an opportunity, not if they had any hope of rising in the ranks of society. "A trap we can lay for him or something about the alliance that will play into our strengths and hide our weaknesses. There's no reason to waste this opportunity with a sleight of hand that doesn't gain us anything."

"What would you suggest?" Marcel inquired.

Jean sighed. "A trap has the advantage of taking as many rebel wizards off the street as we can capture or kill at that one time, but if we can convince him of some misinformation about the alliance that will give us an advantage longer term, that would be even more advantageous."

"Would he believe vampires are taking on all the night patrols?" Orlando suggested.

"That won't work," Antonio disagreed. "I already told the spy that we fought alongside wizards."

"And even if he did believe it, it would only work once," Raymond added. "The first time anyone escaped from a 'vampire' patrol, he'd know wizards were there as well. What if we reveal to her a supposed weakness about vampires, besides the ones Jean mentioned at the press conference, something that would instead play into vampires' strengths?"

Jean considered the suggestion. "Sunlight and fire was what I said that evening, both of which are true." He chuckled. "Maybe the stereotypes are good for something. All the legends say vampires are sensitive to holy water, that it burns us. It doesn't hurt us any more than it hurts anyone, but Serrier might believe it. If he does and uses it, the fact that it doesn't work would only convince him there were no vampires in that particular patrol, at least at first. He'll figure it out eventually, I'm sure—but it sends him to research spells and use resources in ways that won't hurt any of us, other than maybe leaving us cold for a bit."

"What do you think, Raymond?" Marcel asked. "You know the way his mind works better than any of us."

"There's never a guarantee where he's concerned," Raymond mused aloud, "but it would appeal to his narrow-minded xenophobia. It has as good a chance of working as anything else."

"She's expecting me back," Antonio admitted, hiding his eagerness to return downstairs. Even knowing what he knew about the woman waiting for him, he could not slake the desire to taste her blood again. "I suggested she might like something to eat and some wine to help pass the time. I can mention the holy water if you'd like."

"Wonderful," Marcel agreed. "It will be much more believable coming from you than from someone she knows and has reason to distrust."

Chapter 4

"GOD, I thought this day would never end," Thierry groused, collapsing onto the couch. It had been quiet all day, as if the city was holding its breath, waiting for the storm that was sure to come. Thierry knew he shouldn't complain about a routine shift, but between that and the preparations for the ritual the next day, it had been tedious beyond belief. Raymond had been at his most pedantic, insisting on checking and double-checking every little detail. Thierry understood. He simply resented being the one ordered to do the checking instead of the one insisting on such rigor.

"Here," Sebastien said, sitting down next to Thierry. "Enjoy this and relax a little."

Thierry took the glass from his partner and sniffed it to see what Sebastien had served him. "Did Alain tell you I liked kir?" he asked, curious how the vampire had known exactly what apéritif to fix for him.

"No, but you made yourself one a couple of nights ago, so I figured you might enjoy another one," Sebastien explained.

Thierry did not even try to suppress the thrill that shot through him at the thought that Sebastien was paying such close attention to his preferences. He sipped the drink and sighed in delight. The other man had mixed it just the way he liked it. Leaning his head against the back of the sofa, he let the tension of the day seep out of him slowly, marveling at how easy a routine he and Sebastien had developed over the past week. Finish their shift, come home, relax a little before Thierry ate and Sebastien fed, then sleep, the vampire holding him close, keeping him safe. With another deep sigh, Thierry decided he could get used to this, to having someone to share his life again, someone to take care of him sometimes, someone to care for at other times.

On the heels of that thought, warm hands settled on his shoulders. He cracked his eyes open to see Sebastien looking at him critically. "You're tense," the vampire told him. "Turn around a little so I can get to your back. Let me help you relax."

Thierry shifted so he was sitting as Sebastien directed, back to his partner, still leaning against the couch as he sipped his drink and let Sebastien's hands work their magic. He had already learned how talented they were. He started to stifle his groan as they worked the muscles of his back through his shirt, but Sebastien had told him he enjoyed the little sounds the wizard made. The memory sent an erotic thrill down Thierry's back, a sensation that still surprised him at times. How, in nine days, he could have come to trust Sebastien almost as completely as he trusted Alain was hard enough to understand. How, in those same nine days, he had come to desire the vampire defied all logic. He had stopped trying to explain it since their first kiss. Logic did not seem to apply where his feelings for the dark-haired vampire were concerned. Fortunately, Sebastien seemed as baffled at times by their relationship as he did, making Thierry a little less insecure about his inexperience with men. The fact, too, that Sebastien had not pressured him, had not rushed him in any fashion, also helped. The vampire had fed almost every night, with explosive results, but beyond that, they had done little more than kiss, despite Thierry's steadily increasing desire for more. Downing the last of his drink, he decided he had waited long enough for Sebastien to take the next step. It was his turn.

"I need a shower," Thierry declared, setting his glass aside and turning to face Sebastien, determination clear on his face.

"Good idea," Sebastien agreed. "It'll help you relax so you can sleep better tonight. You were restless last night."

Thierry smiled wolfishly. "Why don't you join me? That way we can both relax a little."

"Thierry," Sebastien began warningly, but his words were cut off by Thierry's torrid kiss.

"Don't argue," Thierry insisted, tugging on the vampire's hand.

Already painfully aroused, Sebastien let Thierry lead him toward the master suite and into the bathroom. When the wizard reached for his clothes, though, Sebastien shook his head and stepped back. His control would never survive Thierry undressing him—and regardless of what the blond thought, he was not ready to deal with an out-of-control Sebastien. "Get in the shower," he directed. "I'm not going to disappear."

Thierry complied with celerity, stripping off his remaining garments and turning the shower on hard and hot. Independent of everything else, he did need to relax, and the pounding of the water would help ease the knots in his back and neck. Sebastien paused in his own disrobing to appreciate the wizard's nude form. Broad shoulders, narrow hips, long, long legs… he caught the edge of the sink, his knuckles turning white from the strength of his grip as he struggled to master the urge to push Thierry against the wall and ravish him. He had made a promise to make love to Thierry properly the first time, not just fuck him over the nearest surface. He intended to keep that promise, but the sight of Thierry's bare buttocks as he bent to adjust the water strained his control.

"You can touch me, you know," Thierry said without looking up from what he was doing. "I don't bite."

"No," Sebastien agreed hoarsely, "but I do."

Green eyes glittering with lust, Thierry looked back over his shoulder. "I know. I reap the advantages of it every time you do."

Sebastien almost turned and walked out of the room, not sure he could stay and still keep his promise. Thierry must have read his indecision on his face, because the wizard straightened and approached slowly. "You're not taking anything I'm not offering," he reminded the vampire.

"I know," Sebastien repeated raggedly, "but—"

"But nothing," Thierry insisted, hands settling on the vampire's cheeks to angle his head for a kiss. Sebastien resisted for a moment before giving up that attempt as pointless. Instead, he turned his attention to keeping Thierry too occupied with the meeting of their lips to think about anything else—like touching him.

Thierry knew the instant Sebastien stopped resisting because instead of kissing, he was suddenly being kissed, being taken. Sebastien's kisses stole his breath every time, swamping his senses, leaving his mind reeling. When he was coherent enough to think about it, he wondered if it had to do with having a male lover this time, someone used to being dominant in every aspect of his life, or if it was Sebastien himself with his centuries of experience who was so potent. Those were thoughts for another time, though. Whatever the reason, Sebastien's attentions made coherency an impossibility, his mind and body only interested in arousing Sebastien to the same fever pitch. To that end, he slid his hands down to Sebastien's bare shoulders, reveling in the opportunity to touch the vampire. Even at night when they cuddled together in bed, the dark-haired man rarely removed his T-shirt, much less his shorts, so Thierry was not about to let the opportunity pass to get his hands on bare skin. "You're cold," he murmured, breaking the kiss. "Let's get in the shower. It'll help you warm up."

The water would do nothing for his body temperature—only blood would do that—but Sebastien did not protest when Thierry moved away and stepped into the shower. It gave him a moment's respite to gather his control as he dropped his trousers to the floor. Taking a deep breath and shoring up his eroding self-discipline, he joined the wizard under the hot, stinging spray.

Thierry had spent quite a lot of time over the past week working his mind around the idea of taking a male lover. He knew what women liked, where to touch their bodies, how to read their reactions to guide his hands and lips. He had no idea how to read Sebastien that way, how to touch the vampire to bring him pleasure. In the end, he had decided to try on the vampire what he himself enjoyed. After all, a cock was a cock, regardless of whose it was, and he knew how to make himself feel good when lovers were in short supply. Surely he could use that knowledge to make Sebastien feel good as well. As soon as Sebastien joined him, he turned the vampire under the hot spray, stepping close, intentionally invading his personal space. Sebastien had put him off all week with one excuse or another, and Thierry had let him, not having come to terms completely with the sudden upheaval in his sexuality. The time for waiting had passed, though. He was ready for more than a few—many—soul-stealing kisses. His hands slid over water-slick skin, learning the contours, noticing where Sebastien was hard in contrast to a woman's softness, angular rather than curved. Moving closer still, he felt their bodies brush, skin to skin for the first time.

Sebastien was prepared for many things, but this newly aggressive side of Thierry caught him off guard, arousing him immediately to a fever pitch. Jettisoning his attempts at resistance, the vampire turned his mind instead to guiding their interactions to a mutually satisfying conclusion without breaking his promise. Turning Thierry under the hot spray and pinning him against the wall, he captured his lover's lips, one hand dropping between them to catch their bobbing erections in a snug grip. Thierry's head hit the tiles with a satisfying thump as Sebastien stroked up the matching lengths.

"Merde!" Thierry cursed hoarsely as he struggled not to come on the spot, the sensation of Sebastien's fist and their cocks rubbing together sending his libido into overdrive.

"Problem?" Sebastien teased lightly.

"There will be if you don't start moving your hand," Thierry retorted, pushing off the wall and rocking Sebastien against the other side of the small enclosure. His hand joined the vampire's, fisting the two shafts rapidly.

Sebastien cursed in turn, cock leaking steadily. "Maudit, Thierry!" he gasped. "Where did you learn that?"

"Just because I've never touched another man's cock doesn't mean I don't know how to handle my own," Thierry retorted, letting his own erection slip from his grip in favor of lavishing more attention on Sebastien.

Sebastien's witty reply died on his lips when Thierry's thumb brushed over the head of his cock, teasing the slit as the movement of his hand drew back the foreskin, revealing the sensitive glans. He groaned deep in his throat and did his best to return the favor, not wanting to neglect his lover.

"Need something, lover?" Thierry taunted, his other hand releasing its hold on Sebastien's hip and sliding between his thighs to palm the heavy balls.

Sebastien knew exactly what he needed, but since spinning Thierry around and fucking him against the wall was not on the agenda, he would have to settle for the wizard's hands on him. "Exactly what you're giving me," he replied, reciprocating the caress, determined to make Thierry as mindless as he was quickly becoming.

Thierry's climax caught him off guard, tearing through him suddenly even as he sought to bring his partner the same release. His knees trembled as Sebastien bore him back against the wall again, stroking him continuously through his explosive orgasm and shuddering aftershocks. He did his best to keep his own hands moving, pleasuring his lover. His doubts as to his success disappeared when he felt the hot splash from the vampire's cock. Slumping against the wall, he tilted his head and blindly sought Sebastien's lips for a brief, torrid kiss. "Merde!" he drawled again, his voice thick with satiation.

Sebastien grinned and reached for the soap, his legs only marginally more steady than Thierry's as he quickly washed them both clean. When he was done, he shut off the taps and guided his lover out of the tiny cubicle and toward the bedroom. "We're not done yet."

Thierry went eagerly, not ready for the evening's explorations to end. He fell backward onto the bed, pulling Sebastien down on top of him. "So what else do you have planned for me?"

"I didn't have anything *planned*," Sebastien insisted, "except helping you relax a little."

"You certainly succeeded," Thierry purred, "but you just said we weren't done. So what are you planning?"

Sebastien shook his head indulgently and lowered his lips to his wizard's neck. "I'm hungry."

Thierry's reaction was immediate and unequivocal, his head falling back to bare his neck as his hips jerked upwards, seeking contact. He hissed at the brush of the towel around Sebastien's waist, pulling at it until he had removed the cloth from between them. He wanted nothing to dampen the sensation of his lover's body pressing into his. "Take what you need."

Sebastien froze, struggling against the desire to simply drive his fangs into the offered flesh and feast. Thierry would not stop him, but his own sense of responsibility held him back. Tomorrow, his partner would participate in the balancing ritual, giving of his magical strength to mitigate the threat posed by the elemental magic. The last thing Sebastien wanted was to send Thierry into the ritual weakened. Yet, he needed to feed or he would almost certainly lose his immunity to sunlight and might have to find sustenance elsewhere before Thierry recovered, and that thought was repugnant to him. He would have to walk a fine line between taking enough to last until Thierry had regained his strength and not taking so much that Thierry could not do his job tomorrow.

"Sebastien?" Thierry prompted, not understanding his partner's hesitation.

"Always in a rush," Sebastien teased, not wanting to admit to the possessiveness or the protectiveness he was feeling. He knew Thierry desired him—their interlude in the shower was proof of that—but they had not made any commitments beyond the alliance. Perhaps they would, in time, but Sebastien was not ready to deal with any of that tonight. After the ritual, after they were lovers in every sense of the word—assuming Thierry still wanted him—he would see where things stood and decide then. For now, he lowered his head, licking gently over skin mottled already with bruises and bites. His cock swelled immediately at the proof of Thierry's submission. The last time he had fed from someone so frequently, he had been bound by an Aveu de Sang. He pushed that thought away, knowing he did both his Avoué and his current lover a disservice by comparing them. Instead, he lifted his head enough to comment, "Can you do something to help these heal faster? I hate seeing your skin so torn up."

Thierry threaded his fingers into Sebastien's hair. "I don't," he replied. "I like the reminder of what you've done to me."

Sebastien groaned, fighting the urge to sink his cock as deep as he would momentarily sink his fangs. "You shouldn't say such things," he chided.

"Why not?" Thierry drawled, not even trying to hold back his smile. "Afraid you'll lose control and ravish me?"

A growl escaped Sebastien's throat as he grabbed Thierry's short hair, tilting his head back and pouncing on the long column of flesh. The rush of hot blood into his mouth sent his senses spinning, his own wildly fluctuating emotions mingling with Thierry's desires to leave Sebastien aware of only one thing: his constantly growing lust for the man beneath him.

Thierry gasped in delight when he felt Sebastien's fangs penetrate his skin, his body arching of its own accord, seeking the familiar friction of Sebastien's slender form pressing against his. The sound changed to a moan as bare skin rubbed bare skin. Despite his explosive climax in the shower, his libido was fully alert again. The combination of feeling Sebastien's skin against his own for the first time with his lover's lips and fangs ravishing his neck was enough to send blood rushing to his cock. He tensed again, shivering almost violently when he felt Sebastien's hand sliding down his back, over the curve of his buttocks, fingers delving between the tight globes. When one finger brushed lightly over his perineum and around his entrance, he shuddered with need. "Fuck me."

Sebastien lifted his head, breaking the vampire kiss long enough to meet Thierry's gaze. "Not yet."

Thierry groaned in frustration. "When?" he demanded hoarsely.

"After you've recovered from tomorrow's ritual," Sebastien promised. "For now, let me take care of you another way."

Thierry nodded his assent, head dropping back as Sebastien's mouth returned to his neck, slipping back inside him with practiced ease as his teasing fingers continued to stroke the wizard's most private flesh. Silently, Sebastien cursed his lack of foresight, having nothing at hand to ease his fingers' way into Thierry's body. He considered lifting his digits to Thierry's lips, letting his partner wet them that way. If Thierry had been more experienced, he would not have hesitated. As it was, Sebastien refused to do anything that might make the process of discovery less than enjoyable. He was too eager to sink into his lover's tight depths, hopefully more than just once, to risk having the wizard change his mind.

Thierry was far from changing his mind. The probing fingers that stroked and massaged, working his sphincter diligently, made him squirm, trying to draw them deeper, trying to draw Sebastien deeper. Thoughts of practicalities were the last thing on his mind as he writhed beneath the lash of new sensation, desperately seeking more. He planted his feet, pushing up hard into Sebastien's hand and against Sebastien's body, the delicious friction adding to the desire flavoring his blood.

Even without the untainted lust in Thierry's blood, Sebastien would have known his lover wanted more. He pressed his fingers a little deeper, until the hitch in Thierry's breathing told him that was far enough without lube of some kind. His mouth worked harder on the wizard's neck, the combined sensations enough to catapult Thierry into his release. Sebastien followed quickly as wet heat spread over his hip from Thierry's climax. Carefully, he disengaged his fangs, licking the wounds to close them and then simply resting his head against the wizard's shoulder.

"Relaxed yet?" he asked once his breath had settled.

Thierry chuckled in reply. "But now *I'm* hungry."

Chapter 5

ORLANDO GLANCED at the clock again, as he had been doing compulsively for the last hour. Fourteen hours and twelve minutes. In fourteen hours and twelve, no, eleven minutes, they would arrive at the Tour Eiffel prepared to fight a concerted effort to bring down the metal structure. In fourteen hours and… ten minutes, they would risk their lives for a building. A symbol, yes, but a building. He knew what Alain would say. There would be people there, tourists, employees, innocent bystanders who would need their protection as much or more than the building itself. Orlando only cared about one of them, and that was Alain himself—who would be in the vanguard, leading by example rather than commanding from behind. In fourteen hours and… eight minutes, he would follow Alain into battle and do his best to protect his lover, knowing all the while that there was far too little he could do against the dark wizards. Knowing, too, that Alain's best defense was not there, but was instead risking himself trying to balance the elemental magic. And that thought would be constantly in the back of Alain's mind, nagging at him, distracting him, putting him even more at risk. In fourteen hours and….

"Orlando."

The vampire looked away from the clock and sought his lover's gaze questioningly.

"Stop worrying. Tomorrow will take care of itself."

Orlando laughed shortly. "Easy for you to say. I've only just found you," he explained. "The thought that I might lose you…."

Alain shook his head. "You can't think that way. Yes, I could die tomorrow in the battle. I could also get hit by a car when I walk out the door in the morning, before we ever get to the Tour Eiffel. Life is one big risk. We have to focus on enjoying the moment now, or fear will paralyze us." He drew the vampire into his arms. "I love you, and death is the only thing that will ever keep me from your side." Rolling to his back, he urged Orlando atop him.

Orlando stared down into the azure eyes of his lover, his mate, and knew the truth of that vow. Even without tasting Alain's blood, the wizard's sincerity was palpable. With a groan, he lowered his head, bringing their lips together in a tender kiss. He lingered over his lover's mouth, taking the time to taste, to kiss gently but thoroughly, his tongue twining with Alain's before drawing back to explore his teeth, his palate, every nook and cranny. He could feel Alain's body responding, beginning to stir in encouragement. His own cock was like granite, fear having roused his need to claim, to prove that whatever happened tomorrow, tonight they were well and together and nothing could part them. Instincts he refused to acknowledge urged him to stake his dual claim, to sheath his fangs in his Avoué's neck as he made love to him, but his lingering fears held him back. If he lost control and hurt Alain, he would never forgive himself. Knowing that his lover would eagerly agree to such a suggestion only added to both the temptation and the determination to stay in control. He dared not climax with his fangs still in Alain's neck, but he could use the necessity of feeding as a means to heighten his lover's passion and hope that satisfied both his own instincts and Alain's desires.

Having decided on his path, he slid his lips lower, across Alain's neck, lingering on the brand that proclaimed their promise to the Cours, even if no one outside the world of the vampires would ever truly understand. He still marveled that someone like Alain would willingly bind himself to one cursed, but he realized that sometime in the past few days he had stopped questioning it. In the very depths of his being, he knew that Alain's promise was true. Only death would ever keep the wizard willingly from his side. Overcome by the sudden rush of emotion, Orlando flicked his tongue out to prepare Alain's skin and drove his fangs deep, directly through the symbol that bound them.

Alain gasped in surprise, hands scrabbling in the sheets for purchase as Orlando bit him abruptly. All thought fled as he reacted to the sudden, decadent pull of his vampire's lips and fangs on his skin, to the realization that Orlando had chosen to feed through the symbol of their Aveu de Sang. He tilted his head back farther, baring his neck, body and mind already catapulted into ecstasy. He wanted to reciprocate, but Orlando had taken complete control of this encounter, leaving Alain mentally reeling, assailed by overwhelming passions. In the end, he gave up and simply enjoyed the power of the feelings Orlando visited on him. He still hoped one day to be able to lavish on Orlando all the attention the vampire regularly lavished on him, but until that day came—if it came—he would school himself to giving Orlando whatever his lover could accept. It was hardly a hardship to lie back and let Orlando love him, however selfish that made him feel.

As always, the banquet of flavors inherent in Alain's blood stole Orlando's breath. He drew deeply, the liquid nourishing his body, the emotions revealed therein nurturing his slowly healing heart. He could feel the passion spark between them as it did each time they lay this way, the towel around Alain's hips from his shower and the loose slacks Orlando still wore no impediment to the sensations assailing them both.

Orlando carded his fingers through Alain's hair, massaging the wizard's scalp, relearning the contours of his skull before ghosting across his face again, blindly tracing the lines of his cheekbones, lingering on the scar on his right cheek. Alain had dismissed it as long healed when he first noticed the cicatrix, but Orlando could not help wondering about its origin.

Alain pried one hand away from the sheets to cradle Orlando's head as he fed, urging him to take more, to feed more deeply. Remembering the quietly whispered revelations of his maker's cruelty, he kept his touch light, caressing rather than guiding, but very much encouraging. He felt tension invest his lover's lithe frame and crooned soothingly, whispering words of love and longing intended to remind the vampire of where he was and who he was with.

The fearful tension faded slowly, replaced with a different kind of tension as Orlando's hand moved slowly across Alain's arm, lingering on the curve of his biceps, fingers stroking tenderly.

The sudden tenderness in the gesture helped Alain relax. His grip on the covers eased as his arm encircled Orlando's shoulders, reciprocating the loving touch, his hand moving restlessly back and forth over the vampire's skin. Lifting his head as best he could, he looked down over the slender form of his lover, feeling a rush of heat stain his cheeks as he admired the elegant curve of Orlando's bare back and cloth-covered legs. Then Orlando's hand moved, leaving Alain's arm and making its way to his side and the curve of his hip, the towel having fallen open as they rubbed against one another. Alain's head fell back to the pillow, a groan of unadulterated pleasure escaping his lips. He knew himself cherished as he had never before been, even when he and Edwige had first fallen in love. "Love you," he gasped, feeling his emotions swirling out of his control.

Orlando raised his head, face flushed with the blood he had drunk and the passion it inspired, meeting Alain's glittering eyes. Heedless of his wizard's possible reaction to the taste of his own blood in Orlando's mouth, he captured Alain's lips with his own, kissing him with desperate passion. "Need you," he moaned.

"You have me," Alain promised as he pressed light, nibbling kisses to the Cupid's bow of his lover's lips, their tongues twining as they embraced. He could taste his blood on Orlando's tongue—but knowing how it had gotten there, he found the flavor as intoxicating as Orlando had always claimed to. A part of him would always marvel at the change that had come over him in the past two weeks as he let go of certain preconceptions concerning vampires, but he had stopped worrying about what his new acceptance said about him. "You'll always have me."

Orlando buried his face in the crook of Alain's neck, hiding the pained expression that surely contorted his classic features at the thought of the inevitable day when mortality would claim his lover and make a lie of that promise. Wizards lived longer lives than ordinary men, but even if they both survived this war, even if the Milice wizards triumphed, death would eventually claim the man beneath him, separating them forever. He bit his lip, holding back a sob. Suddenly desperate, Orlando ripped off his belt, uncaring of the torn belt loop, pushing his clothes down and off.

Alain gasped at the sudden contact of skin with skin, his passions, already roused from Orlando's feeding, only augmented now by his lover's body pressing against him. "Please," he begged, already desperate for more stimulation.

Orlando did not wait to be asked twice, rising to his knees to straddle Alain eagerly. Where before, his hands had stayed more or less still, only touching to ground himself and Alain, now they flew across his lover's body, stroking every spot he knew to be sensitive—the wizard's nipples, his lower belly, the inside of his thighs. Alain reacted exactly as Orlando had wished, arching and writhing beneath the caresses as if electrified.

Retracting his fangs with great effort, he lowered his head to Alain's shoulder, kissing along the line of his chest as he worked his way down to take one tight pink nub in his mouth, then the other, his hands still stroking his lover's thighs, coasting slowly higher as they worked their way toward their goal.

He knew the flavor of Alain's blood tonight, knew what emotions colored his mind and heart. Now he wanted to taste the wizard's skin, his sweat, his seed. He would only sense the barest shadow of their true flavor, but he wanted all his limited senses would allow him.

Caught in the storm of passion Orlando was evoking, Alain found himself struggling mentally to keep up, every gesture of encouragement or reciprocation he began already out of place before he could complete it. As much as it went against the prodding of his heart, he had no choice but to lie back and accept the vampire's attentions. "Feels so good," he murmured, settling for words since actions seemed beyond him.

"Good," Orlando declared, lips moving against Alain's abdomen as he spoke. "It's supposed to." He sucked lightly at the skin above the wizard's hip bone, loving the way Alain squirmed in delight.

"Suck me," Alain pleaded. Having Orlando's lips so close to his cock without touching was enough to drive him demented.

"I will," Orlando promised, a shiver running down his spine at the decadent words in Alain's husky whisper. "When I'm ready."

"You have no idea what you do to me, do you?" Alain went on, catching the telltale reaction. If hearing him talk encouraged Orlando to continue, he would talk until he could no longer form a coherent thought. "How you make me feel?"

"Tell me," Orlando suggested, tracing the line where hip met thigh with his tongue.

"Like I could walk on water or float through the air," Alain rasped. "You set me aflame with every touch and make me feel invincible. When you kiss me, I'm Don Juan, Cyrano de Bergerac, Romeo, and D'Artagnan rolled into one."

"You're all those things to me and more," Orlando declared, his hands finally reaching the top of Alain's thighs. One moved toward the mattress to cup his lover's sac; the other moved upward to stroke the hard shaft that bumped his cheek, leaving a trail of sticky fluid. He guided the tip to his lips, smearing the creamy liquid over his lips.

The picture Orlando made straddling his thighs, lips glistening with seminal fluid, sent a fresh surge of lust through Alain's body. "Kiss me."

Orlando complied immediately, stretching out fully atop Alain's hard body so that their lips met and locked in a primordial joining as deep as the magical bond that joined their minds and souls.

As arousing as the kiss was, they both quickly needed more, their passion too heightened to settle for even the most inflammatory kiss. Orlando broke the kiss to lap quickly at the trickle of blood that escaped the bite marks. They were the only ones that marred Alain's neck, the magic that bound them healing the incisions within hours. He was tempted to take more, but he had already drunk enough to satisfy his physical needs and overindulging could be dangerous. Even so, the lust and love he tasted in Alain's blood called to him like a siren's song, luring him in.

Alain's fingers returned to their favorite spot in Orlando's hair. He was pleased to see that the gesture did not even elicit a flinch this time, giving him hope that the vampire would eventually be able to accept, even to enjoy other caresses that currently brought back bad memories. His other hand stroked his lover's back, prelude to taking a more active role, but Orlando caught his hand with a shake of his head, lifting it above his head and pinning it there.

The wizard accepted the limitation, reminding himself that however they came together, however they touched each other, every joining was a sign of their love and devotion. If he could not use his body to give his lover pleasure, he would have to use his words instead. "Do you know what I like better than anything else?" he rasped.

"What?" Orlando asked, lifting his head so he could meet Alain's eyes.

"Your lips on my neck," Alain replied, "on the mark that binds us. Everything else comes from that. No other touch moves me like that one does."

Orlando smiled tenderly, lowering his head and kissing the brand again, his hands braced on Alain's chest. As he shifted, his palms massaged hard muscle and peaked nipples.

Alain gasped. "That's a close second, though."

"This?" Orlando questioned, moving his fingers more deliberately.

Alain nodded. "Does it feel as good when I touch your nipples as it does when you touch mine?" His voice deepened as he spoke, betraying the depths of his arousal.

Orlando flushed and looked away shyly, uncomfortable with the intimate conversation yet beguiled by the tone of Alain's voice into replying. "Everything you do to me feels good."

Then why won't you let me do more of it? Alain thought silently. "Show me how you like to be touched," he said aloud, not wanting to mar the beauty of the moment or risk going into battle with an argument between them.

Orlando hesitated a moment longer, torn between doing as Alain asked and touching him instead. In the end, the eager desire on his lover's face swayed him and he closed his eyes, letting his hands wander over his own skin, finding the dark disks of his nipples and caressing lightly. He circled the outer edge of each aureole, his breath quickening from the stimulation. He could feel Alain's eyes on him, could sense the increasing sexual tension between them as he concentrated on his own pleasure. He tweaked his own peaked flesh gently and then with a little more force as he discovered the joy of his own body. Over the century since Jean had rescued him from his maker, Orlando had brought himself release many times—but always hastily, furtively almost, as if someone might be watching, waiting to criticize him for having needs. Now, under Alain's loving, lustful gaze, those doubts vanished and he let himself linger.

"You look good enough to eat," Alain husked. "I could lie here all night and watch you, except that I want to touch you, too. Let me touch you, Orlando."

Orlando shook his head, his hands lingering. "Tell me what to do."

Alain frowned inwardly, but tangled his hands in the sheets to keep them from reaching from Orlando. "Leave one hand where it is," he directed slowly. "Keep doing whatever feels best. Stroke yourself with the other. Slowly. You make me feel so good when you touch me that way. Make yourself feel good. Show me how you want me to touch you when you're ready."

Orlando's heart clenched at the reminder that he could not simply let his lover do as he pleased. A part of him wanted to say to hell with his fears, but he knew how that would end. With a battle looming, the last thing he wanted was another argument, another misunderstanding that could distract them both at a critical time. He closed his eyes and let his head fall back as his hand slid lower to circle his erection, sliding up and down the hard shaft.

Alain watched avidly, memorizing the motion, the speed, the rhythm. Eventually, he could not stop himself. He reached down and stroked his own shaft in time with Orlando's movements. "Open your eyes. Look at me, Orlando."

Orlando's eyes opened, his gaze glassy with lust. "I want to touch you."

"I'm not stopping you," Alain reminded him. "Just say the word and I'll move my hand. I'm yours. All you have to do is ask."

"Move your hand."

Alain's hand fell away from his cock immediately, settling to the sheets as tension rode him hard, waiting to see what Orlando would do. The vampire reached for his lover tentatively, as if the last weeks had not happened, as if he doubted his right to touch or his ability to please the man beneath him.

"Whatever you want, Orlando. I'm yours," Alain repeated.

Orlando's lips curved into a smile as he lowered his head again to Alain's neck, sucking there gently. "I want to be inside you."

"What are you waiting for?" Alain asked, voice catching on the suddenly violent desire surging through him. He parted his legs, bending his knees to create a cradle for Orlando's body, offering himself to his lover.

Suddenly desperate, Orlando grabbed the lube and prepared Alain as quickly as he dared. "Do it," Alain insisted.

Any hesitation Orlando might have felt fell by the wayside at the sound of Alain's voice, at the desperation to match his own that he heard in the husky rasp. He sheathed himself in one long, slow thrust, joining their bodies in a union as old as time and as profound as the one symbolized by the brand on Alain's neck. "I love you," he whispered against his wizard's neck.

"I love you, too," Alain gasped, body arching into the slow, rhythmic thrusts. He could already feel his climax threatening, the combination of Orlando feeding and the verbal play leaving him on the cusp of release.

"Come for me," Orlando ordered, slipping his hand between them to stroke Alain's cock. "I'm not going to be able to wait."

"Then don't," Alain replied, the first tremors of his orgasm shaking him. "Let go and take me with you."

Orlando thrust frantically, his climax tearing through him, his entire body twitching as he found his release. The repeated prodding to his prostate had the desired effect, and Alain climaxed immediately after as the vampire collapsed on top of him.

Carefully, Alain's arms encircled his lover, holding the slender form against him. "Someday," he murmured against Orlando's ear, "someday, it'll be my turn. When it is, I'll make you as wild with desire as you make me every time you touch me. Someday, you'll trust me enough to let me show you how good it feels when a lover touches you the way you touch me."

Orlando tensed slightly but did not pull away. He wanted the image Alain painted with his seductive words, wanted to be free of his past to the point that he could accept whatever caress Alain bestowed and press his own desires without fear or hesitation. Instead, he nuzzled the smooth skin of Alain's neck, marred only by two tiny wounds that would be gone by morning and by the brand that would bind them always.

Beneath him, he could feel Alain relaxing into sleep and he rolled to one side to allow his lover to rest. He would need all his wits about him when they went into battle in… twelve hours and… forty minutes. In twelve hours and… thirty-nine minutes, they would fight for the continued right to live and love. In twelve hours and… thirty-eight minutes, they would stand side by side against the rebels who sought to bring them down. In twelve hours and… thirty-seven minutes, they would renew the struggle to see who would live and who would die.

Chapter 6

THE VOLUNTEERS for the Rite d'équilibrage gathered in la Salle des Cartes at nine o'clock the morning of Samhain. Looking around the room, Raymond went over the ritual in his mind, trying to best deploy the resources at hand. He was aware of Jean and Marcel talking in the background, of Thierry frowning at him across the room, of Thierry's partner hovering protectively at the blond wizard's elbow, but none of that held his attention. His thoughts focused entirely on the hours to come. Any break in concentration—particularly his own, since he would be in charge of funneling the energy of the gathered wizards—could be dangerous, even fatal. He could not afford any distractions. Unfortunately, his partner constituted one, despite his best attempts to put the vampire from his mind. Deciding he had done all he could until they got to the Opéra Garnier and its subterranean lake, Raymond let his thoughts wander to their current obsession: one Jean Bellaiche.

He had convinced Jean that there was no reason to come with the wizards to the ritual, that his presence could well be a distraction to those wizards not used to him. In truth, Raymond was more concerned that Jean would distract him. It seemed he could not be in the same room with his partner without watching him with eagle eyes. When they were apart it was even worse, the twitchy need to seek out the vampire enough to make him edgy at best, downright surly at worst. In many respects, he needed the balance that would come from the Rite d'équilibrage as much as the elemental magic did. He had to find some way to ground himself again and to control the irrational craving for his partner. Otherwise, he was likely to take some poor fool's head off, or else throw himself into the Seine in a fit of insanity.

The thought brought an ironic smile to his face. He had considered that course quite seriously when he first left Serrier, sure Marcel would never believe him. Cutting his life short by his own choice had seemed infinitely preferable to either a life in prison or one ended by Serrier's tortures. In the end, self-preservation won out and he had thrown himself on Marcel's mercy. The old wizard had taken one look at him and accepted him into the fold. Raymond had never looked back, devoting himself to the Milice with all the power and knowledge at his disposal.

It was all finally paying off, he decided, glancing back at Jean again. Between his own efforts and the mystery that was his bond with the chef de la Cour, he had finally found a true place in the Milice and the alliance. Even Alain and Thierry, who up until a few weeks ago had questioned his loyalty at every turn, were starting to give weight to his opinions and ideas. The coup de grace, though, was this ritual, specifically his role in it. As the focal point, he bore the responsibility for the success or failure of this attempt. The others, even Dumont, were grunts, though as his second, Thierry would step in if Raymond faltered.

"Is everyone here?" Marcel asked, appearing at Raymond's elbow.

Raymond nodded. "Fifty volunteers present and accounted for. We just need to get down there and get started. The equinox started at sunrise. We're wasting time."

"Then don't waste any more," Marcel declared.

"I'll send someone to check in before the patrols go out to la Tour Eiffel," Raymond said, "so you know how we're doing."

"Good," Marcel agreed. "Alain will be more comfortable going into battle if he knows the ritual's going well."

Raymond left unsaid the rather uncharitable thought that of course Alain must not be upset. Marcel could hardly be blamed for wanting his captain in top form for a battle as large as the one at the Tour Eiffel would be, and wildly fluctuating emotions were not conducive to control. Turning his attention back to the gathered wizards, he raised his voice. "We'll reassemble on the banks of the lake beneath the Opéra Garnier in ten minutes," he ordered, revealing the location of the ritual for the first time to all but Marcel's inner circle of advisors. Despite still having the known spy confined for the most part, they had decided not to reveal the true location until the last possible moment in case Serrier decided to disrupt the ceremony by more than just his attack at the Tour Eiffel. "Don't be late."

As the other wizards began disappearing, Raymond crossed to speak to Jean one last time. "You'll be fine here until I get back, right?" he asked unnecessarily.

"I'll be fine," Jean assured him, resisting the urge to lean forward and kiss his partner. He had fed once more since the passionate encounter upon Raymond's return from La Réunion, a less fraught if equally intense session, but he had still not dared any greater intimacy than his fangs in his wizard's neck. Now, in the Salle des Cartes—with Raymond about to leave for the Rite d'équilibrage and with numerous others looking on—was hardly the opportune moment. "Marcel and I have political strategy to discuss. We need to figure out the best way to sway the members of the Conseil des Ministres who still don't want to cooperate with the equality legislation. I'm sure we'll still be at it when you get back."

Raymond snorted. "Yes, I imagine you will be." He glanced at Marcel. "Watch his back for me."

The Milice general and the chef de la Cour looked at each other in bemusement, but before they could ask which one of them Raymond had addressed, the wizard was gone, having displaced himself to the Opéra.

"I don't think I'll ever understand that boy," Marcel commented with a shake of his head.

"I'll never get bored trying," Jean replied.

Marcel refrained from commenting, but a sly smile played across his lips. Raymond had been alone too long. It did an old wizard's heart good to see him have some chance at happiness, though he imagined Raymond would deny both his prior loneliness and his current contentment if asked. That was fine with Marcel. Raymond never had to acknowledge it as long as he did not reject it.

Beneath the city, beneath the catacombs, in the bowels of the Opéra Garnier, the wizards gathered one by one until the full complement had arrived. All levity left the group as they spread out around the banks of the fabled body of water where the Phantom of the Opera had taken his beloved Christine and where, if legend was to be believed, his ghost still lingered. Not being superstitious by nature, Raymond dismissed that, but he could not deny the sense of power that resonated through the cavern. Despite the presence of the water, the room was not dank. While he was sure it would be cool in the summer, now, in late fall, the space was quite comfortable. Taking his position on the north side of the lake, he waited until Thierry stood in counterpoint to him at the water's southernmost edge. Between them, the other forty-eight wizards spread out, equally spaced on the points of the compass, creating a full circle of magic—twenty-five men and twenty-five women to balance the elemental magic that governed them all.

Eyes closing, Raymond began to chant, channeling his magic into the water. Thierry's voice joined his. Then, one by one, the other wizards joined in, moving clockwise around the circle from each of the grounding wizards until fifty voices united. Their magic funneled through the two anchors and from Thierry into Raymond and from Raymond into the void.

Glutted with power, Raymond schooled his mind to form the link with the elemental magic that would let him affect it rather than simply monitor it. The connection slammed into place and he felt himself drawn into the vortex as the source of all natural and magical energy sucked the offering from him. He gasped in surprise as he felt control of the joining wrenched from him, not by any of the other wizards, but by the magic itself. Taking a calming breath, he probed the bond, trying to find the new fulcrum so he could offer his silent support and assistance. Across the lake, he saw Thierry sink to his knees, head in his hands. Muttering a curse under his breath, he drew his focus away from the Rite long enough to break the spell on the wizard next to him. "Get Alain," he ordered harshly before plunging his mind into the breach again, not even looking to see whom he had addressed. He had to end the Rite, even if it meant not completing it, before they lost wizards to the pull of the elemental magic.

He could feel Thierry fighting to hold his own, to retain control of his own magic and the offering of the others, but the pull was inexorable, drawing him deeper and deeper. Hoping to lessen the draw by lessening the magic available, Raymond worked his way mentally around the circle, breaking the thaumaturgic bonds that held the other wizards rapt, being careful to work in a pendulum swing so that the numbers on each side of the lake stayed relatively even. The Rite was all about balance, and anything that disrupted that balance would make his job even harder. One by one, the other wizards' minds came free, most of them slumping to the ground with mental, physical, and magical exhaustion, for all that they had barely initiated the contact with the elemental magic. Finally, only Raymond and Thierry remained locked in the struggle with forces far beyond their ken.

Raymond tried to free Thierry the same way he had freed the others, but the wizard resisted him, blocking him out as he fought to keep himself from being drained body and soul. Raymond cursed again as Thierry rejected him a second time. Giving up that attempt, he simply offered his strength to shore up the blond's waning resources and prayed that Alain would hurry. If he did not, he could well arrive to a burned-out husk.

Hunkered down physically and mentally, Thierry felt his mind and spirit assailed by the elemental magic, colors swirling around him, through him, confusing his attempts to center his mind. Heat washed through him, further muddling his thoughts as memories of lying with Sebastien the night before mixed with the sensation of being tied to the elemental magic. He tried to separate reality from the theurgically induced visions. It seemed, though, that his memories were being used against him, as fodder for the connection that trapped him immobile and out of control of his magic.

Not since he was a boy, first discovering his innate abilities, had he felt this incapable of wielding the power within him. All around him, sensations—sound, color, heat—buffeted him, leaving him completely untrusting of any of it. He pulled in tighter on himself, trying to maintain the integrity of his magical core. He retained enough sense of the world outside of himself to realize that the other wizards were no longer with him—freed from the magic's trap by Raymond, he assumed. He thought he felt the dark-haired wizard's mind brush his, but he dared not trust anything outside himself now if he had any hope of not being burned to a crisp, the magical core of his being extinguished like a match in a windstorm.

"Where's Alain?" Michel Lestrade cried frantically as he reappeared in the Salle des Cartes. "I've got to find Alain!"

"What's going on?" Marcel asked urgently, crossing to the wizard's side. Though not the most powerful wizard, Michel was not usually prone to panic. "Why do you need Alain?"

"Raymond said… get Alain… something went wrong… with the Rite… Thierry's… trapped," Michel panted, trying to catch his breath, his body still shaking from the few moments he had been caught in the magical maelstrom.

"What?" Sebastien exclaimed, grabbing the wizard's arm and pulling him to his feet. "Tell me what happened?"

Before Michel could reply, Alain came running into the room. "Thierry's trapped," Michel managed to say again. Before he had even finished, Alain had disappeared.

Sebastien's howl echoed through the room, head thrown back as the mournful sound resonated, full of anger and fear and helplessness. Orlando exchanged a look with Jean and could read grudging sympathy on the face of the chef de la Cour. Knowing the elder vampire would not make the first move, however, Orlando did, joining Marcel and Sebastien. "Can you send us wherever they are?" he asked the Milice general.

Marcel looked back and forth between the two vampires, seeing Orlando's determination and Sebastien's desolation. With a decisive nod, he cast the spell, transporting them to their partners' sides. He would trust Alain to handle the situation there. He had other fires to put out now that his captain would not be leading the battle at the Tour Eiffel in an hour.

"What the hell is going on?" Alain shouted when he materialized next to the lake to find wizards collapsed around its perimeter. He took in the scene with a single glance. Only Raymond still stood; even Thierry had fallen to his knees.

"He won't let me help him," Raymond ground out, the strain of dividing his attention between Alain and the Rite evident in his voice. "We've got to get him free."

Alain nodded and ran to Thierry's side, kneeling next to his best friend. "Come on, Thierry," he pleaded. "Let me help."

Caught in the maze of visions, Thierry reminded himself that Alain's voice had to be a figment drawn from his memories rather than reality. His friend was fighting at the Tour Eiffel, not here at the Opéra.

"We've got to break the connection with the elemental magic," Raymond called, "cut him off from it completely for long enough to free him. I can't do this alone, Alain."

Reluctantly, Alain nodded. What Raymond proposed was risky. If they cut Thierry off too completely or for too long, he could lose his ability to touch the magic altogether, leaving him bereft of half of himself. If they did not get him free of the vortex sucking the strength out of him, though, they could lose him completely, not only his magical resources, but his physical resources exhausted to the point that he could no longer live. "I'll cast the spell."

"Alain, you know—" Raymond began to protest.

"Yes, I know you can probably cast the spell more deftly, but if something goes wrong, he'll deal with it better if he knows I was the one guiding the spell," Alain reminded the other wizard. "We'll have enough problems if this goes wrong without him attacking you for it."

Raymond could not argue with that logic, so he gestured for Alain to begin.

Closing his eyes, Alain envisioned a loom, stringing it first with tendrils of magic. A moment later, he could feel Raymond's magic join with his, the weft to his warp. He was peripherally aware of a commotion behind him, of other wizards moving to meet the threat or keep the distraction from interfering with his concentration.

"Let me go to him," Sebastien roared as the wizards moved to stop him. He brushed one aside like a fly before Orlando caught his arm, pulling him around. "Let me go!"

"You can't help him, Sebastien," Orlando insisted. "Alain and Raymond have to do this. Don't make their job harder."

"If it were Alain there?" Sebastien challenged.

"You'd be holding me back," Orlando acknowledged ruefully, "but that doesn't mean you're right and I'm wrong. Let them do their job."

The sound of Orlando's voice broke Alain's concentration momentarily. "Focus!" Raymond's voice echoed within his mind. "Thierry's all that matters now."

Pushing aside his worries over why Orlando was here, Alain picked up the strands of the spell he had dropped, working with Raymond to complete the net they would cast across Thierry to separate him from the elemental magic. When the strands pulled tight, Alain met Raymond's eyes across the lake that still separated them, Raymond still holding his place in the magical compass to balance Thierry. As one, they cast the net, blanketing Thierry in their magic.

The maelstrom that had held Thierry tight swirled out of control, seeking some new victim, but the other wizards were prepared, resisting the lure of unimaginable power. Denied a source of new energy, the whirlwind slowly eased. Raymond wondered what that presaged for their future, since they had not completed the Rite d'équilibrage. When it had finally dissipated completely, Alain and Raymond released the magical net as well. Next to him, Thierry slumped into Alain's arms.

Tearing free of Orlando's grip, Sebastien raced to them. "Thierry?" he pleaded. "Talk to me."

"He's unconscious," Alain told the vampire. "We have to wait for him to wake up to see what damage was done."

"Damage?" Sebastien snarled, pulling Thierry from Alain's arms into a protective embrace. No one hurt his wizard! "What do you mean, damage?"

"He was caught by forces too powerful for him," Raymond explained, joining the others. "It may be several days before we can see whether it damaged his magic."

"Give him to me," Alain ordered. "He needs to go to the infirmary where they can take care of him properly."

Sebastien hissed possessively. "Like hell, wizard. Tell me what to do for him, and I'll make sure he gets what he needs."

"There's nothing you can do, vampire," Alain snarled back, fear over all that could go wrong even now that Thierry was free making him snap out at the nearest target. He had told Thierry before the alliance even formed that he could not fight this war without his best friend at his side. Despite all that had transpired since then, that still held true. "He needs magical care."

Realizing this was degenerating into a pissing match, Orlando stepped between them. "This isn't helping Thierry," he told them both. Knowing he would be as frantic had anything happened to Jean, but equally able to understand Sebastien's fears, he touched Alain's cheek, willing his partner to listen to reason. "Send them both where Thierry can get the best care and then make sure Sebastien is allowed to help. Now go."

With a sharp nod, Alain took quick stock to make sure Thierry wasn't bleeding before casting a displacement spell to send Thierry and Sebastien to the infirmary. "Go on," Orlando urged Alain. "I know you want to be there, too. Raymond will make sure I get back to Milice headquarters."

The other wizard nodded his agreement. Torn between his loyalty to his best friend and his desire to stay with Orlando, Alain hesitated.

"Go on," Orlando said again. "I'll be there in a few minutes. He needs you. I don't, right now."

His gratitude visible on his face, Alain cast the spell again, transporting himself to the infirmary lobby.

Chapter 7

"ADÈLE!"

The wizard looked up at the sound of her name. "Sir?" she asked when she realized who had called her.

"You'll have to lead our forces at the Tour Eiffel today," Marcel informed her.

"Me?" she repeated, sure she had heard wrong. "What happened to Alain?"

"Something went wrong with the Rite d'équilibrage," Marcel explained. "Alain had to go help Thierry. That leaves you as the ranking officer in the three patrols assigned to the Tour Eiffel today."

"But," Adèle protested, "I haven't made any plans. I wouldn't know where to begin defending it."

"Here are Alain's plans," Marcel offered, holding out the blond wizard's notes. "I have every confidence in your ability to pull this off. Your people are well trained not just to obey orders but to think on their feet, as are Alain's and Thierry's. You have two goals in this: keep the rebels from bringing down the Tour Eiffel, and take out as many of them as you can. This won't be like our usual strikes where we try to take prisoners. I don't care if you come back empty-handed as long as you come back and the monument is still standing."

Adèle nodded. Marcel had not said the words, but she understood nonetheless. They would be shooting to kill that afternoon, every spell a lethal one if they could cast safely. Now she just had to deal with her partner.

"About time he recognized that we're capable of being in command," Jude griped when she told him of the change in plans.

"Marcel is perfectly aware of what we're capable of," Adèle informed him coldly, "and we'll prove our worth today by following Alain's plans to the letter. I may or may not have made the same plans if I'd have time to work it out on my own, but I'm not about to screw things up—or let you screw them up—by second-guessing his decisions, particularly since I'm pretty sure I saw Thierry's hand in some of those notes, and he's the best strategist we've got."

Jude snorted, but kept his opinion of what any mortal could know of strategy next to a vampire steeped in le jeu des Cours to himself. Inwardly, though, he resolved to nudge Adèle in the right direction if he saw the battle going ill because of lack of foresight on the wizards' part. Then again, they were fighting other wizards, equally ignorant of the layers and layers of sleight of hand perfected by vampire society, so perhaps the battle plans would be sufficient.

Either way, he was determined to see not only to his own survival but to his partner's as well. He did not always care for her attitudes or her actions, but he had grown quite used to being able to ignore the dawn again since the formation of the alliance.

THE FIRST spells flew at exactly noon, and as Adèle countered one after another, she had to admit that had they not been forewarned, the Tour Eiffel would have fallen already. As it was, even with Alain's and Thierry's patrols as well as hers, they were barely holding their own against the onslaught of dark wizards.

"Fouquet, behind you," she shouted, vaulting down a flight of steps to fire off a spell at a dark wizard. She did not even bother to see if she recognized him. He was down. That would have to do for now.

"Thanks," Lt. Fouquet yelled back, turning his attention elsewhere again, seeking the dark wizards where he could find them.

Adèle ducked just in time to avoid an *Abbatoire* that should have hit her in the head. Instead, it went harmlessly into the metal girders, sparking a little as the elements absorbed the magical energy. Dropping to her knees and using a different beam for cover, she sought the source of the spell. Before she could cast again, Jude had leapt the distance, a simple flip bringing him to stand in front of her attacker, and engaged the man hand to hand. Shivering at the sight of the two men, she cast a binding spell, knowing it would pass right over her partner. She should have warned him, just to be polite, but such niceties were beyond her where the vampire was concerned. It was a little bit of revenge for the way he insisted on belittling her at every turn.

A detonation rocked the tower, knocking Milice operatives to their knees as they struggled not to lose their footing and go over the edge. "Guy," she shouted to her lieutenant. "Get down there and find out what's going on."

He waved his assent before winking out and reappearing on the ground, wand at the ready as he searched for the source of the blast. Adèle did her best to cover him from above, but she had the defense of the entire platoon to worry about. Ultimately she lost track of him in the smoke and confusion.

Guy managed to reach the foot of one the supporting girders, using the metal for cover as he searched for any sign of what had caused the explosion. A spell crater drew his attention and he slunk forward to investigate, trying to be as unobtrusive as possible. Kneeling down, he examined the hole. A quick incantation revealed its cause, and he frowned. This kind of land mine spell could have been scattered all around the base of the tower and through the Champs de Mars at any time. Even if they won the battle, they would have to be incredibly careful in the aftermath to make sure they had not missed any.

He would not be able to clear even the sandy area completely by himself, at least not during the battle—but he would at least start around the girders to make sure the force of the blasts did not bring down the tower itself. He cast a revealing incantation so he could see the spells he would need to disarm in order to protect his comrades. The sand lit up like fireworks on la Fête nationale. He muttered a curse under his breath as he contemplated what to do next. He would have to navigate a veritable minefield to even get to the nearest leg of the tower, disarming as he went. He dared not displace himself either, for fear of triggering a spell as he reappeared.

"I'm going to need help down here," he shouted up to Adèle. She waved to let him know she had heard him, but before she could send someone to assist, she was besieged herself. Knowing she would send help as soon as she could, he began the counter spell for disarming the mines.

Slowly, he carved a path toward the second leg of the tower, disarming one mine after the next. A stray cast from above triggered one of the spells near the third footer, though, rocking the tower again and forcing Guy to his knees, hands covering his head for protection. "Merde," he cursed under his breath when the reverberations stopped. He rose again and began working his way forward.

He almost shouted a warning to his fellow Milice wizards to watch their spells, but he did not want any of Serrier's wizards deciding to set off the mines intentionally. Another explosion sent him ducking for cover again—but this time it did not stop with one spell, instead setting off a chain reaction. Guy cast counter spells frantically, trying to slow or stop the explosions. His friends were up there, being shaken like leaves in a gale each time the Tour Eiffel shuddered from another blast. His final spell ended the cascade, but not before it set off the land mine right next to him.

Several stories above, Adèle watched in helpless fury as the explosions drew nearer and nearer her lieutenant and friend. "Guy!" she screamed. "Get out of there!" She thought he looked up at her, as if to tell her he understood—but before he could displace himself, another explosion went off, knocking him to the ground and sending her tumbling over the edge of the girder she was leaning on. She caught the metal cable, holding on for dear life, cursing roundly as her wand slipped from her grasp and fell to the ground below. Without it, she could not effect a displacement to either return her safely to the ground or to the landing where she had been fighting.

The cold air numbed her fingers as she dangled helplessly, an easy target for anyone who cared to fire a spell in her direction. Even if no one saw her, though, she knew she would not be able to hold out for very long. She would lose feeling in her hands, and when that happened, she would fall. Determined not to simply let it happen without trying to do something, she started inching her way down the cable, hoping to get close enough to one of the girders to pull herself to safety.

"Don't move."

Adèle froze at the sight of a wand pointing at her. She refused to cower, though. The wizard, whoever she was, could cast whatever spell she pleased. Adèle was helpless to fight it without her wand, but she would not give the other woman the pleasure of seeing her beg. The woman's mouth opened, but no sound came out, her head jerking around suddenly and her body dropping to the ground. Another head appeared over the edge of the girder. "Perhaps now you'll admit I have some usefulness," her partner drawled.

"Shut the hell up and give me your hand," Adèle growled, not wanting to think about being grateful to the arrogant vampire.

"That's hardly conducive to gaining my cooperation," Jude pointed out, even as he leaned forward and took firm hold of her wrist.

"Just get me the hell off this cable," she griped. "I feel like a sitting duck out here."

Jude did as she asked, pulling her back onto the metal landing and crowding against her momentarily.

"Get out of my way," she snapped. "I've got to get my wand and check on Guy."

Jude frowned, not liking the sound of another man's name on her lips. "One of your conquests?"

"Salaud," she spat. "One of my soldiers, not that it's any of your damn business. Now get out of my way. He could be dying down there."

"He could already be dead," Jude countered.

"Fucking bastard," she ground out, drawing back and slapping him hard. "Maybe he is, but my wand's down there, too, and if I don't get that back, neither one of us is likely to survive this battle. Now get the fuck out of my way and let me go."

Jude's head rocked back from the force of her blow, giving her space to slip by him and start down the steps toward the ground. Recovering, he caught her wrist. "Stay here," he ordered, "and keep your head down. I'll get your wand and check on your precious soldier. As long as you don't have your wand, you're vulnerable to their spells. I'm less so."

Adèle gaped at him. Despite the condescending tone of his voice, he was right, and nothing had forced him to offer. "Thank you."

Jude nodded curtly as he sprinted down the steps, his preternatural speed taking him to the ground in far less time than Adèle could have managed. One glance at the burned face of the wizard on the ground told him all he needed to know, but he dutifully checked the man's pulse to make sure. As he suspected, he found nothing. He carefully shut the blank eyes and bowed his head as he made the sign of the cross, a long-forgotten habit from before his turning.

Coming back to his surroundings, he began his search for Adèle's wand. Fortunately, Guy's revealing spell still functioned despite the man's demise, and Jude picked his way carefully between the dangerous spells. The cascade that had killed Guy and nearly killed Adèle had left the ground cratered but relatively spell free, allowing Jude to navigate his way to where the length of oak rested on the ground. He hesitated for a moment before picking it up, wondering whether it could hurt him—but he had volunteered, and Adèle huddled above, defenseless, while he waffled. The last thing he needed was to lose his partner. He might not like her much, but he did like what her blood could do for him.

Sprinting back toward the girder, he felt a spell hit him, nearly knocking him to the ground. Fortunately, it seemed to be one that did not affect vampires; though winded from the fall, he had no problem rising again and seeking the relative shelter of the metal structure. Climbing as fast as he could, he returned the wand to its owner. “He’s dead,” he told her softly. “I’m sorry.”

Her face hardened as she fought the twin urges to cry and to rail against the heavens. Feeling her magic pressing hard against her control in response to her wildly fluctuating emotions, Adèle turned sharply on her heel, seeking a target for her anger.

Valérie Lavie had no idea what hit her, no time to defend herself or even identify the source of the spell that flattened her. Bewilderment was the last thing she felt before she lost consciousness.

Adèle sought another target as another blast rocked the tower. She grabbed for the closest thing to hand to steady herself, scowling when that turned out to be Jude. “What are you doing?” she snarled as he caught her in his arms until the shaking stopped.

“Trying to keep you from going over the edge again,” Jude snapped back. “Having to save you once was bad enough.”

Adèle glared at him until he released her, refusing to acknowledge the thrill of desire that shot through her at being held so close. Their lives were already complicated enough without adding sex to the mix. Then he shifted and she could feel the hard bulge in his pants. Silently, she cursed herself roundly for the seductive heat that spread through her. They were in the middle of a battle! She had no time for this sort of distraction. Pushing away from him, she refocused on the fight—but all around, the remaining dark wizards began disappearing. Adèle had not heard any order to retreat, but one had clearly been given.

“Secure a perimeter,” Adèle ordered Lt. Fouquet. He called an acknowledgement and led his patrol out to the edge of the Champs de Mars. They worked quickly, erecting a magical barrier that would keep bystanders clear of the area until it was deemed safe again.

“Lt. Gastineau, get your squad to work on clearing any remaining mines,” she continued.

“Yes, ma’am!”

“We’ll have to get an engineering team in here to check for damage before the Tour reopens,” she mused aloud.

“Adèle.” Jude’s voice was low and hoarse as he spoke. She turned to him in surprise. The look on his face sent lust coursing back through her again, despite her efforts to focus on the aftermath of the battle. She could not simply leave. She had responsibilities. His gaze called to her, though, pushing buttons she did not know she had, tempting her to forget everything except the promise in his eyes.

"Captain Rougier!"

She tore her gaze away from Jude to see who had called her. Jérôme knelt on the ground next to Guy's lifeless body. "Take care of him," she told the other wizard, trying to shake off the effects of the vampire's spell. She knew he had no magic the way wizards did, but she also knew the feeling of magical compulsion. That felt very much like what she was experiencing now. She could fight it, for a time at least, but eventually she would have no choice but to give in. Looking back to Jude, she sighed. "Give me half an hour," she requested. "Let me do right by the fallen and then I'll come with you."

Chapter 8

"HURRY UP," a voice hissed behind him. "If they see us, we're dead."

Eric did not bother turning to see who spoke. "If I trip one of Chavinier's wards by mistake, we're dead anyway," he replied coldly, "so unless you think you know his spells well enough to bring them down undetected faster, shut up and let me concentrate."

The other wizard had no reply for that, though he grumbled under his breath nonetheless at the painstaking care Eric took to dismantle each ward. Eric ignored him. He had no desire to have this mission degenerate into a shouting match that would certainly lead to their detection, there in the bowels of the city as they worked their way closer to Sainte-Chapelle and the Palais de Justice. Chavinier had covered his bases well, Eric had to give him that, but even the most painstaking plans could be undone by someone with the patience to outthink their architect. Eric had no illusions that he could do so on a regular basis, but this once he thought he had found the chink in the Milice armor. Only a few more wards separated them from Sainte-Chapelle and a strike at the very heart of the French government.

"Merde!" he heard a wizard spit behind him.

"What is it?" he whispered harshly, turning back to look at whomever had spoken. "What's wrong?"

Jean-Claude Vuillemin, a new recruit from Arles, looked up apologetically. "I think I tripped a ward. I stumbled, and when I put my hand on the wall to steady myself...."

Eric knew how the rest of that sentence went. This close to the Palais de Justice, every inch of the subterranean passages was covered in spells. He had cleared the ground so they could walk but had not bothered with the walls, since they could pass without touching them. "He knows we're coming now," Eric informed the others. "We'll just have to hope our double distraction has him too spread out to rally in time. Let's move!"

With the need for secrecy gone, their passage through the tunnels sped up considerably. Eric no longer worried about clearing alert wards, only those that would endanger them as they passed. They burst out into the courtyard at the entrance to Sainte-Chapelle, wands drawn and spells leveling anyone in their way. He saw a guard on a radio calling for help and sent the device flying, though he expected enough had gotten through to alert the guards on the inside. So they would have the gendarmerie to deal with, maybe even the military, as well as whatever force Chavinier could cobble together at the last minute. Only

Eric and Serrier had known about this attack before the patrol left to execute it, so Eric was confident Chavinier's spy or spies had not revealed their plans.

The screams of the tourists caught in the attack barely penetrated the battle haze fogging Eric's mind. They were no threat to him or the other wizards, most of them running at the first sign of trouble. The rest simply fell cowering to the ground, no impediment to their progress past the admission gate and into the lower chapel. On another occasion, Eric might have paused to appreciate the solid lines of the vaulted ceiling or the elegant blue and gold decorations that evoked the Virgin Mary, but the sound of booted feet approaching focused his attention on the battle. "Vincent, Jean-Claude," he ordered, "seal the door. We don't want anyone surprising us from behind."

The two wizards moved at his command, barring the door through which they had entered and fusing the lock magically shut. Even another wizard would be hard-pressed to separate the mechanism they had just melted closed.

Shouted orders to surrender to the police echoed down the spiral staircase from the upper chapel. Eric looked at his companions and laughed. "They still think their guns can do anything against us?" he asked rhetorically. "Let's prove them wrong."

They started up the stairs until they reached the last curve before they would be visible to the officers waiting for them. On Eric's silent command, they paused while he cast a reflecting spell on the wall in front of them so that their magic would ricochet into the upper chapel. "Spike their guns," he ordered firmly, ignoring the grumbling from some of the wizards who did not see why they could not simply cast an *Abbatoire* at everyone and be done with it.

"Spike their guns," Eric repeated, meeting the gaze of each of his patrol until they had all nodded in acceptance.

He gave the signal and they cast as one, their spells bouncing off the wall in front of them into the chapel above. The magic reverberated through the room, twisting the metal barrels until no bullets could escape. The dismayed shouts made Eric smile. "Let's go."

They burst into the room with every intention of pushing through the doors into the main halls of the Palais, their progress halted not by the soldiers, but by a commanding voice they all recognized too well. "Drop your wands."

"Putain de merde! What's Chavinier doing here?" Jean-Claude whispered desperately.

"Steady," Eric ordered, searching to see if the old wizard had come alone or if he had brought others with him. He had always known a time might come when he would have to face off with his former mentor, but that did not make it any easier now that it had happened.

"You don't really want to do this, Eric," Chavinier cajoled. "Grief makes people do strange things. We all understand that."

"Vieux con!" Eric spat, all the pain of his loss swamping him again at the sight of people he associated with happier times. He told himself again and again that he had moved on, moved past that horrid day, but moments like these showed him just how wrong he was. "It wasn't grief that made me leave, but your refusal to see justice done. Get out of the way and nobody else will get hurt."

"You know I can't do that," Marcel replied sadly. He would give much to welcome Eric back into his fold, but as long as the war raged that seemed unlikely. He still held out hope, though, that someday the situation would be different.

"And you know I can't come back," Eric retorted. "*Abbatez*!"

Before the spell could connect, a dark-haired man Eric did not know pushed the general out of the way, taking the spell in the chest and going down. Eric's spell was the signal the other wizards needed to begin their attack. They focused on the door, knowing their destination was not Sainte-Chapelle itself but the Cour de cassation. From behind them, hidden amidst the gendarmes, spells rang out, the wizards accompanying Chavinier coming to his assistance. Eric's patrol circled up as they had been trained to do, their backs to each other, their wands aiming at all the points of the compass. To their surprise, many of the gendarmes stayed to fight, engaging them hand to hand when the Milice spells let them get close enough.

"The windows," Vincent shouted, casting a spell to shatter the glass walls, the shards cutting deeply as the dark wizard sent them flying into the opposing forces.

The floor grew slick with blood as the fight raged on, neither side able to get a definitive edge. The tide of battle ebbed and flowed, spells flying constantly though opponents changed. Suddenly, Eric found himself face to face with one of the few Milice wizards he would have any qualms about casting on. Caroline had been his wife's best friend, had grieved at his side when Danielle and the children were killed. His ties with her ran far deeper than they had with anyone other than Thierry and Alain. Those friendships had died when Alain's spell killed his family, but he had never been able to make that final break with Caroline. The *Abbatoire* died on his lips as he mentally scrambled to find another spell, one that would take Caroline safely out of the battle without harming her. Before he could cast, a red-haired fury attacked from the side, physically bowling him over—an unprecedented occurrence given his size. Before he could fight her off, he heard Caroline's voice casting a sleeping spell. He tried to block it, but the woman who had tackled him still held his arms, keeping him from moving. Blackness settled over him.

Seeing Eric down, Vincent shouted for the other rebel wizards to retreat, grabbing his friend's arms to take him along before winking out. He hoped Eric's wasn't bleeding—the displacement would kill him—but it was better than letting him be captured. The members of his patrol still standing did the same.

"Stand down," Marcel called as the dark wizards disappeared. "Jean, you can get up now. Thank you for the assistance and the ruse."

The chef de la Cour rose from where he had fallen after taking the *Abbatoire* in the chest. "How many of them escaped?"

"I didn't get an exact count of how many there were to begin with, but enough that they would have been suspicious if my rescuer hadn't stayed dead," Marcel replied with a tight smile. "We need to keep Serrier in the dark for as long as possible."

"Next time, somebody else gets to play dead," Jean decided. "Listening to everything without being able to help isn't my style."

"If I trusted anyone else the way I trust you, I wouldn't have asked you to do it," Marcel assured him. He looked around the chapel at the shattered glass and sighed. "They have no respect for anything other than their own power. Fortunately, some things are within my power to repair. Will you see to the wizards we took down? Georges can help you bind them."

Jean nodded and joined the blond wizard to gather up the prisoners. "Caroline," Marcel called, "see to the wounded."

She waved and started moving among the injured. She could heal simple wounds from the flying glass easily enough, though the spell required enough of her own energy that she used it only on the deepest cuts. Outside, she could hear the sound of sirens approaching, ambulances to transport the injured for medical care. Her first aid notwithstanding, the gendarmes had suffered badly under the rebel attack.

Her heart ached as she tended the wounded, thinking about the wizard who had betrayed them. She had understood Eric's loss and grief when Danielle and the children were killed. She had even understood his anger, though she felt it had been misplaced. She had never come to understand, however, how he could use Danielle's tragic death as a reason to change sides. Danielle would have been horrified if she knew. She had tried telling Eric that the first time she saw him after his defection, but he refused to listen.

"What's wrong?" Mireille asked, appearing at her partner's elbow. "You look distraught."

"The wizard you attacked, the big one, used to be a friend of mine," Caroline explained. "I never thought about what would happen if I came face to face with him in battle, I guess. And now that it's happened, I still don't know how to deal with it."

The secouristes swarmed into the room at that moment, drawing Caroline's attention back to the wounded and the dead. "We'll talk about it later. Right now, we have work to do."

IN the tunnels beneath the city, Vincent paused to catch his breath. He had not dared transport the patrol directly to Serrier's headquarters, just in case Chavinier tried to track their spell. He paused for a moment to position Eric better in his arms. His friend was still breathing, so the spell Bontoux had thrown at him was not fatal, at least. Even so, he wanted someone to check Eric over as soon as possible. He had lost too many friends since this war began to want to lose another one.

Vincent frowned as he mentally tallied the losses from today's aborted raid. If they had succeeded, it would have been a grand gesture, a crippling blow to the government, irrefutable proof of their superiority. Unfortunately, they had not succeeded. He scowled at Vuillemin. The man's ineptness had alerted Chavinier—although how the old man had gotten a defense together so quickly, Vincent did not know. That was not his problem, though. He left the strategizing to Serrier and Eric, and others who were good at it. He knew his role in the war effort: brute force. He had accepted that when Serrier first started preaching his doctrine of magical oligarchy. Vincent did not always agree with the methods the dark wizard supported, but the memories of a childhood friend who had been tormented by bullies until he defended himself with magic, only to find himself severely punished for "crimes" against the nonmagical, were far too vivid to dismiss. In Serrier's new world, such injustice would not be permitted. He only hoped the end of the war would mean the end of some of Serrier's more extreme methods. Otherwise, he feared to find himself as dissatisfied with the new order as with the old.

Reminding himself that Eric needed him to act, he ordered the others to return to Serrier's base by different routes so that anyone following them would, he hoped, decide they had disbanded rather than returning together to a central location. Keeping Eric tight in his arms, he disobeyed his own orders and displaced them directly to Serrier's infirmary, turning Eric over to the care of the medical practitioners.

"What happened?" Serrier snapped, storming into the room almost as quickly as the healers.

"Vuillemin tripped a ward on the way in," Vincent explained apologetically. "I don't know how Chavinier reacted as quickly as he did, but he was waiting for us at the doors from the chapel into the Palais de Justice. Maybe someone tripped a ward earlier and didn't say anything?"

Serrier's face tightened. "I'll deal with Vuillemin. You make sure they get Eric back on his feet as quickly as possible. I want his take on what happened."

Vincent nodded as Serrier strode out of the room, anger sparking around him. Vincent was glad that anger was directed at someone other than him. He could almost feel sorry for Jean-Claude. When Serrier got this angry, heads rolled. Sometimes literally.

"He'll be fine in a few hours," the medic interrupted Vincent's thoughts. "The spell just knocked him out. There won't be any lasting damage, but it's still safer to let him wake up on his own."

"Thanks," Vincent told the woman. "I'll let Serrier know. Contact him or me when Eric wakes up."

"Yes, sir," the woman agreed.

Leaving the infirmary, Vincent winced as a pained scream echoed down the hall. The medics would be busy later, that much was certain. He turned and walked the other way, not wanting to see what remained of the clumsy wizard. He had seen enough bloodshed for the day.

Chapter 9

"WHAT'S TAKING so long?" Sebastien growled. He paced the hall outside the cubicle into which the medics had rushed Thierry as soon as Sebastien had appeared with the injured wizard in his arms.

"I don't know," Orlando replied honestly, more than a little worried himself. Alain was unharmed physically, but the vampire already knew what kind of toll it would take on his partner if Thierry did not recover. Not to mention that Orlando had grown rather fond of the blond wizard himself. So, it seemed, had the man next to him. "You know Alain would've taken him somewhere else if this weren't where he could get the best treatment. He's not going to do anything to harm Thierry."

Sebastien did not totally agree, given that his partner was in the infirmary now because of something Alain had done. From what little he understood of what had happened at the Opéra Garnier, though, the wizards considered that they had no other choice. That did not make it any easier to accept.

"You can come in now," the chief medic said from the doorway. Immediately, Sebastien pushed past him into the room. A low growl escaped his throat when he saw Thierry still unconscious, Alain perched on the edge of his bed.

"What's wrong with him?"

"We won't know for sure until he wakes up," Alain replied slowly, guilt assailing him as he considered again all that could possibly go wrong.

The answer did nothing to assuage Sebastien's frustration. "And when will that be?" he asked, voice clipped.

"We don't know."

Face tightening, Sebastien reached for Alain, pulling him up by the collar of his shirt. "What *do* you know?" he demanded.

Unable to stop himself, Orlando grabbed Sebastien's arm. "Let him go." Taking a deep breath, he reminded himself to stay calm. "This isn't helping," he added, trying to diffuse the clearly brewing fight. Physically, Sebastien would triumph, but Alain's magic would work on the other vampire—and Orlando knew he did not need a wand to cast. Such a fight, though, would benefit no one, least of all Thierry.

Slowly, Sebastien forced his grip to loosen. "What can you tell me?" He knew he was out of control, but he could not seem to temper his reactions. The last time he had reacted this way, Thibaut had been the object of his obsession, the Avoué brand on his neck all the explanation any vampire needed. Thierry's neck was mottled with bruises and bites, but no brand—yet Sebastien felt as truly bound now as he had then.

"He told you about the Rite d'équilibrage, right?" Alain asked.

Sebastien nodded.

"Something went wrong," Alain continued. "Raymond was supposed to be the focal point, but when they made the connection with the elemental magic, it drew from Thierry instead. I guess it caught him unprepared, but whatever happened, he couldn't get free. Imagine him hunkered down against a huge storm. We tried to reach him, but he was so drawn in on himself that we couldn't get to him. We had to break him free by cutting him off from the outside. The danger with that is that he could be cut off permanently, and we won't know until he wakes up. When he does, he'll either be able to sense his magical core again or he won't."

"But you don't know how long it'll take for him to wake up," Sebastien verified.

Alain shrugged helplessly. "It depends on how badly drained he was physically. Magic isn't just out there," he explained, gesturing vaguely to the void. "It comes from inside, too, and that requires a certain degree of physical strength. To have been drained the way he was and then to fight it the way he did required serious exertion on his part. He needs to rest physically as well as magically in order to recover."

"Once he wakes up, even if he's weak, he'll know right away if he still has his magic, right?" Orlando checked, an idea forming in his mind.

"Yes," Alain agreed, "but if he was severely weakened, that could be several days."

"I can taste your magic when I feed," Orlando pointed out. "Wouldn't Sebastien be able to tell if Thierry still has his magic?"

"But if he's already drained, I could make things worse," Sebastien protested.

"You wouldn't have to take much," Orlando reminded them. "A sip would be enough to reassure you both that he will recover, in time." *And maybe you'll stop snapping at each other*, he added silently, not about to let either one know how petty he found their squabbling—as if Thierry only had enough time and attention for one of them.

Alain considered the suggestion, weighing the merits of knowing Thierry's probable prognosis against the risks of possibly worsening both his physical and magical conditions. He tried to remember what it had felt like the first time Orlando bit him, when it had truly been a sip, enough for the vampire to read his heart and taste his magic but not enough to sustain him. He found that the incredible sense of well-being that emanated from their Aveu de Sang overshadowed the details of that first night in the cemetery. "I just don't know," he said finally. "It would probably work, but I have no way to guess how it would affect his recovery."

"It's not that important," Sebastien declared firmly. "I don't want to do anything to make things worse."

"That's just it," Alain replied. "If we know there's damage on a magical level, there are things the medics can try that might help. But they can cause damage if his magical core isn't almost burnt out. It would be like blowing up a tire. If you blow up a low tire, you get a full tire again. If you blow up a full tire, you get an explosion. And the sooner they know, the more effective the treatment will be. That's why we need him to wake up."

"Or Sebastien needs to bite him," Orlando interjected reasonably.

"And if that weakens him more?" Sebastien demanded.

Orlando threw up his hands in frustration. "How do you feel when I feed from you?" he asked Alain, ignoring the flush that colored the wizard's cheeks and neck. "Does it weaken you?"

"It wouldn't," Sebastien argued. "The Aveu de Sang protects him."

"Then find another wizard and ask him or her," Orlando sighed. "While you're debating, Thierry's lying there without treatment that might make a difference in his recovery, if he needs it. I realize it isn't my decision to make, but I don't see the problem here. I can't imagine how one tiny sip could make that much difference."

"What do you think?" Sebastien asked Alain seriously. As much as his primal instincts resisted the idea, at this point Alain was the best judge in this situation. He hoped that would change, hoped it would have the opportunity to change, but at the moment, this needed to be Alain's choice. "You know him better than I do, and if there's anyone he'd trust to make this decision for him, it's you."

What would Thierry want? Alain asked himself seriously. His best friend had always been more about actions than about words, choosing the course that would net them the most benefits even if it meant taking a risk. Sometimes he won, sometimes he lost, but he rolled the dice again and again. If their situations were reversed, he would do anything he could to make sure Alain got the best treatment, the most appropriate treatment, as quickly as possible. "Nothing ventured, nothing gained," he replied slowly. "Take as little as you can so you don't drain him any more than he already is, but find out what you can. We'll give you some privacy."

"It's all right," Sebastien replied. "I don't mind if you stay, not for this. It's just a little kiss."

Alain glanced at Orlando, who nodded slightly. Sebastien was not feeding in earnest, and he had invited them to stay. Alain had made the important gesture by being willing to leave. Orlando did step back to the edge of the enclosure, though, drawing Alain with him so Sebastien could approach the bed unimpeded.

Sebastien walked over slowly, perching precariously on the narrow space at Thierry's side. His fingers twined with his wizard's as he stared down at the handsome face. In repose, the worry lines around the man's mouth and across his forehead had eased, making him look younger, but all the dynamism Sebastien associated with him was gone as well. The lax features showed none of the sharp intelligence or wicked sense of humor he had come to expect from his lover. He reached out and brushed his fingers along Thierry's hairline, stroking tenderly.

Across the room, Alain glanced away. Sebastien may have considered the bite nothing more than a little kiss, but the wizard understood that far more had passed between the two men than he realized. Thierry had admitted his interest in his vampire partner, but they had not had time to talk since then. It appeared he had acted on that interest, because no one seeing Sebastien's tenderness as he lifted Thierry's wrist to his lips could doubt they were lovers. He only hoped Sebastien did a better job of caring for Thierry's heart than Aleth had done. He would hate to have to hurt the other vampire.

Sebastien's gaze flicked sideways to the pair standing nearby, not quite touching but so clearly together. He envied that closeness that came from the soul-deep commitment they had made. Turning his attention back to his own partner, he licked lightly at Thierry's skin before his fangs dipped just beneath the surface to taste. He immediately sensed a bone-deep weariness which he attributed to the physical drain from the ritual. To his relief, he also tasted Thierry's magic, as rich and vibrant as it had ever been in the wizard's blood. He broke the connection with a sigh of relief, closing the wounds tenderly, when Thierry's hand twitched in his.

"S…Sebastien?" Thierry's voice broke on the word as his eyes fluttered open, and he reached for his partner. "Where am I?"

Alain had already taken a step forward automatically when his best friend's words registered. He paused, uncertain of his place now. A few weeks ago, he would have been glued to Thierry's side until the other wizard was completely recovered, but he seemed to have been supplanted. A hand on his elbow drew his gaze to his lover. When Orlando had his attention, the vampire gestured with his head in the direction of the door. Alain nodded and followed him outside.

"Now that he's awake, he'll be able to determine if he needs magical assistance, won't he?" Orlando checked.

"Yes."

"Then let's give them their privacy," Orlando suggested.

Alain was still torn between his need to make sure Thierry was well and the logic of Orlando's words. Finally, he accepted that Sebastien had first claim on Thierry's attention now. He could hardly complain when his own priorities had shifted to the slender vampire at his side. "We need to figure out what went wrong," he said, turning his mind to other problems now that Thierry was awake.

"Then I guess we need to talk to Raymond."

"He'll be in his office, pouring over old tomes, trying to figure out what happened," Alain mused aloud. "Let's go see what he's learned."

They wended their way through the maze of corridors inside Milice headquarters until they reached Raymond's office. They knocked and then waited until they heard a distracted, "Come in."

Raymond looked up when his door opened. "Is there any news on Thierry?" he asked immediately, seeing who darkened his doorway. "I'm trying to figure out what happened. If I understand that, maybe I'll be able to figure out how to help him."

"He's awake," Alain informed the other wizard. "He woke up just a minute ago."

"Is his magic intact?"

"I don't know. We didn't stay to ask," Alain replied.

Raymond's surprise showed clearly on his face.

"His partner's with him," Orlando explained. "We thought it best to let them have some time alone. We vampires tend to get protective of those close to us."

We put things, people, on pedestals, building our very existence around the object of our affection. Monsieur Lombard's words echoed in Raymond's mind, Orlando's comment adding even more weight to their hypothesis that the bond between partners somehow had a salutary effect on the elemental magic.

"He was awake and talking," Alain elaborated. "If he needs magical attention, he'll ask for it. We're more interested in what happened at the lake."

"I don't know," Raymond sighed. "Everything seemed to go fine, then the focus suddenly shifted and instead of us channeling magic, the elemental magic seemed to grab hold and pull it out. I've done that ritual countless times and I've never had that happen before."

"Has the imbalance ever been this bad before?" Alain countered.

"Well, no," Raymond admitted, "but it's been enough to be noticeable."

"So what was different this time?"

"I don't know!" Raymond insisted. "If I did, I'd have kept it from happening."

"What could be different?" Orlando asked. "Have you used that lake before?"

Raymond nodded. "Not always, but yes, when we've needed more than a few wizards involved."

"So it wasn't the location."

"No, I already thought about that, and it wasn't the number of wizards. I've found records of the Rite being done with that many people before, even with more, with no problem."

"I know Thierry wasn't happy about you being the one leading the Rite," Alain admitted. "Could his resentment have interfered somehow? Even unintentionally, could he have fought you for control?" He hated to think Thierry would act that way, but in the heat of the moment, particularly if he had seen something that struck him as odd, he might have done it.

Raymond reviewed his memories of the incident. "It felt like it came from outside," he repeated. "We didn't lose control. The elemental magic *took* control and latched onto Thierry. The question is why. If it had been Marcel, I would've understood perfectly—but Thierry isn't that much more powerful than I am, if he is at all."

"You were still standing when I got there, and he wasn't," Alain pointed out.

"Yeah, but I wasn't the one at the center of the vortex, either," Raymond reminded him. "I felt a little of what Thierry was fighting when we cast the net over him. I wouldn't have fared any better than he did."

"Yeah," Alain agreed. He had felt it, too, felt the force of the elemental magic buffeting his shields when it was denied Thierry's power. "So what made the difference?"

"I can only think of one possibility," Raymond said slowly, hesitating to reveal what he knew without Marcel's consent. "His connection with his partner."

"What?" Alain and Orlando asked in unison.

Raymond sighed and began to explain. "If we're right, the partnerships don't just help the alliance. They contribute to the magical equilibrium too. And if that's the case, then it's possible Thierry might have become the fulcrum instead of me because of the depth of his connection with Sebastien."

Alain's and Orlando's eyes met as they both remembered the incredibly tender scene they had witnessed in the infirmary. "Thierry mentioned at one point that Sebastien tended to feed lightly and often as opposed to deeply and more rarely," Alain offered, not entirely sure his friend would want him to share the rest of his confidences.

"So perhaps that's what brought him to the attention of the elemental magic in a way the rest of us who were there didn't," Raymond mused. "That would make sense."

"There may be another component to it as well," Alain suggested. "I haven't asked Thierry about his experience, but I find myself energized after Orlando feeds. If anything more powerful than I was before, rather than less. If that isn't just the Aveu de Sang, then Sebastien's frequent feedings could actually have made Thierry the better choice for the focal point. If that's the case then the Rite may have gone awry because he was unprepared for it."

"That's plausible," Raymond agreed after a moment's thought, "though I don't particularly care to test it."

"So what do we do then? Make sure no paired wizards participate when we try again?"

"It didn't work?" Orlando asked, hoping Alain would not offer to lead the next attempt.

Raymond flushed. "I've been so busy trying to figure out what went wrong that I haven't even checked."

"Check now," Alain suggested.

"I'll need some water."

"Let me do it then," Alain offered. "My affinity is with air."

Raymond gestured for him to proceed. Closing his eyes, Alain focused his magic on the air in the room, channeling into it much as Raymond had done at the lake. A ripple passed through the room before the breeze settled with no sign of the previous imbalance.

Orlando looked back and forth between the two wizards, seeing Alain's concentration followed by both men's surprise. Much of their conversation had been over his head, a discussion of matters he had never even known existed before a few weeks ago. "What is it?" he asked when Alain's eyes opened. "What's wrong?"

"Nothing's wrong," the wizard replied in amazement. "Nothing's been this right since the war started. I couldn't find any sign of imbalance locally. I didn't want to push beyond that in such a small space."

"Even if it's just a local improvement, though," Raymond commented excitedly, "we haven't managed this level of stability since the war began."

"But at what cost?" Alain asked, thinking of Thierry upstairs in the infirmary. Yes, he had awakened, but that did not mean he was unscathed.

"That remains to be seen," Raymond admitted, "but now that equilibrium is restored, we need only to maintain it again. With the vampires to help fight, we might even be able to assign a few wizards to that task permanently."

"That's for Marcel to decide," Alain said firmly. His conscience nagged at him for abandoning Thierry. "I should go see how Thierry's doing."

Raymond nodded and let them go without another word. He knew how the other wizards viewed him, even now. He was their source of information, their researcher, but not their friend. He had even learned to accept it, but that did not stop him from wanting someone to look out for him the way they looked out for each other. His thoughts slid traitorously to his partner, holed up with Marcel discussing political strategy. Perhaps, given enough time, Jean might come to see him the same way.

Returning to the infirmary, Alain paused outside the little cubicle. "Is it safe to come in?" he joked.

Sebastien's head popped out through the curtains immediately. "He's fallen back asleep, but he said he couldn't feel any difference in his magic. As you said, he's exhausted physically, but it looks like his magic is undamaged."

"Dieu merci!" Alain breathed. "Did the medics check him out?"

"They said he can go home when he wakes up, but that he's on bed rest for a week," Sebastien replied. "He wasn't happy, but he's still too weak to argue."

"He won't stay that weak for long," Alain warned.

"He'll need a lot more than a week to be stronger than I am," Sebastien insisted. "I'll make sure he rests."

Movement inside the curtain drew their attention. Thierry lay on the bed, struggling to sit up.

"Don't try to get up," Sebastien insisted, hurrying back to the bed. "You shouldn't even be awake yet."

"He's always hated the infirmary," Alain said with a smile.

Thierry glared at him.

"How are you feeling?" Alain asked.

"Like I just got hit by a runaway train."

"You look like it, too," Alain teased.

"Fuck you," Thierry retorted.

"That's my job," Orlando interjected before Alain could reply, hand flying to his mouth as he realized what he had said. The other three laughed, though, easing his discomfort.

"Seriously," Alain went on when the laughter died down, "how are you?"

"Tired," Thierry replied. "I don't think I've ever been this tired, but the medics say it's normal, that I'm actually doing far better than they would've predicted since I'm awake and coherent. They can't find any effect on my magic, and I can't feel any difference either."

"Good. Sebastien said they'd spring you when you woke up, so I'll go see about finding a medic to sign your release papers," Alain offered.

Thierry smiled tiredly. "Thanks."

Alain smiled in return and led Orlando back out into the hallway. "Your job?" he teased. Orlando flushed again, but Alain just leaned in and kissed him softly. "Let's get Thierry settled and then maybe we can go home and you can do your job."

That sounded like the best idea Orlando had heard all day.

On the other side of the curtain, Sebastien took Thierry's hand. "We'll get you out of here soon."

"I just want to go home," Thierry admitted, "and curl up in my own bed. I hate the way hospital sheets smell."

"We'll get you there soon," Sebastien promised, "and then you can rest."

Thierry fought his drooping eyelids, knowing the medics could not arrange magical transport for him if he was unconscious. "Stay with me?" he asked.

Sebastien's grip tightened. "For as long as you need me."

Chapter 10

"IT IS time."

Adèle did not acknowledge the vampire who had suddenly appeared at her side, instead finishing the orders she was giving to Charlotte and her patrol.

Impatient, Jude grabbed her arm, swinging her around.

Adèle glared at him. "I'll find you later, Charlotte," she said, pulling free of the vampire's grip. "I have something I need to take care of."

Charlotte nodded and left well enough alone, privately glad to see that she was not the only one who sometimes found dealing with her vampire partner difficult. "Don't worry about anything here. I'll make sure everything's taken care of."

"Thanks," Adèle said as she turned back to Jude. "Can you be any more obnoxious?" she demanded as she stalked past him toward the Métro stop that would take them toward her apartment. She did not ask where he lived or if he would prefer to go there. If she was going to do this—and she still had trouble believing she was—she intended to do it on her turf.

"Oh, I'm quite sure I could," Jude snapped back, clasping her arm proprietarily as they walked. He did not ask where they were going. He honestly did not care as long as it was private. He would even make do without a bed. Any flat surface would suffice, horizontal or vertical.

"Let go of me," she hissed as they descended the steps to the subway platform. News of the battle had clearly gotten out, because the entire station was deserted.

"Make me," he challenged, pushing her up against the wall and grinding against her lewdly.

She could not stop the spike of lust that went through her when she felt the bulge in his trousers and knew she was the cause of it, but she could decide how she would react to it. She refused to simply let him have his way with her. They would do this on her terms or not at all. Hoping vampires were not immune to pain, she grabbed his ear and twisted hard. He jerked away from her as she had hoped, allowing her to slip past him and onto the train that pulled into the station at that moment. The doors had started to close, making her grin at the idea of leaving him behind, but he jumped through at the last second, erasing her smirk and replacing it with a scowl.

Before she could react, Jude was at her side. He pressed her down into a seat, one hand tangling in her hair to pull her chin back so he could reach her neck, the other hand settling heavily on her hip to hold her in place. She started to struggle, out of habit if nothing else. Then she felt his lips and fangs on her neck and found she had no desire to fight anymore. Of its own volition, her hand gripped his shoulder, pulling him closer as the lust his bite inspired welled up within her.

The taste of Adèle's blood exploded on Jude's tongue. He had grown used to tasting her derision, but that flavor was absent this time, replaced by a rush of adrenaline and lust. His head spun with the new, intoxicating combination, making him wonder what it would take to elicit this response more often. The hand on her hip slid upward, caressing the curve of her waist, following the line of her body to the ripe breasts that had caught his attention the first time he saw her. He had dreamed of touching her, of pulling aside the figure-hugging blouses she favored to gain access to the smooth cream of her skin. He would not bare her in public, jealously refusing to share even the sight of her with anyone else, but he would touch, the mixture of his own battle-inspired lust and the taste of her reaction in her blood overriding what few sensibilities he possessed. Adèle was *his* and he had every intention of claiming her in every way known to vampires. In this moment, she would not turn him away. He could taste her acceptance in her blood, feel it in every movement of her lush body against his.

As the train hurtled through the dark tunnels toward Chevaleret, in and out of sparsely populated subway stations, he used every skill at his disposal to augment the passion building between them. He kneaded the taut mound of flesh as she moaned softly, arching against him eagerly, her hands moving over his back, his shoulders, into his hair, encouraging his attentions. Through the layers of her shirt and bra, he felt the tight point of her nipple prodding his palm. Sucking harder at her neck, gorging himself on the sweet taste of desire, he pinched lightly at the little nub, inciting her nerves to riot. Her body jolted against his as fresh lust spiced her blood. Then one of her hands slid lower, cupping his ass through his jeans, and he lost track of everything except bringing her to the peak as soon as possible. Silently, he cursed modern fashion that allowed women to wear pants, wishing for the skirts of his youth which had allowed him easy access to his lovers' tender parts without revealing more of them than he was willing to do. Settling for the heel of his hand against her sensitive nub, he stroked her through the cloth, feeling another jolt of lust hit her in response. Against her neck, his lips curved into a smile. She might spit and hiss, but like any pussy, she purred beneath his hands once he got her in his grip.

Adèle's head fell back against the cold metal of the subway wall as Jude's hand cupped her familiarly. She knew she should protest, especially since the corner of the train provided no privacy, though at the moment, they were alone in the car. It had been so long, though, since anyone had touched her, much less with such forceful mastery, that she could not summon the will to utter the words to stop him. She needed a strong man. Otherwise, she ended up eating him alive, leaving him a mass of trembling nerves and herself unsatisfied. She suspected that would not be a problem today. Through the thin wool of her slacks, she felt one long finger trace the lines of her folds, probing as much as the intervening fabric would allow. Her entire body twitched when he prodded the hood hiding her sensitive nerves. She bit her lip to hold back the pleas that threatened to fall. Not even for this would she let her infuriating partner hear her beg.

She forced her eyes to open as the train pulled into the next station. Pasteur station, one stop before Montparnasse. Even if no one got on now, she knew better than to imagine that Montparnasse would be as deserted. Summoning her concentration with great difficulty, she fumbled for her wand and cast a glamour on the doors, giving the impression that the car was completely full. It would not fool another wizard, but hopefully it would distract the average commuter.

That task done, she turned her full attention to giving as good as she got, her wand falling to the floor as she reached between them to stroke the hard shaft nudging her hip as intimately as he was stroking her.

The sudden surge of magic in Adèle's blood distracted Jude from his current obsession long enough to hear her cast a spell. Then her hand closed around him and he forgot all about magic of any kind except the magic of her touch. The dual assault from his own desire and what he tasted from her rocked his control, but he refused to succumb first. He redoubled his siege of her senses, giving in to the urge to touch her more intimately. A quick tug released the button and zipper on her slacks, his hand diving inside to plunder her riches. With complete surety of his welcome, he pushed aside the slip of her underwear, parting her folds and finding her wet with desire. He smiled smugly and licked the skin around his fangs, determined to lavish so much pleasure on her that she could not hold back.

Her back arched and she cried out wordlessly when one long finger slid into her heated depths, his thumb coasting upward to massage her hidden nubbin. A fresh rush of fluid rewarded his efforts. Lifting his head for a moment, he licked his way up the long column of her neck to one delicately curved ear. "Come for me, my little pussy." He nipped at her earlobe, drawing a drop of blood which he sucked into his mouth along with her flesh, closing the wound with his tongue.

"Bastard," Adèle hissed, the sensual spell he had woven shattering at his coarse words. She wanted to pull away—but the lure of his touch, of the release he could give her, was too strong. "You're not man enough to make me come."

Incensed at the aspersion to his manhood, he wrenched her head back again, attacking her neck with the combination of bloodlust and passion that only she could inspire. A second finger joined the first, spearing her deeply as his thumb pressed harder. He loosened his grip on her hair to see if she would fight his bite. When she did not try to raise her head, he released the dark locks completely in favor of her breasts. Frustrated by the layers of cloth, he tugged at the neckline of her blouse, tearing it until he could get his hand where he wanted it: skin against skin.

"Fucker," she spat, her fingers clawing into his neck, "that was my favorite shirt." In retaliation, she grabbed his hair and pulled hard, breaking the connection between his fangs and her skin. Her other hand pressed harder against his cock, determined to wrest control back from him. If she had known the picture she presented to his lust-glazed senses she might have refrained, for she was the portrait of wantonness, an image that overrode every scruple he possessed. Her color was high, passion and anger staining her cheeks a brilliant shade of rose. Her lips curled in a snarl of protest Jude found nearly irresistible. Blood trickled from the wounds on her neck, beckoning him like a siren's call. Her breasts heaved temptingly above her ripped neckline. Her legs splayed wide open, his hand deep in the apex of her thighs as he sought to drive her wild.

"Not yet," he told her, voice dripping with sheer masculine confidence, "but I will be before long, buried deep inside your dripping body. Say what you want, little pussy. I know what you want, and I'll be the one giving it to you."

"When hell freezes over," she retorted, squeezing his cock almost to the point of pain. "I take what I need, when I need it and where I want it."

"So the cat thinks she has claws?" His free hand circled her wrist, forcing her hand away from his groin and pinning it to the back of the seat. "We'll see how prettily she purrs before I'm done with her." His fingers drove deep inside her again, pressing unerringly on the spot that drove her wild. She fought it, fought him, but her body had been without a lover's touch for too long. While she might have fought him, she found herself unable to fight herself. Giving in to the inevitable, she closed her eyes and let her orgasm rush through her, pointedly ignoring the lascivious noises he made as he withdrew his fingers and licked them clean. "If you taste this good on my fingers, I can only imagine how good you'll taste on my tongue."

Pulling her coat around her to hide her disheveled state, Adèle rose to her feet, refusing to let her knees tremble in the aftermath of such an overpowering climax. "Keep dreaming," she spat, turning on her heel and striding out the door onto the platform. Cursing, Jude sprinted after her, grabbing her arm and spinning her around to face him.

"We're not done yet."

Deridingly, she looked him up and down, the bulge in his trousers looking quite painful. "What?" she challenged. "You didn't get off? Not my fault." She tugged her arm free and kept walking, climbing the stairs to street level two at a time.

Angrily, Jude stalked after her. As tempted as he was to push her up against a wall and fuck her where they stood, there were too many people around in the early afternoon for that to be an option. Even if she did not fight him—and he had no illusions on the likelihood of *that* coming to pass—someone would surely protest on the grounds of public decency. When they got inside wherever she was leading them, he would take his due and show her what she was missing.

She was aware of him following her, but short of shouting rape—she figured the blood on her neck and the ripped blouse would be enough to get him thrown in jail for a few hours at least—she saw no way to get rid of him. When they got to her building, she would get him off and then throw him out. He had reduced her to a helpless mess of quivering nerves. She owed it to herself, to her own dignity, to do the same or worse to him.

The short walk down rue Vincent Auriot to Square Dumois where her apartment was passed in tense silence, neither of them speaking in an effort not to draw attention to themselves. Adèle typed in the code to her building, shielding the touch pad with her body so Jude would not have the numbers, not wanting him to show up on her doorstep unexpectedly. When the outside door closed behind them, she turned on him. "Still here?" she asked derisively.

"I haven't gotten what I want yet," he replied tightly.

"Well isn't that just too bad," she sneered, climbing the stairs to her third floor apartment. When they reached the landing, she spun, pushing him face first against the wall, her hand diving beneath the waistband of his slacks to encircle his still swollen erection. "I'm glad I didn't waste my time," she commented cruelly as she stroked his sizable shaft. "I like to actually feel my lovers when they're fucking me." She felt him start to struggle so she tightened her grip, holding him in place. It only took a moment for him to start rocking into her fist. "Now who's the hungry slut?" she goaded. "Can't stop yourself from fucking my fist, can you? Just like a little boy, no self-control. Go on, cream your pants like a horny teenager. It's not like you're any good to me anyway."

Jude could have thrown her off. Her strength was no match for his, but he could not make himself pull away from her seductive touch. Despite the derogatory words, she made him hotter than anyone had in years. He would just have to show her who held the cards in their little game, and that would be far easier if he had already come once. He did not worry about getting hard again. As exhilarating as he found their battles, verbal and physical, he would be ready again in no time. Relaxing into her touch, he let his climax build until it exploded out of him, coating her hand and his belly, soaking into the fabric.

"Oh, that's going to be a little hard to hide," she crowed, pulling her hand away and wiping it insolently on the leg of his trousers. "Too bad you didn't think to wear a coat."

Turning her back on him, she touched the handle of her door, the wards recognizing her magic. She cursed silently for having dropped her wand on the train. She would have to buy a new one, a hassle she did not need. Frustrated, she started to slam the door behind her when Jude forced his way inside. "I don't remember inviting you in," she snarled.

"I'm not finished with you yet."

"Too bad, because I'm finished with you. You got what you wanted. Now get the hell out."

Jude grinned and grabbed both her arms, crushing their lips together. Her lips tasted as sweet as her blood. He cupped her jaw in one hand, prying her mouth open so he could surge inside to taste more fully, to claim her mouth as he intended to claim the rest of her.

As disgusted as she was aroused, Adèle took the only recourse open to her. She bit him. Hard.

"I wouldn't be a gentleman if I didn't make sure you got what you want," he prodded. "If I slip my hand back down your slacks, I'll find you dripping again, won't I, Adèle? You put up a good front, but you're just like every other round-heeled wench, legs spread for any man strong enough to take you."

Glancing down at the wet stain on his trousers, she scoffed. "Get it up again and maybe I'd be tempted, but I know your type. I'll be here twiddling my thumbs for hours if I have to wait on you to recover. I've got better things to do with my time."

"I didn't need my cock to satisfy you in the train," he reminded her, advancing on her predatorily. "I don't need to be hard to do it again."

Before she could protest again, he grabbed the sides of her coat and pulled it off her shoulders, pinning her arms to her sides. Leering at her, he ripped her blouse the rest of the way, exposing her torso. "Just lie back and relax, little pussy. I'll show you a good time."

She struggled against the leather coat, against his confining arms, but she could not get her arms free to push him away as he lifted her from the waist so her breasts were at the level of his mouth. She kicked at him ineffectively, too close in his tight embrace to get any force behind the movement. Then his lips closed over her nipple, wet heat surrounding her through the thin lace of her bra, and she lost any desire to fight.

Feeling her capitulation, Jude backed toward the wall, catching her between his hard body and the plaster, freeing one hand to pull the lace cup away from her breast, baring her completely to his gaze for the first time. The full globes made his mouth water and he lowered his head again to taste smooth flesh without any barrier. To his surprise, Adèle's legs circled his waist as he suckled. Not sure he trusted her seeming submission, he grazed his fangs lightly across the upper swell of her breast, blood welling to the surface. Licking at the scrape, he tasted nothing but desire, the spice a jolt to his own system as his cock started to reawaken. He switched to the other breast, giving it the same attention with lips and tongue. When she shifted restlessly against him, he bit her, letting the tips of his fangs break the surface, surprising a needy moan from her throat. "Like that, do you?" he goaded. "Does it arouse you to bear my marks? My own little pet wizard."

"I'm nobody's pet," she snarled, renewing her struggles.

"Sure you are, pussy," he crooned. "All it takes to tame you is the right touch, the right bite." He pierced her again, leaving a mark to match the first on the underside of her breast this time. "See," he said when she moaned and squirmed again, "and don't bother denying it. I can taste your feelings in your blood. You're so turned on right now you'd do whatever I asked as long as I keep touching you, biting you."

"Fuck you."

"No, no, pussy, you've got that backwards. I'll be the one fucking you before the afternoon is over. But first, I think I'll make you beg for it."

"I don't beg," she snapped, digging the heel of her boot into his back. "Ever."

The gouge of pain startled him into pulling away enough for her to get out from between him and the wall. She tore the jacket from her shoulders, ready to fight him in any way she could. She rued the loss of her wand now for more than just the frustration factor of buying a new one. Her magic would not work on him, but she could have used it to barrage him with objects until he got the message and left. "And I don't see you walking away either," she goaded. "If this means so little to you, why are you still here?"

"I never denied I desire you," Jude reminded her. "Surely I'm not the first to tell you you're beautiful enough to rouse the dead. I don't have to like you to want to fuck you through the mattress."

"So this is revenge?"

"Not at all," Jude countered, stalking her slowly. "This is lust, pure and simple, and I'm not leaving until I get what I want: you, wanton and willing beneath me."

"In your dreams," she spat, putting the couch between them.

"I won't need to dream. I'll have the real thing." Before she could move away again, he vaulted lightly over the couch, catching her in a steely embrace. One arm circled her torso while the other pinned her thrashing legs. Biting her breast again, he smiled at the lust that still surged through her system. She could say what she wanted; she needed this as badly as he did.

Stalking through her apartment, he found the bedroom and carried her inside, tossing her on the bed and following her down before she could escape. "You can let me take your pants off or I can tear them like I did your shirt," he informed her, his burgeoning shaft grinding against her pubic bone, "but either way, I'll have you naked in the next thirty seconds."

Adèle warred with herself, knowing she should not give in so easily, but knowing as well that she could not overpower him. She could continue to fight, but their joining was as inevitable now as it had been when they first left the battlefield. When this was over, she would have a few choice things to say to Marcel about the magical compulsion she could feel pressuring her, but in the end, she would give in. At least if she cooperated, she might get some pleasure out of their encounter as well. Jude had already proven he could make her fly, and she could not deny the temptation to feel that way again.

"I can't very well get undressed with you lying on top of me," she groused, pushing at his shoulders.

Jude looked down at her suspiciously. Yes, she was still trying to manhandle him. Yes, she still thought she could control things, but the fight seemed to have gone from her. Deciding to make sure, he caught her chin, baring her neck and biting her again, tasting her acceptance in her blood.

"Bastard," she insulted him when he rocked back on his knees enough to let her move. "You fed this morning and again on the train. How often do you need to bite me?"

"You enjoy it, pussy," he drawled, some of the tension leaving his voice now that she had stopped fighting him. "And blood doesn't lie."

His eyes never left her body as she levered off her boots and slid the wool slacks down her legs. She peeled off the tattered remnants of her blouse and stood before him proudly nude. "Your turn," she informed him coolly. "If you get a peep show, so do I."

"Cheeky wench," he scolded, rising to his feet and beginning to unbutton his shirt. "You could help."

"I'm not your servant," she reminded him, sitting back on the bed and ogling him openly. She might not like him much, but there was no denying his physical appeal. Dirty blond hair, green eyes, powerful muscles as his smooth torso came into view, an absolutely delicious ass—she copped a feel when he bent to pull off his shoes—and, as he turned to face her, his pants falling to the ground, a thick, erect cock that left her throbbing to be filled.

"I've seen worse," she observed, injecting a hint of scorn into her voice to prick his pride. He did such delightful things to her when he was angry.

"Bitch," he ground out, pushing her back onto the bed.

"I thought I was a pussy," she goaded as she felt his weight pressing her into the mattress, his skin cool against her heated flesh.

"You are," he retorted, fingers sliding between her legs to prove his point, "a sopping wet pussy, but it doesn't make you less of a bitch."

Done with conversation now that she had him where she wanted him again, she pulled his head down to hers, biting at his lips to silence him.

He growled possessively, tongue plunging between her lips again to explore the cavern of her mouth. Her tongue dueled with his, forcing its way into his mouth as well, refusing to give in to his attempt at dominance. His hips rocked against hers steadily, leaving a streak of fluid against her lower belly and into the nest of curls at the juncture of her thighs. The smell of sex rose to wreathe her senses in desire.

Breaking their kiss, she pretended to yawn. "I wonder where I left my vibrator," she mused aloud, trying to keep her voice from breaking as his lips skated across her collarbone toward her breasts. "Since you're obviously incapable of fucking me."

Anger at how easily she pressed his buttons roiling inside him, he rocked back on his heels and glared down at her. "I should leave you to it."

She shrugged. "Then do it. I don't need…." Her words were lost in a long, low groan as he plunged his fingers inside her again, lowering his head at the same time to suck strongly at her clit. She bucked beneath him, fighting for more now.

Every possessive instinct he owned urged him to bite her again, to claim her in every way he could. Already, her neck and breasts bore the sign of his presence, but her attitude made it clear she had no qualms about sharing her favors with any man who caught her eye. He could not tolerate that. His fangs dropped as he fought the urge to mark her most private flesh. Turning his head, he bit hard into the smooth skin of her inner thigh, the desire for blood warring with the desire to be sheathed inside her. Her answering desire slammed into him, sending his emotions swirling out of control. Pulling his fingers from her tight sheath, he attacked her with his mouth, his tongue driving as far inside her as it could reach to catch every taste he could. The beast inside him, barely civilized by vampire law, fought his control, wanting her blood as well. Unable to stop himself, he let his fangs graze her folds, barely enough to scratch. She cried out sharply above him, but made no effort to pull away as her blood mixed with her fluids in his mouth.

Pulling away before he lost control and hurt her badly, he slammed into her dripping sheath, his mouth seeking her neck as his hips pistoned in and out of her wildly. Her head fell back invitingly as his lips closed over her skin, fangs sliding home as easily as his cock had. She fought him for completion, their bodies racing toward the pinnacle outside their control. He tasted her building orgasm in her blood even as he felt the contractions begin around his cock. He thrust harder, wanting her so mindless with need, with desire, that she would willingly come back for more.

The explosion took them both, searing through their bodies, leaving them panting harshly on the edge of consciousness before finally giving in to the blackness assailing their senses.

Chapter 11

"DO YOU want to talk about it?"

Caroline looked away from the blank spot on the wall where she had been staring for at least the past hour, probably longer, since she had no idea what time it was now. They had done all they could at Sainte-Chapelle, for the wounded and dead and also to repair the building itself, before Marcel finally ordered them all home. She had been ridiculously grateful not to have to finish her shift, even though she knew without a doubt that Marcel had returned to Milice headquarters—where he would not only work until the change in patrols, but probably far into the night as well. Her guilt at leaving could not compete with the relief of avoiding questions about Eric.

She had known—they had all known—that he had switched sides; but seeing him in battle with his wand pointed at her, hearing his usually gentle voice casting an *Abbatoire* at Marcel, had shaken her far more deeply than she was willing to admit to anyone else.

"Caroline? You have to let it go or you won't be able to function," Mireille said softly, drawing her partner's attention. "Talk to me."

"Brother against brother, a house divided," Caroline murmured, eyes still mostly vacant. "That's what we are now, what this war has made us. I knew most of them, you know, before this stupidity started. We weren't all friends, but we had more than a passing acquaintance with the other wizards in the city. There are too few of us not to have some contact. And then Serrier started this wizarding supremacist bullshit and suddenly friends were enemies."

"The wizard who attacked you?" Mireille pressed gently.

"He's the one I knew best, anyway," Caroline agreed, "although I was far closer to his wife than I was to him. I introduced them, you know, after Danielle and I both came to Paris from Nantes. We were roommates at the university there, and then we shared an apartment when we first got here. Until she married Eric, actually."

"And what does she think of his choice?" the vampire asked curiously.

"She never knew," Caroline explained, tears welling in her eyes as she remembered the terrible aftermath of that first open attack. "He sided with us first, you see, until Danielle and their children were killed. She wasn't a wizard, couldn't defend herself when Serrier attacked the house where she was visiting another friend of ours. My only consolation is that she probably never knew what hit her." Caroline hoped to all the gods that was true, because it was the only way she lived with knowing Danielle had died magically. The idea that she might have suffered, might have known anything more than a moment's shock as the spell hit, would cripple Caroline beyond functioning. "I lost my best friend that day and her husband, all I had left of her, a week later."

Mireille's arms closed around the weeping woman, drawing her into a tender embrace. She forcibly ignored the tendrils of jealousy that her wizard might weep over another, an emotion she was at a loss to explain. The two had been friends, not lovers, and the other woman had been happily married, a mother more than once. Her jealousy was ridiculously unfounded, and even if they had once been more than just friends, the war had started over two years ago and Caroline said Danielle died early on.

"If she died in one of Serrier's attacks, why would her husband change sides? Wouldn't that be added incentive to fight for the Milice?" That was the one part of it Mireille did not understand.

"Serrier's wizard didn't kill her," Caroline explained. "Alain did. Not intentionally, but it was his spell that hit her, and that was something Eric simply couldn't forgive."

"You obviously did, though," Mireille observed. She had witnessed her partner working with the other wizard. She would not have described them as close, but they had seemed on friendly terms.

"She wasn't a wizard, but Danielle hated prejudice or intolerance in any form. She would have hated what Eric did. He let his anger lead him down a dark path, but I couldn't do the same. It would've been a complete betrayal of her memory, and I couldn't do that to her, not when Eric had already made that choice," Caroline replied. "Alain's spell hit her, but he was crazed with grief at the time, having found his ex-wife and son already dead. He didn't know she was there or he would have been more careful. I don't always agree with him, but I know he's an honorable man. He lives every day with the knowledge that he's killed innocents, the people we're supposed to use our magic to protect. There isn't anything I could do to him that's worse than what he does to himself every time he thinks about that day."

"You're a lot more forgiving than I would be," Mireille commented honestly.

"Maybe if Danielle had been a different woman, I might have felt differently about it, but she didn't have a vengeful bone in her body," Caroline said with a watery smile. "I've never known someone with a kinder heart. She would hate the thought that her death—the attack that included her death, anyway—started this war. She would hate the thought that anyone has been hurt in any way because of her." She turned in Mireille's embrace, burying her face against her lover's shoulder. "When we first came to Paris, Danielle and I visited the Conciergerie. There's an altar there, where Marie-Antoinette was imprisoned before her death. All around the room, words from her last letter have been inscribed, a memorial to her life and death. In one she implored her children not to revenge her death. '*Que mon fils n'oublie jamais les derniers mots de son père que je lui répète expressément : qu'il ne cherche jamais à venger notre mort,*' it said on the altar. I have no idea what prompted Danielle to say anything, but she told me that day that she felt the same way, that if she ever died tragically, she didn't want anyone to be blamed for it, just to let her go and make peace. How could I do anything but what I've done in the face of that attitude?"

"A premonition of some kind?" Mireille wondered aloud.

"It's possible," Caroline admitted, "though she never showed any other signs of it. Still, she lived her entire life surrounded by wizards and magic. Her grandmother who raised her was a wizard, she married a wizard, and I'm pretty sure her children would have been if they'd lived long enough for their power to manifest. She didn't have any overt magic, but I've heard of stranger things."

Caroline buried her face in Mireille's neck. "I miss her," she sobbed brokenly. "It's like this ache I've learned to live with, but it never really goes away. I won't think of her for a few days, then something will happen to remind me of her. We lived here in this city together for six years, did everything together. The only place that doesn't remind me of her is Milice headquarters, because she was never there. The Milice was barely forming when she was killed, and the building was just another government office."

Mireille held her partner tightly, letting her grieve. The vampire knew the loss of loved ones, having lost everyone when she was turned, but that grief was muted by time and choice. Some small measure of time had passed for Caroline, but it seemed to provide her no consolation. She rocked the sobbing woman gently, hoping to provide some comfort by her presence.

"Help me prove we're still alive," Caroline said suddenly, raising watery eyes to meet Mireille's. "Danielle always said you had to celebrate being alive. Help me do that."

"How?" Mireille asked.

"Take me to bed and make love to me," Caroline pleaded. "Make me forget everything but the touch of your hands and the taste of your lips."

Mireille frowned, unsure if this was the best course of action given Caroline's wildly swinging emotions, but her instincts reared their head at the invitation, eager to feed on the tender flesh and hear the wanton cries flow from the long, slender throat. The force of her reaction surprised her, especially given her own doubts about the wisdom of the request, but she found she could not deny it. The words simply would not form on her lips.

Instead, she wrapped her arms around Caroline more tightly, lifting her easily and carrying her toward the bedroom. Gently, she laid her lover on the bed, stretching out next to her and stroking her face tenderly. She would give Caroline this gift, this reassurance, and sate her own desires in the process. She marveled, when she had time, at how quickly the relationship had developed, but it felt so damn right to be here in Caroline's arms, in her bed, comforting her and being comforted in return. For the first time since she was turned, someone saw her as more than either a competitor or a freak or an illicit thrill. Caroline related to her as another woman first instead of merely treating her as a fellow soldier.

The fact that she was a vampire did not seem to matter at all. Lowering her head, she kissed the wizard gently, beginning the slow seduction that was her hallmark.

Caroline burrowed her hands into Mireille's long red hair, pulling their heads together forcibly. "I don't want soft," she purred against the smooth lips. "I want wild and fast and so hard I pass out when I come." She nipped at Mireille's jaw. "I want your fingers and your tongue and your fangs until you've wiped every thought but you from my mind."

Mireille's fingers trembled as lust hit her like a physical force, leaving her fighting not to rip Caroline's clothes as she peeled them away, letting the clothes fall carelessly to the floor. Her fangs dropped so fast it hurt, a hiss escaping her lips that was part pain, part lust. She pinned Caroline's shoulders to the bed as, still fully clothed, she straddled her naked lover. Caroline writhed beneath her, one knee bending to bring her thigh against Mireille's mound, rubbing provocatively over the sensitive region. She tilted her head back, offering her neck, but the vampire was focused on more sensitive flesh. One hand making sure her partner stayed where she wanted her, the other circled the creamy globes of Caroline's breasts—one, then the other, tugging urgently at the already peaked nipples. She would never have used such a rough caress normally, but there was nothing normal about this interaction. Caroline had never been so desperate; Mireille had never felt so out of control. Lowering her head, she sucked strongly on one taut peak, hands catching Caroline's torso as she arched off the bed. She licked and nipped, careful to keep her fangs from scoring the tender flesh.

"Bite me," Caroline pleaded, shifting as best she could beneath Mireille's implacable grip. "Let me feel your fangs."

Mireille resisted, knowing that once she settled in to feed, she would not want to stop, and she still had other plans for her mouth before they were finished. With one last lick to the sensitive point, she skimmed her lips down the flat plane of Caroline's stomach, inhaling the scent of desire underlaid by the pulsing blood running hot and heavy through the wizard's body. Her fingers found damp folds, exploring the outer lips through the blond curls. Caroline thrashed beneath her, parting her legs wider, obviously inviting a more intimate touch. "Patience," Mireille counseled, glancing up to meet her lover's green eyes.

"Fuck patience," Caroline replied crudely, sliding her fingers where she wanted Mireille's. If the vampire would not give her what she needed, she would give it to herself. She should have been surprised at her actions, but she had no thought to spare for anything but assuaging the lust riding her hard.

"Oh no," Mireille purred, catching Caroline's fingers and licking them clean before capturing both wrists in an implacable grip and pinning them to the bed, "but I will fuck you. When I'm ready." She punctuated her words with butterfly kisses down the length of the wizard's slit, her tongue plunging deep on the last word. She smiled into the soft bush as Caroline cried out her pleasure, hips lifting off the bed in search of more contact.

The wizard's heels dug into Mireille's shoulders as she tongue-fucked her partner, the blonde's head tossing back and forth wildly on the pillow. "Bite me," she pleaded again.

Again, Mireille shook her head. She had known vampires who claimed to have so trained their lovers that they could feed from their sex with impunity, but Mireille had no desire to mix that level of pain with Caroline's pleasure. When she had tasted her fill of her lover, she would find a spot to feed that would sate her need for blood without damaging her wizard's delicate folds.

Letting her tongue slip from the drenched sheath, she slid her fingers deep instead, stroking the walls of the passage, seeking the spot that would drive Caroline wild. Her tongue worked upward, burrowing beneath the hood of flesh to lick the sensitive nub until Caroline's thighs trembled on either side of her head. "Bite me," the wizard begged a third time.

Turning her head, Mireille did, driving her fangs deep into Caroline's inner thigh. The rush of blood hit her senses like the metaphorical ton of bricks. She worked her fingers deeper into Caroline's body, twisting them slightly as she pulled them out before plunging in again, determined to fulfill the wizard's request.

Caroline's orgasm caught her off guard. It ripped through her with the force of the typhoon that had struck La Réunion days before, stealing her breath and her consciousness as she came.

The taste of the wizard's release in her blood triggered Mireille's own climax, the flavor of passion an aphrodisiac like none other. Carefully, she pulled her fangs from Caroline's thigh, closing the wounds carefully with her tongue. They had torn in the tremors of orgasm, making her glad she had not given in to Caroline's earlier demands to be bitten. These wounds would be painful enough. Lifting her head, Mireille smiled softly at the relaxed and sated woman beneath her, too energized from the infusion of blood to relax into satiation herself quite yet. Quietly, she rose from the bed and removed her own clothes. They were stained with blood from the earlier battle, reminding Mireille of all that had transpired. She shivered in the cool room, the heat of Caroline's blood making her more sensitive than usual to temperature. Deciding she would rest better if she was clean, she pressed one last kiss to Caroline's bare breast before heading into the bathroom to take a quick shower. Perhaps if Caroline awoke, she would join her. And if not, she would return to bed when she was done and pass the quiet hours in her lover's embrace.

Chapter 12

ANGÉLIQUE WAS twitchy.

Her hands itched. Her fangs pressed against her gums, trying to drop. Butterflies danced in her stomach, lust skittering along her nerves even though she was alone in the room. She might have understood the feeling if she were with a lover, but nothing in the empty room should have inspired such sensations.

She should not have been hungry, having fed from David just the night before in preparation for going out on patrol, but that interlude had been as generally unsatisfying as the others. He gave her his blood and nothing else. She took it and nothing else. She had no idea how that made him feel, but it left her wanting more. Perhaps that explained the odd emotions assailing her. If so, a visit to any of her occasional lovers might scratch the itch and help her settle back into her routine. She picked up her address book, flipping through it to find someone she could call in the middle of the day, someone who would be free to come to her since she could hardly explain her sudden immunity to sunlight to anyone outside the alliance. Bertrand Avéline worked third shift at one of the bars in the neighborhood and rented a room above it. Furthermore, he was one who had never tried to turn their occasional liaison into anything more than a means of releasing pent-up passion for both of them. Yes, he would be a perfect choice. Picking up the phone, she dialed his number, smiling when his sleepy voice perked up as soon as he realized who was calling.

They chatted for a moment before she cut to the chase, inviting him over for the afternoon. "I'll see you in fifteen minutes then," she purred as they hung up the phone.

Deciding there was no need for pretense, she changed out of the functional outfit she had worn for the patrol into a silk kimono that hugged her curves in all the right places, revealing her full cleavage and parting as she walked to give glimpses of long, creamy legs. Brushing out her long, black hair, she examined her face in the mirror, trying to decide whether Bertrand would prefer a natural look or a sophisticated one. She started to rise from the dressing table without applying even a coat of lipstick when she realized where that impulse came from. Scowling, she sat back down and painted her face with an expert, subtle hand. She refused to conform her behavior to her partner's priorities, especially since he had made it obvious that he wanted no part of her outside the alliance.

A knock on the door drew her attention, and she consciously replaced the frown with a welcoming smile. Bertrand might not be her partner, but he was an undeniably attractive man willing to indulge her in bed in any way she pleased. She opened the door and ushered him inside, relaxing into his embrace when he immediately drew her to him. He was already aroused, much to her delight. She returned the kiss, backing toward the bedroom, her hands shedding his clothes as they walked. She tumbled him onto the bed, the folds of her robe opening as her mouth lowered to his neck, biting eagerly. His blood was sweet as always, but without the zing she had grown accustomed to. Pushing all thoughts of David from her mind, she sucked harder, enjoying the eager way Bertrand's hands moved over her body.

DAVID PACED his apartment. The urge to go find Angélique was nearly overwhelming, but he knew better than to push his luck. If all she did was slam the door in his face, he would be lucky. Given what he really wanted to do, she would probably not be nearly that nice.

He had known from the first time he saw his partner that she was a beautiful woman, just the kind he appreciated. Full figured without being fat, dark hair, dark eyes, a body made to seduce a man. If he had been in the market for a lover, she would have been the perfect choice. Unfortunately, the exigencies of the alliance had precluded that sort of approach, and now he was stuck with a partner he did not want and without a lover he would have gladly embraced.

All he had to do was close his eyes to imagine her henna-painted hands moving over his body. She would know just how to touch him, just where to linger for maximum effect. She had been a pleasure slave. She surely knew all there was to know about the art of making love. Her hands would be soft, her skin fragrant, redolent of incense and exotic perfumes. She would taste sweet beneath his lips as he kissed every inch of her skin, and she would not be shy in returning the favor, leaving him mindless with passion.

The vividness of the image surprised him enough to break him out of the lust-inspired trance. Yes, she was beautiful. Yes, she was even very much his ideal, but he had consciously avoided thinking about her as anything other than his partner precisely because she was his partner. The sort of fantasy that had overtaken him just now had no place in their relationship—and he knew that, had deliberately refused to let his mind go there. So why now? Why had he failed today where he had succeeded before?

He quickly cast a revealing spell on his apartment to make sure no stray charm was affecting him. He found only his own wards, but the gut feeling that something magical was going on remained with him. Lighting a fire in the grate with a flick of his wand, he channeled his magic into the flames, searching for a magical disturbance that would explain the uncharacteristic lapse, but the elemental magic was far more balanced than he had seen it since before the war began. Deciding he enjoyed the warmth of the flames, though, he left the fire burning as he continued to pace.

Concentration evaded him, fleeting images of Angélique entwined with a faceless man haunting him. He told himself they were groundless, but he could not shake the feeling of betrayal that accompanied them. Angélique was *his!*

That thought brought him up short. He had no claim on Angélique outside the alliance and had indeed been one of those who protested the possibility of the vampires wanting more than just a military relationship. He had no idea where the impulse to claim had come from, but he knew one thing for certain: he had to talk to Marcel, and soon.

Pulling on his coat, David locked the door to his apartment and reset the wards before heading to Milice headquarters to see what the general knew about all of this.

HAVING SEEN Bertrand out, Angélique slumped down on the bed, body sated, mind completely unsatisfied. She should have been a boneless, mindless heap, as well as Bertrand had taken care of her, but the twitchiness remained. An image of red hair flashed into her mind, but she pushed it aside. David already thought she was a wanton slut. The last thing she needed was to prove him right. Besides, she had no idea where to find him.

Deciding a walk would do her good, she dressed and wandered out into the city. She wandered up the boulevard de Clichy toward place Clichy, a smile teasing her lips at the freedom to visit her adopted home in the daylight. Montmartre was a very different neighborhood by day than by night. Reaching place Clichy, she let her feet guide her, ambling aimlessly into the residential neighborhood north of the boulevard des Batignolles. She froze in front of one of the many apartment buildings along rue Nollet, resisting the urge to go in. Finally, her curiosity won over her good sense and she examined the names next to the various buzzers.

D. Sabatier.

IN HER tiny studio north of Paris, Monique paced restlessly. She had failed to infiltrate Chavinier's ranks the way Serrier wanted, a failure she was still feeling in the lingering pain in her muscles. She knew the only reason it was not worse was that she had brought back some information he could use. He was already plotting how to arm his ranks with enough holy water to be effective as a weapon in battle.

It was not the pain that kept her from settling, despite Serrier's best efforts to leave her with a lingering reminder of the cost of failure. Nor was it war strategy. No, she could not settle because she could not get a certain Spanish vampire out of her mind. She had seduced him quite thoroughly in the little room in the basement of Milice headquarters, even letting him bite her again as they lay entwined. It should have been as easy to forget as any other meaningless romp.

Yes, he had left her as mindlessly sated as she could remember being recently, but it was still just sex, the stuff of masturbation fantasies when she hit a drought, but otherwise not enough to spend time thinking about. Yet she could not get him out of her mind. She had tried sleeping with someone else—but while she had enjoyed it, as soon as the man left her bed, visions of Antonio haunted her again. She had asked the medic to check her for compulsion charms, even though the vampire should not have been able to do any magic, but the doctor gave her a clean bill of health. The urge to walk out her door and keep going until she reached Milice headquarters was nearly undeniable, but she knew what would happen if she gave in to that impulse. Chavinier had sent her on her way kindly last time, telling her to keep a low profile so Serrier did not find her but declining to offer his protection, much less a place in the Milice. If she showed back up now, demanding to see Antonio, she would surely end up thrown in jail. The vampire was not worth that. He could not be worth that.

BEHIND HIS closed volets and heavy curtains, Antonio cursed the sunlight that imprisoned him far more effectively than any jail cell could ever do. He had known the taste of freedom for one short morning, in a tiny impersonal room. He had planted the false information as requested, seduced her because she had so obviously wanted it, and fed from her as deeply as he dared because he had needed it. He could still taste her blood. He had fed since then, but it had been flat in comparison, a biological necessity rather than a soul-searing pleasure.

He wanted to rage, to throw things, to release some of the pent-up frustration that had grown within him in the past few hours. He had long since accepted the limits of his vampiric existence, but today, the urge to go out, to find the woman whose blood would free him from those confines, was nearly overwhelming. Only the certainty of dissolution held him back, for the magic in her blood had long since worn off. In this moment, he would have forsaken all vows of loyalty to Jean, all responsibility to the Cour, all sense of right and wrong if only he could taste her again. He knew what she was, could guess what she had done—but he wanted her anyway, with a force that left him surly and frightened. How could a single feeding steal his reason to such an extent? Was it because he could not have her, or were all the paired vampires prey to such a debilitating need? And if they were, what would happen when the war ended and the alliance was no longer a necessity? His mind shied away from such possibilities, preferring to dwell on the woman who had hijacked his very being with one taste of her blood.

He could not abandon all he was, all he believed in, for a dark wizard who had no desire to switch sides. He simply could not.

RAYMOND'S SENSES had been so battered by the elemental magic that when he first felt the pressure against his shields, he ignored it. As high as he had raised his defenses, nothing would be able to get in anyway. Only when the sensation did not fade did he realize that this was more than just a stray bit of magic. Something wanted in. Lowering his shields enough to sense the compulsion, lust instantly assailed him. Slamming his defenses back into place, he frowned. They had checked the elemental magic after the ritual and found it back in balance. Unless it had been only fleeting, that could not be the source of the pressure on his shields.

Determined to be methodical, he went into the bathroom and filled the tub with a few inches of water, channeling into the basin, but just as in his office, he found no sign of a magical imbalance.

Not a disequilibrium, then. That was good news, at least. A quick spell showed that all his wards were intact, which meant that whatever this was, it was probably not something Serrier had concocted. The dark wizard was twisted, but not terribly innovative. Unless someone new had started creating spells for him, nothing in his arsenal should be able to get through the more arcane of Raymond's protections.

That meant wild magic. Raymond almost wished it were a spell of Serrier's. Then he could simply find a counter spell and be done with it. If it was wild magic, that meant it could be influencing any magical creature anywhere in the city, possibly beyond, depending on how strong the flare was. Lowering his shields again, he ignored the lust that flamed in him and the compulsion to go to Jean's apartment in search of the vampire.

A sickening realization hit him. This was his fault, his and Alain's anyway. This was the remnants of the ritual gone wrong, the vortex they had pulled Thierry from. They must have severed the vortex as well, leaving the power in it ungrounded, free to wreak havoc on any magical creature unprepared for the onslaught. And since they had kept the ritual a secret, that would be every magical creature in the city. Not just the wizards and vampires, but any werewolves, goblins, gnomes, or any other magical race. He did not know if the effect would be the same on everyone as it was on him, but he feared it would be. The nearly uncontrollable urge to seek out his partner returned even though his shields remained high. He shuddered at the thought of the lower order creatures—the trolls or fairies who had less developed consciences—rampaging under the influence of magical lust. This was a disaster in the making.

Thumping his head against the table, he cursed his carelessness silently. He knew better. Ending a spell or ritual properly was one of the first lessons a fledgling wizard learned. Alain might have been excused under the circumstances since it was his best friend collapsed on the floor, but Raymond had no such excuse. He had been in charge of the ritual. It had been his responsibility to end it properly.

He needed to find Marcel, to tell him what had happened and see what they could do to corral the vortex and ground it properly. Stomach churning at the thought of admitting his mistake and dealing with the possible fallout, he took a couple of deep breaths, calming himself as best he could before displacing himself to Milice headquarters.

DEEP IN the cellar of the old mansion, the vampire stirred, brought out of his reverie by a feeling he had not known in more than fifteen hundred years. His dark eyes opened, piercing the blackness with their steely stare as he assimilated the sensation and compared it to his memories of a time gone by.

Then, it had been a wizarding king who was trying desperately to stop the westward halt of the Alamanni, an alliance of Germanic tribes led by unscrupulous wizards. It had been a less civilized time, a less enlightened time, and the magical repercussions of the war had been far more far-reaching than this time around. Lombard would give Chavinier that much credit, at least. So far, he had managed to keep the war from affecting the other magical races beyond the politics of Serrier's propaganda. In an attempt to help the devil they knew and see the end of the magical influences on their behavior, the vampires of his past had agreed to attack the Alamanni under cover of night, only to find themselves ambushed and decimated. It had taken hundreds of years for the Cour de Reims to recover from the war's depredations.

Even in Paris, leagues from the heart of that war, the vampires had felt the press of magical coercion. They had found their instincts strengthened and their reason overridden, until they went on rampages that resulted in their arrest and execution.

The compulsion now was not as strong as it had been then: enough to rouse his instincts, but not enough to override his good judgment. His thoughts strayed to Mireille, the daughter his fate had never allowed him to have. Would she be caught up in the madness such magic could inspire?

He spared a thought that perhaps the magic that drew the paired vampires to their partners would also protect them from this new compulsion. If it did, at least some of his kind would be safe. Unfortunately, if this set off a new round of persecution, the authorities might not care whether the vampires were involved in helping the alliance or not.

He could do nothing now while the sun ruled the hours, but the next time Mireille came to check on him, he would warn her to be on her guard. She did not have his strength, but she was not without reserves of her own. As things stood now, being aware of the influence would be enough to help her keep control.

If matters grew worse, he would contact Jean and warn him as well, though he imagined Mireille would take his warning to the chef de la Cour. If worst came to worst, he would speak with Chavinier himself. He refused to see what had happened in Reims happen here.

Chapter 13

PASSING INTO the courtyard of Orlando's apartment building, Alain pulled the vampire into a quick embrace, hands running down his lover's sides. "So now that we're off duty and Thierry's safely home, you've got another job to do," he teased lightly.

"Oh?" Orlando replied in similar vein, his heart beating faster at the thought of pulling Alain up the stairs and into their bedroom, of pushing aside the barriers of clothing that separated them, and of joining them as one flesh again.

"Yes, oh," Alain insisted firmly, a shiver running down his spine at the thought of making love with the object of his affections. It had only been a few hours, but between the ritual and Thierry being hurt, so much had happened that it seemed like far longer.

"I guess we should go upstairs, then," Orlando smiled, "unless you have an exhibitionist fantasy you've never told me about." His own boldness surprised him. He chalked it up to finally feeling comfortable in his own skin, most of the time anyway, and having a lover who accepted him exactly as he was.

"I don't want anyone seeing you naked but me," Alain growled possessively, pulling Orlando toward the stairs, the thought of sharing the vampire's beauty with anyone complete anathema to him.

Orlando's eyebrows shot up at the unexpected tone in his lover's voice, but he followed willingly enough. When the door to the apartment closed behind them and Alain spun him against the hard wood, pinning him against it, the vampire frowned at the uncharacteristic action—but the kiss that followed was as tenderly persuasive as Orlando could have wished, so he relaxed into it, letting Alain have control for the time being.

The rush of lust that swamped him at feeling Orlando's body against his came as no surprise to Alain, but the urge to keep the vampire there, to spin him around and take him there against the wall, came out of nowhere. Reminding himself not to push too hard, he kept the kiss and his lingering caresses gentle as Orlando began his own rediscovery of the wizard's body.

"Why are we here when there's a perfectly comfortable bed just down the hall?" Orlando teased when Alain kept him pressed against the door.

Again, the urge to stake a claim asserted itself, Alain's hands squeezing hard on Orlando's hips before he could stop them. He forced himself to take a step away even though Orlando had not protested, staring down at the disobedient limbs.

"What's wrong?" Orlando asked, concern growing when he saw bewilderment rather than passion on Alain's face. He moved to his lover's side, taking the wizard's hands in his.

Alain spun them around to catch Orlando between his body and the wall again, the kiss not so gentle this time.

"Alain!"

The sound of his name, the concern in Orlando's voice broke the spell, giving the wizard the strength to step back. His hands scrubbed at his face.

"What's going on?" Orlando demanded.

"I don't know," Alain replied honestly, a tremor in his voice as he fought the urge to silence the questioning with a kiss that never ended, to push the slighter man down and claim him, "but I don't like it. The problem is, I can't seem to control it."

"Control what?"

"Myself," Alain said slowly. "It feels like a *Forçage*, a compulsion spell, but I haven't been around anyone who would use one." His hands itched to touch, but he did not trust himself now. They cramped in pain from the effort of not reaching out and grabbing. "Don't let me hurt you," he warned. He knew he should leave, but he doubted he could make himself walk out the door. "I mean it, Orlando," he added insistently. "Whatever's going on, I don't know how long I can fight it, and I don't want to drive a wedge between us because I do something you don't want. Don't let me hurt you, even if that means holding me down."

Orlando frowned at the obvious pain Alain was in. He had moved forward in their relationship because of the bone-deep assurance that the wizard would never hurt him. To think that now Alain would do him harm, however inadvertently, shook the foundation of their relationship in ways that made him incredibly uncomfortable. "Maybe I should leave," he suggested.

Alain wanted to agree, but he could not make the words come out of his mouth. "I'd just follow you," he admitted honestly. "This spell is fixated on you or on us, and I don't know how to break it."

Instinctively, Orlando started toward Alain, intending to comfort him, but the wizard shook his head. "Don't trust me right now," he warned, the words tearing at him. Why did this have to happen so soon after they had finally gotten their relationship back on track? "It's taking all the strength I have just to stay still."

"What do I do, then?" Orlando asked seriously. "If I can't leave, but it isn't safe to stay, what do I do?"

Magic crackled the air around Alain as he fought the spell on him, going to his knees with the effort. "Tie me down. If I can't move, I can't hurt you."

Orlando shook his head even as the image of Alain tied to the bed triggered his own bloodlust. It was too much like the tortures Thurloe had inflicted on him.

"Do it, Orlando," Alain insisted. "I don't know how much longer I can fight this, and I don't ever want to give you reason to distrust me."

Orlando nodded slowly, then pounced, catching Alain's arms in his so that the wizard was essentially helpless. He could feel his lover's struggles, and it tore at him to the point that he almost let go, but he reminded himself that this was different than what had been done to him. While he might tie Alain's hands until the spell passed, he had no intention of hurting his lover while he was bound.

Pulling two ties out of a drawer, he forced Alain's hands above his head to the slatted wood of the headboard. The wizard struggled with him, giving Orlando no choice but to use the weight of his own body to hold his lover in place as he affixed the first of the bonds. He gasped in surprise when Alain's teeth closed over his nipple through the shirt and sweater he wore. His grip slipped with his attention, allowing Alain to pull his second hand free. It promptly tangled in his hair, dragging Orlando's head toward his for a hungry, bruising kiss.

Without breaking the kiss, Orlando caught Alain's hand again and finished tying it to the bed.

"What do I do now?" Orlando asked.

"Kiss me again," Alain demanded roughly, testing the strength of his bonds. They held him tight, giving him very little room to move his arms. He relaxed a little, giving in to the forces driving him now that he knew he could not hurt Orlando. He could ask, plead, demand, but he could not take unless the vampire gave.

"That isn't what I meant," Orlando protested, though he found he wanted to do as Alain asked. "How do I help you now?"

"Kiss me again," Alain repeated, trying futilely to clear his mind enough to concentrate on a better answer to Orlando's question. The magic befuddling his senses had one goal and one goal only: Orlando, preferably writhing beneath him as Alain pounded into him. Without conscious thought he tried a spell to release his bonds, but he could not connect with his own power, the sorcery controlling him seemingly interfering with his innate magic. Given that he could not get free to take what he wanted, he would have to make do with what he was likely to get. The one still rational corner of his mind noted with interest that even though he wanted more, even now he was capable of adapting to reality rather than fighting his bonds until he was free to do as he truly wanted.

"I don't know how that's going to help," Orlando protested even as he did as the wizard asked, lowering his head so their mouths met. Alain nipped hungrily at his lips, causing Orlando to startle slightly before relaxing again into the kiss. He feasted on the hot cavern, tongue dueling with Alain's as they battled for dominance. The struggle aroused him in a way their usual, tender kisses had never done.

With a determined hiss, he took control, his body pinning Alain's to the bed from shoulders to knees, his hips grinding down against his lover's hard cock. “You like that, don’t you?” he demanded. “Like knowing you’re completely at my mercy.”

“I’d like it even better if our positions were reversed,” Alain growled back.

“Dream on,” Orlando retorted before he could stop himself. His eyes widened as he realized what Alain had said and how he had reacted. He knew Alain’s words came from whatever spell he was under, but he was not suffering from the same spell. Was he? Alain bucked beneath him as if trying to dislodge him, and he turned his attention back to his lover.

“Stay still,” he hissed, rising up on his knees so he could grab Alain’s hips and hold him in place.

“Make me,” Alain goaded, out of his mind with the combination of the lust Orlando always inspired and the desperate, magically inspired need that demanded heat and power and passion, not their usual tenderness. He only hoped that giving the magic what it demanded would break its hold on him.

Instincts roused at the challenge, Orlando felt his fangs elongate, peeking out between his lips. The urge to sink his teeth into tender flesh and assert his dominance once and for all blindsided him, leaving him reeling. He jerked away, hands trembling as he fought himself.

“What?” Alain demanded from the bed, wanting to feel those fangs in him. “Not man enough to take what you want?”

“Don’t,” Orlando whispered, so softly the wizard had to strain to hear him. “Don’t make me hurt you.”

“You couldn’t hurt me if you tried,” Alain snarled, hating the tone of his voice, hating the way Orlando’s face tightened at his words, but he could not call them back, could not stop himself from prodding the vampire.

“No, I couldn’t,” Orlando agreed quietly after a moment, “because I won’t try. I won’t ever do anything that might hurt you.” He closed his eyes for a moment, struggling to overcome his instincts, to retract the dangerous incisors. It took longer than it ever had since he first learned to control himself, but finally he felt them withdraw. Returning to the bed, he looked down at Alain, saw the lust riding him still, the unusual glitter in his eyes that he attributed to whatever magic had his lover in its thrall.

“Is it roughness you need?” he asked seriously, hands hovering an inch above Alain’s body. “Is that what it’s going to take to break this spell?”

Yes! Alain’s instincts shouted, but he made himself pause and consider. As a rule he preferred a gentler touch, a lover’s caress—but they seemed paltry and weak at the moment. “I don’t know,” he forced himself to admit. “It’s what I crave, but I don’t know if giving into it will help or make matters worse.”

“What do you want me to do?” Orlando asked helplessly.

“Fuck me,” Alain declared. “As fast and hard as you dare.”

Orlando felt the prick to his pride, felt his fangs start to drop again. He would not bite Alain, though he knew the wizard would not protest if he did, but he would withhold only that. Grabbing the neckline of Alain’s turtleneck, he pulled hard, ripping the fabric away. Alain's gasp was music to his ears as he lowered his head and sucked hard on one dusky nipple, loving the way the wizard bucked beneath him. "Bite me," he pleaded.

"Anything but that," Orlando promised. "Don't ask that of me."

Alain subsided, teeth puncturing his lower lip as he fought back the urge to insist. Orlando's lips closed around his other nipple, drawing his attention as his body tensed with lust. It would not take much for him to go off like a rocket. "Fuck me, then," he demanded.

Rocking back on his heels, Orlando unbuttoned Alain's jeans and swiftly pulled them down and off. The long legs parted eagerly for him as he reached for the lube on the table next to the bed. With trembling fingers, he prepared Alain as cursorily as he dared, relieved to find the muscle still somewhat relaxed from last night. He wanted to linger over the preliminaries, to make sure he did not hurt Alain the way he had been hurt too many times, but his lover was not in the mood for slow. For that matter, neither was he, though he seemed to be doing a better job of resisting the violent side of whatever was driving them.

"Do it," Alain goaded. "Stick it to me like you mean it."

Orlando hissed his displeasure even as he moved between the widespread thighs. Alain subsided marginally as the vampire pushed his cock past the guardian muscle. His fingers closed tightly around the ties holding his arms, knuckles turning white as he rode out the burn of that first moment of penetration. Orlando did not give him time to catch his breath, picking up a steady, pounding rhythm.

Alain's heat burned away the last of Orlando's inhibitions, leaving him fully in passion's thrall except for one thing. His fangs dropped again, but he kept his head well away from Alain's skin, the mechanics of the hard fucking making it all but impossible for him to kiss his lover anyway.

Levering open eyelids that had fallen shut as Orlando drove into him, Alain groaned at the vision above him. Orlando's fangs had dropped again, beckoning to the wizard with all their destructive beauty, the perfect gleaming counterpoint for the dark beauty of his vampire lover. A light sheen of sweat glossed Orlando's brow and dampened his hair as it fell forward to cast shadows across his olive skin. The classic features were a graven mask of lust and concentration, making Alain wish his hands were free so he could augment the lust and shatter the concentration. He wanted those fangs as badly as he wanted the cock currently driving him out of his mind. He knew how good they could make him feel, knew that bite would be all it took to shatter his mind and build him anew. Then Orlando's hands gripped his thighs hard enough to leave bruises as they pushed his knees almost to his ears, bending him double as the fucking became even more frenzied. For the first time, Alain thought perhaps he understood Orlando's caution. As strong as the vampire was, the fangs he so desired could damage him if Orlando's will failed to keep them in check. It took seeing the vampire nearly out of control to make Alain realize how tight a rein he kept on his desires most of the time. While he would never stop hoping Orlando would eventually trust himself enough to take all the wizard had to offer, he finally accepted the seriousness of his lover's concerns.

Having Alain helpless beneath him was a potent aphrodisiac, a realization that disgusted Orlando even as it aroused him. He did not want a helpless victim. He wanted a lover, an equal. Yet in this moment, he could not reject the power of the image his wizard presented—bound, bent double, helpless to do anything except take the reaming he was delivering. The feral growl that escaped Orlando's throat—as he pulled Alain's buttocks still higher onto his thighs to give him more leverage while he pounded into the willing passage—startled him, but he could not hold it back. His instincts prodded him to lift one thigh to his shoulder, to turn his head and feast. Alain would not stop him. Even without whatever magic currently drove them, the wizard would not have stopped him, but Orlando fought down the impulse. His own fears were too deeply ingrained for even this odd compulsion to overcome. He would not hurt his lover. Period.

His hips pounded faster, harder, driving them toward a climax that hovered just out of reach as if waiting for something more, some final signal. He tossed his head as the urge to bite grew stronger. That had to be what the spell wanted, but Orlando refused to give in. "Come for me," he ordered, hoping to push Alain into his release despite the demands of the magic. "Come for me now."

Alain undulated beneath him, body aching with the need for release, but his orgasm hovered just out of reach. *Bite me.* The words hovered on his lips, but he held them back, remembering his promise to Orlando. Anything but that. "Touch me," he said instead.

Orlando closed his fist around Alain's neglected cock, stroking it in time to his rapid thrusts. That gave Alain the final stimulation he needed to climax, thick cream spattering his chest. The wizard's contractions milked Orlando's erection, triggering his release as well. He collapsed forward, releasing his hold on Alain's thighs. To his surprise, he felt his lover's arms go around his shoulders.

"How?"

"Magic," Alain quipped with a tired smile as he felt the last tendrils of the compulsive power leave him. His eyelids drooped.

"Sleep," Orlando murmured, stroking Alain's eyebrow with the pad of his thumb. He refused to be worried by his lover's ability to free himself. Alain was asleep now. If he woke again still prey to whatever spell, Orlando would simply overpower him again if that was what it took. "I'll guard your dreams."

Chapter 14

ALAIN SLEPT hard, waking two hours later feeling as if he had rested far longer. Eyes opening to the now familiar sight of his lover's dark head resting on his shoulder, he smiled tenderly until the memory of what had happened earlier returned.

"Oh, God, I'm sorry," he gasped.

"What?" Orlando asked, the words startling him out of his reverie. "What are you talking about?"

"Earlier. I all but attacked you," Alain reminded him.

"No," Orlando corrected, "you fought yourself to the point of pain to keep from attacking me."

"You had to tie me down to keep me from hurting you!"

"But you didn't hurt me," Orlando pointed out reasonably. "Even prey to whatever had you in its grip, you didn't hurt me."

"And if next time I can't fight it?"

With a sigh, Orlando pushed up to his elbow and peered down at his lover. "You're determined to make this into something, aren't you?"

"Orlando! The things I wanted to do to you—they're part of me. It brought out in me things that were buried, but they were still there."

Orlando shrugged, the image of Alain clenching his fists to keep from touching him roughly still fresh in his mind. "You fought it today. You'll fight it again. And if you can't, I'll fight it for you. Tell me now, free of any magic, that you want me to bind you again if this happens a second time. As long as I know you want me to help you, I'll do whatever it takes."

"Don't ever let me hurt you," Alain insisted, reaching out and taking Orlando's hand in his. "Whatever you have to do, do it, but don't ever let me hurt you. You're not the young soldier you were then. You're strong enough to fend me off if you have to. I pray it'll never come to that, but nothing you do to me could be worse than knowing I caused you a moment's pain."

"I promise. Now, what came over you?"

"I don't know," Alain replied. "It felt like a *Forçage*, but I haven't been around anyone who would have cast one on me. Nobody outside the Milice knows I'm here, so Serrier's minions shouldn't have been able to target me from afar—and even if they did find me, they shouldn't have been able to get through the wards I put up here."

"So what could it have been?"

"I don't know, but I think we need to report it to Marcel. Even if it is a fluke, he needs to know about it—and if it's some new trick of Serrier's, we need to counter it as quickly as possible."

"Take a minute and clean up first," Orlando urged as Alain rose from the bed and reached for his slacks. "You don't want to go in there smelling of sex. It'll only bring up questions you probably don't want to answer."

Alain frowned and cast a quick cleaning spell on himself.

"That won't work on me," Orlando reminded him. "Give me five minutes and we can go."

Alain nodded, wishing he had not been so quick to use his magic.

As if reading his lover's mind, Orlando paused in the doorway to the bathroom. "You can still join me if you want."

With a relieved smile, Alain followed Orlando into the bathroom and shut the door.

THE SIGHT that met Adèle's eyes when she regained consciousness could not have been less welcome. She hurt all over, and not in a pleasant, satiated way. The bites on her neck, breasts, and thighs stung, far more than when Jude had fed from her in the past. And the cause of that pain was lying peacefully in her bed. She lay still a moment longer, doing a quick inventory of her feelings. The compulsion that had pushed her into bed with him earlier had disappeared while she slept, leaving her free to rise and to try to figure out what had happened.

Silently cursing being deprived of her wand, she showered quickly and dressed without the benefit of a healing spell. Maybe it was better to leave the marks anyway, proof of what had happened should anyone question her. Jude still had not stirred on the bed. Deciding he could not hurt anything, she left him there, gleeful at the thought of him waking alone. It seemed a fitting revenge for the way the afternoon had gone. He had fed, so he would not be trapped in her apartment even if night had not fallen yet, relieving her of any concern on his behalf. Despite the interlude earlier, they were not lovers and could never be unless he lost the attitude. She pointedly ignored the fact that he had given her exactly what she needed in bed. There was far more to a relationship than mind-blowing orgasms. Knowing her wards would reset automatically at her departure, she headed out, slamming the door behind her, filled with mean satisfaction at the idea of disturbing him as she did.

She spent the ride to Milice headquarters trying to separate her emotions about the sex with Jude from the events themselves. Marcel would need more from her than just her anger, however justified, to figure out what had happened and to keep it from happening again. The battle itself had gone much as usual, as far as her interactions with Jude were concerned. They had sniped at each other the entire time, but had still managed to work together well enough to hold off Serrier's wizards. The spell, a *Forçage* or whatever it was, hit after the battle was over—though in retrospect, she could identify an increased awareness of Jude and his presence during the latter part of the fight. She could easily imagine one of Serrier's wizards casting such a spell on her, but she could not imagine what purpose sending her home to fuck her partner hard and fast would serve. She could think of far more detrimental compulsions a dark wizard could cast. The only consequence of the spell that she could think of was the delay in her report to Marcel, but she had sent Charlotte to report in—so even then, only her personal impressions were missing. Pursuing that line of thought, she tried to remember anything she had seen or heard that might have been time sensitive, but she could come up with nothing. Unless the wizard who cast the spell had done it for personal kicks, for the simple knowledge of putting her in a sexual situation she would otherwise have rejected, she could see no reason for anyone to have used a *Forçage* this way.

She was not sure if that thought reassured her or not.

"Where's Marcel?" she asked when she found David outside the older wizard's office.

"Inside with Raymond," David replied with a scowl. "He arrived right before I did. They've been closeted for over two hours."

"You know he wouldn't make you wait if they weren't discussing something important."

"I know," David shrugged, "but there's something going on, not quite a *Forçage* but close."

"You felt it, too?" Adèle verified, surprised. "You weren't at the Tour Eiffel."

David's scowl deepened. "I don't like this at all. What did you feel?"

Adèle flushed. "What did you feel?"

"An almost irresistible urge to go find my partner," David replied vaguely. "You?"

"Close enough," Adèle agreed, turning to knock on the door. "I don't care if we're interrupting. Marcel needs to know about this. Now.

"Sorry to disturb you," she began when Marcel opened the door.

"Marcel!" Alain's voice interrupted from down the hall, Orlando directly behind him. "Something's going on at the magical level. Either Serrier has a new spell or we've got a problem."

Marcel looked from one concerned face to another and sighed, opening the door to let the four newcomers inside. "We have a problem," he agreed, shutting the door behind them. "Raymond, Jean and I have been trying to figure out how to contain it before it spreads. Obviously, we're too late."

"What, exactly, is the problem?" Alain asked coolly, memories of how he had wanted to act making him tense. Even Orlando's calming hand on his lower back did nothing to ease the tension. If his lover had not been a vampire… he shuddered even to think of what he might have done.

"Wild magic," Raymond replied. "When we broke Thierry free, we didn't ground the vortex that held him captive. That magic's now loose in the city."

"So all the wizards are affected?"

"And at least some of the vampires as well," Jean added. "I haven't talked to any who don't have partners, but those who do also seem to be feeling it."

"So what do we do about it?" Adèle demanded. "And why the hell did it make me want to have sex with a man I despise?"

Raymond and Marcel exchanged a resigned glance. "It would seem that the exchange of magic that allows your blood to protect your partner creates a bond between you," he said slowly. "One benefit of that bond is a balancing of the elemental magic. One downside, apparently, is a susceptibility to each other and, it seems, to outside magical influences."

"So every time the elemental magic gets out of balance, I'm going to have this uncontrollable urge to…." Alain trailed off, not even wanting to put into words the urges that had assailed him. He did not want anyone, least of all Orlando, to know how close he had come to breaking nearly every promise he had made to his lover.

"No!" Raymond assured him immediately. "This should be a one-time occurrence. The next time we have to do a Rite d'équilibrage, we'll be better prepared and we won't leave the magic ungrounded at the end."

"It will, however, continue to happen to anyone not on their guard until we can mop up this mess," Marcel elaborated, "which is what we've been discussing since Raymond and Jean got here."

"Why are the vampires involved?" David asked curiously.

"Because this wild magic is affecting us, too," Jean replied sharply. He had little patience with the superior attitude that even some of the Milice wizards had toward the "lower" magical races. Having become more aware of Serrier's true intentions through his time spent with Marcel at the Conseil des Ministres, he was more determined than ever to help win this war. If his response was even less tempered than usual, he chalked it up to the insistent desire to chase everyone from the room and ravish his partner. That feeling had grown steadily since he had joined Raymond in Marcel's office. "We're magical beings, as you should have assimilated by now, and fluctuations like this one affect us as severely as they affect you."

"Perhaps even more in some cases," Raymond added, "given that we're used to maintaining some degree of magical shielding, and the vampires can't do that."

"So what have you come up with?" Alain asked, heading off the ensuing argument.

"A couple of different options," Marcel said. "I'll let Raymond explain, since this is his area of expertise."

"The question," Raymond began, "is quite simply what's the best way to gather back up the bursts of wild magic and neutralize them. The problem is that the longer we wait, the more scattered the wild magic becomes, so it isn't just a matter of dispersing the initial vortex safely. We also have to gather up and disperse the bits of magic that hit each of us today as well as the ones that are hitting others all over the city."

"How do we do that?" Adèle asked suspiciously.

"Have you ever broken a thermometer?" Raymond asked. "One with mercury in it?" Adèle nodded. "The wild magic is like those drops of mercury, looking for something to attach to. My suggestion is twofold. First, we need a paired wizard to represent each of the four elements."

"You felt that vortex!" Alain protested. "There's no way four of us will be strong enough to ground it."

"Not if we had to deal with it alone or all at once," Raymond agreed, "but we won't be dealing with it all at once. The more time passes, the more it breaks apart, leaving more manageable bits of magic. More importantly, though, if our partners will agree to help, I believe we could handle even the vortex."

"How?" Alain challenged.

"What do you feel, magically, when Orlando feeds?" Raymond asked. "Can you feel the magical transfer?"

Alain nodded. "But I don't feel weakened. Are you saying feeding actually makes us stronger?"

"I don't know how long the effects last," Raymond admitted, "but I'm pretty damn sure that in that moment, our power increases exponentially."

"So by feeding during the ritual, we can help protect our partners from whatever happened to Thierry?" Orlando verified.

"That's the theory," Jean agreed. "The problem is that we can't test it without doing it." He marveled a little at the power of the partnership bond. Only a few weeks ago, he had insisted Thierry leave the room before Orlando took even a little taste of Alain's blood. Now he was seriously suggesting what amounted to an orgy, four pairs feeding at the same time, in the same place. Even more amazing was that he doubted the vampires involved would question it any more than he did. It needed to be done. It would protect their partners. They would do it.

"And we can't do that today because everyone is exhausted, either from the Rite d'équilibrage and its aftermath or from one of the two battles we fought this afternoon," Marcel interjected. "We're not risking more wizards by rushing into something unprepared."

"And the risk from this wild magic affecting more people?" David protested.

"Which would you prefer?" Marcel countered pragmatically. "Sex with your very lovely partner or losing your magic because you weren't prepared for the demands of this new spell?"

David's scowl suggested he did not care for either option.

"And what about this susceptibility?" Adèle demanded. "What do you do about that?"

"Whatever you want," Raymond replied. "Resist it, give in to it… it doesn't seem to affect anything either way."

"How do I get rid of it?" she insisted irritably.

"As long as Jude feeds from you regularly, I don't think you can get rid of it," Jean informed her. "But you don't have to do anything about it."

"Easy for you to say," she scoffed. "You weren't just all but attacked on the train." To prove her point, she pulled down the edge of her blouse, revealing the still oozing bite marks on her breasts.

"Keep your shields up as if you were in battle until you know the wild magic has been controlled," Raymond advised. "If you keep it from getting a foothold in your psyche, you can resist even the wild magic." He flushed slightly and looked away, not meeting her eyes or Jean's. "I am."

"You're still feeling it?" Alain asked sharply.

Raymond nodded. "You're not?"

"Not since I woke up."

"No," Orlando corrected, "it was before that. You were yourself again before you fell asleep, after we…."

"I think the term you want is made love," Jean inserted gently, seeing the flush beneath Orlando's skin.

"Are you still feeling it, Adèle?" Marcel asked.

"No," she replied. "It would seem that sex releases the compulsion, at least for a while." She would make sure she kept her shields as high as she could, though, because she had no intention of falling prey to the wild magic again.

"I NEED to check on Thierry," Alain told Orlando when they finally left Marcel's office. "I put up a dampening ward to keep him from forgetting he wasn't supposed to do magic for a few days, but I need to make sure he wasn't hit by this wild magic. The state he was in, he wouldn't have been able to resist it."

"I'll wait for you at home, then," Orlando agreed, knowing Alain could go faster by himself and figuring as well that the other wizard might take Alain's news better without Orlando looking on.

Given the revelations of the past hour, Alain almost hesitated before leaning over to kiss Orlando, but he refused to let anything shake his faith in their relationship. Whatever forces had brought them together, they were together now and only that mattered. The way Orlando leaned into the kiss made Alain wonder if he was as disturbed by everything they had learned. They would need to talk, too, to validate the strength of their bond, but that could wait until after he had talked to Thierry. "Love you," he murmured before casting the displacement spell that would send him to his best friend's doorstep.

The whispered words brought a smile to Orlando's lips as Alain disappeared. A moment later, Jean appeared at his elbow. "I haven't talked to you in a few days," the older vampire said with a smile. "How are you?"

"A little unsettled," Orlando admitted. "Hearing that the emotions I'm feeling aren't really my own…."

"Don't go there," Jean interrupted. "Maybe the magical push sped things up between you, but Alain doesn't act like a man under duress. And neither do you. I have never seen you as happy as you've been since you met him. I don't see Adèle or David or their partners looking the same way. Or my partner. We're learning to work together, but it isn't the same as what you obviously feel for Alain. There's a big difference between lust and love."

"How do I know for sure?"

Jean smiled. "Youngling," he teased as Orlando scowled. "Come visit with me for an hour or two and I'll see if I can help you understand."

"I promised Alain I'd meet him at home," Orlando hesitated.

And that's the proof of the difference right there, Jean thought with a smile. "You're still allowed your own separate interests," he reminded Orlando. "He's gone to talk to his friend, I'll bet. There's no reason why you can't go talk to yours."

Half an hour on the subway saw them safely ensconced in Jean's apartment. The chef de la Cour poured them each a glass of wine, though he knew they would barely taste it, and then settled in a comfortable armchair, waiting for Orlando to settle as well. "Do you want a fire?"

"No," Orlando replied with a shake of his head. "I want you to tell me how to be sure I haven't made a mistake."

"Lust might drive you into bed," Jean said bluntly, "but I'm going to guess that your Avoué isn't covered with bloody bites the way Adèle is."

"Of course not!"

"That's what untempered lust looks like, and I'd bet those aren't the only marks on her body. She's bruised and bloody from the lust the wild magic inspired, and angry and resentful because of it. If I read Alain correctly, he's angry at feeling out of control, but it's directed at himself, not at you and your lack of control."

"That's right."

"Then it's not just lust," Jean declared. "His concern is for you and his anger is self-directed, which it wouldn't be if he didn't care about you genuinely. You obviously retained at least some control since he isn't covered in bites, which means you obviously care about him enough to retain your scruples even with the wild magic pushing you."

"I didn't feel it," Orlando admitted. "At least I don't think I did. I was too focused on him and his obvious distress."

"And you doubt your feelings?" Jean questioned. "I felt that magic, Orlando. I'm still feeling it. It took all I had not to go in search of Raymond or

Karine or someone, and when we sat in Marcel's office together, it was even worse. For you to say you didn't even feel it… that's all the proof I need of your true feelings."

"Then why was he affected? Or does that mean he doesn't really love me the way he says he does?"

Jean sighed. He had thought Orlando was getting over his insecurities. "Alain's a wizard," he reminded his friend. "Magic affects him differently than it does us. Neither of you said exactly what you felt or what happened between you, and that's fine, but if it's bothering you, maybe you should tell me."

"We were just joking around at first," Orlando recalled. "I'd said something earlier, to Thierry, and it turned into a running joke between Alain and me. Everything was fine and then suddenly he grabbed me. Almost immediately, he pulled back, but it cost him, and it seemed only to get harder for him to hold back."

"Did he hurt you?" Jean asked sharply. He doubted the wizard would do anything to hurt Orlando physically while in his right mind, but that level of wild magic hardly counted as normal circumstances.

"No, of course not," Orlando exclaimed. "He'd never hurt me. He'd sooner hurt himself."

"And again, I say, how can you doubt his feelings?"

"I guess I still have a lot to learn," Orlando said slowly.

"It's easier to see from the outside than from the inside, no matter how old you are or how much experience you have," Jean assured him. "You never know. One of these days, you might be giving me advice."

Orlando chuckled, shaking his head. "That'll be the day."

Chapter 15

ALAIN BREATHED a sigh of relief as he stepped through the wards he had erected around Thierry's house. The *Vide* charm still held. Hopefully that meant Thierry had not also been a victim of the wild magic. In his delicate state, that could have been extremely dangerous.

"Is everything all right?" Sebastien asked by way of greeting when he answered Alain's knock. "I didn't expect to see you again today."

"I didn't expect to be back," Alain agreed. "Is Thierry okay?"

"As far as I can tell. He's slept pretty much since you left."

"Good," Alain declared, "but I need to talk to him for a few minutes, if that's all right with you."

"He's a grown man," Sebastien replied easily. "He can make his own decisions."

Alain laughed softly. "That may be, but I know what it's like having a vampire for a lover."

"I'm not Thierry's lover," honesty compelled Sebastien to admit, however regretfully.

"Not yet," Alain shrugged, "but I doubt he'll make you wait much longer."

"Que Dieu t'entende," Sebastien replied fervently.

Alain laughed again, more heartily this time. "I'll put in a good word for you." Turning serious, he added, "When I'm done talking with Thierry, I'd like to talk to you, too, about the Aveu de Sang, specifically about your relationship with your Avoué, if you don't mind."

Sebastien swallowed hard, memories of Thibaut swamping him again as they always did when he allowed his mind to dwell on the past. "I'll be here," he replied vaguely. He would let Alain ask his questions and then decide which ones he would answer.

It was not exactly the answer Alain had hoped for, but he would take what he could get. "Thanks. I'll go see Thierry now." He walked deeper into the house with the familiarity of friends, as comfortable in Thierry's space as he had ever been in his own. Memories he had not let surface earlier assailed him as he walked past the living room and down the hall toward Thierry's bedroom. He and Edwige had spent countless hours here with Thierry and Aleth, happy hours of shared friendship and a lifetime of devotion. He had grieved here after Edwige and Henri were killed, holding on to the memories as if they could bring them back. He had even come here once after Thierry had moved out, to confront Aleth. He had seen how badly Thierry was hurting and would have done anything to alleviate that pain. Aleth had been blunt, telling him she would not take second place in Thierry's life to the war effort, and that as long as he had that as his mistress, he would not have her. Alain had argued for what seemed like hours, but she would not be swayed. Either she was first in Thierry's life or he was no longer part of hers. Alain had no answer for that—the dead bodies of his ex-wife and child, of Eric's wife and children, too fresh in his mind for him to contemplate anything less than total dedication to stopping Serrier. Now, two years later, he would be just as vehement, he realized, if for different reasons. The dark wizard's blight was spreading. The only good that had come from it was the new alliance with the vampires. And now this revelation of the effect of the bond between partners could possibly strain, even shatter, that.

Looking around again, he frowned. He had no idea why Thierry had brought Sebastien here, why he and the vampire seemed to be making it their home, but he was not sure it was such a good idea to start a new relationship in a place filled with Aleth's ghost. Opening the bedroom door, he pulled the stool from the dressing table to the side of the bed. "Thierry," he said softly, shaking his friend awake.

"Alain? What are you doing here?" Thierry's voice cracked drowsily, bringing a smile to Alain's face. The other wizard had never been easy to awaken.

"I just thought I'd come check on you."

"Tell me another one," Thierry retorted. "I'm sleepy, not crazy. What's going on?"

"I really did come to check on you," Alain protested. "There's been a rash of wild magic left over from the Rite d'équilibrage and I wanted to make sure it hadn't affected you."

"I've been asleep since you left," Thierry promised, "but Sebastien could have told you that, so what else is going on?"

"I got hit by it," Alain said after a long pause.

"Are you all right?" Thierry exclaimed.

"Physically and magically, yes," Alain assured him, "but I'm still unsettled by it. I had no control of myself for the time it had me in its grip. I couldn't do magic and I felt…."

Thierry waited patiently for Alain to continue. His friend was clearly upset, and pressing him would not help. When the silence started to stretch, though, he frowned and pushed himself up to sitting.

"Orlando had to tie me up," Alain said finally. "If he hadn't, I don't know what I would have done to him."

Thierry shook his head. "You'd never hurt him."

"Not now, I wouldn't," Alain agreed, "but then… if he hadn't been strong enough to stop me, I could have. Not with the intention of hurting him, maybe—but certainly given his past, if I'd done what I wanted to do, I'd have lost him for sure."

"What, exactly, did you want to do?" Thierry pressed.

"Take control," Alain replied. "Press him up against the nearest stable object and fuck him so hard he'd feel it for a week. Ravish him… and if he were willing, there'd be nothing wrong with any of that, but he wouldn't be willing, and that would have made it rape. God, Thierry, I'm as bad as the bastard that tortured him."

"Stop!" Thierry interrupted harshly. "Stop right there. Did you actually do anything that hurt him in any way?"

Alain shook his head. "He stopped me before I could."

"Then what happened?"

"He did to me what I wanted to do to him."

"And were you willing?"

"Of course! He wouldn't touch me if he thought I didn't want him to."

"So if I understand you correctly, the wild magic got a hold of you and you got a hot, hard fucking out of it, just like you wanted."

"But that's just it," Alain insisted. "Yes, it was amazing, and yes, it was what it took to break the hold the wild magic had on me, but it wasn't what I wanted when it started."

"You're a naturally dominant man," Thierry pointed out reasonably, "who I'd venture to guess is usually the one doing the fucking, not the other way around. And despite his actual age, Orlando doesn't look much like a top."

"Looks don't have anything to do with it," Alain reminded his friend. "Sebastien's older than Orlando, but he's not an especially big guy. I'll bet he shows you a good time the first time he gets you under him, though."

Thierry flushed and looked away, thinking of Sebastien's fingers stretching him and how good it had felt. He would have to wait a few more days now to feel the rest, but he had no doubt Alain was right. "That's beside the point. You're used to being the top, Alain. It's only natural you would want that with Orlando. Doesn't mean you're going to take it by force, but there's nothing wrong with wanting it. What does Orlando think of this? Is he upset?"

"Amazingly, no," Alain marveled. "He's focused on the fact that I fought the magic's hold long enough for him to get me tied to the bed. And once he'd done that, it didn't matter what I wanted to do. I couldn't do anything but lie there."

"So he's not hurt, he's not upset, the wild magic's broken and all cleaned up. What's the problem?"

"It's not all cleaned up. Marcel won't do another ritual today with everyone exhausted from the Rite d'équilibrage or from battle, so it could hit again—although Payet said he was able to fight it off by keeping his mental shields high, and the *Vide* charm here kept it from hitting you."

"Then it wasn't an isolated incident?"

"No. At the very least, Adèle and her partner, Payet and Bellaiche, and Sabatier were affected as well," Alain explained. "Adèle apparently got quite a ride."

"You know that's the way she likes it."

Alain shook his head. "Not this time. She wasn't happy at all. You could see torn bite marks on her neck and below her neckline. She looked like she'd been savaged. If it had been any other circumstances, I'd have been asking her who I needed to hunt down."

Thierry chuckled. "As if she needed any of us to take care of her."

Alain had to smile. "Too true. Regardless, though, the wild magic seems to be targeting the paired vampires and wizards. The exchange of magic that lets your blood protect Sebastien makes you a target, too."

"What do you mean?"

"There seems to be a certain… sensitivity to our partners, and the wild magic blew that out of control—so that Adèle ended up sleeping with a partner she hates, and I ended up trying to take something I know rationally I can't have."

"Are you saying the attraction I'm feeling for Sebastien is a side effect of my magic protecting him?"

"I don't know whether I am or not," Alain admitted, "but I don't think so. From all I know of Sebastien, he seems an admirable man. I have eyes so I know he's an attractive one. I think maybe you were drawn to look at him by the magic—but until the wild magic hit her, Adèle hadn't touched her partner, I'm sure. David's partner still isn't talking to him—or just barely—so I'm sure he didn't get laid, even if he wishes he had."

"Maybe not, but you fell for Orlando so fast it made *my* head spin, and I'm contemplating a relationship with a man for the first time ever. You don't find that a little odd?" Thierry challenged.

Alain sighed. "I love Orlando. So maybe I fell in love more quickly because of the bond between partners, but it's gone way beyond that. You know as well as I do that there's no such thing as a love potion. Human behavior can be forced, but not human emotions. The elemental magic, wild or not, can't force me to love Orlando. And I do."

"So it might make me end up in Sebastien's bed, but it can't make me respect him in the morning?" Thierry quipped, hiding his unease behind a joking façade.

"With the *Vide* charm in place, it can't even make you do that," Alain reminded him, "at least not when it hit everyone else. Enjoy this time of discovery. You can pick the experience apart later if you want."

"You say that so easily, but do you remember how you anguished over your first crush? Do you remember how hard it was the first time you tried to approach a man instead of a woman?"

Alain nodded. Thierry had been there the whole time, urging him to take the risk, to act on his feelings—once he had worked up the nerve to come out to his best friend. "I remember, but you don't have to worry about Sebastien rejecting you. You know that, right?"

Thierry snorted. The vampire had already had his fingers up Thierry's ass. Rejection was definitely not the issue. "That's not the point. It's unsettling to suddenly find this out about myself at my age. I thought I had my sexuality figured out, and then Sebastien touched me. He makes me go off like a kid again. Aleth never learned my body as well as Sebastien already has."

Alain grinned wolfishly. "Isn't it a wonderful thing?"

Thierry flushed bright red. "Yeah," he drawled slowly, thinking about how good Sebastien could make him feel. "Yeah, it's an absolutely amazing thing."

"It'll be even more amazing when—I suppose I should say if, but he seems like an equal opportunity lover—you slide inside his tight heat. No woman has ever squeezed you the way a man's ass will, especially if it's been a while since he's had a lover."

Thierry squirmed uncomfortably on the bed. "Will it hurt?"

"If he's careful, if he prepares you right and takes his time, it'll just be a little sting the first time and then nothing but pleasure," Alain promised. "And if he doesn't, I promise to take it out of his hide for you."

"He'll be careful," Thierry said without thinking.

Alain grinned. "Oh? Has he started prepping you already?"

Thierry flushed again, but kept his silence.

"You're hardly going to shock me, Thierry," Alain reminded him. "I'm not the one with the virgin ass." He sobered and added, "All teasing aside, you know you can talk to me about anything, right?"

"I do know. It's not that. I trust Sebastien, but I'm not sure I trust myself now. Aleth just died a couple of weeks ago. And up until the day she died, I still dreamed of being reconciled with her," Thierry explained. "But it's so easy to just let go and feel good when we're alone and he touches me. He's the reason we haven't made love all the way yet, you know. He's got this idea that he has to make that first time perfect, and so he's holding back, waiting for I don't know what."

For you to be ready, Alain mused privately. He simply nodded his understanding, though, and admired Sebastien's restraint. He doubted he could have been so noble with a man as attractive as Thierry ripe for the taking. The only reason he had not put the moves on his friend years ago was Thierry's patent interest in women. Before the past few weeks, Thierry had refused any details of Alain's sex life, beyond the fact that he had one, whenever his partner was male.

"Why are you here?" Alain asked after a moment.

"What do you mean?"

"Why are you in Aleth's house? There wasn't anything wrong with your apartment, so why did you bring him here?" Alain clarified.

"It was warded and my apartment is so small. Here, at least, I could offer Sebastien a bed instead of just a couch. I wasn't ready to offer anything more when I first brought him here," Thierry reminded his friend.

"Take him to your apartment," Alain advised, "or take the time to put up wards at his place, but don't stay here. You don't need to start this new life surrounded by Aleth's ghost."

"At the moment, I'm not starting anything," Thierry reminded him, "unless you've also come to release me from durance vile."

Alain chuckled. "You've got a drop-dead sexy man sharing your bed and you want to leave it? Shame on you."

Thierry scowled. "It's one thing to spend a day romping in bed with a lover, but I hate being confined this way."

"Another day, two at the most," Alain insisted. "You know it's safer this way."

"Doesn't mean I have to like it," Thierry griped. He did not relish the enforced idleness, chafing at the restrictions that confined him to his bed and gave him far too much time to think. He did not want to think, to worry about his feelings. He wanted to exhaust himself during the day and fall into a dreamless sleep in Sebastien's arms at night, preferably after finding pleasure at one another's hands. He was a man of action, not one of deep thoughts: a warrior, not a philosopher. Such introspection made him uncomfortable, but he had no distraction now. Sebastien had already made it clear he would not touch the wizard again until Thierry was well.

"I know," Alain sympathized. "Just rest, get as much sleep as you can, and you'll be back on patrol before you know it."

"Not soon enough."

Alain chuckled and rose. "Get some rest. I'll be back tomorrow to check on you."

"That's what you said this morning."

"Let's hope there isn't a repeat of this afternoon," Alain said fervently. "Call me if you need me or if anything makes you think the *Vide* charm is weakening. I don't know that you can fight off the wild magic on your own right now, and I want Sebastien to be able to keep his promise about that perfect first time."

Thierry grumbled under his breath, but Alain caught his shoulder, making his friend look up at him. "I'm serious, Thierry. Whatever you think you want, you don't want your first time with him to be driven by magic neither of you can control."

Thierry had to admit Alain was right in that respect. He would prefer it if magic had nothing to do with his relationship with Sebastien at all. That seemed to be asking too much, though, so he would settle for knowing they were not under the influence of wild magic. "I'll call you if anything feels off, I promise." He tried to stifle a yawn and failed. "I guess maybe I do need a little more sleep after all."

"Told you," Alain joked, walking toward the door. "À demain."

"Salut."

Closing the door behind him so his conversation with Sebastien would not disturb Thierry, Alain sighed deeply. That had gone both better and worse than he feared. Thierry had not run screaming for the hills, but neither had his counsel settled Alain's own concerns.

He had just entered the living room again when Sebastien appeared from another room. "Is Thierry all right?"

"He seems to have dodged the bullet," Alain replied honestly, thinking how that applied in more ways than one. "Now he just has to rest and get his strength back."

"So what was so important it couldn't wait until he got his strength back?" Sebastien asked civilly. He did not believe Alain would disrupt Thierry's recovery unnecessarily, which meant something was going on, and he did not intend to be left in the dark.

"I needed to make sure the wards protecting him were still in place," Alain explained vaguely. "There's been an outbreak of wild magic that could have hurt him in his weakened state."

"You didn't need to talk to him for that," Sebastien pointed out, "much less for half an hour."

Alain sighed. This had been difficult enough with Thierry. Trying to have this conversation with a virtual stranger was even worse. "The wild magic seems to be preying on the partnered wizards and vampires. It got through my wards at Orlando's apartment, although I didn't have a *Vide* charm in place. It wasn't enough just to make sure the charm held. I needed to make sure the magic hadn't gotten through."

"It hadn't, I take it," Sebastien verified.

Alain shook his head, "No, the *Vide* worked." He took a moment to screw up his courage and bring up the rest of his concerns to the one man most likely to have answers to his questions. "Are all Aveux de Sang as… powerful as mine seems to be?"

Sebastien chuckled. "Ask a hard question, why don't you?" He paused and considered the question. "I can only speak for myself, of course, but my attraction to my Avoué was instantaneous, even though it took me a couple of weeks to give in to his desire for an Aveu de Sang. From what I've heard, though, neither you nor Orlando realized what you were doing when you made your vow."

Alain flushed. "No, apparently not, but I would have made it anyway, probably more willingly, if I'd understood. I thought… well, it doesn't matter what I thought. I don't regret the promises it entails, and at the time it seemed perfectly logical and right to make them, but in retrospect, the speed is breathtaking. I'd known him less than thirty-six hours when he put this mark on me. He'd only truly fed from me once, though he'd bitten me a couple of other times. I guess a part of me worries that it was too fast."

"Why now?" Sebastien asked, not surprised at the sentiment, but definitely surprised it had come up this long after making their pledge. "What's changed that you're asking these questions now?"

"Because, while I'm the only one with a brand on my neck," Alain replied, "I'm not the only one with a sudden, and at times inexplicable, attraction to my partner. In forming the alliance based on the partnerships as we have, we've meddled with something that we didn't understand and maybe still don't. Whatever it is, though, it's creating relationships that might not be as consensual as we think." He wondered briefly why he was being so honest with someone he barely knew, but no one else had Sebastien's unique perspective on the Aveu de Sang. No one else could tell him how much of what he felt was magically inspired.

"What do you mean?" Sebastien demanded.

"The magic that protects you from sunlight, the magic in Thierry's blood, predisposes you to be attracted to him, as far as I understand it," Alain explained, still trying to get his mind around the afternoon's revelations, "but we didn't know that when we started this. I don't believe it can make one person fall in love with another—that goes against everything we've ever been taught about the way magic works—but it can influence people's actions."

"When did you find all this out?"

"This afternoon," Alain assured him. "I haven't been keeping it from you or Thierry or anyone. The burst of wild magic I told you about seems to have a much stronger influence on everyone than just the magic involved in feeding, which is what brought it to light."

"And so now you're wondering if you have a brand on your neck because of some outside magical influence instead of your own personal preferences," Sebastien postulated.

Alain nodded, shamefaced. He would never admit it to Orlando, not even to Thierry, but to this relative stranger, the only person he knew who had ever been part of a relationship like his, he could give voice to the doubts that had not left him since Raymond first mentioned the partnership bond. "I just can't seem to do anything right where he's concerned, and it makes me wonder if he made a mistake choosing me. I want to be with him, but I can't seem to give him what he needs."

Sebastien laughed incredulously. "Is that what you think an Aveu de Sang should do? Oh, Alain, you've got it all wrong. Yes, the Aveu de Sang binds you together, but it's not some outside force picking two people to belong together. It's a magical covenant that two people enter into, just like any other covenant. It doesn't make you perfect for each other or do away with all misunderstandings or anything like that. It's a promise. The execution of that promise is up to the people involved—fallible, imperfect people who do stupid things and say things they don't mean and yell and shout and sometimes wish they'd done anything but make that promise. The Aveu de Sang just means you have to work it out because the vampire can't survive without his Avoué."

"Yes, but—"

"No buts," Sebastien interrupted. "I've been around long enough to see a lot of things, and I'm pretty sure there's no such thing as a 'perfect' couple. Everyone has their flaws, and in every relationship there are rough spots. From what little I know of Orlando, the fact that he's in a relationship at all speaks volumes for just how good you are for him. I don't know whether this partnership bond influenced your decision. I don't know if you'll ever know that, but it *doesn't matter now*. The decision is made and it can't be undone. Put the doubts behind you and figure out how to live together. If there's a problem, deal with it. If there's a misunderstanding, clear it up, but don't let 'what ifs' interfere. The only other choice is to turn Orlando out to starve, because as long as you live, he can't go anywhere else for sustenance."

"I could never do that!" Alain protested.

"Then you have to learn to live together," Sebastien informed him. "It's as simple as that."

As simple as that. Alain almost laughed at the absurdity of that statement. There was nothing simple about anything involving him and Orlando, as that afternoon had proven once again. "Thanks," he said. "I'd better get home. I don't want him to worry."

"I'll make sure Thierry stays in bed and rests," Sebastien promised.

"Why don't you make sure he stays in bed and doesn't rest instead?" Alain retorted. "At least he'd be in a better mood when I come to visit tomorrow."

He cast the displacement spell before Sebastien could reply, leaving the vampire shaking his head at the apparent contradictions in Alain's behavior. He had no trouble encouraging an unprecedented relationship between Thierry and Sebastien, yet he could not accept the validity of the relationship he had formed. That was a concern for another day, though. Despite the wizard's encouragement, Sebastien fully intended to wait for Thierry to recover before taking the next step in their relationship, especially since he imagined Thierry was as unsettled by Alain's news as Alain was. They had time. They could wait until they were both ready.

Chapter 16

LUST RODE Claude hard as he surveyed his handiwork. The woman beneath his lash had been beautiful even before he started: thick blond hair just brushing her shoulders, limpid blue eyes, alabaster skin, svelte curves. Now that hair was matted with sweat, the eyes rimmed red from her tears, the pale skin crisscrossed with vivid welts and flecked with blood. He slipped his hand inside his pants, rubbing his erection as he examined the erotic tableau, trying to decide where to direct his attention next.

He circled her slowly. At first, her eyes had followed him as he moved, begging him silently to have mercy on her. He had spelled her to silence, except for her screams, hours ago, but that had not stopped her from turning pleading eyes his direction. She had given up on that, though, her head hanging limply between her widespread arms.

He had done all he could do with the whip, he decided, tossing it aside and picking up a wickedly jagged knife instead. He ran the flat of the blade down the inside of her arm, turning it sharply as he reached the juncture of limb and torso, slicing cleanly through skin and muscle.

She screamed.

His lusty smile turned feral, the hand on his cock picking up speed, as he moved to the other side, the asymmetry of only one cut offending him. She knew what to expect this time, flinching away from the knife as much as her bonds allowed. "Don't bother," he told her, his voice raspy with cruel desire. "You can't get away from me. I'm going to take care of you, sweetheart. I'm going to make you so beautiful."

His gentle crooning might have soothed her in other circumstances, but she had learned not to trust him in any way. Since the night she was taken, her life had been reduced to moments of incredible pain followed by hours, even days, of confinement. At first, she had held out hope that they would realize their mistake and let her go. She knew nothing of any use to them. They had no reason to hold her.

Then, she had clung to the thought that Jean would rescue her, but she did not know if he even realized she was missing. They saw each other infrequently enough that he might not go by her apartment for weeks still.

The knife caught her again, wrenching another moan from a throat raw from screaming. They had stopped asking her questions a few days ago, giving her to this monster instead. He looked so harmless, boyishly cute almost, but that face hid a soul as black as night and as twisted as the gargoyles of Notre-Dame. She had learned quickly not to expect any mercy from him.

The bruises from the first time he brought her to his torture chamber five days ago had almost faded. He had gone relatively easy on her then, though she had not thought so at the time, still questioning her between beatings. The thin metal cane he used had hurt, leaving bruises mottling her fair skin, but it had never drawn blood. He left her alone the next day, bringing her out of her cell again three days ago. Then it had been matches, never quite enough to actually burn, but enough to leave her covered in red patches. She had gotten two days' respite after that, but she was clearly paying for it now.

Claude slipped his hand from his pants to finger her bare breast speculatively. He had spared the soft swells when he wielded the whip earlier, preferring the smooth planes of her back, belly, and buttocks where he could lay down long, even stripes. The blade in his hand, though, allowed for far finer work. Changing his grip, he dragged the tip from the top of her breast to the nipple, raising droplets of blood in its wake. Lowering his head, he licked the wound, pausing to suckle on the pink teat.

Karine sobbed brokenly, this new violation of body and spirit somehow worse than the ones that came before. When it was just pain, she had accepted that they were cruel, sick men who got off on torturing people. As awful as it was, she had come to terms with it, but this was a different kind of torment.

Deciding he liked that sound, Claude lifted his head and repeated the action on the other breast, biting at her nipple this time to see if it would elicit a louder sound. To his delight, it did. "I knew I'd find a way to please you," he crooned as he drew the next line on her body, connecting her nipples this time.

Karine whimpered, closing her eyes against the sight of his lips on her skin, like a lover's. She did not want that image in her mind. This perverted bastard was not her lover, would never be her lover. Jean was her lover. He might not love her, but he always took care of her, not like this. She could feel her mind slipping away, into precious memories, the continuing pain a physical reality that could not touch her soul.

Claude frowned when the sounds stopped. The tops of her breasts were decorated in a starburst pattern, but he had not completed it on the undersides yet. The thought of leaving his work unfinished bothered him, but he needed something to bring her back to him.

He was not done with her yet. There was so much he could still do to her body, since Serrier had given him permission and since no one else seemed to care, but he had to show her that she had to participate, too. It was no fun, otherwise. With a frown, he looked from the knife in his hand to her body. He would have to choose where to bury it in her or else she could die, and he did not want that. Shifting his grip again, he stabbed the blade hard into her thigh. Her scream rent the air, the sound such a pleasure on top of the attentions he had been lavishing on her that he could not wait any longer. He pulled his erection from his trousers and jerked it hard a couple of times, spattering her bloody skin with his release.

The scream was so sharp, so unexpected that both Eric and Vincent stopped in the hallway outside, looking at each other in confusion before opening the door to the room from where it emanated. Vincent took in the scene with one quick glance, the woman's bloody body, Claude's lax face, hand still on his cock, and felt his stomach roil. "You're disgusting," he told the other wizard flatly before he could even consider the possible consequences.

Eric did not repeat the sentiment, though his face mirrored it clearly. He had intervened the last time Claude was torturing someone. He could not afford to do so again. Serrier trusted him for the moment, but the dark wizard was fickle at the best of times. Eric had no desire to make him question his decision.

"Clean up your mess when you're done," Vincent ordered as he turned back into the hallway, drawing Eric with him. "We have to use this room in the morning."

Claude made a rude gesture but said nothing as the two men left.

"He's a rabid dog," Vincent mused to Eric as they walked toward the exit to Serrier's lair. "I don't know why Pascal doesn't just put him down."

"He's occasionally useful," Eric replied with a shrug, feigning a casualness he did not feel. "If she'd been holding back information, she'd have told it by now."

"You can't tell me you approve of that kind of cruelty," Vincent asked disbelievingly.

"No, of course not," Eric replied quickly, "but it amuses Pascal, and as long as it does, it won't do any good to complain about it. It's different for you. You've been with him from the first, but there are still people who don't trust me. I don't want to give them a reason to question my loyalty."

Vincent shrugged. "There are people who question everyone's loyalty. I imagine Chavinier has the same problem."

Eric shook his head. "Chavinier is a trusting old fool. He believes everyone has some goodness in them. He'd find a way to redeem Claude if he could."

"Do you ever think about going back?"

"God no!" Eric spat. "They had their chance and they blew it when they let Magnier get away with murder. I may not always agree with Serrier's methods, but a regime that lets a murderer walk free despite the evidence against him is a regime that needs to change. I'll see justice done or I'll die trying."

Vincent bit his tongue for a moment, not sure he should share the thoughts in his head, but they pounded at him until he finally took the chance. "I'm just afraid that 'justice' will end up looking a lot like what we just saw."

Eric's eyes were cold. "If Magnier's the one in chains, you won't hear me complaining."

"And if instead it's Danielle's friend, Caroline?" Vincent asked softly, not sure why he was challenging Eric this way.

"She chose her fate when she sided with Chavinier," Eric declared, squirming inwardly beneath Vincent's serious stare. Beneath the piercing gaze, he felt an odd curl of desire in the pit of his stomach. Why had he never noticed the color of Vincent's eyes before? Or how long his eyelashes were?

Blinking in surprise, Eric looked away.

"What's wrong?" Vincent asked immediately, seeing the odd look on Eric's face.

"Nothing," Eric replied with a shrug, ignoring the way his friend's solicitude added to the rush through his body. "Just…."

"Just what?" Vincent asked, giving in to the impulse to touch Eric's broad shoulder. The little jolt that traveled up his arm surprised him, but he had more important concerns at the moment.

Eric shivered and met Vincent's eyes, seeing the same uncomfortable desire he was sure darkened his own gaze. "Are you feeling it, too?"

Vincent nodded slowly. "I was afraid it was just me."

Eric shook his head. "We shouldn't do this," he reminded his friend. "If Serrier finds out…."

Vincent chuckled, his grip on Eric's shoulder tightening. "There's no reason for him to find out. We're off duty and we're off base. No one's around to see."

"Your place is closer," Eric observed, making a decision he hoped he would not regret.

"So it is," Vincent agreed, a slow smile transforming his usually intimidating face. "Meet you there?"

Eric nodded and cast the displacement spell with an inviting glance.

"Shit," Vincent muttered as he followed Eric to his apartment. "I don't know where this came from, but I hope it doesn't go away any time soon." He had learned early on to keep a low profile where his interest in men was concerned. Serrier had made his views on homosexuality as clear as he had on the subject of equality for nonmagical races. Vincent had no desire to run afoul of the dark wizard's twisted morality.

Already outside Vincent's apartment, Eric asked himself the same question—but while his sudden sexual interest in his friend surprised him, it was strong enough and felt good enough that he did not try to fight it. When Vincent appeared beside him and opened the door, he shoved the other man inside ahead of him, kicking the door shut behind them.

"Tell me the wards reset automatically," Eric requested as he attacked Vincent's mouth, his hands sliding over the curve of the other wizard's closely shaved scalp.

"Ngnnn," Vincent tried to answer, his words impeded by Eric's tongue. Deciding talking was overrated—and incredibly turned on by the idea of being with someone big enough to manhandle him the way Eric had—he let actions speak for him, turning them so he could walk Eric backward down the hall toward a bed.

Eric gasped as Vincent took control, moving him as easily as if he weighed half his 120 kilograms. He grasped at the powerful muscles of Vincent's arms, not to stop him, but to steady himself against the torrent of need that washed through him. They stumbled blindly into the bedroom, falling onto the bed in a tangle of long limbs and hard bodies, wrestling slightly for control.

Vincent rolled to his back, Eric's weight pressing him down hard. He bucked up beneath his friend turned lover, nearly dislodging him, but Eric recovered quickly, pinning him. Vincent grabbed the thick brown hair and pulled Eric's head down for a kiss, using the distraction to flip them over and pinning Eric neatly beneath him.

"Fuck, you're strong," Eric gasped, breaking the kiss to catch his breath.

Vincent chuckled huskily and ground his swelling shaft against Eric's matching hardness. "You ain't seen nothing yet," he drawled cockily.

"Promises, promises," Eric griped, his legs wrapping around Vincent's hips to hold him in place.

Pulling his wand from his back pocket, Vincent cast a quick spell, leaving them both suddenly, deliciously naked. "Oh, God," Eric groaned, the feeling of flesh against hard flesh enough to have his eyes rolling up in his head. He planted his feet and pushed hard, wanting out from under Vincent so he could explore the magnificent expanse of naked man.

Vincent reared back obligingly, only to catch Eric's hips and flip him onto his stomach, coming back down on top of him so that his cock rubbed along the crease of the other wizard's ass.

Eric froze. He had not considered the reality of sex with Vincent until now. They were two alphas fighting for dominance, and he was quickly coming to the conclusion that Vincent would win. He swallowed hard even as he felt his body opening in welcome. "Go easy on me," he requested softly.

"You've got to be kidding," Vincent scoffed, rummaging in the drawer of his bedside table for something he could use as lube. With a muffled curse, he reached for his wand again, summoning a bottle of lotion from the bathroom. "You want it just like I do—hard and fast and as deep as I can get."

Eric groaned, the image evoked by the words leaving him trembling. His fear warred with his desire, the conflict freezing him in place as cool fingers parted his cheeks and probed at his untried entrance. He bit his lip against the groan that threatened at Vincent's rough preparation. The fingers delved confidently inside his clenching passage, finding his prostate almost immediately and surprising a yelp out of Eric.

"See?" Vincent goaded. "Hard and fast and dirty." He nipped roughly at the curve of Eric's buttocks as he added a second finger. "Fuck, you're tight. You're going to feel so damn good around my dick. I can't wait to feel you squeezing me."

He scissored his fingers quickly, stretching the guardian muscle enough to admit him. Another day, he might have spent hours playing with Eric's ass this way, the picture his friend presented, head down, back bowed, ass in the air begging to be taken one he would not soon forget, but he had no patience for that sort of extended play today. He needed the raw physicality of his cock inside that eager hole, stretching it wide as he pummeled the man beneath him.

Lining himself up, he pushed home hard, seating himself in one long drive. Eric bucked violently beneath him, nearly knocking him off the bed. "So that's the way you want it?" Vincent growled, his hands settling hard on Eric's hips, fingers digging deep enough to bruise. "Never let it be said I disappointed a lover."

"No," Eric gasped as Vincent started to move. "Fuck. Give me a fucking minute."

Vincent froze, his hand slipping around to find Eric's wilting erection. "What's this?" he asked in surprise.

"It fucking hurts," Eric ground out. "It better damn well get better than this."

Frowning, Vincent stayed where he was, fondling Eric's cock and balls in encouragement. When the shaft did not immediately begin to swell, he caught Eric's shoulder with his other hand, pulling the man up against his chest, tweaking the still peaked nipples and biting firmly at Eric's shoulder. "Tell me when you're ready."

Eric nodded, the pain radiating from his aching channel slowly fading, leaving him with an odd sense of fullness, not unpleasant, but definitely different. "Slowly, yeah?" he asked. "Let me warm up to that hard and fast and dirty."

Vincent's frown deepened even as his hips began to move again, lured by the seductive heat and tightness of Eric's body. "You have done this before, right?" he verified.

"What, sex?" Eric scoffed, not wanting Vincent to withdraw. The pain was almost gone, his desire rekindling with each slow pass of the other man's cock over his gland. "Of course."

Somewhat reassured, Vincent let his body move more freely against Eric's, though he kept one hand on his lover's resurgent erection, a bellwether of his interest in the proceedings. The other hand urged Eric back down onto the mattress. He did not want to be an inconsiderate lover, but the need to fuck the man beneath him wildly rode him hard.

Bracing himself on the bed, Eric began to push back against Vincent's thrusts, meeting him halfway, silently encouraging a harder, deeper pounding. Vincent delivered, abandoning restraint and pummeling the upturned ass with all his considerable strength. Eric grunted with each thrust, hands grabbing the headboard to keep from hitting it each time.

"Not gonna last long," Vincent gasped as the constrictive passage worked his shaft constantly. "You feel too good."

"Don't need you to last," Eric admitted, feeling his orgasm bubbling in his balls. It would not take much more and he would shoot all over Vincent's hand.

Eric's comment broke what little reserve Vincent had left. His hips stuttered roughly through his climax, coating Eric's insides with creamy fluid.

He pulled back quickly, watching his spunk seep from the stretched hole. "Fuck, you look sexy this way," he groaned, tracing his finger through the remnants of his orgasm.

Eric moaned huskily. "Get me off," he demanded, his own release beckoning but just out of reach.

"Pushy bottom," Vincent griped, reaching between Eric's legs to fist his cock as he lowered his head to suck on the other wizard's sticky balls.

Eric threw his head back and came with a hoarse shout, collapsing forward into the puddle of his own release, all strength and thought deserting him.

With a self-satisfied grin, Vincent curled up behind his new lover and wondered if Eric would be up for another round in the morning.

Chapter 17

SEBASTIEN PACED the confines of Thierry's living room restlessly. The sun had set hours ago, though its rays no longer penned him in the way they once did. No, it was magic that kept him inside like a caged tiger tonight. Wild magic. Magic that could make people act in ways they would not when they were not under its influence. Magic that could hurt his partner if it made it past Alain's wards and inside the house. So far that had not happened, but waiting to hear that it was safe to leave again was driving Sebastien mad.

Deciding the balcony off the living room would be safe—Alain had warded the whole house—he opened the door and stepped onto the stone terrace, breathing deeply of the crisp night air. To the northeast, he could see the lights of Paris blurring the horizon, but away from the city, the sky above him was dark, the atmosphere clear of the city smell that sometimes hovered over the capital.

He could feel his senses sharpening as he stood there, letting the cold breeze wrap around him before moving on. The hint of winter in the air brought a smile to his face. He had always loved the dark season, as a child because of the escape from heavy labor in the fields, and as a vampire because of the additional hours free from the sun's lethal rays.

The bells of the Cathédrale Saint-Louis tolled the midnight hour. Samhain was officially ended and la Toussaint had begun. All over the country, people would spend the day visiting the graves of lost loved ones. The war had increased those numbers in the past two years. Sebastien wondered if Thierry would want to visit Aleth's grave. He doubted the wizard would be strong enough to leave his bed even if Alain gave the all clear on the wild magic—but if Thierry wanted to go and Alain said it was safe, Sebastien would see that he made it there, even if he had to carry his lover himself.

He always visited Thibaut's grave on the anniversary of their Aveu de Sang, preferring to celebrate the beginning of their love rather than its end, but Thierry could well make a different choice. Sebastien was determined to respect whatever choice Thierry made, no matter how much it bothered him to think of his lover mourning for a lost love. He recognized the hypocrisy of that statement as he fingered the locket in his pocket, which Thibaut had given him, but it did not change his emotions. It was in his nature to be a possessive, jealous lover.

Thinking of Thierry's dead wife, of Thibaut, and of anniversaries roused his instincts. His fangs dropped swiftly. He frowned at the unexpected reaction. A mature, powerful vampire, he rarely lost control of his appetites these days, only releasing his fangs when he intended to feed. He shivered suddenly as the desire to do just that, to return into the house and sink his fangs deep into Thierry's neck, nearly overwhelmed him.

"What the fuck?" he muttered, bracing his hands on the railing as he struggled to bring himself back under control.

Wild magic. The realization came to him as his knuckles turned white from the force of his grip.

Alain had warned him, but Sebastien had not realized that the *Vide* charm truly protected only the house or that the balcony was not part of the house. Releasing his hold on the balcony railing, he stepped back across the threshold, short fingernails cutting into his palms as he waited for the *Vide* to take effect and negate the influence of the wild magic.

Seconds passed. Then a minute. And then two, with no lessening of the urges driving him to barge into Thierry's room and take what was his. Cursing himself for a fool, he returned to his pacing. He was no neophyte, newly made and out of control with his lust for blood. He had long ago mastered those desires. He refused to give that control up now, especially not when his most feasible option for sating them was his partner—who needed to rest, not to pander to the magically driven needs of an unreasonable vampire.

His body ached with the effort of resisting the lure of the man down the hall. He briefly considered leaving again, going out and hunting as he had done before meeting Thierry, but he rejected that thought as quickly as it came. This need was not a general one. He was not hungry for blood. He was hungry for Thierry, the need more for sex than for nourishment. That was even more out of the question, though, than feeding. He would never be able to cherish Thierry the way he deserved with his passions out of control this way, and he had made the wizard a promise he would not break.

He would simply have to ride it out.

"Sebastien?"

The vampire was halfway down the hall at the sound of his name before he could stop himself. "Yes, Thierry?" he called, forcing himself not to take another step. "Did you need something?"

"Could you come in here, please?" Thierry's voice requested.

Sebastien stifled a curse and walked to the threshold of Thierry's bedroom, his hand clenching on the door jamb to keep from going inside. Seeing the blond lying there in the bed, green gaze soft and unfocused from sleep, ratcheted up the tension infusing him. "What is it?" he asked more gruffly than he intended.

"You're feeling it, too, aren't you?" Thierry asked. "I don't know how it got through Alain's wards, but the wild magic has us both."

"Merde!" Sebastien cursed roundly. "I'm sorry, Thierry. I stepped out onto the balcony. I didn't realize it wasn't safe."

Thierry shrugged. "What's done is done. Now we have to figure out how to deal with it."

"We ignore it," Sebastien replied immediately.

"That's only going to work for so long," Thierry informed him softly. "And the longer we wait, the deeper its hold will be. Alain and the others will get it mopped up tomorrow so it can't affect others, but I don't know if even that will break its hold on us."

"So what do we do?" Sebastien asked hoarsely.

"Alain said sexual release broke the spell."

"No," Sebastien replied flatly. "I am not making love to you for the first time with this… spell driving me. I won't take the risk of hurting you."

Thierry chuckled despite the equally powerful urge pushing him. He should have known his lover's indomitable will would fight this to the bitter end. "You don't have to make love to me to make us both come," he reminded the vampire cheekily. "All you have to do is feed from me."

Sebastien shuddered, the desire to take what Thierry was offering nearly driving him to his knees. "We can't."

"Better to do it now than later when the magic will be that much more difficult to control," Thierry reminded him reasonably.

"Putain de merde!" Sebastien cursed. "You're supposed to be helping me resist this, not tempting me. This is hard enough as it is."

"My point exactly," Thierry said seriously, pushing up on his elbow. "If I thought we could fight this—if I thought we could hold out until the cleaning crew takes care of this tomorrow—I wouldn't have said a word, but I know I'm not that strong right now. I also know what it does to me when you feed from me. There's far less danger to me magically in that than there is in fighting this compulsion."

"Thierry."

The wizard could not decide if his name was intended as discouragement or capitulation. It did not matter. He pushed up on one elbow, the sheet falling to his waist to reveal his bare chest, nipples already hardened from the effects of the wild magic. One hand stretched out to his lover. "Get undressed and come to bed."

"This is not a good idea," Sebastien muttered as he pulled the old sweatshirt over his head, revealing his pale skin to his lover's gaze. "I'm going to have enough problems staying in control fully dressed."

"Keep going," Thierry insisted when Sebastien started toward the bed with his trousers still in place. "The faster we get off, the faster we'll be free of the magic. Surely that will be easier skin to skin."

"And when I lose control?"

"Then I'll be well and truly ravished," Thierry replied with a confidence he did not completely feel. He trusted Sebastien, though. Even if the vampire did lose control, he knew his lover would not hurt him. Lifting his hips, he pushed his boxers off, lifting the sheet to welcome Sebastien into the bed and giving the vampire a glimpse of his nakedness at the same time.

Sebastien gave in, sliding between the sheets and pouncing on Thierry's neck with no other preliminaries. The wizard's head fell back with a lusty groan as he felt Sebastien's fangs penetrate him. He angled his lower body so their groins met, erections brushing lightly. The hiss that escaped the lips attached to his neck fired his blood even more. "Touch me."

Sebastien frowned through the vampire's kiss, feeling his control slipping as the passion in Thierry's blood added to the desire simmering in his loins. He ran his hand up Thierry's arm and back down his midline, the light coating of hair doing nothing to hide the lines of hard muscle or the pink nipples that seemed to beg for his attention. Sucking harder, he let the ebb and flow of desire in Thierry's blood guide his hands as he toyed with the puckered flesh, tweaking the buds gently and then with more force when Thierry squirmed beneath him, moaning softly.

He promised himself the opportunity to linger later, when wild magic did not have them in its grip—but for now, he slid his hand lower to encircle Thierry's straining cock. The sooner he brought them both off, the sooner they would be free of this madness.

As good as Sebastien's hand felt stroking him, that was not the touch Thierry wanted. The last time they had been together this way, Sebastien had teased his entrance. He had wanted more then, and his conversation with Alain only increased that desire. Grasping Sebastien's wrist, he guided his lover's hand where he wanted it. "Touch me," he said again.

Groaning, Sebastien lifted his head, breaking the connection between them for a minute. "I don't have any lube," the vampire husked regretfully. "I don't want to hurt you."

Thierry frowned, mentally ransacking his drawers. The expression changed suddenly to a smile. "Will this do?" he asked, rolling toward the dresser next to the bed and rummaging through the top drawer until he found a tin of ladies' hand cream that Aleth always kept there.

Sebastien made a little moue at the smell of lavender as he opened the tin, but the cream was thick and slippery. "If you don't mind smelling like a perfume factory."

"I'll wash," Thierry shrugged, pulling Sebastien's head back down to his neck, his pulse thundering in his ears and his loins as he waited for the familiar bite and the less familiar press of fingers against his most private flesh.

Neither was long in coming. Sebastien's fangs sank back into the holes they had made earlier, his fingers spreading the thick cream generously over Thierry's balls and between his buttocks, massaging constantly but with varying pressure until Thierry was thrashing wildly on the bed. Only the connection between Sebastien's mouth and his neck kept him somewhat in place.

Then strong hands caught his hips as Sebastien shifted to straddle one of his legs, pinning him in place. One hand slid down his leg, urging him to bend his knee, spreading it wide so he lay completely open to his lover. Sucking harder on Thierry's neck so he could make sure his wizard felt no pain, Sebastien dipped his fingers in the cream again before pressing one slowly past the tight ring of muscle. His lover gasped, but Sebastien could taste no pain, no fear—so he continued, his finger delving deeper until his knuckles rested between Thierry's buttocks.

Having something up his ass felt as odd as Thierry had imagined it would, but it was not painful as he had feared. Rather, as Sebastien started to twist his finger in the tight hole, he felt full. Then that seeking finger brushed something inside him and he yelped as fireworks went off behind his closed eyes.

Against Thierry's neck, Sebastien smiled and pressed again on the spongy little bump, tasting the jolt of passion in Thierry's blood each time he did. He could feel the wizard's cock leaking against his stomach and the desire to replace the taste of blood with a different flavor filled him. Trusting Thierry to tell him if anything hurt, he released his lover's neck and slid lower to lap at the cloudy fluid anointing the tip of the wizard's erection.

Thierry's hands flew from their place tangled in the sheets to Sebastien's head, gripping tightly as the vampire teased him. He undulated between the probing finger that never pressed quite long enough on his pleasure point and the lapping tongue that probed the slit and beneath the foreskin, generally driving him wild.

Sebastien wanted the silky cock in his mouth, but his fangs stubbornly refused to retract and the vampire refused to risk scoring the hard length with his sharp teeth. He would have to settle for using his tongue. Another night, he would give Thierry a real blow job. He worked his way up and down the hard shaft, the smell of lavender assaulting his senses as he neared the thick curls at its base. Making a mental note to buy lube, he nuzzled the fragrant nest, the hint of Thierry's scent beneath the overwhelming floral aroma adding to his desire. He ground his aching cock against the sheets as he licked once at Thierry's sac, the taste of lotion making him change his mind. Another pleasure to save for a later date.

Resting his head against Thierry's stomach, he pressed a gentle kiss to the expanse of soft flesh stretched tight over hard muscle. "I need to taste you again," he admitted, looking up and meeting Thierry's eyes. "Can I bite you here?"

Thierry nodded, too lost in passion to question. Sebastien's tongue lapped over the skin just to the left of his hipbone, preparing it for the bite to come. Thierry felt the now-familiar pinch and then the rush of lust he had come to associate with Sebastien's fangs. The finger inside him started to withdraw, eliciting a moan of protest, but Sebastien's free hand soothed him, the other dipping into the cream again before returning, two fingers stretching him this time. They bumped against his prostate almost immediately.

With a broken shout, Thierry found his release. The burn, offset by the intense pleasure of those magical fingers against his prostate, was enough to push him over the edge. Sebastien's fangs did not leave him, though, continuing to suck strongly on his hip as he shuddered and shook in the throes of a magically driven climax.

The sweet flavor of satiation brought a smile to Sebastien's lips even as his own orgasm hovered frustratingly out of reach. Tenderly, he slid his fingers from their snug berth, despite a nearly overwhelming desire to add a third finger and rouse Thierry again for another round. Next time he would sheath his cock in that tight passage. That day would come, but not tonight. Not like this. They had enough magic in their lives, in their relationship, without this wild magic further complicating things.

Thierry's fingers carded gently through the vampire's dark hair. "Let me help you," he requested. "Let me return at least some of the pleasure you gave me."

Sebastien lifted his head, blood-stained fangs shimmering in the low light. He nodded and scooted back up the bed, lying flat where Thierry's hands guided him, resisting the urge to flip his lover beneath him and bury himself in hot flesh. The hands that moved over him were firm, confident as they moved over his chest, just brushing his nipples before sliding lower to lift his cock from the stickiness on his lower abdomen. One hand gathered fluid from his belly to ease the way while the other reached between his legs to fondle his heavy sac. He tensed, wondering if Thierry would try to reciprocate caress for caress, but his hands did not wander beyond their current positions, stroking and squeezing to maximum effect.

The thought of returning all the pleasures Sebastien had given him crossed Thierry's mind, but his hands stayed where they were, the combination of his own inexperience and the sudden tension in Sebastien's body enough to dissuade him. Another time, perhaps, but not tonight with the situation already as fraught as it was. Tonight, he would go with what he knew and help break the magic driving Sebastien as quickly as possible.

It did not take much for Sebastien to reach his peak, his orgasm rolling through him in long, deep waves, his cock spurting fluid over his chest in sharp bursts. Thierry's hands did not still, prolonging his pleasure until his erection began to wane and all tension seeped from him. "Feeling better?" the blond asked when the vampire's eyes opened again.

Sebastien paused for a moment to take stock. The restlessness that had plagued him was gone, along with the irresistible desire to seek Thierry's company despite knowing the dangers. He still wanted to be right where he was, but that feeling was not new. He had wanted to be here, sharing Thierry's bed, since the first time he had tasted the man's blood—but the force of that desire, augmented by the wild magic, had returned to its normal levels. "I think so. You?"

"Yes," Thierry replied, "it worked. I could feel the spell dissipate as soon as I came." He yawned suddenly. "I think I need to rest some more."

Sebastien sat up, reaching for the sheets to leave so Thierry could rest, but the wizard caught his hand. “No, please stay. I sleep better in your arms. Besides, what are you going to do to me you haven’t already done?”

If you only knew, Sebastien thought darkly, images of rolling Thierry beneath him and claiming him completely still lurking in his mind. He relented, though, lying back down and welcoming Thierry into his arms. “Go to sleep,” he ordered grumpily, softening the command with a kiss to the top of Thierry’s head.

Against Sebastien’s shoulder, Thierry smiled and drifted back to sleep.

Chapter 18

ERIC WOKE slowly to the foreign sensation of strong arms holding him and an equally odd soreness in his ass. Memories returned slowly, leaving him with the uncomfortable realization that he was in Vincent's bed, having let the other wizard fuck him thoroughly the night before. He wondered what else was fucked besides his ass, hoping they had not damaged their friendship or endangered their positions in Serrier's ranks.

"Stop thinking so loud," Vincent grumbled behind him, startling Eric into sitting up. Strong hands immediately pulled him back down to the pillows. "It's too early for thinking."

Eric subsided, having learned last night the futility of fighting those hands. Vincent was his match physically, a true rarity for a man of his size. Was that the attraction, he wondered? If so, though, why had he only noticed last night? They had been friends almost since he had arrived at Serrier's lair two years ago. So what had changed? He had known for some time that he found some men attractive, too, but he had loved Danielle to distraction, far too much to experiment on the side. Once he switched allegiances, he had not even considered the option, seeking female lovers when he sought one at all, not wanting to risk his newfound position for a meaningless fling. Was that what last night had been? It had not felt meaningless at the time, he knew that for sure. *And now?* he asked himself. Before he could answer his own question, Vincent's hands moved, sliding down his back to knead lightly at his heavily muscled backside. He flinched.

"What?" Vincent asked, opening his eyes. "Did I misread you last night?"

"No," Eric mumbled, "just sore."

Vincent frowned, pushing up on one elbow. "I wasn't that rough."

Eric shrugged and looked away, unwilling to muddy the waters further by telling Vincent that last night had been his first experience with a man. "I guess I'm out of practice."

Vincent caught his chin and met Eric's eyes seriously. "Something you want to tell me?" he pressed. When Eric stayed silent, his eyes narrowed dangerously. "You told me you'd done this before."

"I have," Eric retorted, "just not with a man."

"And you let me pound you that way? You're either a fool or a better man than I am. I could have hurt you!" Vincent scolded.

Eric shifted on the bed, feeling the lingering soreness. "Yeah, I realize that."

"Turn over," Vincent ordered, flipping Eric onto his stomach before the other wizard even had a chance to move. His hands went to the hard cheeks, parting them firmly, noticing as he did the ritual scar on the back of Eric's leg. His own matching scar bisected his chest. He wondered sometimes what they had gotten themselves into, accepting those marks and all they had come to represent. If he had known then…. That train of thought did not bear completion. He had not known and now he was committed.

Eric started to pull away, but Vincent stopped him with a sharp smack. "I have to make sure you're not bleeding," he explained, examining the inflamed flesh carefully. While he was sure it was painful, he could not see any tears in the tight pucker. Rolling Eric to the side, he looked at the sheets, finding no trace of blood there either. "Good," he declared. "You'll be sore for a few days since you didn't have the good sense to tell me you were a virgin until after I'd fucked you through the mattress, but it doesn't look like there's any real damage." He flopped back down on the mattress. "So much for round two."

"What?" Eric challenged, coming up on his elbow and smirking down at his friend. "You can dish it out but you can't take it?"

"You want a piece of me?" Vincent retorted with a grin. "Better men than you have tried."

"We'll see about that," Eric replied, his own grin making his eyes dance with lust and laughter as he grabbed Vincent's wrists in one hand and pinned them to the pillows. "Stay there," he ordered.

"Why should I?"

"I'll make it worth your while," Eric promised, lowering his head and nipping at Vincent's lips. "Just give me a chance."

Vincent smiled. He would struggle enough to make it interesting, but this was one man he would not mind bottoming for occasionally—especially if it meant he got another shot at Eric's tight, virgin ass. And next time, he would cherish that gift.

SHE CAME to him on a shaft of moonlight, her voluptuous breasts barely contained by the scrap of red silk that draped over her shoulders and fell loosely to brush the tops of her thighs, swaying with her movements. The hem beckoned to him, tempting him to slide his fingers beneath it and sample the delights it so tantalizingly hid. Her henna-painted hands caressed her curves through the thin fabric, as if daring him to pull them away and touch her himself. He sat up, uncaring that the sheets fell away to reveal his nude form. He had every intention of having her there next to him in exactly the same state as soon as possible.

Her lips curved at the sight of him as she sashayed toward the bed, every gesture screaming seduction. He ached just from the sight of her. He could only imagine what touching her, feeling her touch him, would do to him. He opened his mouth to speak, to invite her to join him, but her fingers caressed his lips, silencing him with a single look. He nodded his agreement and leaned back on the bed as she knelt on the end and slithered up over him, pressing him into the sheets.

His hands moved automatically to her hips, sliding over smooth silk and luscious curves. She was soft, but not weak. Then she lowered her mouth to suck at one nipple, her fingers combing through the strawberry curls on his chest to find the other one, and he stopped thinking altogether. Of its own volition, one of his hands slid beneath the silk, seeking skin and finding it, smooth buttocks completely bared as he pushed the nightgown up to her waist. His other hand moved to the clasps holding the chemise on her shoulders, releasing them so that her breasts tumbled free. He licked his lips eagerly, wanting to feast on the succulent globes. As if reading his mind, she lifted her head and straddled his waist, her thighs hugging his flanks snugly, her cleft lining up perfectly with the length of his swollen erection as she leaned forward to offer him her breasts.

He tangled one hand in her thick black hair, pressing her closer as his other hand cupped the breast he was not currently suckling. He kneaded the tempting mound, toying with her pert nipple as he nipped at the other one, surprising a pleased gasp from her slender throat. He rocked his hips, shunting his cock along her nether lips, hoping she would lift up so he could slide deep inside her. She was already dripping wet, anointing his erection with the proof of her passion.

An annoyingly insistent beeping broke the spell, dragging David back to consciousness. With a muttered curse, he slapped off the alarm and fell back onto his pillow, staring at the ceiling in disgust. He had spent the entire night this way, tangled in the sheets, victim of sweaty, erotic dreams that always faded just before he could flip Angélique beneath him and sate himself in her body. He already knew jacking off would not help. He had tried it last night, several times, after hearing Alain and Adèle both admit to breaking the magic's hold through an orgasm. Apparently, that only worked with one's partner, and his was nowhere to be found. He supposed he could have sought her out—he knew where she lived and worked—but that would have been admitting more than he cared to about the magic's ability to control his behavior. If Raymond could resist, so could he. He just hoped Marcel got the cleanup ritual underway soon, because good intentions only went so far.

THIERRY STIRRED in bed, memories of the night before assailing him instantly. He groaned as his cock hardened. Shifting on the bed, he was relieved to feel Sebastien's arms tighten around him immediately, the vampire's body still spooned the length of his, an inexplicable source of comfort. Not wanting Sebastien to get up yet, as the vampire inevitably did when he knew Thierry was awake, the wizard closed his eyes and settled back down as if he had only stirred in his sleep. It either worked or Sebastien was no more eager than he to start the day, because the dark-haired vampire neither moved nor spoke.

Taking stock, Thierry was relieved not to feel the same pressure of the wild magic he had felt the night before. He in no way regretted how it had ended, but he knew it was dangerous given the magical trauma he had suffered the day before. He could still feel the magical void of the *Vide* charm Alain had left in place, so the wild magic had not destroyed it. It must have come inside with Sebastien instead. He would have to make sure his lover did not go out again until Alain gave the all clear, even just onto the terrace.

His hip stung slightly, a smile hovering on his lips as he glanced down at the two red pinpricks just inside his hipbone. Come to think of it, his ass stung a little, too, not surprising since Sebastien had finger-fucked him thoroughly the night before. The thought sent desire curling in his gut again, not magically induced this time, but the simple result of lustful memories. At the same time, he could feel a nervous flutter at the thought of anything larger inside him. If those two fingers left him feeling this sore, what would the full girth of Sebastien's cock do to him? Pushing that thought aside, he reminded himself firmly of Alain's promise that it would not be painful if Sebastien did it right.

An unexpected tickle in his throat caused him to cough experimentally, bringing a frown to his face. Forcing his thoughts away from sex, he took a quick inventory of the rest of his body, groaning as he felt the building congestion in his head and the lethargy that always accompanied a cold. He did not have time to get sick. It seemed his body had other ideas, though.

Coughing again, a little harder this time, he sat up slowly, groaning again at aches that had nothing to do with sex.

"What's wrong?" Sebastien asked lazily from behind him.

"Sick," Thierry replied before he started coughing again. He stumbled toward the bathroom, hoping he had a cold remedy of some sort to ease the symptoms that had come on far too quickly. With a sinking stomach, he wondered if this was a side effect of magical and physical exhaustion. If it was, last night had only made matters worse, for he had expended more than a little energy in his oh-so-pleasurable wrestling match with Sebastien. Rummaging through the medicine cabinet, he found a bottle of cough syrup that had not passed its expiration date and took a long swig, feeling it soothe his scratchy throat.

"Sick?" Sebastien repeated from the doorway. "But you were fine yesterday."

Thierry nodded. "And now I'm not. I guess it's going to be a longer recovery than we thought."

Sebastien frowned, not liking the idea of Thierry being sick. He liked the potential ramifications even less. "Did we cause this?"

Thierry shrugged. "We might have. It might have happened anyway. There's really no way to know."

Sebastien's frown deepened. "When it's safe for us to leave, I'll find someone else to feed from until you're well. I don't want to make you worse."

Jealousy reared its ugly head, twisting Thierry's heart and contorting his features. "Don't even think about it."

"If I made you sick…."

"That's a risk we'll just have to live with," Thierry insisted. "I don't share."

RAYMOND OPENED his eyes slowly, coming out of the light trance he had sunk into in place of sleep last night. He knew he needed the rest, but he could not risk letting the wild magic take hold if his shields slipped. He had too much to do today and he could not afford the distraction—any distraction—if he intended to fix the mess he had created yesterday with his carelessness. He had burned the midnight oil deep into the night, studying every reference he could find to the sort of wild magic they would be dealing with today, as well as to anything that could safely boost a wizard's power. Nothing he found showed as much potential as the vampires and the partnership bonds, particularly since those relationships also seemed to attract the wild magic even without any additional incantation.

Looking down at the spell he had written out the night before, he examined it again with fresh eyes, searching for any weakness that would allow the wild magic to escape or to influence the wizard doing the spell as it worked. He could not find any way to improve it, but he would swallow his pride and ask Alain and Marcel to look at it as well before they began. The last thing he wanted was for some careless oversight on his part to wreak havoc on still more people's lives.

He forced his mind away from wondering how Jean was dealing with the continuing compulsion. He knew the vampire had felt it, the expression on Jean's face when he and Raymond had first entered Marcel's office yesterday one of bemusement and frustration. The chef de la Cour had not known what was driving his desires, but he knew something was. Raymond snorted softly. Of course something was driving him. He found it far too easy to resist the former dark wizard, who had nothing to recommend him but a love of books and old lore. He had certainly given up easily enough when Raymond drew back from further intimacy after his return from La Réunion. Apparently, one taste of intimacy with Raymond was enough for the vampire.

And that was ridiculous, and he knew it. Jean had promised to respect Raymond's limits and had done just that from the very beginning, with the exception of that one memorable interlude—proof of an innate nobility to which Raymond could never aspire, not with his checkered past. That Raymond wished he would insist again was irrelevant. Until he was ready to admit to those feelings, Jean would surely do the honorable thing and keep his distance. The wizard reminded himself he should be flattered that his partner had such respect for him. It did not stop loneliness from eating at him as he thought of the other partners in the alliance and how close most of them were becoming.

That was a problem for later. Much, much later. He had a ritual to plan and execute, a war to fight, and far too many other responsibilities to dwell on the impossible. Stepping into the shower, he scrubbed at his face, washing away the last of his fatigue, determined to keep his focus where it belonged.

"HOW ARE you this morning, my boy?" Marcel asked when Alain entered his office.

"I'm all right," Alain replied slowly, though in truth he was still more than a little unsettled from the day before. He had slept in Orlando's firm embrace but had shied away from any other intimacy, afraid either feeding or sex would bring back the wild magic, perhaps even more strongly than before. He had considered putting a *Vide* charm on Orlando's apartment until they knew it was safe again, but he did not want Orlando to realize how truly worried he was. He needed his lover's trust too badly to risk anything that might shake that.

"No more bouts of wild magic?" Marcel verified.

"No," Alain answered. "I don't know if that means it doesn't come around a second time or if it just couldn't get through my shields this time. Either way, I'll be glad when it's no longer an issue."

"I'm sure you're not the only one," Marcel agreed. "Speaking of that, I wanted your thoughts on who to include in the ritual today. You missed the discussion Raymond and I had yesterday. He believes the best way to do this, besides including your partners, is to have one wizard for each of the four elements working independently but at the same time and in the same place. He would represent water. You and Orlando would represent air. Normally, I would ask Thierry to represent earth, but as he is under the weather at the moment, that won't be possible."

Alain frowned. For whatever reason, earth was the rarest of the elements among wizards, making Thierry's current infirmity even more damaging to the Milice. "You only want paired wizards, right?" he verified. His first thought was of his own lieutenant, Hugues Fouquet—but however good a wizard he was, he had not found a partner the day the alliance formed.

"Raymond is quite convinced your partners will increase your strength to the point that only four of you will be able to handle the entire process, so yes, only paired wizards."

"That leaves out Fouquet," Alain mused aloud. "Or you, for that matter. Are you sure you couldn't participate even without a partner? You're stronger than any two of us put together."

"I would, even without a partner, if I didn't have to be at the Palais de Matignon today for meetings," Marcel explained. "I suggested a delay but was overruled."

"The only person who comes to mind is Magali Ducassé, but she transferred, didn't she? To Amiens?" Alain suggested finally.

"I can arrange for her to return for the day easily enough," Marcel replied, "but I wasn't sure how the vampires would feel about that. At least if it were you and Raymond and Thierry, you and your vampires know each other well enough to allay some of the issues brought up by feeding with others in the room. Your vampires don't know Magali at all, and her partner doesn't know you."

"Do you have a better suggestion?"

"No," Marcel admitted. "I'd hoped you would think of someone I'd forgotten."

"If we call Magali back, then we would do better to have a woman for fire as well," Alain commented. "Two men and two women, at least for the wizards."

"Adèle would probably appreciate the opportunity to put the wild magic to rest," Marcel suggested ruefully. "Would that suit?"

"I think so," Alain replied, "as long as her partner keeps his arrogant mouth shut."

"If he's busy feeding from her, he won't have time for talking anyway," Marcel quipped.

Alain chuckled and shook his head. Even the weight of his role in the Milice could not completely break the old reprobate of his bad habits, it seemed.

Chapter 19

ALAIN NODDED to Magali and Luc as they walked in. "Do you know everyone?" he asked the wizard.

"All except Adèle's partner," she replied, offering her hand to the blond vampire. "Magali Ducassé."

"Jude Leighton," he replied with a curt nod, shaking her hand as briefly as possible. He was not completely able to hide his disgust at having to deal with yet another woman who did not know her place.

"Leighton," Luc growled from Magali's shoulder, not pleased with the other vampire's reaction to his partner. He knew Jude by reputation, but the other vampire had another think coming if he thought he could treat the partner of any chef de la Cour shabbily.

"I don't think you've met the rest of the wizards," Jean intervened, breaking the tension. As much as he would love to see Jude taken down a notch or two, the cost of letting the big vampire be the one to do it was higher than he was willing to pay.

Luc let it go with a final glare at Jude, turning to meet the other wizards in the room.

Jean introduced Raymond, Alain and Adèle, deliberately introducing his own partner first. He wanted it quite clear that in however high esteem Luc held Magali, Jean valued his own partner just as much.

Though his nods to all three were polite, Luc clearly got the message Jean had intended to send, taking a moment longer to greet Raymond than the others.

"Let's get started," Raymond declared when they had finished the introductions. "We have a lot to do."

They spent the next hour debating suitable locations and rehearsing the incantation Raymond had written until he was satisfied each wizard knew it perfectly. To his delight, Jean had not even had to correct his pronunciation this time.

Once they knew the spell, they shuffled partners to gather again around the underground lake. The large cavern provided everything they needed: water for Raymond, earth for Magali, air for Alain, and a safe place for Adèle's fire.

Raymond took his place at the west side of the lake, directing Adèle, Magali and Alain to move into position to complete the circle. Magali's power grounded them and Alain's sent their magic outward into the air. The four vampires waited until the space thrummed with gathering power before taking their places behind their wizards, tension high in all four of them as they contemplated the semipublic nature of what had heretofore been an incredibly private act.

This was not the quick taste they had accepted in public as the alliance was forming, though only Jude had even participated in that. This would be a serious, prolonged feeding as they combined the inherent magic of the partnership bonds with the intentional magic the wizards would perform during the grounding ritual.

"You don't have to do this," Raymond reminded Jean softly, sensing the unease in the room. "It will take us longer and be harder without you, but we can do the spells alone."

Jean shook his head. "You're already taking a risk by doing the ritual with just four wizards. You can't seriously expect us to walk away when we can help minimize the danger."

Raymond smiled gratefully. "I'm glad you're here."

"There's nowhere I'd rather be," Jean replied, returning the smile. Stepping closer to his partner, he settled his hands on Raymond's hips, feeling the tension invest his partner's muscles at the unexpected touch before relaxing again. He pushed the collar of Raymond's turtleneck lower, licking conscientiously at the smooth flesh. He put everything else out of his mind but the man in front of him. The other three pairs were far enough away around the edges of the lake that he could not even hear the wizards murmuring the spell that would draw in the wild magic and ground it safely in the earth's core. He could only hear Raymond's voice chanting steadily, with just the occasional hitch in his breathing as Jean prepared his skin.

The rhythmic intonation faltered when Jean's fangs slid beneath tender skin, probing deeply as he found a vein. He stroked one hand reassuringly up Raymond's side as he waited for his partner to pick up the threads of the spell again, so he could time his suction to the words.

Raymond leaned back slightly against Jean as he felt the vampire's fangs penetrate his neck. His partner took his weight easily, supporting him physically as he supported him magically. The surge of power that hit when he resumed the spell surprised him in its intensity. If the other wizards were feeling the same exponential increase in their magic, they probably could have tackled the original vortex alone. The scattered bits of wild magic would pose no problem whatsoever.

Gathering his tattered concentration, Raymond caught Alain's eye, making a quick gesture to indicate that the other wizard should start his search for the wild magic. Alain nodded back and closed his eyes, casting the accumulated power out into the atmosphere. The spell worked on the simple theory that like attracts like, and so the wild magic would be drawn to the incredible strength that coalesced around them. And when it was, they would catch it and ground it. They simply had to maintain the spell and their concentration until they could deal with all the individual drops.

Almost immediately, they could feel the influx of wild magic. It was channeled through Alain into the other three, to be consigned to earth, water, or flames and thus grounded and unable to wreak havoc anymore.

Magali swayed slightly as wave after wave of wild magic came at her. Luc's arms came around her immediately, one large hand on her hip, the other splaying across her stomach, settling and supporting her as she concentrated on the stone beneath her now bare feet. His breath was hot on her skin and his hair brushed her cheek, subtle sensations that could have been distractions but instead helped center her further. She was not alone in dealing with the onslaught. Luc was right there with her, adding his power to hers, a synergy that flooded through her and rocked the ground beneath her feet as she channeled into it, trapping the wild magic within.

Adèle had to resist the urge to pull away when Jude first moved into place behind her, his closeness reminding her of things she wanted to forget—but she had agreed to participate, knowing what would be required. She focused her anger at his whispered "Hello, pussy," into the flames she conjured in a circle all around them, not bothering to hide her satisfaction at his instinctive flinch. She would not let the fire get close enough to hurt him, but she did not mind making him a little uncomfortable. His fangs sank into her neck immediately with no preparation, his hands gripping possessively at her hips as he pulled her back against him hard. She wanted to squirm away from him, but he would either take it as encouragement or as a sign he had discomfited her, neither of which was acceptable in her mind. Instead, she set the flames dancing even higher as the sudden burst of energy surged through her. When the first drops of wild magic slid down the connection with Alain, she almost laughed at their pitiful strength as she banished them neatly, a little flare in the circle of fire the only indication of their passing.

Alain's mind flew outward with his magic, sweeping across the city in great, wide strokes, gathering up the bits of wild magic that had caused him such grief, capturing them and funneling them back to his friends who were waiting to deal with them. He could feel Orlando's arms around him, his lover's fangs in his neck even as his mind soared above the city, the sensations grounding him in a way nothing else had ever done. He felt invincible at that moment, ready to take on any threat, any obstacle. He knew that feeling was an illusion, just like the feeling of flying was an illusion, but he reveled in it nonetheless. For these few minutes, the world appeared stretched out at his feet.

The part of Jean's mind not buzzing from the sudden inrush of Raymond's magic marveled at the resonance in the air as power flooded the room. They had posited that this would work, though they had not dared test it because of the wild magic they would surely attract, but he had not even imagined it could work this well. He could taste the steadily increasing power in Raymond's blood, could feel it transferring to him and back to Raymond, an infinite loop that would continue as long as the spell and his feeding did. He resisted the urge to move closer, to grind against Raymond to work off some of the lust that sparked in him as he fed, not tasting any comparable awareness in Raymond's blood. As much as he wanted his partner, he would not trespass where he was not welcome, and Raymond's reaction the last time he had fed from the wizard's neck had made his feelings on the matter quite clear.

Luc had known the diminutive woman in his arms was a powerful wizard. He had watched her as she did her job before, but as she channeled the wild magic into the ground, pulse after pulse of energy flowing through her—and through him by extension—into the solid stone beneath their feet, he realized just how deep her strength extended. When she swayed in his arms, he tightened his embrace, supporting her weight without thought. She leaned against him pliantly, the relaxation of her limbs belied by the concentration he could taste as her blood flowed steadily down his throat. Her trust in him humbled him, for he had seen enough of her to realize she trusted rarely and slowly. Supporting her weight with one arm, he brushed her hair back from her forehead, feeling the sheen of sweat that dotted her brow as she deftly met the demands of the spell. Her head tilted ever so slightly into the caress, bringing a smile to his lips.

Adèle's power was as potent an aphrodisiac as anything Jude had ever tasted, every nerve in his body on high alert as the flames flickered all around them. He pressed as close to her as he could, not wanting to be burned by her magic, the contact only adding fuel to the lust raging inside him. She arched away from him, pricking his pride. His hands closed roughly on her hips, pulling her back against him. He slid one hand forward, splaying firmly across her lower abdomen just above her pubic bone to hold her in place. The other hand climbed up her ribs to her breast, squeezing roughly. He felt the jolt of annoyance and lust that hit her through her blood. He sucked harder on her neck, feeling the power raised by his feeding augment even more. Curious to see what would happen, he kneaded her breast again. He felt the same mixture of annoyance and lust, followed by the same boost in her power. Grinning around his fangs, he thrust against the curve of her buttocks in time with his suckling mouth and the pinch of his fingers on her nipple.

Orlando had tasted many things in Alain's blood in the almost three weeks since he had first tasted it, but for the first time, he tasted his lover's unleashed power. In its latent state, Alain's magical ability underlay every exchange of blood from their very first meeting in the Père Lachaise cemetery, but Orlando had never tasted its total expression until now. As it flowed through Alain's blood and into him, it seemed to amplify a cycle of give and take that only increased the magic instead of ebbing and flowing, leaving Orlando feeling glutted with the force of it. And with that flush of power came the hot surge of lust that only Alain could inspire. Orlando could feel his body reacting to Alain's closeness, his cock swelling in his trousers as he pulled his lover even closer, one hand moving up and down Alain's side in time to the pull of his lips on the wizard's neck. The other hand stroked over the brand that joined their lives, the oldest and deepest magic between them. He swore he could feel another jump in Alain's power at the gesture so he cupped his palm over the mark. When he felt it again, he disengaged his fangs for a moment, switching his head to the other side and biting right where he had first claimed Alain as his own. Alain's body arched beneath his, lust and love and elemental power pulsing through him and through their bond into Orlando.

The last burst of power as Orlando changed where he bit Alain's neck drew the last of the wild magic, channeled from him to Adèle to neutralize. A sudden cry drew his attention as the flames she had summoned suddenly flared out of control.

"Raymond!"

The sound of his name drawing his attention, Raymond looked around the lake to the unexpected sight of Adèle fighting to bring her magic back under control. Cursing silently, he sent a shockwave of magic through the lake, water splashing up to douse the flames.

"Bastard!" Adèle shouted, struggling in Jude's embrace as he resumed his unwelcome attentions the moment the flames died around them. "You could have killed us both!"

Frowning, Alain waited for her partner to acknowledge her words, to admit his fault and cease his clearly unwelcome actions, but the vampire showed no reaction to Adèle's words or her struggles. With a frustrated shake of his head, he cast a binding spell at the vampire, a variation of the one they had used to hold the dark wizards at the Gare de Lyon the morning the alliance formed.

"What did you do to him?" Orlando asked drolly.

"Stopped him," Alain replied with a shrug. "She should be able to undo my spell even though she couldn't have cast it on him."

"Did the ritual work?" the vampire asked, putting Jude out of his mind.

"I think so," Alain answered. "I couldn't feel any wild magic remaining. Let's see what Raymond thinks."

Ignoring the bound vampire, they walked around the edge of the lake to join Raymond and Jean. "Well?" Alain asked. "How did we do?"

Raymond smiled, still feeling the aftereffects of the surge of power. "We did it," he assured them. "I couldn't feel anything left when we finished."

"Good," Alain and Orlando declared in unison. Turning to Magali and Luc, who had also joined them, Alain addressed Magali. "Can I help your partner get back home?"

"Thanks, Alain," Magali smiled, "but I think we're going to stay in Paris tonight. We'll get ourselves home tomorrow." She had expected to be too drained after the ritual to be able to transport herself home and so had convinced Luc to spend the evening with her in the capital. The surge of power still connecting her strongly with the earth beneath her feet, and the possessive hand that had not left some part of her body—belly, back, elbow—since the ritual began, brought a smile of feminine delight to her face. She considered the romantic delights of strolling along the Seine before retiring to the room they had reserved at the L'hôtel du 7e art, just a few blocks off the river in the Marais.

"In that case, maybe you'd send Orlando back to Milice headquarters so we can go home," Alain requested, the pinch of Orlando's fangs through the Avoué mark making him hungry for more intimacy.

"Of course," Magali agreed. "Are you ready?" she asked Orlando.

Orlando looked to Alain for confirmation, feeling the lingering desire that always swamped him when he fed from Alain. At Alain's nod, he answered Magali. With a flick of her wrist, he disappeared, Alain right behind him.

"Shall I… dispose of your partner as well?" Magali asked Adèle.

"Don't bother," the dark-haired wizard replied. "I have a few things to say to him while he can't do anything but listen. I'll free him before I leave and he can find his own way out. He fed so he doesn't have to worry about the sunlight if he gets out of this maze before nightfall."

Magali chuckled. "Remind me not to cross you."

"Maybe this'll teach him that, too," Adèle muttered hopefully.

"Don't count on it," Jean murmured beside her. "You could oblige me, though, if you don't mind, unless you still need me here, Raymond?"

Raymond shook his head, knowing he would not ask for what he really needed, the power flooding him needing an outlet. He would have to find some other way to release it.

Magali sent Jean back to Milice headquarters, glancing at her watch, surprised at how much time had passed. The sun would be setting soon, if it had not already. "Shall we go?" she asked Luc, heading toward the exit. She had tracked a dark wizard through the coulisses one day, her eidetic memory providing her with the path out now.

"Thanks, Magali, Luc," Raymond called after them. "Adèle, do you need me to stay?"

Adèle shook her head. "No, I'll be fine, and I won't hurt him too badly. He just needs to learn a little respect."

Raymond shrugged and winked out directly to his apartment.

Chapter 20

JEAN RACED down la rue du 4 septembre toward rue de la Michodière. The Piège-Pouvoir, the second ritual, was finished, the wild magic that had so strongly influenced the various partnerships safely dispersed, but the power that sang in his veins from feeding while Raymond had worked the spell demanded release, and he doubted he would be welcome in Raymond's bed. The wizard had kept him at arm's length since the first time he fed after returning from La Réunion. He had let Jean feed, but only from his wrist again, as if he feared letting the vampire closer—until today at the ritual.

He needed more than that, not because he was hungry but because he needed the release that came from the combined power of feeding and sex. For that, he needed Karine. He took the steps to her apartment two at a time, all momentum stolen when he saw the wilted flowers by her door. She had not even taken them inside.

He had told her repeatedly that if she could not be satisfied with what he could offer, she should tell him to leave. He did not need to be told twice. It appeared Raymond would be receiving a visitor tonight after all. Jean spared a passing thought to visiting Sang Froid instead—but he needed a connection, not the anonymity Angélique provided. He needed a lover tonight, not a victim.

Minutes later, he pounded on the door to Raymond's apartment, uncaring that the noise might disturb the neighbors. There were only two other doors off the garret hallway, and he could not sense anyone within.

Not at all surprisingly, a wand greeted him as the door cracked open. "It's me," he told his partner. "Let me in."

The chain holding the door shut clanged against the doorframe as Raymond released it and opened the door wide enough to let Jean enter. "What are you doing here?" he asked. "Even more importantly, how did you find me?"

"I found your apartment while you were still in La Réunion. I was wandering the streets and ended up here," Jean explained, eyes raking over the vision Raymond presented in a pair of dark sleep pants and a hastily donned robe half-open to reveal a strong, smooth chest. "As for why I'm here now…." He would never be able to find the words to explain the emotions riding him. Replacing words with actions, he caught Raymond's wand hand, setting the length of birch aside and lifting the wizard's wrist to his mouth. He brushed his lips over the mottled skin. "I need you."

"Y… you fed already," Raymond stuttered, hating the way his body betrayed him. Even with the wild magic dispersed, his partner asserted a magical pull on him that Raymond found increasingly difficult to resist. "You shouldn't be here."

"Yes, I should," Jean insisted, sliding his lips up the muscular arm. "We've been dancing around this for long enough."

Raymond shook his head. "It isn't us," he protested. "It's the partnership bond pushing us to feel this way."

"Is it?" Jean challenged. "Or is the bond as powerful as it is because of the way we feel?"

"Adèle—"

"Adèle is a very beautiful woman in an absolutely untenable position, I agree," Jean interrupted, "but she's not you, and I'm not Jude. Give me tonight to convince you. If you still want me to leave in the morning, I will, and I won't ask anything of you again beyond the minimum of the alliance."

Raymond swallowed nervously, feeling rather like the mouse hypnotized by the cobra, knowing he should flee but unable to move away. One long, slender finger traced the line of his throat, following his bobbing Adam's apple, surprising a soft moan from his lips. It had been so long since anyone touched him with any sensual purpose. *Except Jean*, a little voice reminded him. The vampire had respected Raymond's wishes most of the time, feeding as impersonally as possible. It was proof that they could resist the magical compulsion if they chose—but the memory of the one time Jean had not been so clinical stayed with Raymond, tantalizing him with all that could be between them. Slowly, he nodded and started toward his bedroom.

Breath catching in his chest, Jean followed, shedding his light jacket and dropping it on the back of the couch as he passed. Raymond's bedroom, like every other room in the apartment, was cluttered with books. Only Raymond's half of the bed was not completely covered.

Having reached the bedroom, Raymond's nerves faltered again and he shifted nervously back and forth from one foot to the other. It had been several years since he had last taken a male lover and he was not completely comfortable with the idea of taking one now, particularly with the extenuating circumstances.

"Easy," Jean soothed, stepping smoothly into Raymond's personal space, letting their bodies brush together. "You know I'm not going to hurt you. Remember what monsieur Lombard told you? It goes against everything I am to hurt anyone I care about. I can fight some of my instincts, but not those. I don't want to fight those. You're safe with me, Raymond. You always will be."

It helped just to hear that Jean wanted more than simple release, that he had come to Raymond deliberately. Turning, he disappeared into the bathroom, coming back out with a thick hand cream. "This'll have to do for lube," he said apologetically. "I don't keep—"

Jean's lips on his silenced his words. He gasped in surprise, somehow not having expected kissing from the vampire chef. The other man's lips were soft and warm, another unexpected sensation. If he had thought about it, Raymond would have guessed they would be cool.

"Stop thinking and kiss me back," Jean scolded gently against Raymond's mouth. "You can analyze everything tomorrow. Now, I just want you to enjoy."

Raymond chuckled softly. "It's my defense mechanism," he admitted.

"I know," Jean replied. "That's why I told you to stop."

"That's easier said than done," Raymond observed. "Why don't you see if you can make me?"

"Is that a challenge?" Jean asked, eyebrows lifting in surprise.

"If you're up to it," Raymond teased.

"I'm up," Jean assured the wizard, bumping their hips together so Raymond could feel his arousal. He found an answering one. "So are you, it would seem."

"So it would seem," Raymond admitted. "What are we going to do about it?"

"We're going to clear enough room on your bed for both of us and then we're going to get rid of some of these clothes. We'll see what develops from there," Jean declared.

A flick of Raymond's wrist sent books flying back to their correct locations. "Very efficient," Jean commented drolly. "Are you as good with clothing?"

"With my own, I am, but I don't know if it'll work on yours since you're immune to my magic," Raymond replied.

Jean considered suggesting they find out, but he wanted the pleasure of stripping Raymond's clothes off himself. To that end, he reached for the robe covering his wizard's broad shoulders. "I don't mind doing things the old-fashioned way." The silk was smooth beneath his hands, warm from Raymond's skin. Pulling the fabric free, he lifted it to his face, inhaling the scent of soap and man.

Raymond squirmed uncomfortably, not sure how to react to the incongruities of the situation. They were not lovers despite what they were about to do—yet Jean acted like they were, leaving Raymond flailing internally.

Setting aside the robe, Jean turned his attention back to Raymond. His partner was an undeniably attractive man: short, dark hair, lightly spiked; strong features with surprisingly light eyes; a full, lush mouth Jean intended to learn more completely before the night was done; strong, well-defined muscles without being overly bulky. As far as Jean could tell, he was perfect. Then Raymond turned and Jean caught sight of a long, jagged scar down the left side of his wizard's back. "Who hurt you?" he hissed.

"Serrier," Raymond replied shortly. "All of his top lieutenants, and yes, I was one, have a similar scar somewhere. It's a test of our loyalty, to prove we'd stay with him no matter what."

"He's a dead man," Jean growled, insides clenching at the thought of the pain Raymond must have endured to bear such a mark. "I'll kill him myself."

"Don't," Raymond insisted. "Not over this. Not over me. I don't even remember it most of the time. It's not like I can see it. Most of the time, I forget it's there."

Jean accepted Raymond's statement, but he would not forget. He would never forget what his partner had suffered at Serrier's hands. He had plenty of reasons to oppose the rebel wizard already, but this made it personal. Despite Raymond's pleas, it had just become his personal vendetta to see Serrier dead. No one hurt his wizard.

Stepping up behind the other man, he ran tender fingers over the ridged flesh, learning every inch of this badge of honor. How many lives had Raymond saved since he switched sides? How many people still lived and breathed because this man understood the workings of Serrier's twisted mind? He lowered his head and kissed the cicatrix, his tongue tracing the white line at the center of the scar as if his saliva could erase this mark as easily as it healed the bites he inflicted to survive.

Raymond's breath caught in his throat. For the first time since Serrier had marked him, he stood bare-chested before someone else, someone who could see the scar and judge him for it, who could have found him repulsive for bearing the scar. Jean seemed to have a completely different reaction, enthralled with the mark rather than repelled by it. His heart clenched in gratitude and desire as the vampire stroked the disfigurement tenderly, and when his lips replaced his fingers, Raymond melted beneath the caress.

Feeling Raymond leaning into him, Jean encircled his soon to be lover in an eager embrace, his hands wandering over the strong planes of Raymond's chest. To his delight, Raymond arched into his hands. Lifting his head, he urged the wizard to lean back against him as he continued to stroke every inch of hard muscle and smooth skin. Eventually, his hands settled over the bulge of pectoral muscle, kneading at the firm planes while his fingers tweaked at the diamond-hard points of Raymond's nipples. He had been a lover of women often enough to have developed a fetish for the little bumps even on his male lovers. If his reaction was any indication, Raymond shared that interest, his breath hitching with each pinch and pull.

Continuing his explorations with one hand, Jean let the other hand slide lower, over the planes of Raymond's flat abdomen and beneath the waistband of the black sleep pants to cup the generous endowment hidden therein. A groan escaped the wizard's throat, bringing a smile to Jean's lips. "Do you like that?" he taunted lightly.

"Merlin, yes!" Raymond exclaimed, hips bucking forward into the channel formed by the vampire's fist.

"Think how much better it'll be when it's my ass clenching around you," the chef de la Cour teased.

Raymond's knees went weak at the thought even as his mind protested. "But I thought…."

"You thought that because I'm the leader of the vampires, I'd want to top in bed?" Jean verified. When Raymond nodded, he explained, "But that's exactly why I don't want to. If you were a vampire, that would be different, but you're not. I can let down all my defenses with you, let go of le jeu des Cours for a few hours and just be Jean. And Jean wants—needs—to be fucked through the mattress tonight. Will you give me that?"

Raymond bit his lower lip as he turned in the vampire's embrace, fighting not to come in his pants like a green youth just at the thought of being allowed such intimacy. On the few occasions he had let himself imagine being with Jean, the vampire had always been the one firmly in control, firmly on top. "Yes," he murmured hoarsely. "Anything you want."

"That's a pretty broad offer," Jean teased.

"I meant it," Raymond replied, his earlier hesitations fading in the wake of Jean's willingness to share control of their encounter. He had been so sure that any potential lover, seeing the mark on his back, would change their mind, that he had not let himself hope for anything more than an occasional chance encounter. Everything within him vibrated now with the certainty of this being more than just a one-night stand. Even if their partnership did not survive the end of the war, Jean was committed to that effort. Furthermore, his offer to leave in the morning if Raymond insisted suggested that if Raymond did not, the vampire intended to stay. Lowering his head, he nipped gently at the thin lips as he finally allowed himself to relax and accept what was happening between them. He would always wish it had happened without magical impetus, but he knew in his heart that he had made his choice because of Jean's words, not because of some outside pressure.

Jean parted his lips, offering Raymond entrance, but the wizard did not immediately take advantage, instead lingering over the tender flesh he was currently exploring. In the meantime, his hands wandered over the vampire's lightly clad form, learning the contours through the cloth that separated them.

"You can take them off," Jean offered breathlessly, breaking the kiss when his head began to spin from lack of air. Knowing how his limitations had changed after he was made, he marveled that Raymond had not felt the need first, but the wizard seemed not to notice anything except his diligent perusal of the vampire's body.

"How old were you when you were turned?" Raymond asked curiously as he began unbuttoning Jean's shirt to reveal the lithe lines of his torso. He had seen the strength that resided in the sleek body beneath his hands, the deceptive strength of the cheetah that appeared slender next to its heavier feline kin but could explode in a burst of speed that put the others to shame.

"Twenty-eight," Jean husked, arching into a caress that mimicked the ones he had bestowed only moments before, "but it was a time of privation, with

Viking attacks every summer until the king made Rollon a duke in exchange for warding off the Norsemen who sailed up the Seine to pillage. The abbey wasn't spared any more than the rest of the city, and we starved along with everyone else."

That explained the slender frame beneath the man's face, Raymond decided as he explored further, his hands eager to learn every inch of Jean's body. Pushing aside the fabric that separated them, he bared the vampire to his eager gaze. Jean stood still beneath his perusal for a moment before reaching for the sleep pants Raymond still wore, sliding them down and off as well. The wizard's lower half was as perfectly formed as his upper half, leaving Jean more than pleased with his decision on how to spend the evening. The elegantly curved cock would fill him delightfully. Now it remained only to see if Raymond was as well versed in the erotic arts as he was in the esoteric ones.

The hands that guided him toward the bed were as confident as Jean could have wished, easing him down onto the smooth sheets that had cooled in the time since Raymond had risen to answer his door. The body that pressed his into the mattress was just heavy enough for Jean to feel its presence without being uncomfortably heavy. Interestingly, Raymond aligned their bodies in such a way that Jean's cock was trapped between them, caressed with every movement, however slight, while his own did not touch Jean at all, leaving the vampire hyper aware of its absence. "There's nothing quite like being pressed into the mattress by the weight of a man," he purred, shifting beckoningly beneath his lover.

Raymond smiled down at the vampire, leaning on him a little more fully. "Be careful," he teased. "I might decide to keep you here."

"I might decide to let you," Jean retorted, arms languidly circling the wizard's neck and pulling his head down for a kiss. "After all, I have everything I need right here in this bed." He nipped lightly at Raymond's jaw, letting his fangs just brush the skin without leaving the slightest trace of their passage.

Raymond's eyes closed helplessly at the words. To be needed… to be the center of someone's world. Monsieur Lombard had told him anyone who gained the devotion of a vampire would be cared for beyond their wildest dreams. Raymond had not asked Alain if he was happy. He had not needed to. To be offered some small measure of that same devotion from his own partner was more than he had let himself hope for.

Determined to give Jean some of that same sense of belonging, he mated his lips to the vampire's, kissing him tenderly, passionately, offering his mouth in exchange for the other man's. Their tongues twined, a writhing, clashing tangle, vying for dominance of the kiss. Keeping their lips joined, Raymond rolled to the side so he could reach Jean better, his free hand skating over smooth skin.

Remembering how the vampire had lingered on his chest, Raymond did the same now, his fingers circling the taut nubs of flesh, plucking at them gently when Jean writhed against him. "Just like that," Jean gasped, pulling free from the kiss to nuzzle at the line of Raymond's jaw. "You make me feel so good."

Tipping his head back, Raymond offered the curve of tender flesh to his partner, trusting that the vampire would not hurt him. His hand slid lower, along Jean's flank to his hip and then lower still, lifting his thigh so it draped over his own legs. Jean rolled slightly onto his side, the new position giving Raymond access to his back and buttocks, the tight crease parted slightly as if in welcome.

Squeezing one globe of flesh in acknowledgment, Raymond ran his hand up and down the long leg that inched its way up toward his waist. He could feel the play of strong muscle beneath smooth skin, the allure of matching his strength against the vampire's growing in him with each stroke. Jean was not some retiring flower in need of delicate restraint. He was Raymond's match in power and intelligence, his equal in every way, capable of meeting him thrust for thrust. With that liberating thought, he fumbled for the container of lotion he had retrieved from the bathroom, squirting some onto his fingers so he could begin to prepare his lover.

"Do you want to roll over?" he asked considerately.

"No," Jean replied, nipping at Raymond's jaw again. "I want to see you, watch you, the entire time you're inside me." He did not add that he hoped Raymond would let him bite him at the same time. Blood was such a part of sex for the vampire that he had a hard time imagining not feeding at the same time, but he would wait to ask. No need to overwhelm Raymond with everything all at once.

"Putain," Raymond groaned, the thought of taking Jean face to face like true lovers making him shiver in anticipation. "You keep saying things like that and I won't last long enough to get inside you."

"I'd just have to get you hard again," Jean assured him, but he subsided onto the bed, parting his legs in invitation so Raymond could reach his entrance more easily. He would enjoy licking and sucking on the wizard's sated cock until it was hard again, but Raymond had been so skittish tonight that Jean did not want to do anything that might shatter the mood between them now. He would see how many times he could make Raymond climax some other time, but not tonight.

Groaning again at the sinful image, Raymond sought the furled rosette, testing its resilience with tender fingers. It gave way slowly, making the wizard wonder how long it had been since Jean had last let someone take him this way. The thought that the vampire trusted him to such an extent fired his blood even more. "Relax," he urged, the tip of one digit working its way in to the first knuckle.

"I'm trying," Jean gasped. "It's been… awhile." It had been more than awhile. It had been almost four hundred years, but Raymond did not need to know that detail. Not since Thibaut betrayed him had he trusted a male lover outside the vampire community—and within the Cour, he could not let anyone top him.

The invading finger sank deeper, brushing over the bundle of nerves, and Jean felt everything inside him give in to the pleasure it evoked. His eyes closed, lips parted, lower lip caught between his teeth. Raymond's breath caught at the mask of pleasure on his face. To know that he could bring such joy to his experienced partner gave him the confidence he needed to work his finger the rest of the way in, rocking it sideways to stretch the still tight guardian ring before adding a second one.

"All right?" he asked as he withdrew his finger to slide back in with two. Jean's face was set, making it impossible for Raymond to determine if he was hurting his lover.

In reply, Jean captured Raymond's mouth in a hard kiss, lifting his hips in invitation. Raymond slid his fingers deeper, scissoring them slowly until he felt the resistance fade.

"Now," Jean said with a last nip to Raymond's lips. "I need you now."

Raymond nodded, withdrawing his fingers and using the last of the lotion on his hand to slick his cock. Rolling to his knees between the widespread thighs, he rocked his hips against the tight portal, seeking ingress. It took a moment, but then gave, allowing him inside. His eyes rolled back in his head as he assimilated the incredible heat and tightness that held him, caressed him, welcomed him.

Jean's head fell back and he fought not to tense against the burn as Raymond's cock split him wide. To his relief, the wizard paused when he hit bottom, giving Jean a chance to catch his breath and relax into the stretch. When Raymond did begin to move, he did so subtly, just stirring his shaft in the clenching channel, not enough to abrade the delicate tissue, just to let Jean feel his presence.

Wanting the taste of his lover on his tongue, Jean nipped at Raymond's neck. "Let me bite you," he requested, licking the skin he hoped to mark.

Raymond froze, all the ingrained fears rushing back at him, but he pushed them aside. Jean had fed from him before, countless times, had even used his fangs to make love to him once. The fact that they were intimately joined now changed nothing. If he could trust the vampire once, he could trust him every time. They had proven only hours before that combining feeding and magic strengthened the wizard. Surely this would be no different. "Y… you fed already," he stuttered.

"I know our limits," Jean assured him. "I won't take too much."

With a slow nod, Raymond assented, eyes closing as he anticipated the bite.

Some day, Jean swore to himself as the taste of Raymond's blood hit his senses, some day he would bite his lover and not taste fear along with whatever other emotions flavored his blood. Pushing that thought aside, he concentrated on using that point of contact to lavish as much pleasure on Raymond as the wizard was lavishing on him. If the sudden spike of lust in Raymond's blood was any indication, he was succeeding.

Raymond shivered, his thrusts unconsciously matching the rhythm of Jean's lips on his neck. He kept his movements abbreviated, not trusting the lotion to provide sufficient lubrication for any kind of energetic pounding. There would be other chances. Jean had asked for the night to convince Raymond, but Raymond did not need that much time. He would not ask Jean to leave.

Lust beginning to spiral out of control, he reached between their bodies to encircle Jean's cock, stroking it at the same deliberate pace. Against his neck, the vampire moaned, encouraging Raymond to speed his movements, hand and hips. Moments later, he felt the hot spurt of creamy fluid over his knuckles and between their bellies. The tight sheath contracted around him, milking his erection until he climaxed.

Carefully, Jean slipped his fangs from Raymond's neck, licking at the little wounds to seal them. Raymond lay still on top of him, his breath coming in hot pants against Jean's neck. Smiling gently, he stroked the strong back, fingers finding the scar again, caressing it repeatedly as if he could soothe away the pain that caused it.

Raymond shivered as the vampire's fingers explored the scar. He would never have imagined the mark of his shame could be an erogenous zone—but with Jean's fingers lingering there, the symbol of all he had come to hate became something else, something more. He let go of the anger he had nursed as his shield against the world and let the power of their partnership replace it.

Chapter 21

ADÈLE STALKED back around the lake to where her partner lay bound by Alain's spell. His eyes followed her, making it clear Alain had not dulled his senses, only bound his body. "I think I like you this way," she observed, nudging him with the toe of her boot.

He glared at her, but could do nothing to stop her.

"I could do whatever I wanted to you," she mused aloud, eyes raking his bound form. "Beat you, burn you, throw you in the lake." The power conjured up for the ritual still burned inside her, seeking an outlet. She smoothed her hands over her sides, watching lust flare in his eyes as her gesture outlined her figure. "Get you all worked up and leave you high and dry."

She pulled the thin sweater she wore over her head, leaving her torso clad in only a lacy camisole that covered her skin but did nothing to hide her form. Smirking down at him, she cupped her breasts in her hands as if offering them to an unseen lover. "Do you want to touch me?" she taunted. "Pull my chemise down and play with my breasts?" Her hands mimicked her words, giving him a swift glimpse of her nipples before her palms covered them, rubbing firmly, eyes closing as her desire mounted swiftly. She knew this feeling, the combination of adrenaline and lust that came from the concentrated, prolonged exercise of her magical abilities. It would fade on its own, given enough time, or she could release it in a most pleasurable way.

Letting the stretchy fabric slide back into place, she moved her hands, pulling free the band that confined her hair, a quick shake of her head sending it tumbling out of its braid and over her shoulders. "Or maybe you'd bite me again," she mused, fingers stroking the smooth skin he'd marked the day before. As soon as she had bought a replacement wand yesterday, she had healed those marks as well as the others he left on her body, not wanting the reminder of her weakness. Today, though, he was the weak one, the one completely at her mercy, and she fully intended to exploit the opportunity, knowing she might well never get another one. "You'd like knowing I was marked, wouldn't you?"

Casually, she reached for her wand, casting a healing spell on her neck to erase even the bite marks from the just completed ritual. "Too bad," she sneered, moving to stand over him. "I don't choose to be marked by any man."

Staring down at the bound vampire, she considered her options. She could release him and find her own satisfaction elsewhere or she could drive him crazy by making him watch what he wanted and could not have. She knew it was petty of her, but after yesterday she needed to be in control again, of herself and him. Stepping back, she bent to peel off her boots and pants, shivering against the chill in the air. With an impish smirk, she called back up the circle of flames Raymond had doused. The heat of the fire roared through her, bringing a flush to her skin.

Jude would have flinched if he could have when the fire burst from the ground again, but the spell the interfering blond wizard had placed on him kept him from moving at all. He could see, hear, feel, blink, but that was it. His skin buzzed with lust, an itch that demanded scratching except that he could do nothing about it. Nor could he demand that she, little slut that she was, do anything about it. She stood brazenly in front of him in nothing but her underwear, long legs and arms bare, her hair tousled as if someone had run passionate fingers through it. A light blush stained her cheeks and the tops of her breasts, proof of the lust raging in her blood. Lust he had not inspired. Silently, he fumed at the sight of her unblemished skin. His marks should have still been there, at least for a few more days, proclaiming to any who looked that she belonged to him. She had removed that claim, rejected it as she had tried to reject him. She would learn the folly of trying to reject a vampire.

Her bare toe nudged him between his legs. "Are you paying attention, little prick? Oh, wait, that's part of a man and you're not man enough to please a woman like me, are you?" She turned away, giving him a view of her bare buttocks, just the string of her thong parting them. Glancing back over her shoulder, she ran her hands over the smooth skin. "See something you like?" she teased, running her fingers beneath the thong and lifting it away from her body. "Too bad you never learned how to respect other people's limits. If you had, maybe you wouldn't be in stasis and would be the one with your fingers in my hot, wet cunt." As she spoke, she fitted her actions to her words, bending slightly so he could see her fingers moving slowly into her body, stroking the walls of her slick passage.

Mouth watering with desire, Jude grunted, the only sound he could make, drawing her attention as she continued to shunt her fingers in and out of her folds. "Did you want something?" she taunted. "All you have to do is ask, you know, little prick. I'm a reasonable woman when I'm treated with decency and respect." Looking away again, she plucked at her nipples through her chemise in time with her stroking fingers.

"Putain, that feels good!" she groaned as she worked her fingers deeper. Pulling aside the fabric of her camisole, she pinched her nipple more firmly, aware of his eyes on her, aware of the swelling hardness in his trousers that even Alain's spell could not negate. The sense of her own power flooded her, tightening the silken bonds of desire even more. His green gaze flashed black at her when she turned a little to make sure he could ogle her bare breast. "Did you say something?" she nudged.

He glared and stared pointedly at her still-clothed body. "Oh, you want me to take them off? Why don't you come help me?" she teased, her hands pausing in their ministrations to toy with the hem of her camisole. His expression darkened with frustration, bringing a joyful laugh to her lips as she pulled the garment over her head and tossed it onto his chest followed by her thong. "Little prick," she drawled almost affectionately. "You're burning with frustration, aren't you?"

She knelt next to him on the ground, her hand hovering a hair's breadth above his cock. "That looks painful," she observed drolly. Bending forward, she brushed her breasts across his lips. "You want to taste, don't you? You're salivating like a rabid dog just to open your mouth and bite my tits until they're bloody, aren't you?" She sat back again, stroking herself contemplatively. She was deft enough with her magic to release just his lips so he could suck her nipples or her clit—but that would be giving him power over her again, something she had sworn never to do. She would use his hard cock the way she would use her vibrator at home, but he would get nothing more from her, now or ever.

"Too bad you're a little prick. I like having a lover suck my nipples, but you already proved I can't trust you to respect my limits. My fingers are preferable to your fangs." Reaching for his trousers, she unbuckled his belt, popped the button and pulled down the zipper, hand sliding inside to free his cock from his briefs. She stroked him a couple times to make sure he was fully hard. "I seem to have left my vibrator at home," she told him coldly. "I can go home and use it there, leaving you high and dry, or I can use you here instead. Blink twice if you want me to stay."

Jude stared at her for a long moment, seriously considering telling her to go, but his body was afire from her little show and he knew a random fuck would not satisfy it. He could feel her hand on his cock, which meant he would be able to feel her pussy as well, hot and slick around him. She would do all the work since he could not move and he would get the vision of her riding him until she came. He blinked twice, slowly and deliberately.

Immediately, Adèle straddled him, sinking down on the hard flesh, arching her back as he penetrated her all the way to her core. Closing her eyes, she rode him hard, letting her magic flow unchecked through her and out into the crackling flames. They leapt and danced with the ebb and flow of her desire. Feeling her orgasm approaching, she slowed her movements, opening her eyes to meet Jude's leering glare. "When *I'm* ready," she informed him haughtily, pressing his cock deep inside her and holding it there as she slid her fingers over her clit, the other hand pinching her nipples in alternation.

She was as hot and wet and tight as he remembered, squeezing him perfectly. Physically, sexually, she was the perfect match for him, not turned off even when he got rough, not disgusted by his bite. If only she were not so flamboyantly independent.... Then again, he admitted silently, if she did not prick his temper quite so much, the sex would probably not be nearly as interesting. She aroused him to a boiling point just by existing. The desire to tumble her beneath him and ravish her completely was growing nearly unbearable, only the magic he could not counteract keeping him from giving her what she really needed. She might talk about decency and respect, but what she really needed was a man strong enough to put her under him and fuck her senseless. That would obviously not happen today, but his years as a vampire had taught him patience. He would bide his time. The next time he caught her alone, he would show her what happened to little pussies who did not know their place.

Feeling the imminence of her orgasm fade, Adèle began to move again, letting the frenzy build in both of them again, reveling in her power over the man beneath her. Motionless as he was, he could do nothing to enhance his own pleasure. He was completely at her mercy, and today she had none.

Twice more, she drove them nearly to the point of no return, only to stop and let release slip through their grasps. Finally, though, her self-control shattered and she rode him hard until she came in long, pulsing waves, collapsing forward onto his chest, her elbows digging painfully into his sides.

Levering herself off him, she retrieved her scattered clothes, dressing slowly in front in him until only her tousled hair and higher than usual color revealed the way she had spent the past hour. Glancing down at him, she smirked at the sight of his still swollen erection. "Sorry about that," she taunted, dragging sharp nails up the thick length, a cat toying with its prey. Standing, she closed off the fire spell, extinguishing the flames that had warmed them and accepted her magic. "See you around."

She walked the length of the lake, casting the spell to undo Alain's binding at the same moment she cast an invisibility spell. She knew she should simply leave, but she wanted to see what he did when he was finally free.

Feeling the release of the magic that had held him, Jude did the first thing that came to mind, reaching for his aching cock and jacking himself off rapidly. His eyes closed as he conjured the image of her beneath him as she had been the day before. It only took a few strokes for him to climax, his cock pulsing long and hard as he released all the tension and frustration and desire that no one else could rouse in him the way she did.

Unaccountably disturbed by the sight of Jude's orgasm, Adèle whispered the displacement spell, arriving back in her apartment with the unsettling image of her partner's hand on his cock haunting her thoughts. She had no interest in him outside the boundaries of the alliance. Hell, she had no interest in him at all!

None.

Chapter 22

ORLANDO STUMBLED slightly as he arrived back in Alain's office, Magali's touch with the displacement spell marginally different from Thierry's. Even before he could catch his balance, Alain was at his side, steadying him. "We should have had her send me home," Orlando muttered, turning into Alain's arms and capturing his lover's lips in a passionate kiss. "I don't want to wait the time it would take for the subway to get us there."

Alain did not have to ask what Orlando did not want to wait for. The lingering effects of the ritual sang in his veins, leaving him aching for the release that only his lover could give him. "We could go downstairs," he suggested between desperate kisses. "There are rooms—"

"With tiny little beds not meant for the kind of energetic lovemaking I need right now," Orlando interjected, vetoing the idea, his hands moving restlessly over Alain's body. "There has to be somebody here who can send me to the apartment."

"If you don't mind the entire Milice knowing what we're going home to do," Alain chuckled. "You're throwing sparks left and right, and I'm sure I'm the same. Thierry's still at home and the door's locked," he went on, urging Orlando toward the couch. "Let me take the edge off so we can at least get home. Then you can take me as hard as you want."

Orlando tensed for a moment at Alain's guiding hands, but while he could still feel the magic crackling in the air around them, this was not the wild magic from the day before. This was Alain's own magic. His lover had not hurt him yesterday in the grip of a much less benign force. He would not hurt him now. Letting the wizard settle him on the couch, Orlando's breath caught as Alain sank to his knees between the vampire's spread thighs, unbuttoning his pants and drawing out his erection. His head fell back, eyes closing on a deep groan, as his lover's mouth wrapped around the tip of his engorged cock, sucking him deep into his throat. It was still a new enough sensation to make his head spin. He grabbed the edge of the cushions, as much to keep from forcing Alain's head deeper onto his shaft as to steady himself. Then Alain's lips brushed the base of his cock and he gave up holding back. His fingers burrowed into the red-gold hair as Alain swallowed around his length, bobbing up and down before pulling back to tongue the sensitive head. "Alain!" he groaned.

"Yes, angel?" he asked, lifting his head. "Do you need me to stop?"

"No!" Orlando husked immediately. "It feels so good."

Alain smiled, licking the weeping slit as his hand continued to stroke up and down the shaft. "It's supposed to feel good."

Orlando laughed softly, the sound cut off by another moan of pleasure as Alain pushed the foreskin back, his tongue sliding beneath to play over the sensitive frenulum. His eyes closed as he marveled at how far they had come now that he had exorcised most of his fears. A week ago, he would have found it all but impossible to relax beneath Alain's ministrations, but the intervening days had reminded him again and again how completely he could trust his partner. If Alain had not hurt him yesterday when the wild magic would have given him an excuse that even Orlando could not have argued with, he never would. He barely even flinched now when Alain's hand slid between his legs to fondle his sac as he slid his lips back down, taking Orlando into his throat again.

With a startled shout—for he had not realized his release was so close—Orlando climaxed, back arching, his cock twitching in Alain's energetic mouth. His lover milked every drop from his heavy balls, continuing to lick and suck all the way through his orgasm.

Licking his lips lasciviously, Alain smiled up at his lover from his place between his knees. "Feeling better?"

"Oh yeah," Orlando sighed, repletion obvious in his heavy voice. After a moment, he opened his eyes and looked down into Alain's glittering eyes. "Can I return the favor?"

Alain shook his head, a flush of embarrassment staining his cheeks. "No need," he said, looking down at the wet spot on the front of his trousers. "It seems to have taken care of itself."

Equally bemused and flattered, Orlando tugged on Alain's hands, pulling him up onto the couch. He kissed Alain hungrily, tasting himself on Alain's tongue. "We need to go home," he growled. While the blow job had indeed taken the edge off, his need for his lover was in no way sated.

Alain shuddered in delight at the rasp of Orlando's voice, at the hunger he could still hear in its dulcet tones. Of its own accord, his hand covered the Avoué brand on his neck, pierced by the marks of Orlando's fangs. They would heal by morning—but for this short time, he was doubly claimed, a thought that moved him to the depths of his being. "Yes," he agreed huskily, no longer caring that the other wizards might guess why they were in such a hurry. If what Raymond and Marcel had said was right, any other paired wizard was feeling some degree of the same draw to their partner as he felt for the precious man in his arms. He muttered a quick cleaning spell to remove the evidence of his passion. "Let's find someone to send you home."

In a few short steps, they were in the Salle des Cartes, the on-duty wizard keeping a straight face as Alain gave the orders to send Orlando to his apartment before blinking out so his répère would give the location. A moment later, the wizard's spell sent Orlando to join his lover in their living room.

"Bedroom, now," Orlando ordered, hands pulling at Alain's clothes.

"Get yourself undressed," Alain proposed, herding Orlando eagerly in the direction of their room. "It'll be faster than fighting with each other's clothes."

Nodding, Orlando shed his shirt before they reached the hallway and his shoes before they crossed the threshold into the bedroom. Dropping his pants, he turned to face his equally naked lover. "On the bed," he commanded, the magic-inspired lust still gripping him despite his climax at Milice headquarters. He wondered how many times it would take to expend all the energy that still hummed inside him from feeding during the ritual. He wondered as well how much more strongly Alain was feeling it, since he was the one who had been channeling the magic.

Alain hastened to comply, climbing onto the bed. He yelped in surprise when Orlando appeared behind him, nipping at the curve of his upturned ass. His fangs did not penetrate. Indeed, Alain could not feel them at all, but just the thought of Orlando biting him there, indeed anywhere, as they made love left him trembling with need. "Bite me?"

"Next time," Orlando answered regretfully, even those fears easing somewhat in the wake of the realizations of the past two days. "I took too much during the ritual. I know I can't hurt you by overfeeding, but that doesn't mean I can't hurt myself."

Disappointed but accepting the explanation, Alain rolled to his side. "Then come make love to me instead."

Orlando grinned widely. "I can certainly do that." He crawled up the bed next to Alain. His lips captured his lover's, plundering his mouth. When Alain's tongue twined with his, he sucked it into his mouth possessively, taking control of their interaction. He could feel the lingering magic pulsing in his blood, imagined it was the same for Alain. "What do you need?" he asked, though he thought he knew.

Alain flushed. He needed a repeat of yesterday, hard and fast, but he had scared himself the last time and so was hesitant to ask now.

"Tell me," Orlando urged. "You're not going to drive me away. You didn't yesterday and today you don't even need me to help control your magic. What do you need?"

"You," Alain said simply. If his magic had as powerful a grip on Orlando as it did on him, he would get what he needed because Orlando would need it too. And if not, he had dealt with a glut of power before, when he had no lover. He would deal with it again.

"You have me," Orlando promised. "For as long as you live, you have me."

"Then take me and prove it," Alain urged, rolling to his stomach and pushing up onto his hands and knees.

Orlando clenched his hands, trying to control the urge to pounce. However aroused Alain was, he would not appreciate a dry penetration. Mastering his desire for the moment, he reached for the lube on their bedstand, squeezing some onto his fingers and beginning to stretch the tight portal.

Alain's head dropped to his hands as he felt Orlando's fingers on him, in him. It was not quite enough, not quite what he wanted, but even that connection sang along his nerves, leaving him hot and panting with desire. He knew part of it was his magic and the magical connection between them, but he did not care. They were and would always be connected magically, the exchange of blood whenever it occurred linking them in a way no other bond ever could. They shared one bed, one home, one life. He trembled with the potency of that thought, his need increasing exponentially, stealing any thought of waiting. “Now, Orlando, please!”

Given the choice, Orlando might have waited a little longer, preparing Alain more thoroughly, but he was not proof against his lover’s pleading voice. Withdrawing his fingers and slicking his cock with the lube that remained on them, he nudged the clenching muscle. “Relax and let me in,” he directed, voice tight with the restrained need to bury himself deep. He knew this congress would not be slow and sweet—but even so, he could not bring himself to do anything that might hurt Alain, however inadvertently. Some actions were simply beyond him.

Alain tried. The combination of desire and magic, though, had him strung so tightly that he could not force the tension from his muscles. “Just do it,” he begged. “I need you so badly.”

Pushing past the resisting ring, Orlando gasped as he felt his lover’s heat surround him. Nothing felt like this. Nothing compared to this. He tried to pause and savor the first moment of joining, but his control wavered, his hips beginning to move despite his best efforts. Leaning forward, he draped himself along Alain’s back, covering his wizard as completely as he could. Almost immediately, his movements took on a desperate stuttering as he strove for release. Pushing himself back up to sit on his heels, he drew Alain with him until his lover rested his head on Orlando’s shoulder and sat across his thighs. His hands roamed over the wizard’s chest, stroking firmly, tweaking lightly at his nipples before sliding lower to stroke his cock and balls. Alain’s harsh groan increased the rapture Orlando felt at each sign of the pleasure he could give to Alain.

To his surprise, Alain thrashed in his arms almost immediately, his cock twitching and disgorging a torrent of creamy fluid. The clenching of his passage left Orlando shaking as he continued to chase his own orgasm. Alain moaned in his arms, falling limply against him. Orlando supported his weight easily, hands stroking again, trying to rouse the softening shaft to full hardness once more. “Again,” he demanded as he strove to drive even deeper into his lover’s now lax body. “Come for me again.”

Alain almost protested that he could not after climaxing in his office and again just now, but to his surprise, he felt his body reacting to Orlando’s continuing thrusts and caresses. He tossed his head against Orlando’s shoulder, moaning when his lover’s lips closed over his earlobe, sucking in time with his plunging hips. Eyes closing, he gave up all pretense of control, letting his magic rampage through him, sparking around them as his arousal spiraled higher and higher. Another orgasm shook him like a dog with a bone, his cock jerking dryly in Orlando’s grasp. Drunk on sensation, he cried out for release, for relief, but Orlando’s grip was inexorable, holding him in place, rousing him again until he could do nothing but hang there, caught between the vampire's cock and his hands, a conduit for the outrush of magic and the inrush of desire. "Please!"

Orlando was flying, his body overloaded with sensation and his mind lost in Alain's eager submission. He had doubted, when they first became lovers, whether he could care for a lover as he deserved, whether he could give pleasure instead of pain. Those doubts had faded after the first few times they made love, but a part of him always feared Alain was humoring him in some way. Seeing Alain now, he could not doubt anymore that there was pleasure to be found in giving oneself to a lover. Suddenly, with a ferocity that stunned him, he wanted that, wanted to give that gift to his wizard as Alain had given it so generously to him.

That thought was enough to send him spinning out of control, body and mind seizing with the force of the climax that tore through him and out. Every muscle going lax, he fell to the side, only barely catching himself and Alain. He shivered with the implications of his sudden desire, so out of character with anything he had let himself even consider, much less want, before now. Feeling Alain lying limply at his side, he decided he could worry about it later. Alain was certainly in no state to do anything now but sleep. He turned his lover's chin gently toward him so he could press a tender kiss to the soft lips. "I love you."

"Love you, too," Alain whispered, voice barely audible, trying to open his eyes and reach for his lover.

"Sleep," Orlando chuckled. "I'll be here in the morning."

Alain's eyes closed immediately, his face relaxing into slumber. Orlando relaxed against him, holding his wizard in his arms and trying to comprehend the sudden change in his attitude toward two things he had feared since the moment his maker first touched him.

Certainly, Alain's patience had helped. His lover had not pressured him into something he was not comfortable with, even though at times he was obviously frustrated with Orlando's fears. His equally obvious desire to be bitten, to be taken, helped as well. Each time he fed, he could taste Alain's desire, and each time they made love, Alain's pleasure was palpable, visible in the way his body reacted. He was here, in Orlando's arms, because he wanted to be. And if he also wanted more, Orlando wondered if maybe he could finally give his lover those things.

A yawn surprised him, fatigue not usually being a problem for vampires. The ritual, the feeding, and the lovemaking had clearly taken more out of him than he realized. He snuggled down next to Alain and drifted off with a smile on his face.

Chapter 23

THE FEELING of a hand stroking his hair startled Raymond awake, every muscle going tense until memory returned and he remembered what had happened, where he was, and whose hand was touching him.

"Good morning," Jean murmured, leaning over to kiss the wizard softly. "Did you sleep well?"

Raymond hummed in his throat as he returned the kiss. He had slept better than he had since the war started. It seemed having a bedfellow agreed with him. "Morning," he husked when Jean drew back. "I slept very well. What about you?"

"Like the dead," Jean quipped with a crooked grin. "What time is Marcel expecting you this morning?"

"At nine," Raymond replied. "What time is it?"

"Too late for a repeat of last night," Jean sighed before winking playfully at Raymond. "I guess I'll just have to come back here tonight if I want a piece of you."

Raymond chuckled, giving in to the teasing, even as he thrilled at the thought that Jean still wanted him without the magic driving them. "I guess you will," he agreed, pushing up onto one elbow so he could see the clock. Eight o'clock. Jean was right, especially since the vampire would have to take the subway to get to Milice headquarters.

Smiling at Raymond's simple acceptance, Jean tugged on his wizard's shoulder, bringing his head back down for a tender kiss. Raymond had not sent him away. In Jean's eyes, that meant they were lovers now. If the way Raymond returned the kiss was any indication, that feeling was mutual—but as much as Jean wanted to linger and prove it, they had a meeting to attend and he knew better than to suggest being late. Ending the kiss with a quick nuzzle to Raymond's bite-riddled neck, Jean rolled onto his back and stretched languorously. A quick sniff revealed the smells of blood and sex.

"I need a shower." Had their agenda for the day been different, he would have left the scents to bring back the memories at odd times, but the chef de la Cour de Paris could hardly meet with the Milice general in such a state.

"The bathroom's through there," Raymond offered, pointing to the door. "I don't think my clothes will fit, but I can try a cleaning spell on yours. It should work if you're not wearing them. I'd join you, but if I do, we'll never make it to our meeting on time."

Jean grinned. "Another morning, when we don't have anywhere to be, I'll take you up on that. Try the spell. We haven't lost anything if it doesn't work."

With one more quick kiss, he rose and walked unashamedly nude into the bathroom, reveling in feeling Raymond's gaze on him until the door shut behind him. He showered quickly, wanting to leave Raymond time to complete his own ablutions the traditional way if he so desired.

Coming out of the bathroom, he found his clothes neatly folded on the bed and no sign of Raymond. Dressing quickly, he walked into the living room, smiling at the mess of papers and books there as well. Raymond undoubtedly knew what every single one was and could find anything he needed without even having to search.

The smell of coffee drew him toward the kitchen. He drank the beverage when not doing so would place him outside the norm, but he had no experience of it as a mortal and so did not truly understand the appeal. His partner, though, clearly did, if the way he was inhaling the first cup was any indication. He hung back, watching as Raymond puttered around the kitchen, pulling out a baguette and frowning at it when he realized it had gone stale. With a muttered expletive, he tossed it aside, opening cabinets and looking inside.

"Nothing appeals?" Jean asked curiously as Raymond shut the doors without taking anything out.

"Nothing in them," Raymond replied, looking up. "I haven't been here often enough to buy anything. Most days, I'm lucky to grab a pastry for breakfast and a sandwich from the charcuterie for dinner."

"That'll never do," Jean tutted. "You need to eat properly to stay healthy. I don't care what anyone else says or thinks. We're turning the tide here in large part because of you."

Raymond flushed and looked away. "You're just biased because you're my partner."

Jean shook his head emphatically. "I'm sure I am, but it's more than that. From what I understand, Alain couldn't have saved Thierry alone after the Rite d'équilibrage went wrong. I know you wrote the spell you used yesterday to ground the wild magic. Maybe it isn't grand gestures and big battles, but I see the value even if you don't."

Raymond shrugged. "I'm glad, but don't feel like this is a battle you have to fight. The others are too aware of my past to think of anything else."

"Their loss," Jean replied firmly. "Now, let's find you some breakfast, and today I'm making sure you eat a real lunch and a proper dinner."

"Yes, sir," Raymond teased with a mock salute. He could hardly believe himself, but it felt so right to relax and joke with Jean this way. Even before the war, he had not been involved in l'ANS, preferring to spend his time with his books and his research rather than with people, publishing one paper after another in scholarly journals. Jean seemed to bring out the best in him, though, the part that usually hid beneath the veneer of academic disdain. Giving in to impulse, he reached for the vampire's hand, pulling him close for a quick kiss. "Thank you."

"For what?"

"For believing in me, for making sure I take care of myself, for coming to me last night and being here still this morning," Raymond replied with a flush. "I'm used to being alone. This is nice for a change."

Jean draped his arms around Raymond's waist. "I've spent most of my thousand years as a vampire essentially alone. It's a fact of my existence, unfortunately. To find someone I want to be with for more than the few minutes it takes me to feed is a rare gift." He had found it once before, only to have the man stolen out from beneath his very nose by another vampire. He pushed that thought aside, reminding himself that Sebastien remembered the incident very differently, claiming not to have known of Jean's interest in Thibaut before branding him. At least this time, he did not have to worry about anyone else claiming the object of his interest.

Raymond shook his head, the scope of Jean's experience amazing him yet again. "When this is over, if I survive the war, we're going to sit down and I'm going to pick your brain," he declared. "A living witness to a thousand years of history… I'll never find a better primary source!"

Jean's arms tightened at the thought of Raymond not surviving. A couple of weeks ago, the thought would have disturbed him because of what it would have meant to his own ability to go out during the day, but it had grown far beyond that now. He wanted Raymond with him, magic or no magic. "You'll survive," he swore. "I'll make sure of it."

Raymond just smiled, appreciating the determination in Jean's voice. He had no illusions, though. No vampire would be a match for Serrier if it came to a fight, and any student of biology knew a rabid animal was at its most vicious when cornered. "We should go if we're going to make it to Milice headquarters on time," he reminded Jean, deliberately changing the subject.

Jean let the matter drop, though he had every intention of keeping Raymond within arm's reach any time there might be danger. If nothing else, most of the spells he had seen the dark wizards cast so far had been things that would do far more damage to mortals than to the undead.

They stopped at the nearest boulangerie to get breakfast for Raymond, then descended into the subway for the ride north. The cars were too packed to allow for any kind of private conversation, the throng pressing them from every side leaving Jean incredibly edgy by the time they finally left the Métro and walked back to street level. His possessive, protective instincts had clearly latched onto his partner. Once they were free of the mob and he could relax again, he mentally took a step back, considering the matter as objectively as he could, trying to determine how such an attachment would affect him not only personally but also as chef de la Cour.

Certainly no one could deride him for having a plain lover, not with Raymond's darkly handsome looks, a perfect match for Jean's own dark hair and eyes. Nor would the vampire community find fault with him having a male lover, the rules of morality that governed mortal society losing their influence when a vampire was changed. Raymond's obvious intelligence would allow him to participate in le jeu des Cours, or at the very least help him avoid the kind of mistakes that would cause Jean to lose face. Even Raymond's somewhat outcast status would not be any real detriment since the vampires as a whole were already outcast from society, although he had hopes that would change after the equality legislation passed. Still, vampires had long memories and they would not quickly forget what it felt like to be cast aside simply because of who they were. As chef de la Cour, he had nothing to lose by having Raymond at his side, not just now but for as long as Raymond was willing.

On a personal level, if he could get Raymond over the fear he felt every time Jean bit him, he was pretty sure he could feed exclusively from his partner for as long as Raymond could support him. At his age, he did not need to feed nearly as often as a younger vampire—so with careful management and a little bit of self-control, they could probably remain together for most of Raymond's life.

He shook his head, reminding himself not to jump ahead. Even though Raymond had accepted him as a partner and lover, that did not mean the wizard was ready for the kind of permanence Jean's instincts were pushing him to seek. A thought crossed his mind, bringing a smile to his face. Instead of pushing Raymond for a commitment the other man might not be ready to give, he would simply begin as he meant to go on. He would treat Raymond with all the care and devotion he would give to a true consort, until such time as the wizard rejected that role.

"What is it?" Raymond asked, seeing the smile on Jean's face.

"Just thinking about what comes next," the vampire replied, smile widening.

"And that makes you smile?"

"It does indeed," Jean insisted enigmatically. "It's almost nine. Let's not keep Marcel waiting. He might want explanations you'd rather not give."

"Last night was between us," Raymond said immediately. "That is…."

"Yes," Jean agreed before Raymond could even voice his hesitation. "It's not anyone's business what we do on our own time. As long as it doesn't affect the alliance, our affair doesn't concern them."

Raymond nodded, walking inside. He put everything personal from his mind as he focused on making his report to Marcel and planning what came next. For the first time since he had switched sides, he finally felt like the tide was turning in their favor, and he hoped Marcel would press their advantage while they could. He doubted it would take Serrier long to regroup and plan to counter the alliance now that he knew about it. They would need to be ready.

And later, when he was alone, he would ponder everything that had happened with Jean and try to decide what it all meant.

"Good morning, messieurs," Marcel greeted them as they walked in, not blinking an eye at seeing them arrive together. "I take it everything went well yesterday."

"It seemed to," Raymond agreed. "Have you had any more reports of wild magic?"

"Not a single one," Marcel replied with a smile. "I've been thinking about the vampires, though, now that the alliance is public knowledge, and monsieur Cabalet is trying to involve his Cour as well. We need a procedure to find partners for vampires hoping to join the alliance. The two of us won't always be available when people approach us, and we need something in place so whoever's here will know what to do."

Jean nodded thoughtfully. "That makes sense. We vampires tend not to be that regimented in our approach to things, and time isn't usually an issue for us. If something doesn't happen one night, it'll happen the next."

"Not a luxury the war allows us," Marcel agreed. "So do you have any suggestions?"

"I have one," Raymond interrupted. "You and Jean both have enough to worry about without adding this to the list. Delegate it to someone who can handle both the development and the implementation, even if you have them wait to implement it until you can approve it. There's no reason to make your lives even more difficult than they already are, especially if the equal rights legislation goes in for a vote soon. I know you'll both have to be there for that."

"Angélique could handle something like that," Jean mused aloud. "With all the work she puts into Sang Froid, something like this would be easy for her. Do you trust her partner to handle the Milice side of things?"

Marcel sighed. "David is a good wizard. He just has his blind spots. Maybe having to work with her more closely will help him see past them."

"If she doesn't kill him first," Jean laughed, thinking about the last time he had confronted the volatile vampire over her partner. "Then again, I think things have been better between them since he apologized. I haven't been around much when they are, though."

"David and I talked a few days ago, and he seemed willing to work with her and make amends for his attitude. He even suggested she might be able to help recruit new vampires since those who come to her now will be primarily unpartnered vampires."

"I hadn't thought of that," Jean commented, "but it makes sense. She's generally a very good judge of character—she has to be to keep her employees safe—so she would probably be able to smell a rat if one came in with foul play in mind."

"Too bad wizards can't read vampires' hearts the way you can read ours," Raymond observed. "Then we'd be able to check for sure."

"The magical affinity should be at least some indication," Marcel pointed out. "I'd find it difficult to believe there would be an affinity between a wizard firmly in our camp and a vampire who would do something to sabotage our plans."

"Don't be too certain of that," Raymond warned. "If we understood better why the pairs matched up, we might be able to make that generalization, but we have a few dysfunctional pairs. That means there could be mismatches in loyalty as well."

"Merde! I hope that doesn't become an issue," Jean breathed. "Can you imagine what it would do to a vampire to be torn between the strength of a partnership bond and his sense of right and wrong?" He shook his head. "I honestly couldn't predict which would win."

"That's far more likely to be a problem if the vampire were paired with one of Serrier's wizards, though," Marcel reminded them. "Even if it is a mismatch, if a vampire is paired with one of our wizards, they aren't likely to switch sides to join Serrier. Other than our rogue, there aren't any vampires with Serrier's forces nor do I expect him to recruit any. His xenophobia is legendary. I'm not sure how he's managed to keep the rogue from realizing."

"Probably by providing him with victims and a safe place to toy with them," Jean postulated. "As horrid as it sounds, that would be enough to buy his loyalty, at least for a time, and probably enough to keep him too entertained to care about Serrier's politics. The body that was found two weeks ago had been savaged, you said, not just drained dry. That requires time, space, and privacy, all of which Serrier could surely provide, but it also indicates a focus on that alone. My guess would be this vampire doesn't care about anything unless it interferes with his games."

Raymond grimaced at the thought of being at the mercy of a vampire the way that girl must have been before she died. Jean had always been careful with him, and he was beginning to believe the vampire always would be, but even so, his ingrained fear ran deep. "So how do we make sure we aren't welcoming a spy into our midst?" he asked. "Now that Serrier knows about the alliance, he might try to find other vampires like the rogue and send one to us. He already tried and failed with a wizard. It makes sense he'd try a vampire next, xenophobic or not."

"We don't," Jean replied honestly, "unless you know of some kind of truth spell that we could try on them."

Raymond shook his head. "Truth serums are as much a myth as love potions. If they existed, I would have used one a long time ago to convince everyone here that I'd truly switched sides."

Chapter 24

"THERE MUST be a less humiliating spell we can use to test for partners than a levitation spell," Angélique mused as she sat at her desk, her wizard across from her. "If they find a partner quickly, it might not matter, but I don't see vampires being thrilled about floating through the air hundreds of times. And if it's another chef de la Cour, it really won't work."

David shrugged. "Every spell has an effect. That's the point of it. I can tickle someone or goose them or turn them blue or send them from one place to another, but it's going to do something to the person I cast it on, unless that person is you. I don't want to insult anyone's dignity, but that's hardly the only consideration at the moment. We're fighting a war here, in case you've forgotten."

"And you need us to win it, in case you've forgotten," Angélique snapped. "If you run them off before they ever join, you aren't going to help your cause."

"As far as I can tell, it doesn't take anything to offend a vampire anyway, so it won't matter what spell we use," David retorted.

"Well, insulting me doesn't help," Angélique snarled.

"Fine," David said, throwing up his hands, "but I really don't know what you want from me. I've already apologized once."

"A little respect would be nice."

"That goes both ways, you know," David reminded her. "I'm sorry I offended you. I'm trying not to do it again, but it's a little difficult when you so clearly resent every interaction with me. You don't even seem to enjoy feeding from me anymore."

"You made it perfectly clear you didn't want my attention," she countered.

David snorted in disbelief before he could stop himself.

"No?" Angélique questioned. "Did I misunderstand when you sneered at me for owning Sang Froid?"

"I misunderstood," David told her again. "I thought…. It doesn't matter what I thought. I was wrong." Slowly, he tipped his head back. "Taste for yourself if you don't believe me."

The expanse of skin beckoned. Angélique knew she should refuse and do the work Marcel had assigned them, but she had spent the last two days imagining him beneath her fangs again. Ever since Bertrand had left, she could think of little other than David, however illogical that seemed on the surface. He had offered. She would take him up on it and get rid of this ridiculous obsession.

Bracing her hands on the back of his chair on either side of his shoulders, she bent over him, her lips just brushing the skin, waiting to see how he would react. His breath hissed out, ruffling her hair, but he did not pull away. Pushing aside her lingering doubts, she licked his pulse point, letting her saliva prepare his skin. His head dropped back further in invitation. Tempted beyond her control, Angélique bit deeply into the vibrating vein, blood flowing rapidly onto her tongue.

She had expected to taste sincerity and remorse, given that he had offered to let her feed for exactly that reason, but she had not expected the sudden inrush of desire nor her visceral reaction to it. One knee settled on the chair next to his thigh as she leaned closer. She did not lift her head to ask him if he was ready to act on the desire she could taste in his blood. She simply reached for his hand and moved it to her hip, fingers trailing seductively up his arm.

David froze when she moved over him, his body reacting to her nearness as the memories of his dreams while under the influence of the wild magic rushed back. He knew she would taste his desire if she bit him, but she was used to men desiring her. It would be far more detrimental to their relationship to change his mind about letting her feed than it would be to let her taste his desire.

He hoped.

Her hand took his, setting it where the curve of her waist flared to her hip. He steadied her as she leaned closer, not quite daring to believe this was an invitation. Then her fingernails brushed over the back of his hand and worked their way up his arm, brushing lightly, and he gave in to his desire, his fingers tightening, his other hand lifting as well to draw her down onto his lap. She shifted at his urging, settling across his thighs, her breasts brushing his chest just as they had in his dreams.

Fingers caressing the nape of David's neck and teasing the ends of his red hair, Angélique lifted her head to meet his blue eyes. "I believe you," she said slowly, "but I tasted more than just your sincerity." She rocked her hips slightly against his erection. "If you want to ignore this, tell me and I'll go back behind my desk and pretend not to notice. Or we can move to the chaise where we'll be more comfortable and see where this goes. The choice is yours."

David squirmed uncomfortably, his body warring with his morals. She had been a sultan's concubine with no control over the disposition of her body. It felt wrong to take that control from her again now, even if she had offered. "What do you want?"

In reply, Angélique took his hand, lifting it to her breast so he could feel her peaked nipple through the thin bra and gauzy blouse she wore. "You're the one with hang-ups about my past, not me."

"We're supposed to be working," David reminded her weakly.

"We'll get it done," Angélique promised, caressing the back of his hand lightly.

"You still haven't told me what you want," he replied hoarsely, finding it harder and harder to fight his desire. "You complain about me making assumptions, but I can't read your mind the way you can when you feed from me. So you have to tell me what you want. I don't want to make the same mistake twice."

Angélique laughed huskily. "Don't tell me you can't tell when a woman desires you," she teased, eyes sparkling as she glanced from him to the heavy brocade chaise against the far wall of her office, a rolled arm at one end the perfect height to support his head. "I want you on your back on the chaise over there, completely naked, while I ride you until we both come so hard we can't remember our names—but I'd rather sit back down behind my desk and ignore it all if doing that will make it harder to work with you. So again I say it's your choice."

"We get off duty in two hours," he flailed, eyes following hers as his body reacted to her words. "Let's get our work done for Marcel and then we can talk about it when our time's our own."

As much as Angélique wanted him now, she respected his dedication to duty. A smile played around her lips as she rose slowly, brushing against him in every way she could as she stood. She would just have to use the intervening time to ruffle his senses so that by the time they were done, he would be unable to refuse.

David's eyes stayed riveted on the sway of her hips as it set the long, flowing skirt she wore dancing around her ankles. Everything about her screamed sensual indulgence and he wanted desperately to wallow in it, but duty called and he had already failed Marcel enough since the alliance began. Taking a deep breath to calm himself—a pointless enterprise since the room smelled of incense and patchouli, the same scents he had come to associate with the beautiful vampire—he tried to focus on Angélique's earlier request. "Maybe a spell the vampires could feel," he said slowly. "A heating or cooling spell. Or something they could smell."

"Could the wizards heat something up for them to touch?" Angélique inquired, toying idly with the top button of her blouse, drawing David's attention to the depth of her cleavage.

"That's certainly possible, but would it work for determining a partnership?" David countered, swallowing around the lump in his throat. "The magic wouldn't be directed at the vampire but at an inanimate object."

"It's easy enough to test," she observed, looking around for something he could work his magic on. An impish smile crossing her face, she gestured to the couch. "Why don't you cast a warming spell on the chaise? I'll sit on it and see if I can feel it."

David's eyes narrowed but he could think of no reason to refuse. He cast the spell quickly and gestured for her to test it.

Hips swinging seductively, Angélique crossed the room to the couch. She ran her hand over the patterned cloth before stretching along its length, one leg on the chaise, the other on the floor so that her skirt rode up slightly, revealing a shapely calf to David's avid gaze. "I may have to get you to cast this spell on all my furniture," she mused as she shifted, her skirt sliding up even more. "I'm always cold here in the winter."

"That won't work then, will it?" David said, trying to summon a frown instead of imagining himself warming her bed with more than just magic.

"Not to match up partners, no," Angélique agreed, not returning to her desk. She knew full well the picture she presented, draped artfully over the elegant lines of the furniture, but she had told David the truth, too. The heat felt good against the chill of the room. She was one of the few vampires who seemed bothered by the winter weather, a fact she attributed to having been born and turned in a desert climate. "Is there such thing as a magical field a vampire could walk through so that they came in direct contact with the magic instead of just with an ensorcelled object?"

"I can make the room, or a portion of the room, warm or cold," David mused aloud, "but that's still magic acting on the air instead of on you. Again, we can try it."

"Let's try it," Angélique agreed, pleased at the effort David was making to take the vampires' feelings into account.

He cast the spell and felt the temperature in the room increase several degrees. Angélique smiled for a moment before a frown replaced it. "I can feel that, too."

David kicked the desk in frustration, the ink in the old-fashioned inkwell on her desk sloshing out. Cursing under his breath, he searched for something to mop it up with. Immediately, Angélique was at his side, handing him a sheet of paper and taking one herself, using it to blot at the ink.

When they had finished, the desk was clean, but their fingers were stained black. Rolling his eyes, David muttered a cleaning spell, watching as the ink disappeared. "Now if only that would work on…," Angélique began.

"On you," David finished, casting the spell again to make sure. Angélique's fingers remained tipped in black. "Would that work? Would the vampires be willing to get their hands a little dirty if it meant not having to float through the air hundreds of times?"

"I think it's a reasonable compromise," Angélique agreed, moving around the desk so her skirt brushed the leg of David's trousers. "Now that we have that figured out, can I persuade you to come back to my warm chaise with me?"

David swallowed hard. "We still have details we should work out. It's not just the spell we use. Where will they meet? Will we bring the wizards here or take the vampires to Milice headquarters? And how do we make sure we don't miss a wizard while the vampire is there? And if we have vampires from out of town…?"

Angélique silenced him by the simple expedient of kissing him, stopping the flow of words with her lips. After a moment, he stopped trying to talk and kissed her back, tongue tracing her soft lips, which parted eagerly for him. Her body pressed pliantly against his, her curves molding to the hard planes of his body. Giving up on finishing everything now, he pulled back enough to meet her dark eyes. “Let me take you out to dinner first,” he suggested. “Let me treat you with the respect you deserve.”

Charmed, Angélique smiled up at him. “If you wish,” she agreed, “but only if you promise I can have you for dessert.”

David flushed, not sure he would ever become comfortable with her blatant sexuality, but wanting her too badly to refuse.

THIERRY SNEEZED again for the third time in as many minutes, nose red, eyes watering. He was an absolutely pathetic sight, but Sebastien still found him desirable. He knew what the wizard would say if he realized what Sebastien was thinking, but he could not completely rid himself of the guilt he felt at seeing his partner this way. If he had paid closer attention to what Alain had said, he might not have gone out on the balcony while the wild magic was still loose, might not have exposed Thierry to that stress in his weakened state. Thierry had told him repeatedly that the illness could have happened anyway, but that did nothing to reassure Sebastien. As far as he was concerned, it was his fault Thierry was sick and he would make amends any way he could. Setting the tray on the table next to the bed, he helped Thierry sit up.

“I hate being sick,” Thierry groused.

Sebastien chuckled. “One of the advantages of being a vampire. No more runny noses.”

Thierry batted at his partner. “Don’t rub it in.”

“I’m sorry,” the vampire apologized immediately, guilt assailing him again. “Let me take care of you.”

Thierry grumped a little bit more, but accepted the tea and soup Sebastien had brought him gratefully. He was not all that hungry, but the warm liquid eased his throat and soothed his stomach. If past experience was any indicator, he had another two, maybe three days, of absolute misery and then he would start feeling better. Not great right away, but good enough to get out of bed and go back on light duty. It would be a week, probably, before he could go out with his patrol again, but he could at least relieve Marcel and Alain at the Milice base.

“Maybe you are good for something,” he allowed after a few minutes.

Sebastien grinned. If Thierry could tease him, he was not too badly off, easing some of Sebastien’s worries. “Something besides earth-shattering orgasms?”

“Yeah,” Thierry replied, deliberately keeping his expression neutral despite his body’s immediate reaction to Sebastien’s comment. He shifted on the bed, still feeling the aftereffects of their most recent bout of lovemaking. He no longer hurt, but he could definitely still feel that Sebastien’s fingers had been inside him. “Something, you know, important.”

Sebastien laughed and kissed Thierry playfully. With each passing day, he found it harder to restrain himself, particularly since Thierry's hesitations seemed to fade more each time they touched. Two nights ago, he had almost broken his promise to Thierry. He did not know how much longer he would be able to wait. "You really need to get well," he husked, cradling Thierry's cheeks in his hands. "I want to make love to you, just you and me, without magic driving us on or anything else holding us back."

"You have no idea how much I want that," Thierry replied, a shiver going through him at the thought. Then a second shiver wracked him, triggering another attack of coughing. "But we might have to wait a little longer."

"As long as you need," Sebastien assured him immediately. "I won't risk you."

Chapter 25

MALIKA ROBIN looked up and smiled automatically as the door to her cybercafé opened for a new customer. Her smile tightened when she saw the vampire, backlit by the flickering candles and the blue reflections of a multitude of computer monitors. "Can I help you?"

Glancing at the prices indicated on the posted placard, the vampire nodded and took out a one euro coin. "I need an hour's access," he said.

Malika took the money and printed out the access code that would let him log on to the computers. She watched nervously as he scoped the room, clearly on the hunt. After a moment, he took a seat next to a university student who frequented Café Techno. Hackles rising, Malika debated whether to confront him herself or just keep an eye on Nicole and stop her if she tried to leave with the vampire. Remembering Jean's admonition, she gestured for the other employee on duty to take the register while she went into the back to call Jean.

THE BUZZING of the phone startled vampire and wizard alike—Raymond because he did not realize Jean had a phone in his apartment, Jean because so few people had his unlisted number. Rising from his seat, he crossed the room to the converted dumbwaiter that hid the phone from view, raising the sliding door and lifting the handset to his ear.

Raymond watched in silence as Jean's expression hardened, taking on an edge he had never seen in his partner before. It sent a curl of dread through him at the same time that lust sparked low in his belly. Keeping his own expression steady by force of will, he waited until Jean replaced the receiver. "What's wrong?"

"Get your wand," Jean ordered, not answering the question. "We've got a rogue to catch."

Raymond nodded, grabbing the length of birch and pulling on his trenchcoat. "Where?"

"At Café Techno. Malika said he bought an hour's access—but she also thinks he's just trolling, so we need to hurry."

"Do you want me to go on ahead?" Raymond offered. "If he tries to leave, I can stop him."

"He's dangerous," Jean warned.

Raymond shrugged. "So are all the dark wizards we fight on a regular basis. My spells will work on him."

"Don't hurt him. I want to talk to him first," Jean decided.

Raymond grinned. "No torture, I promise, just a binding spell to keep him there until you arrive."

Jean shook his head, grabbing Raymond's hand and pulling him close for a hard kiss. "Go, but be careful."

Raymond could not help the thrill of desire that went through him at the kiss and Jean's obvious concern. Maybe there was hope for them beyond the alliance. "I'll see you there."

AS SOON as Malika hung up the phone, she hurried back out to the cashier, hoping the vampire would still be there. The girl was gone, though, and the other vampire as well. Rushing to the door, she looked left and right, hoping for some indication of which way they had gone. She strained to catch some glimpse of Nicole so she could call the girl back, shout a warning, anything to keep the rogue from catching her—but the street was deserted except for an old bum lying in the doorway of one of the apartment buildings. If he had noticed something, she would at least know where to begin searching. She approached him, but his drunken snores dashed her hopes.

"Nicole," she shouted anyway. If the girl was within earshot, even if the rogue already had her, perhaps she could make some noise that might bring Malika to her aid. "Nicole!"

She heard only silence.

With a defeated sigh, she walked back into Café Techno to wait for Jean and report the rogue's disappearance. She did not know if the rogue would return again, but if word came that another young woman had been killed by a vampire, she would take down the bastard herself, consequences be damned.

RAYMOND ENTERED the café, his presence less likely to draw the attention of the rogue and cause a scene than Jean's. He had watched Jean move at full speed. He wouldn't be more than moments behind. Raymond recognized the café owner from their previous visit, but glancing around, he saw no one else he could tag as a vampire.

"He's gone," Malika told Raymond sadly. "He'd already disappeared by the time I got off the phone, and I'm afraid he's about to kill again."

Frowning, Raymond turned and went back out to see if Jean had arrived. "He's gone," he said when Jean came into view.

Anger showed on Jean's face as they walked inside. "You said he was trolling," he said to Malika.

"Yes, and I think he found a victim." She described the young university student.

"That sounds like a lot of his known victims," Jean agreed. "I assume you searched for them."

"A little, but I had nothing to go on, no way to know which way they'd gone. If I find out he's killed her, I'll destroy him myself if he comes back in," she swore.

"You know that's not the way we handle things," Jean warned. "Don't make me have to convene a court for you."

"Then convene one for him," Malika demanded hotly. "He's endangering us all, even if you don't count what he's doing to the poor mortals he victimizes."

"Don't you think I know that?" Jean retorted. "It's not that easy. First of all, we have no proof. Even if the girl you saw him with turns up dead, that's not proof he was responsible. And even with proof, he hasn't broken our laws. But you will if you act against him."

"If you can't do anything against him under vampire law, then we need to capture him under French law," Raymond interjected. "He's killed, twice that we know about before tonight. That's enough to get him locked up for a good, long time."

Jean sighed. "But we can't prove it was him. We know it must have been, but there's no conclusive evidence against him. The police wouldn't be able to hold him for more than a day or two unless they've found evidence we don't know about." His fist pounded hard on the counter, startling the remaining patrons. "There has to be a better way than this to catch him." He turned to Raymond, eyes hard. "I'm going after him. You're welcome to come along, but you'll have to keep up."

"Let's go," Raymond agreed with a nod for the patronne. Outside, he looked up and down the quiet street. "Is there a way to track him?"

"I wish there were. We'll just have to search and hope we get lucky," Jean replied tightly, his lithe frame vibrating with repressed anger. "If we find them and the girl's still alive, get her and get the hell out of there. I'll deal with Couthon."

"Fuck that," Raymond retorted. "I'm not leaving you to face this bastard alone. I've seen how dangerous he is."

"Raymond," Jean growled dangerously, prowling down the sidewalk, peering down shadowed alleys and into darkened doorways with his preternatural vision. "Don't cross me on this."

"Or what?" Raymond demanded, pacing alongside his vampire. "We're partners, stronger together than either of us could be alone. We proved that yesterday when we took down the wild magic."

"This isn't your fight," Jean insisted, turning into an alley too long for him to peer down from the street. "He's a vampire and that makes him my problem."

"And you're my partner, and that makes him mine."

They found nothing in the alley but overflowing trash cans and a couple of stray cats. “I don’t meddle in wizarding business,” Jean reminded him. “I don’t want you involved in Cour business.”

“That’s a load of bullshit.” Raymond blocked the exit to the alley, hands on his hips. “You know I could help you.”

“How?” Jean demanded, spinning Raymond against the wall and pinning him there, body rubbing against the wizard’s intimately. “However strong you are, you’re not as strong as even the weakest vampire.”

“I don’t have to be stronger than he is,” Raymond reminded him, pulling out his wand. “It won’t work on you, but it would on any other vampire.”

In a move too fast for Raymond to anticipate, Jean captured his wrist, squeezing until the fingers went lax and the wooden shaft fell to the ground. “And when he disarms you?”

A piece of paper jumped from the trash can, forming a tight ball and flying through the air to hit Jean on the side of the head. “Be glad you’re my partner. I could have used something harder,” he replied coolly. “I’m not defenseless, even without my wand, and I know far fouler spells than simply bombarding him with garbage.”

“You can’t be involved in this,” Jean insisted, pulling back and stalking down the street again, resuming his search for Edouard and the missing girl. “If it looks like I need your help to maintain order in the Cour, others will start wondering if I’m strong enough to hold my position. I fought too hard to get where I am. I don’t want to go back to that constant power struggle, even without the alliance and the legislation. To have that kind of disunity in the Cour right now would be disastrous.”

“Stupid jeu des Cours,” Raymond griped as he kept pace with Jean. “It’s going to have to adjust to having wizards around. The partnership bonds are strong enough now, I don’t see many of the vampires letting their wizards go.”

He flushed immediately, realizing what he had said. “Sorry. That wasn’t a request for reassurance. I know you’ll be glad to see the last of me when the alliance is over.”

Jean stared at him in disbelief for a moment before backing him against the wall of the closest building. “I don’t know what gave you the idea I was looking to get rid of you,” he snarled, his body holding the larger wizard in place. “That certainly wasn’t the impression I intended to give when I showed up at your apartment last night and asked you to fuck me. But if you didn’t get that message, maybe you’ll get this one.”

His hands grabbing at Raymond’s short hair, Jean’s lips crashed down on his partner’s. He invaded the hot cavern roughly, plundering his lover’s mouth with a millennium of experience, leaving the wizard gasping and squirming beneath the onslaught. Jean paid no attention, though, weaving a sensual web tighter and tighter around his partner’s senses until Raymond cared for nothing other than reaching the peak that hovered just beyond his grasp. Hands opened his trousers, one sliding down his abdomen to encircle his aching cock, the other down his back to cup his buttocks before delving between them. A single, long finger probed his entrance and slipped deep inside his clenching ass. With a deep, low groan, he climaxed, viscous fluid coating his belly and staining the front of Jean's pants.

His head was still spinning from the speed of his orgasm when Jean pulled away and stalked on down the street. Raymond put himself back together as best he could and raced to catch up with his partner. He did not ask any of the hundreds of questions rushing through his head as they strode the length of the street, then worked their way up and down the cross streets, still with no sign of the rogue.

Eventually, they had no choice but to accept that they had lost this round before it ever truly began. Raymond followed Jean back to his apartment, the scowl on the vampire's face deepening with each step. Finally, the door shut behind them, enclosing them in the safety of Jean's palatial retreat. The wizard opened his mouth to demand an explanation for their interlude in the street, but the words never reached his lips.

Before he could begin to react, Jean had backed him down the hall and into the Renaissance-style bedroom. Raymond tumbled onto the heavy four-poster canopy bed, the black, ornately embroidered curtains parting to let them through and then falling into place again, leaving them in semi-obscurity. Jean's hands flew over his body, pushing clothes aside in their search for skin. Raymond gasped and writhed and wondered fleetingly where the teasing, tender lover of the night before had gone, but he could not make himself care—not with his head spinning from the attentions of this passionate, amorously dominant creature above him.

He tried to return some of the pleasure he was receiving, but for once in his life, his brain completely disengaged, leaving him at the mercy of the bone-deep lust his vampire whipped up in him. He shifted one way and the other in response to the promptings of Jean's hands until he was completely nude on the black silk sheets, his body putty in the hands of his masterful lover. Jean rolled him onto his stomach, pulling him to his knees, hands chasing one another over his chest, stopping only to tweak his nipples before moving lower. Lips sucked at his earlobe, then skated down his neck to his shoulder, sucking hard but not breaking the surface. Raymond shuddered in delight at the thought of wearing a lover's mark on his body instead of just the functional bite marks of partnership that regularly adorned his wrists and neck. Then his lover's fangs pierced his flesh and he cried out, back arching in surprise and pain and pleasure all rolled into one overwhelming sensation. His untouched cock throbbed. His hands were free. He could have reached for it, stroked himself to completion with only a touch or two, but it was not his own touch he craved. He needed Jean's hands on him, around him, in him.

Bending forward, he braced his elbows on the mattress, lowering his forehead to his wrists so his buttocks lifted in obscene offering to the creature of the night behind him. He groaned as hard hands parted his cheeks, a wet finger probing his opening. He did not question where the slickness came from. It did not even matter. He squirmed back against the invading digit, trying to entice it deeper inside of him. A sharp slap across his buttocks, hard enough to get his attention but not to truly hurt, stilled his movement. He got the message. Jean was in control.

Expert fingers stretched his guardian ring, opening him slowly but inexorably for the reaming he was sure was coming. He undulated beneath the thorough fingering, letting his moans and pleas fall unchecked, giving Jean the gift of his submission. Last night, it had not been necessary or even desirable. Tonight it was, and he gave it willingly, eagerly even, a small token compared to the rich whirlwind of change Jean had brought into his life.

The fingers withdrew, tearing a moan of protest from his lips, but his lover's strong hands steadied his hips as the tip of the vampire's cock nudged his clenching opening. "Yes!" he hissed as the shaft began its long, slow slide deep into his body, hollowing him out, then filling him up again.

He thrashed beneath the lash of pleasure when Jean's cock hit his pleasure point unerringly with each pass in and out, leaving Raymond trembling on the cusp of release. "Please," he wailed, uncaring of how desperate or needy he sounded.

The hands on his hips moved to his shoulders, pulling him up to sitting again, lips returning to his neck, lingering over the oozing marks from the earlier bite before the fangs plunged deep again, sucking in time with the ever more enthusiastic thrusts.

Shuddering, Raymond's orgasm tore from him, but the sensations continued to mount, driving him up the peak again, and then again. He was caught between Jean's pillaging shaft and his plundering fangs, so high on pleasure he could hardly breathe. "Please," he begged again, a soft mewl this time, so different from his usual, strident tones.

One more hard thrust, one more deep pull on his neck and he felt Jean climax behind him, the skin on his shoulder tearing slightly as the orgasmic tremors destroyed the vampire's control.

Folding beneath the force of their passions, they fell forward onto the bed. Jean's body partially covered Raymond's, his cock still nestled between the taut globes of the wizard's buttocks, his tongue still swiping idly at the bleeding incisions on Raymond's shoulder, his arms cradling his lover against him as if he intended never to let go.

Raymond lay still, panting harshly through the postcoital haze, images and feelings assaulting him from every direction as he tried to assimilate the two completely different facets of his lover's personality. He wanted to roll over, to curl into Jean's embrace as he had done the night before, but this was not the same carefree, welcoming man he had shared his bed with last night.

"Are you all right?" Jean asked after a few moments. "I didn't mean to get so rough."

Now Raymond did roll in his arms, wanting to see Jean's face as they talked, as heartened by the complete lack of guidance from his lover's hands as he had been aroused by his dominance earlier.

"So what happened then?" Raymond asked, kissing the vampire softly. "Not that I'm complaining, but if I didn't know better, I'd think I had two different men in bed with me last night and tonight."

"You didn't just take up with a vampire," Jean explained ruefully. "You took up with a chef de la Cour. I didn't get where I am by being passive. I was monsieur Lombard's choice for a successor, but I had to fight to hold my position when he stepped down. The same primal instincts, the same primitive drives that let me win then still take over sometimes. Not catching the rogue tonight seems to have triggered them, and you bore the brunt of it. I'm sorry."

"I'm not," Raymond replied honestly. "I wouldn't want it this way every time we had sex, but being desired that powerfully… it's a real boost to the ego."

Jean shook his head in disbelief, relieved beyond words that he had not lost his new lover in his carelessness. "I try to be a civilized man, but the bloodlust that dwells inside me doesn't always give me a choice."

Chapter 26

ANGÉLIQUE LEANED back in her chair, sipping at the coffee she could barely taste as David finished the last of his dessert. They had flirted lightly through the entire meal, eyes rarely leaving each other's faces, fingers brushing occasionally. The warm hum of sexual tension curled low in her stomach, leaving her ready for more, but not urgent yet. Then David set down his cup and shifted his chair so he was closer to her, fingers stroking deliberately over the henna on her hands. They traced the lines of light brown ink that covered her hands and disappeared beneath the sleeves of her blouse. Slowly, but with no hesitation, David's fingers moved to her wrist and up her forearm, pushing the cloth out of the way. "I've wanted to do this since the first time I saw your hands," he admitted. "I'm dying to know how far they go."

Angélique's smile was rife with feminine power. "So find out," she offered huskily, knowing what the suggestion would do to David's libido. He was not the first man to be fascinated by the marks left by her past. Her eyes closed in pure pleasure as he stroked her skin, working up her arm to the fold of her elbow where the design ended.

David's pout at finding unpainted skin was almost boyish. "Is that really as far as they go?"

Angélique chuckled, a low throaty sound that went straight to his cock. "That was as far as the harem mistress had gotten when I was turned," she explained. "Had I remained in the harem, she would have painted my entire body since the sultan had a guest expected in a few days who enjoyed my company and preferred his women adorned. The sultan needed al-Marbruk's good favor and so always made sure I was ready for him."

Jealousy seethed foully in David's stomach at the thought of her being prepared for another man, along with the sick reminder that she had belonged to any man. "How can you speak of it so lightly?" he asked. "You were a slave!"

Angélique sighed. She thought they had moved beyond that, but apparently not. "I lived in the Middle East in the fifteenth century, David," she reminded him. "First of all, I had no real choice in the disposition of my life, but even if I had, I'm not sure I would change it. I was pampered, well fed, protected from the weather and from the scoundrels and thugs who roamed the city. If I hadn't caught the sultan's eye as a young girl, I would have had two other choices in life—working myself to an early grave on some poor man's farm, or whoring myself on the street at the mercy of whatever unscrupulous men wanted to use and abuse me, hoping they didn't damage me so badly that I couldn't work for a time afterward. If my family had been rich, if my options had been different, if

I'd had a different master, if I had been born in this era instead of the one of my birth, I might feel differently about the harem, but my master didn't abuse me and in fact protected me from that because I was the favorite of a powerful, frequent guest. Given my other options, occasionally having sex to help him curry favor with visiting lords was a small price to pay for a life of relative luxury."

"The idea of anyone having that kind of power over another is abhorrent to me," he explained haltingly, trying to make her understand his reaction as she had tried to explain her viewpoint. "I'm as much a product of my time as you are of yours, and the world you accept so blithely goes against everything I believe."

"And if I still lived in that kind of slavery and wanted out, I would appreciate your concern on my behalf," she promised, "but that's all in the past. The very, very distant past. I haven't had sex with a man for any reason other than for the pleasure of it since my maker turned me and brought me out of the harem."

Even that thought made David's stomach roil jealously, but he reminded himself that he had no claim on her past or even truly on her present. Nonetheless, he still wanted to pull her into his arms and erase the memory of every man who had ever touched her.

Some of what he was feeling must have shown on his face, because she pulled her hand away gently with a shake of her head. "Don't look at me that way. Regardless of what happens between us eventually, I won't be owned. I've been a man's chattel once in my life and while it was the best option for me at the time, I also swore to myself I would never again belong to any man. If we went back to Sang Froid tonight, or to your apartment, and had sex, either you'd still look at me and see the harem girl/whore or you'd have the idea that I was suddenly your little wife, at your beck and call. I'm neither of those things. As much as I would undoubtedly enjoy the sex, I think we need to wait until you can accept me as I am."

"And what about you accepting me the way I am?" David challenged, though he kept his voice even. "Am I not allowed to have wants and needs, too?"

"Of course you are," Angélique replied, "but at the moment, what you want and need isn't something I can offer. And what you're offering isn't something I can accept, either. We could go back to one apartment or the other and fuck each other silly, but we'd both end up regretting it. I've survived too long to intentionally do something I know I'll regret. When what we can offer each other is something we both need and want, we'll talk about it again. Until then, I think we should stick with being partners, not lovers."

"But…."

Angélique shook her head and rose from her seat. "Walk me home now," she instructed gently. "I have work to do."

David's face tightened at the thought of the work that awaited her, but he refrained from commenting. She knew how he felt about it, though his attitude had softened somewhat as he came to understand the true nature of her business. Paying the bill quickly, he followed her out of the restaurant and onto the street.

As soon as David joined her, Angélique threaded her arm through his, walking next to him as they returned to Sang Froid. They reached the side door marked "Employees Only" and paused. Angélique turned to face David, one shoulder brushing against his in the darkness broken only by the quarter moon.

David felt like nothing so much as a teenage boy walking his first date home, wondering if she would let him kiss her or if she would slip inside with nothing more than a thank you and a smile. His cock twitched when she leaned closer, tilting her head up and drawing his down so their lips met. He gasped into her mouth as her heady scent wreathed his senses, wrapping him in burning lust. He drew her tighter against him, letting her feel his growing erection. She rubbed against him provocatively, breasts brushing his chest through his open trenchcoat, one thigh slipping between his legs to press firmly against his groin. He moaned, hands going to her waist and then lower to grab her buttocks and lift her against him. "Inside," he whispered, breaking the kiss long enough to speak.

Angélique shook her head, taking a step back and opening the door. "Not until these"—she held up her hands—"are no longer a mark of shame in your eyes."

Before he could protest again, she sent him one last steamy look over her shoulder and shut the door, leaving him alone with a raging erection and no outlet besides his own hand. "Fucking tease," he muttered as he stalked away toward home.

Inside, Angélique leaned against the door, breath coming in little stuttering pants as she listened to the fading footsteps cross the courtyard and move down the alley to the street. Her body thrummed with unfulfilled lust, a sensation she had not endured for more than a few hours since she began her training at the hands of the sultan's slave master. Tonight, she knew better than to think she would find any satisfactory release. She had sent away the only lover who would satisfy her.

Pushing away from the door, she navigated the dim corridors until she came to the main parlor where her employees waited for their clients for the evening. She surveyed the room, seeing familiar and unfamiliar vampires talking with several of her people. She knew she should stay and oversee business since she did not have a night shift, but as unsettled as she was, she would be no good to any of them. Gesturing for François to join her, she whispered her excuses to him, asking him if he could stay later than usual while she attended to some personal matters.

Ever the good friend, he assured her he had everything under control and to take all the time she needed.

She thanked him with a smile and slowly climbed the stairs to her rooms, trying to puzzle out what made David different from the long line of men who dotted her past. From the time she had first discovered the power of her body to influence men, she had always known her own mind where the men in her life were concerned. Desire, disdain, devotion, disgust… her reaction had always been immediate and accurate, even when she had hidden it to serve men who evoked disdain or disgust because her sultan commanded it. With David, though, her reaction varied as widely as the tides at Mont St-Michel, and that left her feeling adrift.

Reaching her rooms, she locked the door, though she knew none would disturb her here. Methodically, she hung up her cape, then removed her skirt and blouse, shaking them out and leaving them to air before returning them to their place in her closet, slipping off her shoes and tucking them away. Clad in only her underwear, her nipples peaking in the cool room, she went into the bathroom to perform her bedtime ritual, though she knew she would find rest elusive.

She took her time brushing her hair, washing her face, and smoothing fragrant oil onto her skin to leave it smooth and lustrous. Her eyes returned frequently to her hands, the swirls and sweeps of color contrasting with the pale skin of her legs, belly and breasts as she coated them with the oil.

An idea came to her, bringing a smile to her hips. She grabbed a washcloth and cleaned the oil from her breasts. Leaving her bra in the hamper, she returned to her bedroom and sat down at the dressing table, opening drawers until she found her henna kit. She lifted a thin brush from the wooden box, tracing it over her skin sensuously. A slow smile spread across her lips. This would do the trick. Setting the brush down, she went into the kitchen to retrieve the henna paste she kept for when she wanted to decorate herself. Returning to the bedroom with the small bowl, she settled in front of the mirror again, dipped the brush in the dye, and began to paint.

Often when she adorned herself thus, she concentrated in great detail, making sure that each stroke was perfectly placed on the canvas of her body, creating elaborate designs to rival the ones she had seen as a young woman in the harem. Tonight, she cared less for the results than for the affirmation of her position. The marks on her arms, like the new marks she added now to her breasts, were simply marks, not signs of disgrace or moral turpitude as David seemed to think. They did not by their mere presence make her any more or less than she would have been without them. They were decorations, erotic enhancements of her beauty that she took pleasure from. This mantra resonating in her mind down to the depths of her soul, she painted from the tops of her breasts, down her belly to the edge of her pubic curls. As she sealed the designs and wrapped them in bandage tape to keep them in place until the stains had set, she smiled at the memory of painting a belly blessing on the breasts and belly of a pregnant concubine in the harem. The young woman, a Norse slave who had fascinated the sultan from the moment he saw her blonde hair and blue eyes, had taken a long time to settle into the life of the harem. Finally, impending motherhood had mellowed her mood and for once she had participated willingly in the decoration of her body, a ritual too foreign for her most of the time. When they had finished the designs and she next saw the sultan, he had spent hours simply tracing the dark lines on her pale skin. She had shared the whispered confidence that she had never felt so desired as in that moment.

Now if only David would feel the same way, seeing the marks as a beauty enhancement, nothing more. Reminding herself to give him time and that she had painted her body tonight for her enjoyment, not his, she settled in bed to rest while the henna set.

Unfortunately, her mind would not still, returning to thoughts of David, of his reaction to the henna, of kissing him. She should have been able to dismiss him, she thought waspishly. She had never before had trouble getting a man out of her head when she did not want him there.

That was the problem, though. She did want him in her head, and in her bed, despite all the reasons why she should not. He would not be satisfied, as Bertrand was, with her visiting occasionally when she desired a man's attention. He would not be satisfied with knowing that she did not always choose him. He was everything she had sworn never to allow in her life again, and yet she could not stop thinking of him. Beneath their protective wraps, her breasts tingled with the memory of his hand on them earlier. She was tempted to stroke them, only the thought of displacing the henna and ruining the designs enough to stop her. Her body throbbed at the thought of how close they had come to having sex in her office. He had wanted her, but his sense of duty had outweighed his desire. She should not have given him a choice, she thought wryly, except that if she had taken that path with her mind muddled by passion, she would have regretted it the next time he reacted to his misperceptions of her.

Shifting on the bed, she slid her hand between her thighs, her fingers stroking her damp flesh. She would never be able to rest with this lust riding her. One long finger worked its way into her body, her eyes closing as she imagined David kneeling at the foot of her bed, staring up at her henna tattoos, touching them, touching her, worshipping her body as the sultan had worshipped Valda. She added a second finger, her thumb massaging her pleasure node, letting her fingers work her to frenzy and into release—but as she withdrew them and wiped them clean on the sheet, she knew it was a hollow climax, a physical release that did nothing to truly satisfy her.

For the moment, however, it was all she could have.

A few blocks away, David tossed restlessly in his empty bed, images of Angélique torturing his mind. He could see with all too vivid detail her buxom form riding a faceless man as she had suggested doing earlier in her office, her head tossed back, her hair trailing down her back, brushing the swells of her buttocks and the thighs of the phantom lover beneath her, tantalizing them both as she rocked them to completion. His mind tossed up images of her henna-painted hands stroking a muscular chest, driving her lover to sweaty, passionate heights.

His hand wrapped around his cock, stroking in time to his mental image of Angélique riding her lover. Her hands moved, leaving her lover's body and stroking her own—from her long, slender neck over her full breasts, pausing to tweak her nipples, then down to where they were joined, her fingers seeking her clit and rubbing it as she moved. His hand sped up as his orgasm approached, trying to imagine himself in place of the mystery lover. He wanted to be that man, whatever that took, and as his climax hit, he decided he did not care that some of that impulse came from a magical bond.

Chapter 27

"HELLO, PUSSY."

The hated words in that hateful voice grated in Adèle's ears. She spun around, looking for her partner, but she did not see him. "Prick," she retorted, walking on down the corridor toward the exit. They had just finished their shift and she wanted to go home, close the volets against the daylight, and get some sleep.

She had nearly reached it, so close she could almost touch the door, when hard hands closed one around her arm, the other over her mouth. She struggled automatically, but she was no match for his strength. Even so, she kicked out at him, determined to find some way to break free. "Struggle all you like, pussy," Jude purred in her ear. "You can't get away."

As if to prove his point, he nipped at the tender lobe of her ear, piercing it with his fangs. The sweet, hot tang of her blood rushed through him, the twin taste of anger and arousal firing his blood like nothing else. He had bided his time since the second ritual, the thrill of the hunt sharpening his mind and senses like nothing else. To have her blood, he need only hold out his hand, but he wanted more than just her neck or her wrist. He wanted her naked and writhing beneath him, wanted her clinging heat and heaving breasts, wanted her marked with his bites so thoroughly and intimately that any man who looked at her would see proof of his prior possession. He would have all those things before he let her go again this morning. Pulling her into an empty room, he locked the door and spun her hard against it, back to the wood.

"What do you want?" she hissed indignantly, though she suspected she knew. Her heart sank at the thought even as her body reacted in anticipation.

"Revenge."

"So what?" she challenged. "You'll just tie me up and fuck me whether I want it or not?"

Jude smiled confidently. "You'll want it," he assured her. "Deny it all you want. I know just how to get you hot and bothered. You'll ask me for it before we're done, pussy." Anticipating her reaction, he caught her wrists before she could swing at him, pinning them behind her back in an implacable grip. His other hand toyed with the buttons on her shirt, opening the first three swiftly so that the tops of her breasts, outlined in black lace, came into view. "Making it easy for me?" he drawled, lowering his head and grazing her skin with his fangs. "You'll look beautiful covered in my marks."

Even knowing it was futile, Adèle struggled, lashing out with booted feet. "So you want to play rough?" Jude responded immediately, spinning her away from the door toward the mahogany table in the center of the room. "If that's the way you want it, pussy, never let it be said I disappointed a lady."

They rammed up against the hard wood, the edge cutting into Adèle's belly as she fell forward, arms still pinned painfully behind her.

"Bastard," she spat. "Let me go."

"Not until I have what I want."

"What about what I want?" she demanded.

"You took what you wanted after the ritual with no concern for my desires," Jude reminded her. "Now it's my turn." He popped the button on her slacks, pushing them and her panties down her legs far enough to impede any future kicks, giving him a perfect view of her buttocks. With a grin, he slapped them hard enough to raise a reddened handprint to their pale surface.

"I'm not going to just stand here and let you fuck me," she warned him, renewing her efforts to get free, twisting her body in an effort to break his grip.

"I didn't think you would," he agreed, using his weight to pin her to the table as he reached beneath her to finish undoing her shirt. If some of the buttons popped in his haste, she had only herself to blame for fighting him. Pulling it from her shoulders, he tightened it around her elbows, effectively immobilizing her arms.

"Sale con!" she yelled when she realized what he had done.

Jude clucked his tongue disapprovingly. "Such language," he scolded. "Ladies should not talk that way." He reached between her legs and grabbed her panties, ripping the fabric on either side so he could pull them free. "Sluts who do talk that way don't get to talk anymore." Before she could say another word, he stuffed the cloth in her mouth.

"How do you like it, pussy?" he demanded, flipping her over so he could have access to the front of her body. "Bound, silenced, completely at my mercy." Her glare answered his question but he ignored it. "Now, let's see what I remember from two days ago." He ran his hands over her lace covered breasts. "I think you said you liked having a lover suck your breasts, didn't you?" He licked a path tenderly over the upper swells, wetting the skin almost lovingly. "Is that the way you want it?" he inquired, lifting his head just enough to meet her gaze. She gave no indication to answer his question. "It's not, is it, pussy? You don't want tender. You want someone strong enough to take you." He turned his attention back to her skin, his fangs piercing deeply as he marked her, sucking blood to the surface, swallowing swiftly and lifting his head again with a satisfied grin as her body bucked beneath him, rubbing her folds against his still-clothed groin. "Someone strong enough to bend you to his will," he gloated, biting again and again, leaving bloody tears over the tops of both breasts. She writhed beneath him—but he could taste the desire in her blood, so he took her struggles as encouragement and pulled the cups of her bra down so he could reach her nipples. Piercing her flesh right above one rosy aureole, he sucked the teat into his mouth, his lower teeth biting at it as he swallowed mouthful after mouthful of hot, life-giving blood.

Adèle fought to spit the makeshift gag out of her mouth as he savaged her breasts, wanting to rail and shout at him for treating her this way, but she could not get enough leverage with her tongue to remove it. Then he bit just above her nipple, sucking hard, and she was glad for the gag because it silenced the moan of pleasure just as it did her protests. She bucked beneath him, trying to get more of his weight against her body. As much as she hated him, she could not deny what he did to her with his rough touches and the cut of his fangs. Bound as she was, she could do nothing to stop him, so she would enjoy what he did to her now and repay him for his audacity later.

Misinterpreting her squirming, Jude lifted his head and smirked at her, shifting so his weight pinned her more completely against the table. "It's no use fighting me, pussy," he scolded. "You can't get away. You'll just have to lie here and bear it until I'm done with you. And I'm nowhere near done with you." His fingers tracing over the bloody bites, he turned his attention to her other breast, biting it as he had the first, smiling at the sound that escaped even with the gag in her mouth. It could have been protest or pleasure. He did not care which. She had used him callously two days before. He had every intention of using her just as much today.

Forcing a hand between her legs, he pinched the delicate flesh sharply, letting his nails dig into her. She cried out through the gag, but he could taste the jolt of lust in her blood along with the pain. "So the little hussy likes being hurt?" he goaded. "Shall I hurt you some more, pussy? Blink twice, was it, if you want it. Don't bother lying to me. I can taste how badly you want it in your blood."

Adèle glared at him, but she could hardly deny what he already knew. She blinked twice, eyes closing tightly on a flinch as his nails dug into her cruelly before he crammed his fingers into her passage. She tilted her hips as best she could with her legs still tangled in her pants, trying to move his fingers to change the angle of penetration. His free hand slapped at her thigh. "Stop fighting, pussy. You can't throw me off and you know you don't want to. You're sopping wet, a regular bitch in heat. Don't worry. I'll fuck you as hard as you could possibly want."

He withdrew his fingers and replaced them with his cock, thrusting hard and deep a few times before pulling out and flipping her over. He slapped both buttocks sharply again, smiling at the sounds she made. Parting the pale globes, he pressed the two fingers slick with her fluids into her rear passage, stretching the muscle perfunctorily. She squealed through the gag, widening his smile. "You used me and left me unsatisfied," he informed her. "We'll see how you like it when I do the same to you. Your wet cunt all empty and needy while I fuck your ass. Too bad you're not a man like you pretend to be. Apparently, this feels pretty good when you're a man." He pushed into the tight passage. "All I need is a hole, pussy. It doesn't have to be the one that feels good to you."

Behind the gag, Adèle smirked. Let him think what he liked. He did not need to know how much she enjoyed being taken this way. Not every time, but one of her more adventurous former lovers had introduced her to the pleasures to be found in this kind of sex. It usually took her less time to come this way than the other way. Since the noises that escaped her made him fuck her even harder, she stopped trying to silence them. If he got off thinking he was hurting her, all the better for her as he pounded into her enthusiastically.

Jude's eyes closed as her body opened to him slowly, enclosing him in hot, velvet heat. She was still bucking beneath him, bringing a feral smile to his lips as he thrust harder, his hands leaving bruises where his fingers dug into her skin. Her ass was so tight around him, far tighter than any cunt could ever be, and her squeals and moans aroused him to a frenzy. Grabbing her hair, he pulled her upright so he could bite her neck, the taste of desire in her blood snapping what remained of his control. He pounded into her body, uncaring of her response, needing the release that hovered just out of reach and the knowledge that he had taken what he wanted without regard for her pleasure.

The sudden taste of her orgasm in her blood, the sudden clench of her passage around his cock, sent him over the edge, his body shaking and shivering through his climax. He pulled back immediately, disgruntled beyond words with the unexpected turn of events. Lashing out at the perceived object of his disdain, he smacked her buttocks again. "Disgusting slut," he spat. "You even like it up the ass."

He righted his clothes and walked to the door. "I hope someone finds you soon. You might get a little uncomfortable with your arms tied behind your back, my spunk running down your legs and my marks all over the rest of you. Then again, maybe you'd like someone to find you that way and give you another good fucking. Shall I send someone else in? You wouldn't care, would you? Another cock to fill up your empty hole, that's all you care about."

Adèle fumed silently, working her hands free of her shirt now that he no longer held her in place. He could say what he liked now, while he was nominally in control, but she knew the score. It had taken her climax to trigger his, despite his obvious intention of leaving her unsatisfied. Let him think he had won. She would show him the error of his ways before all was said and done.

DAVID COULD not remember a word he said to Marcel as he explained their plan for dealing with vampires who wished to join the alliance. He hoped he had not sounded like an absolute idiot, but he figured he probably was one anyway. He had met Angélique at Marcel's office for the scheduled meeting. His eyes were drawn immediately to her cleavage, on display in a scooped neck blouse, not because of the dark valley between her breasts but because he could see the edge of henna tracings that had not been there the day before, he was certain. That had shattered his concentration. The thought of her painting herself—

heaven forbid someone else had done it!—be it for her own pleasure or for a lover, was too erotically charged for him to focus on anything else.

As soon as Marcel dismissed them, David grabbed Angélique's hand, pulling her through the halls and down the stairs to his office. "What's this?" he asked angrily, his jealousy growing with each glance at the designs decorating her skin. "All tarted up for another man after you refused me?"

Angélique shook her head in frustration. "This is exactly why I didn't sleep with you," she retorted. "You think you have the right to claim me, to own me, and that's before we've had sex. It isn't any of your business who I sleep with, but for your information, I used the henna for myself, because it makes me feel feminine and powerful, not to entice a lover."

"Sorry," he mumbled, his eyes still fixed on the edge of the swirls visible above the neckline of her blouse. They had a hypnotizing effect, his hand moving to touch without his conscious awareness. She caught her breath as his fingers traced the bit of brown he could see.

"Let me see the rest," he whispered, eyes never leaving her breasts. "Let me see you."

Angélique hesitated. She had been hesitating since she woke up that morning and washed away the henna paste, leaving only the marks where it had been. She had hesitated over which blouse to wear, one that would show some of the marks or one that would hide them completely. She had hesitated over whether to wear a scarf. In the end she had worn the lower cut blouse without a scarf, reminding herself that she had nothing to be ashamed of, no reason to hide the pleasure she took in her own body. She had known he would notice, had hoped he would notice, but she had not expected his boldness. His accusation, yes, but not the daring touch, not the whispered plea. Not the apology.

Hands trembling, she lifted the hem of her blouse, baring her pale stomach covered in russet swirls. His fingers traced the lines immediately, as he had done with her hands the day before, not waiting for permission, but touching her with all the intimate confidence of a longtime lover. Her eyes closed involuntarily as she gave herself over to the sensation of his rough fingertips on her smooth skin. Eventually, they reached the point where fabric still covered her breasts. Without asking, he pushed it higher under her arms so he could follow the designs over the generous mounds. The snick of the front clasp on her bra was the only warning she had before that covering fell away as well, leaving her open to his gaze, his touch, from waist to neck.

She trembled beneath his touch, frozen in time and space as he explored the pattern on her skin, his fingers never lingering, even when they brushed across the tips of her breasts where the lines intersected. They touched the sensitive peaks but paid no more attention to them than to any other place, leaving her equally frustrated and aroused. Eventually, his hand came to rest on the waistband of the slacks she wore. "How far does it go?" he asked softly.

In reply, she flipped the button from its hole and lowered the zipper, parting the fabric so he could follow the motif around her navel and below to the edge of her underwear.

He dropped to his knees in front of her, resuming his erotic exploration, tracing the newly revealed lines as he had those higher up. When again fabric frustrated him, he did not wait for, or even ask, permission. He simply pushed it out of the way so he could follow the lines to their end amid her nest of curls. "You're a goddess," he murmured reverently, pressing a tender kiss to the top of her mound.

"No," she corrected, her hands holding his head in place for a long, fraught moment before falling to her sides again. "Just a vampire." Slowly, completely unsettled, she backed away and turned, righting her clothes. She had promised herself she would not do this until he saw her as she was, and yet here she was, twelve hours later, breaking her own promise. Even with his apology, his first thought on seeing her new tattoos had been to accuse her of sleeping with another man. As soon as he knew they were not, he assumed they were for him, touching them—and her—as if he had every right to them, as if he were the intended beneficiary of their erotic allure, as if she were his concubine to touch and claim how he wished. That she had accepted, enjoyed, his touch did nothing to negate the fact that he had not asked, had simply taken as if by right. As much as she wanted him, as much as her body fought her mind's control, she could not let him think she was an odalisque for him to use and discard at his whim. "We can't do this. I'm sorry."

David surged to his feet, hands closing on her shoulders, spinning her around to face him. "Why the hell not?" he demanded. "You weren't complaining when I touched you. I may not be able to read your blood, but I think I can tell when a woman's unwilling."

"I never said I was unwilling," Angélique reminded him. "That doesn't mean it's a good idea. I told you last night that I can't do this while you still see me as a sex object."

"And yet you come in today painted like a harem slave. That's a bit of false advertising, you know. Tease is the nicest word that comes to mind."

"Henna is used to paint brides on their wedding days, too, you know," Angélique reminded him tartly. "To bless mothers about to give birth. Harem girls were hardly the only ones who wore such designs."

"I know you're no virgin and unless you're hiding something, you're not about to give birth, so tell me what I was supposed to think when you walked in today with new designs after I had specifically expressed my disappointment that they didn't cover more of your body. If you didn't want me to see them, if you didn't mean them for me, you should have covered them better," he snapped.

"My world doesn't revolve around you," she snapped back. "I did this for myself, because it makes me feel good. And I wore this blouse because I wanted to, because I like the allure of it."

"So you're a tease," David declared, lips pursed in disapproval. "I should have known not to expect anything better. You say you want me to see you, to accept you as you are, but you play up your sexuality to the point that I have to see it and react to it. Then you accuse me of treating you like a whore. I'm not a saint, Angélique. I'm just a man, and it's perfectly natural that I'd see and react to a beautiful woman. You said outright you did this to increase your sense of beauty and power, but I'm not supposed to notice. Is that it?"

"You're supposed to notice," Angélique replied. "But you aren't supposed to take without even asking if you can."

David shook his head. "Find some other shmuck to play games with. I don't have time for this." With a final glare in her direction, he left her alone in the office, determined not to give her—and her tattoos—another thought.

Angélique's face fell and she slumped into the nearest chair, face in her hands, all the enjoyment she had gotten out of painting herself last night gone now in the face of David's anger. He was not right. She had not done the tattoos for him, but for herself. He could not be right. She had not wanted to see his reaction to the marks. She refused to let him be right. She had not set out to tempt him.

He was right. She was punishing him because it had worked.

Chapter 28

ANTONIO MEANDERED along the banks of the Seine. At this early hour of the morning, the quais were deserted, not even the early morning joggers up yet to disturb his thoughts or impede his sporadic progress toward home. The patrol Jean had assigned him to had fought victoriously last night and captured several dark wizards. Antonio had helped with the interrogation as he always did, but his heart was not in it, not when he wanted only one wizard's blood. Of course, he could hardly tell his chef de la Cour that, given that the wizard he wanted fought with the enemy.

Fortunately, she had not been with the wizards his patrol had stopped from breaking into the Bibliothèque Nationale. Antonio was honestly not sure how he would react if he came face to face with her again, in battle where he might be forced to choose between her and his loyalty to Jean, not to mention violating his sense of right and wrong. He wanted to believe he would make the right choice, but he hoped he never had to test that because he truly could not be sure he would.

His entire being ached with his need for her. Everyone else's blood—even the woman he had fed from at Sang Froid who had no magic instead of dark magic—tasted wrong now. Every woman who caught his eye and flirted with the darkly handsome man paled in comparison to Monique, even when objectively the other woman was more beautiful. His bed felt empty in a way it had not only a week before despite the fact that she had never been there. He lay in bed during the day and caressed the cool sheets, remembering what it had felt like to caress her warm flesh instead. He kicked savagely at a stone on the ground, sending it bouncing across the cobblestones and into the river. There had to be a way to fight this susceptibility. He just did not know who or how to ask without giving away his reasons, and he dared not do that. He doubted Jean would condemn him blindly—he had hardly chosen to be partnered with a dark wizard—but it would throw every choice he made into doubt.

The sensation of a wand being pressed against the base of his neck shocked him back to awareness of his surroundings. "What the hell have you done to me?"

He did not even have to look to recognize her voice. "What do you mean?" he asked, though he knew exactly what she was talking about. Apparently, she had not been able to banish him from her thoughts any more than he had been able to stop thinking about her. He was not about to admit that susceptibility, though, to her any more than to Jean or the other vampires. If she had been sincere in her desire to switch sides, perhaps… but she was not.

The wand jabbed into his skull more firmly. "What kind of magic do vampires have that I can't get you out of my head?"

"Liked it that much, did you?" Antonio drawled, the knowledge that she was his partner allowing him to disregard the threat her wand would pose to anyone else. He reached for her wrist, angling the wood away from him. "I'd be glad to offer you a repeat performance."

"Fuck you," she spat, pulling her arm out of his grip and keeping her wand between them.

Antonio grinned, feral heat in his eyes. "I think you have that backwards, darling. I'm the one who gets to fuck you."

"Oh, so you just take what you want?" she challenged. "I don't get a say in the matter?"

"You were willing enough last time," he reminded her. "And you're the one who came looking for me, not the other way around."

"To find out what kind of spell you cast on me, not for anything else."

"No spells, no magic, just good old-fashioned charm," he assured her. "Vampires can't cast spells. Would it be so terrible to admit you liked being bitten?"

"Yes," she retorted. "I don't want anything to do with vampires."

"That wasn't the impression I got when we met the last time," he countered. "Shall I bite you again to see if you're telling the truth?" As soon as the words crossed his lips, he cursed the slip silently. She did not know about that particular vampiric talent. Until now.

"So that's why you bit me before?" she demanded. "So you could report to Chavinier that I was really a spy? Was any of what you told me true? And did you have to fuck me, too?"

"You were flirting, too," Antonio reminded her, grabbing her arm and pulling her toward him. Her hiss of pain startled him. He did not think he had grabbed her that roughly. "What's wrong?"

"Nothing," she sulked, pulling her arm out of his grip. "Just a little sore."

"Who hurt you?"

"It's none of your damn business," she hissed. "You fucked me and then made sure I was sent away. Failure has consequences, you know."

"I'll kill him," Antonio growled. "I'll rip his head off."

She should have blasted him for such a chauvinistic attitude, Monique knew, but her usually neglected feminine core found it flattering. She deliberately kept her male compatriots at bay, not wanting to show any sign of weakness that might cause them to discount her, but that façade came with a price, and Antonio's reaction appealed to a deeply buried need. "Why should you care?" she asked, but her tone had softened considerably.

Antonio sighed and ran a hand through his hair. "There's a bench a little farther down the river," he said, avoiding the question. "We can sit there and talk." He held out his hand in invitation, not sure she would take it.

She did, her slender fingers dwarfed by his much larger palm.

Side by side, they strolled down the river, looking like nothing so much as a pair of lovers heading home after a night on the town. Antonio refused to let himself wish that were true as he led her to the secluded bench. A wrought iron fence separated them from the river, the overhanging row of trees enough to provide a layer of privacy even with only the last autumnal leaves clinging to their branches. In the summer, he would come here often to soak in the smell of the flowers that filled the beds behind the wooden bench, but in the winter, the only smells were of bare, damp earth and the river that ran at their feet. At this hour, no tourist-filled bateaux-mouche with floodlights to illuminate the city's monuments made their circuits, leaving the river bank cloaked in darkness. The water lapped softly at the stone jetties, but Antonio was used to that sound. Sitting, he pulled her onto his lap. She resisted, but he just tugged harder. "The bench is cold and you're not wearing a long coat. I won't do anything you don't want. Just let me hold you."

"But why?" Monique asked even as she sat. "I'm the enemy."

Antonio shook his head. "You might be the Milice's enemy. You might even be Chavinier's enemy, but you aren't mine."

"I should be."

"You aren't."

"But why not?" Monique asked in exasperation. "I feel like there's something going on here I don't understand."

Antonio shrugged. "Do you need to understand it? Can't you just enjoy it?"

"Enjoy what?"

"Enjoy being here with me, my arms around your waist, keeping you warm. Enjoy knowing I'm here with you—that I want to be here with you—even though I probably shouldn't be." He nuzzled her neck, hoping she would not reject him. "Enjoy the fact that I haven't wanted anyone's blood but yours since I tasted you."

She told herself she did not care whom he fed from, but her body quickened at the feeling of his lips on her neck, at the thought of his fangs in her skin. Slowly, she tipped her head back, giving him uninhibited access to the long column of flesh. One hand immediately cradled her head so she would not strain her neck, the little gesture warming her heart even more as she felt his tongue on her skin followed by the sharp prick of his fangs.

She gasped as his lips drew on her neck, sucking her blood into his mouth. The hand not supporting her head rested hot and heavy on the curve of her waist, steadying her across his lap. She wanted it to wander as it had before, caressing and claiming, but he made no attempt to touch her more intimately. Just one hand on her waist, one in her hair, and his fangs in her neck.

She was not sure she had ever been so thoroughly seduced.

With every mouthful of blood, Antonio fell deeper under her spell, this tough woman with a soft heart. She could deny it—and would, he suspected—but he had tasted what lay beneath the surface and he played to that now as he fed, keeping his touch circumspect despite his desire to burrow his hands beneath her clothes and find bare skin. He was taking too big a risk already, just feeding from her. Seducing her again would go beyond the pale, and he found he did not want to start something with her that he could not in good faith continue. He had watched the vampires around him, those with partners in the alliance, and he had seen the bond growing between the pairs, even the ones who fought each other. From the outside looking in, he could see the chemistry between them, see how they matched each other. If magic sped along their recognition of that fact, he accepted it philosophically. His very existence was based on magic. He saw no reason to question its other influences in his life. That was his choice, though, not the choice of the woman in his arms. She did not know what forces had driven her to seek him out and he could not tell her. And until he could, to take any more than this—truly, even to take this—was to trick her into something she did not understand and had not accepted freely.

He drank more deeply, feeling her body melt against his. He tasted the consent he had not asked for, but he kept his hands still, supporting her as she relaxed more fully into his embrace.

The sound of a boat engine broke his concentration. He pulled Monique against him tightly, shielding her face from view as the barge motored slowly by. He doubted the ship's crew even looked toward them, but he was aware of their visibility. When the boat had passed, he tipped her chin up to look at him, kissing her pouting lips gently. "It's too open here, even at night, for me to do more than feed from you."

"Then take me somewhere more private," she suggested, her nerves still singing from his attentions.

He shook his head regretfully. "It's not safe. For either of us."

"I don't care."

"I do," he replied, stroking her cheek with one gentle finger. "Go home where it's safe and heal the marks on your neck. Serrier would recognize them for sure and I can't stand the thought of him hurting you because of what we've done tonight."

"I'm not stupid," she began.

"I know you're not," he interrupted, "but I also know it's easy to forget. I hate the idea that you have to hide them. I want to lie in bed during the day when I can't go out and think of you bearing my mark, but you can't. Not as long as you fight for him."

"Don't try to 'convert' me," she said bitterly. "I chose my side."

"Just be careful," he pleaded. "I won't hold back if I meet you in battle. As much as I would hate to hurt you, I have to fight for what I believe in."

She rose and looked down at him sadly. "So do I." With a muttered spell and a flick of her wand, she was gone, leaving Antonio alone on the bench. He slammed his fist against the wood, ignoring the flash of pain that radiated up his arm. He had tasted the blood of too many dark wizards since agreeing to help Jean interrogate any captured enemy fighters. Their darkness tasted like oil, obscuring everything else with its foulness, but while he could taste anger and even dark magic in Monique's blood, her blood did not have the same fetid flavor as her captured compatriots.

Why, then, was she holding so firmly to that path? Did she think she had no other choice? Did she doubt anyone would accept her sincerity, particularly after he had revealed her to be a plant the last time she came to Milice headquarters? Did Serrier have some other hold over her, some leverage that kept her serving him even when her heart was not in it fully?

His frustration grew with his unanswered questions. She did not belong in the ranks of the dark wizards, but he did not know how to break her free. His loyalty to Jean insisted he should stay away from her until she came to her senses and switched sides, but his heart refused to listen. She needed an incentive to switch sides, a lure stronger than whatever Serrier held over her head. He did not know if he could provide it, but he did know he had to try. Her blood beckoned like the nectar of the gods, offering safety from the sun, offering a rich bouquet of flavors to set all other offerings to shame. He would always regret it if he did not at least try to convince her to defect. He would not pressure her, but he would point out the benefits, seek out the reasons holding her back and eradicate them. Somehow, he would see her at his side.

Now he just had to convince her of the rightness of that plan. Without giving away more information than Serrier already knew.

He had messed up there tonight, revealing his ability to read her feelings in her blood—but he could not see how such information would be useful to Serrier, particularly since it was not limited in any way to the alliance or the partnerships. If he had thought about it, the dark leader could have asked the vampire he had recruited to his cause.

Antonio shook his head in disgust as he thought of the rogue, rising from his cold seat and beginning the short trek toward the houseboat that had been his abode for the past generation. The loner was clearly deluded if he thought Serrier was out for anyone but himself and perhaps the wizards who fought at his side. Antonio had seen delusional dictators come and go in the time since his turning. They were all alike in the most fundamental of ways, using those around them for their own ends while preaching a greater good that in fact benefited only a select few, if even those few ever saw any rewards. More times than not, society rose up against them before they could in any way repay their supporters. This would be one of those times. The alliance would see to it.

Chapter 29

"WHERERVER WE go, they're there before we even arrive!" Serrier shouted at his hapless seconds. "The Tour Eiffel, the Palais de Justice, the Bibliothèque Nationale. He's always had the devil's own luck, but this is beyond ridiculous! Someone is passing him information and I want to know who!"

Everyone in the room blanched, sinking lower in their chairs as if they could make themselves invisible. The last time Serrier had gone on a rampage about a spy, he had ordered a purge of his ranks, killing fifteen supporters before he was convinced he had found the turncoat. "Vuillemin tripped a ward on the way in to Sainte-Chapelle," Eric reminded the rebel leader. "Unless that was intentional on his part, I doubt there was any treachery in Chavinier's presence at that battle."

"That doesn't explain the fact they were waiting for us at the Tour Eiffel. There weren't any wards there," Vincent observed, "and the patrol didn't get close enough to the Bibliothèque Nationale to even see if there were protective wards."

"It's gotten worse in the past few weeks," Claude commented. "Who might Chavinier have recruited in that time?"

"He was at the battle at the Gare de Lyon," Serrier mused aloud. "Wasn't there one wizard who escaped that debacle?"

"Yes," Vincent replied, "little more than a boy." He paused and wracked his memory for a name. "Daniel, Denis, no, Dominique. Dominique Cornet. I remember being surprised he'd escaped when everyone else was captured or killed."

"There's also Monique," Serrier added. "She said she didn't see Chavinier, but she was inside the Milice base."

"And that was right before the attack at the Tour Eiffel," Claude pointed out. "Did she know about it?"

"She might have," Serrier replied. "She wasn't scheduled to participate since she was supposed to infiltrate Chavinier's ranks, but it wasn't a secret mission. Any number of people could have told her. Dominique wasn't scheduled to participate either."

"Were either of them aware of the attack tonight?" Eric inquired.

"Not as far as I know," Serrier answered, "but again, I told the patrol leader a couple of days ago so he could plan. If he told his patrol, one of them could well have told either of the possible spies. Every mission he's anticipated has been, relatively speaking, common knowledge—certainly not limited enough to narrow down who the spy might be, even between just the two we've already mentioned."

"Let me have them for a few hours," Claude offered. "I'll break them for you."

"And by the time you're done with them, they'll both have confessed to avoid your torture," Vincent retorted. "If you want to know which one it is, smoke them out. Give them, or one of them, information you know the other doesn't have and see if Chavinier shows up. If he does, there's your proof."

"And if he doesn't?" Serrier countered.

"Then either the one you told isn't your spy or couldn't get the information to the old fool fast enough. In the meantime, don't announce your plans to anyone you don't trust until right before you put them into effect. That way the spy, whoever it is, won't be able to reveal your intentions to Chavinier until it's too late."

Serrier's laughter was cold. "And who exactly do you think I trust?" he demanded.

"I think we've proven our loyalty," Eric reminded him, deflecting his interest from Vincent, "more than once."

Serrier scowled at the impertinence, lifting his wand and sending a jolt of magic arcing along Eric's nerves. The big man flinched visibly but refused to bow beneath the agonizing onslaught, holding the rebel leader's gaze even as his body twitched reflexively in its effort to flee the grating sensation. Eventually, a pained gasp escaped his lips. As if that were the sign he had been waiting for, Serrier's wand moved again, ending the spell and leaving Eric panting in relief. "One of these days, Simonet, you're going to push me too far."

Eric shrugged, muscles still twitching as they relaxed after the uncomfortable knotting brought on by the sudden attack. "One of these days, maybe you'll actually believe in our loyalty. In the meantime, are we going to try to catch this spy or not?"

"In a few minutes," Serrier replied, eyes narrowing as he tried to decide if there was another challenge in Eric's latest words. "We're not done yet."

"What else is there to talk about?" Vincent asked.

"The bloodsucker has proven less than effective at getting me the information I need," Serrier explained. "Obviously we now know why the vampires assembled that morning, but that doesn't tell us how the alliance"—a sneer marred his bearded face—"works or help us defend against them. We can't keep losing battles the way we have been. We won't have anyone left."

"So what are you suggesting?" Eric asked.

"We need a guinea pig, a vampire to experiment on so we can determine how best to defeat them. I was tempted to just use the one we have, but he might still prove useful if we don't alienate him completely."

Claude's grin bordered on mad as he rubbed his hands in anticipation. "Can I do it? Please?"

Eric and Vincent glanced at each other and rolled their eyes.

"Eventually," Serrier soothed, "after we've found their weaknesses."

"Where do you plan on finding another vampire?" Vincent asked. "We had enough trouble getting this one to talk to us, and they'll be doubly on their guard now that they've sided with the Milice."

"We'll have to capture one," Serrier replied. "Preferably one who's involved with Chavinier, so we can find out their strategies as well as their weaknesses. I think an attack on Montmartre is in order. That seems to be where the majority of them hang out. And in an effort to make sure we get a Milice vampire, we'll make sure our potential spies know about it as well so that Chavinier is sure to send people to defend his new pets."

"That's suicide," Vincent blurted out before he could stop himself.

"It may well be," Serrier agreed, "but anything for the cause, right? I think I'll give you the honor of leading the attack. You and Eric did such a good job finding a vampire the first time, you can make sure you bring me back another one this time."

The two wizards looked at each other in resignation. "When?" Eric asked.

"Tomorrow night," Serrier declared. "We wouldn't want to give Chavinier too much notice or he might find a way to clear the area entirely. Tell the spies in the morning, slightly different versions of your plan so we know which one passes the information on. Dismissed."

The three wizards rose and left the room, Claude returning deeper into the warren of rooms that made up Serrier's lair. Eric and Vincent watched him go, disgust marring their handsome faces. "Does he ever leave?" Vincent muttered. "He's like… Quasimodo or something, hiding his twisted self from the world in here."

"Where else would he go?" Eric asked dismissively. "Anyone else would have him in jail or in a mental institution in a heartbeat. Let's get out of here. We've got a kidnapping to plan." That was not all he had planned, if he was going on what could well be his final mission tomorrow night, but the battle strategy would come first. He could come later.

"Whatever we tell the suspect wizards, I don't think we should tell either of them the truth," Vincent said softly as they walked down the street. "Do you want something to eat before we get started? My cabinets are empty so we'll have to stop somewhere."

Eric paused for a moment and contemplated his own apartment before shaking his head. "I'm pretty sure anything edible I had is now worthy of a school science experiment. What's good near your place? Or would you rather come back to mine? There's a creperie around the corner that's pretty good."

"Crêpes, Eric?" Vincent teased.

"What?" Eric retorted. "I'm from Bretagne. It's comfort food."

Vincent's face sobered. "We need that tonight, don't we?"

"If there's somewhere else you'd rather go…."

Vincent shook his head. “My grandmother used to make crêpes when I was little. Let’s go pretend the world’s as safe now as it was then.”

“Meet me outside my apartment and we’ll walk from there,” Eric suggested. “It’s just a short walk.”

Vincent nodded as they each cast the displacement spell, reappearing outside Eric’s apartment on rue du Hameau. Ten minutes later, they were settled at a table in the café, a bottle of cider between them and their crêpes on the way. Glancing around at the empty room, Vincent leaned forward so they could talk quietly. “Do you have any idea how we’re going to do this?”

“Yeah,” Eric replied slowly. “Ourselves. We’re going to give someone else the command of the patrol and the battle and we’re going to hang back until we can grab a vampire. And as soon as we have one, we’re getting him back to Pascal.”

“Who?” Vincent asked. “I’m not sure who’s left that I trust to watch our backs. I’ll keep fighting as long as there’s a war, but I don’t see how we can keep this up much longer. Chavinier’s decimating our ranks. He’s probably imprisoned more wizards in the past three weeks than since the war began!”

“Which is why Pascal wants us to get him a vampire,” Eric pointed out. “If we don’t find a way to counter the advantage they seem to have created, we’re all dead.”

“Are you really okay with this?” Vincent challenged. “You know what will happen to whatever poor creature we capture.”

“You know what will happen to us if we fail,” Eric reminded him. “I’m still hurting from what he did at the meeting. I’m not eager for a repeat.”

“That was nothing,” Vincent agreed. “It’ll be far worse if we don’t do as he’s ordered.” He sighed. “Sometimes I wonder if it would be worth it to just disappear.”

“And go where?” Eric demanded. “We’re wanted men. Even if Pascal didn’t hunt us down, how long would it be before some little old lady in the apartment next door recognized us and turned us in? We aren’t exactly inconspicuous. I won’t go to prison, Vincent.”

“Would you, though? Get out? If there were a way to be sure?”

Eric snorted derisively. “Find me a way to be sure and then we’ll talk about it. We chose our side. Now we have to make sure we win.”

“Yeah,” Vincent agreed slowly. The arrival of their dinner interrupted the conversation momentarily. When they were alone again, he seemed to have set aside his pensive mood. “We need to figure out how Chavinier’s using the vampires so we can decide where to lie in wait and set our trap. Place Pigalle is too big for the two of us to cover randomly.”

They spent the rest of their meal discussing recent battles and laying their plans. Their crêpes consumed, their coffee savored, they paid the bill and climbed the narrow steps back to street level. “Come home with me?” Eric offered as they walked back toward his apartment.

Vincent grinned. "I thought you'd never ask."

Eric chuckled as he opened the door to his apartment building and led Vincent inside. The bald wizard had been there before, but not since they became lovers, leaving Eric unaccountably nervous. Vincent took the key from his trembling hand and fitted it into the lock, pushing the door open and ushering Eric inside. "Relax," he murmured, pressing a kiss to the side of Eric's neck. "It won't be like last time. I promise."

"I'm not nervous," Eric protested, but the tremor in his voice belied the words.

"Of course you're not," Vincent agreed, his hands burrowing beneath Eric's leather jacket to pull the other man against him. He ground their hips together, feeling the slowly swelling bulge in the dark man's pants. He ran his hands up Eric's back to slide his jacket off, tossing it in the general direction of the coat stand by the door.

Eric shivered in the cool air, but Vincent's hands on his body warmed him quickly, slipping beneath layers of clothes to find the skin of his chest, tweaking at his nipples until his back arched and a gasp escaped his lips. He wanted to return the favor, but his arms refused to obey his mind's feeble commands. Vincent had stolen his wits that quickly.

"Bedroom," Vincent directed authoritatively. "Now."

Eric nodded dumbly and led the way to the one room in the apartment Vincent had never seen before. Until now, he had no reason to bring his friend there. He hesitated on the threshold, but Vincent had no such qualms, pushing Eric gently into the room and shutting the door behind them. "Trust me," he urged, bearing Eric down onto the bed. "Let me show you how good it can feel."

"It felt good the last time," Eric felt compelled to say, not wanting Vincent to feel guilty for the roughness of their first joining.

Vincent just smiled. "This time it'll feel even better." He tugged off Eric's shoes and pants, then straddled his lover to strip his shirt and sweater from him as well, leaving him bare to Vincent's gaze.

Eric let himself be manhandled as Vincent undressed him. Truth be told, he wanted what the other wizard was offering. His body still ached from Serrier's assault, even after the time that had passed and the cider that had taken the edge off. The thought of a lover's touch was comforting, particularly since Vincent seemed determined to keep this interlude as gentle as their first had been wild. Each jolt of lust replaced pain with pleasure, easing his burning nerves and soothing the angry pride within him. Vincent did not think of him any differently now for the spell he had suffered or for the challenge that had earned it. He did not let himself dwell on the possibility of escaping, of simply disappearing and never coming back. That was a pipe dream. But the feel of the big man's hands on his body was real, as was the passion that sparked between them. He needed that passion to wipe away everything else. Tomorrow was soon enough to deal with the rest.

Fingers probing between his legs brought his attention back to the matter at hand, his hips lifting of their own accord into the slick caress. He did not even bother to ask where Vincent had found lube. For all he cared, the other man could have had it in his pocket since that morning. He knew what to expect this time when the invading digits found his prostate, but instead of rushing through the preparation in their haste to get to the final act, Vincent lingered, shunting his finger in and out slowly, teasing the sensitive bump until Eric thought he might come just from those touches.

If they would just stay against his prostate a second or two longer.

He growled in protest, but Vincent ignored him, leaning forward to kiss him tenderly. "I'm not fucking you through the mattress until I know it won't hurt you again," he chided with a smile. "Let me do this right."

Eric subsided slightly, giving control of their lovemaking back to Vincent. His lover stretched him a little bit longer before finally removing his fingers with a last, lingering sweep across Eric's prostate, leaving him trembling and moaning for more. Fortunately, Vincent seemed to have reached the limits of his patience as well. His hand swiped quickly over his own cock before he lined up with the clenching aperture and pushed quickly inside, pausing as soon as the head passed through the still tight ring of muscle.

Eric gasped harshly as his body struggled to accept the new invasion, but the burn faded much more quickly than it had the first time Vincent had taken him this way. Eyes opening to the mind-boggling sight of his friend and lover above him, Eric marveled at the sight of Vincent's face contorted with ecstasy as he fought to stay still, to keep from pounding into Eric's tender ass as roughly as he had the first time.

Reaching up, Eric smoothed away the lines of tension. "Move," he murmured breathily.

Vincent did, starting slowly, his eyes never leaving Eric's face as he sought a rhythm that brought them both pleasure without inflicting any of the inadvertent pain of their first time together. It only took a few seconds before Eric met him thrust for thrust, the powerful body taking all he had to offer and asking for more. Rising to the challenge, Vincent eased up on the iron control he had been exerting, bringing some of his own strength to bear, not to hurt, but to add an additional layer of pleasure. Eric responded, planting his feet against the mattress and pushing up forcefully into each downward movement of Vincent's hips until their groins crashed together with each ingress and they all but separated with each egress.

He almost paused when Eric suddenly collapsed beneath him, but his lover's legs went around his waist, pulling him close with an implacable grip as his arms encircled Vincent's neck, bringing their heads together so their lips met in a passionate, soul-stirring kiss. All hope of control gone, Vincent rocked frantically against Eric, giving in to his passion and striving for the rapture that hovered just out of reach. Eric's fingers dug into his shoulders and Vincent shuddered, his climax tearing through him. Pulling out, he rocked back onto his knees and grabbed Eric's cock, swallowing it down without preliminaries, sucking for all he was worth.

With a hoarse shout, Eric came hard, filling Vincent's mouth and throat with his boiling release, back arching violently with the force of his orgasm. He collapsed on the bed, panting harshly as Vincent settled back beside him.

They did not speak. There was nothing to say, truly, not with their lives under constant threat. The promises they might have whispered at another time, in another place, remained locked in the hearts they were not allowed to have as long as they followed Serrier.

Chapter 30

"HE'S BARELY more than a boy," Vincent muttered as he and Eric watched the young wizard, whom they were supposed to try to trap on the off chance that he was spying for Chavinier. "I feel guilty for bringing him back to Pascal's attention yesterday."

Eric shrugged, though he could sympathize completely. "Pascal hadn't forgotten about him, just his name. He'd have remembered it eventually whether we said anything or not. Monique is the one that bothers me. I suggested Pascal send her to Chavinier to try to spy on him, and now she's a suspect because of it."

Vincent shook his head. "If one of them is the spy—if there really is a spy—they took that chance when they chose their path. And if they aren't the spy, they don't have anything to fear."

Eric snorted. "If only that were true. You know what happened last time. He killed more loyal wizards than spies the last time he went on a witch hunt. And even that debacle wasn't enough to deter someone from switching sides since then."

"We could just not tell them," Vincent suggested softly. "If Chavinier doesn't meet us, Pascal will look elsewhere for his spy."

"And maybe kill someone else instead," Eric reminded him. "Like it or not, they're the two best candidates simply because we know they've had some contact with the Milice since the tide turned in their favor. We have to do this and hope they're smart enough to cover their arses."

"I know," Vincent agreed finally, "but that doesn't mean I have to like it."

"No," Eric replied with a final shrug. "We just have to live with it. You talk to Dominique. I'll find Monique, and then we can be done with it, at least until after the battle when we have to see whose intelligence Chavinier was working with."

Vincent glanced back at the boy hunched down over a cell phone, obviously texting someone. Putain, the kid was young. With a frown, he nodded at Eric and went to plant the message for Chavinier, hoping to hell that Dominique was not the spy. He did not know what he would do if this resulted in the young man's death.

DOMINIQUE GLANCED behind him one last time before stepping into a phone booth near the jardin des Tuileries and dialing the number Chavinier had magically spelled into his memory. Simple was best, Dumont had insisted when they discussed ways for him to pass information to the Milice wizards.

Dominique did not know whose number he dialed, only that it was a Paris number, not a cell phone. Every time he called with information he went to a different payphone, but never one that took him out of his way—so that if anyone was following him, they would not suddenly wonder why he was detouring across town to make a phone call.

Occasionally, no one would answer and he would be invited to leave a message. He never did. Usually, though, Chavinier picked up the phone on the second or third ring, listened to his news, asked a few questions, thanked him, and urged him to be even more careful the next time he called.

Dominique did not need the warning. He could feel the tension rising among Serrier's ranks as Chavinier anticipated more and more of their attacks. Dominique wondered where else Chavinier was getting his information or if the Milice general just had the devil's own luck, because Dominique knew he had not passed on enough information to account for all the foiled attacks.

The phone rang, and again, and a third time. Dominique was almost ready to hang up when Chavinier's voice answered.

"Serrier's planning an attack," Dominique said immediately. "Tonight, in Montmartre."

"He's going after the vampires?" Chavinier's voice betrayed his concern.

"I think so," Dominique agreed. "I wasn't part of the planning. I was just informed to show up tonight at ten for patrol and that we were going to place Pigalle, but I know Serrier's frustrated at how little information he's been able to get about the vampires and the alliance. I overheard him yelling at Edouard, his pet vampire, the other day because he hadn't gotten the information Serrier sent him to find."

"What information did Serrier want?" Chavinier inquired.

"He didn't say, at least not that I heard," Dominique apologized. "I was afraid to hang around too long. When Serrier's in that kind of mood, people get hurt, even when they didn't have anything to do with his bad mood."

"Did the wizard who told you to report for duty tell you how many others were being sent?"

"No," Dominique replied, with an automatic shake of his head. "But he's been increasing the patrol size because of the number of attacks you've countered recently. And I don't know if this means anything or not, but it wasn't my usual patrol leader who ordered me on duty tonight."

"Who was it?" Chavinier asked sharply. "Serrier?"

"No, Vincent Jonnet," Dominique explained. "Big bruiser, bald head, muscles like balloons."

"I know him," Chavinier interrupted. "Be careful, Dominique. Changes in routine like that always make me nervous. This could be a trap for you as much as for the vampires."

"I'll be careful, but I don't think it's anything to worry about," Dominique assured the Milice general. "Serrier's been reorganizing everything recently because he's lost so many people who have been arrested or killed. And the few patrols that have been successful when they've met Milice forces have been that way purely because of numbers."

Chavinier's chuckle could have been interpreted a variety of ways, but Dominique did not ask. The less he knew, the less he could reveal to Serrier if he was discovered. He did not want to see Serrier win and he was proud of doing some small thing toward seeing the dark wizard defeated, but he had no illusions about his own courage in the matter. He knew he would squeal like a stuck pig the moment Serrier started any kind of magical interrogation. He would never be able to hold out against the kind of torture he had seen the dark wizard employ on people who had failed him or whose loyalty he questioned. Dominique just hoped it never came to that.

ORLANDO FLIPPED idly through the magazine in his hands as the RER rattled out toward Versailles. Alain had given him careful directions on how to find Thierry's house from the train station, though in the end Sebastien had simply offered to come get him. It was Sebastien Orlando wanted to see anyway. He had questions for the older vampire—and until he knew what the answers were, it was not a conversation he wanted anyone else to overhear.

He had debated with himself repeatedly since the Piège-Pouvoir and the realizations that came after it. He had committed himself to Alain completely even before he understood what it meant. And that was both the blessing and bane of his current existence. The Aveu de Sang that bound them guaranteed a lifetime of commitment between them, but it also skewed their interactions in ways Orlando was still discovering. He needed advice—blunt, practical, sexual advice—from someone who understood not just his past but also his current situation. Unfortunately, such a vampire did not exist. Jean knew his past as well as anyone did, but he had never had an Avoué and so knew about that bond only in theory. Sebastien had made an Aveu de Sang but knew only sketchy details of Orlando's past. And given the tension between them, he could not suggest talking to them both at the same time. He doubted either of them would be willing to have this sort of intimate conversation with the other present, though they had reached the point of not staring daggers at each other every time they were in the same room.

Even so, Orlando was quietly glad Thierry and Sebastien had not participated in the Piège-Pouvoir. He doubted Jean or Sebastien would have been comfortable with that. Jude was an annoyance and Luc an unknown, but either was better than a rival.

After going back and forth in his head for two days, still so glutted from the feeding at the ritual that he continued to use that excuse for his ongoing hesitation as he and Alain made love, he decided that it would be better to tell Sebastien some portion of his past than to trust to Jean's theoretical knowledge of the effects of an Aveu de Sang. He did not believe Jean would intentionally deceive him or keep anything from him, but he was not convinced his friend would truly understand what he needed to know or have the answers even if he did understand, never having experienced it himself.

Sebastien had previously been willing to talk to Orlando about his bond with Alain, although that had been more in general terms than about any specific issues unique to them. Still, it gave Orlando hope that the older vampire would be willing to help now as well. Orlando had simply said on the phone that he had some questions he wanted to ask, and Sebastien had agreed to meet him at the train station so they could talk.

The train rattled to a stop at his station on the C7 line, and Orlando stepped out of the car onto the sunlit platform. His smile widened as he felt its warmth before the winter wind bit into his cheeks. Even that could not dampen the good mood that came from being free from the constraints his magical nature had imposed on him for so long. He hoped this simple joy never became mundane.

"Orlando!"

Jarred out of his musing by the sound of his name, Orlando turned and saw Sebastien standing just on the other side of the turnstiles, waiting for him. "Sorry," he apologized as he jogged toward the metal barriers and slid his ticket through. "My head was in the clouds."

"So I see," Sebastien joked. "So, you said you wanted to talk. Do you want to go back to Thierry's house or would you be more comfortable talking somewhere else?"

"How's Thierry doing this morning?" Orlando asked before answering. He would prefer the privacy of Thierry's house, but only if their presence would not disturb the recovering wizard.

"He was sleeping when I left," Sebastien replied easily. "He says his cold's getting better, but he still tires easily. He won't disturb us if that's your concern."

"I didn't want to disturb him," Orlando demurred.

"I don't think we will," Sebastien assured him. "If we do, we can always leave again."

Orlando nodded. "Let's do that, then. I don't relish the idea of discussing my personal life sitting in a café where anyone might overhear us."

Sebastien chuckled. "I don't blame you. You were pretty vague on the phone. Is something wrong?" he asked as they walked up the place Raymond Poincaré to the rue Benjamin Franklin where Thierry's house was located.

"Not wrong, exactly," Orlando replied. "It's just… complicated. I don't know how much you know about my past, but it's left me less than comfortable with a lot of things—things that I'm suddenly having to deal with because of my relationship with Alain and the Aveu de Sang. I needed to talk to someone who understands the Aveu de Sang, even if yours wasn't with a wizard."

"I can extrapolate," Sebastien assured him. "After all, my Avoué might not have been a wizard, but my current lover is. I understand the seduction of his magic. With the demands of the Aveu de Sang on top of that, it's a miracle you ever let him out of bed, much less out of your sight." He opened the gate to Thierry's garden, ushering Orlando inside. "We can go inside, or we can sit on the balcony if you want."

"I can't believe I'm saying this given how novel it still is to be able to sit in the sun, but it's a little chilly even for me today. We should probably go inside."

Sebastien laughed. "I'm so glad I'm not the only one who doesn't want to go inside during the day if I have a choice."

"I don't know if everyone would be willing to admit it, but unless they're newly turned, I'm pretty sure there isn't a partnered vampire who feels differently," Orlando replied ruefully. "And it would probably be a huge lure to bring new vampires into the alliance if it were something we were willing to make public."

Sebastien shrugged. "I'll leave those decisions to Chavinier and Bellaiche. So what's going on?"

"Alain wants me to bite him while we're making love," Orlando explained bluntly, "and the thought that I might lose control and hurt him scares me to death."

Sebastien blinked in surprise. "How long ago did you make your Aveu de Sang?" he asked in confusion.

"Three weeks," Orlando replied. "Why?"

"Your control must be phenomenal, both in bed and out," Sebastien said with a shake of his head. "Feeding from him as you make love stabilizes the bond between you, helps extend the amount of time before you need to feed again and gives you more control over your reactions to other vampires where he's concerned. It never occurred to me…. What happened to you exactly, Orlando? Why would you even try to control that urge?"

Orlando looked away, unable to meet Sebastien's questioning gaze as he contemplated trying to explain his past to this vampire he barely knew. Maybe he had made a mistake in choosing Sebastien as a confidant after all.

"Please, Orlando," Sebastien pressed. "I can't help you if I don't know what's driving you. While I know about the Aveu de Sang and about the temptations a wizard presents, I don't know what gave you the strength or the desire to hold back in the way you've obviously done."

"My maker took great pleasure in breaking an innocent boy and turning me into a vampire, then keeping me too weak to fight him. He abused me for over a hundred years before Jean rescued me. By that point, I was too… beaten down to think about any kind of normal relationship. I've fed enough to stay alive, but until Alain, I've never wanted to do anything more than drink what I need and then get away. Every time I touch Alain, a part of me still fears this will be the touch that turns him against me—that this will be the moment when he'll look at me in disgust for trespassing where I'm not wanted."

"That wizard couldn't be more devoted to you if he tried!" Sebastien protested. "I can see it, and I only see his public face. Surely you know how much he loves you."

"Probably not," Orlando replied ruefully. "He's very good about telling me, but it's hard for me to believe it. Not because I don't believe him, but because I have trouble believing anyone could possibly want me. I know, that makes me sound like a pathetic crybaby, but it's a feeling I can't seem to shake."

Sebastien nodded slowly, trying to assimilate Orlando's history. "You can't hurt him," he said finally. "I don't know how else to say it except to promise you that if you ever tried to do something to intentionally hurt him, you wouldn't be able to carry through."

"That's not right," Orlando countered, shaking his head. "I did hurt him once. When I passed out that night and you told him I had to feed, I came awake to the feeling of him holding me down and forcing me to drink. I threw him off the couch and pounced on him. I could taste how much it hurt in his blood."

"Did you know it was him when you pounced?" Sebastien pressed.

Orlando shook his head.

"And when you realized it was him, what did you do?"

"I stopped."

"Exactly," Sebastien said. "As soon as you realized you were hurting your Avoué, you stopped. You didn't think about it. You didn't wonder if you were doing the right thing. You just stopped. You can't hurt him knowingly. You can trip and knock him down by mistake, but if you tried to knock him over intentionally—with foul ends in mind—you wouldn't be able to do it. You wouldn't be able to make your hand connect with his body."

"I'd never do that!" Orlando protested.

"No, I don't think you would," Sebastien agreed, "but that isn't my point. My point is that you don't have to worry about losing control and hurting him. Period. You can't. Your nature, the magical bond between you, whatever—it won't let you. It didn't occur to me that you wouldn't already know that."

Orlando snorted. "My maker wasn't interested in teaching me anything, just in torturing me."

"So what else can I ease your mind about?" Sebastien asked.

Orlando hesitated for a moment before bringing up the other change in his mindset where Alain was concerned. He could talk to Jean about the rest, Jean who had seen him broken and bleeding, who understood how truly shattered Orlando had been. But Jean was not here and Orlando did not know when he would next see the chef de la Cour. "Could he hurt me?" he asked instead, skirting around the subject.

"Why would he do that?"

"I don't think he would, intentionally," Orlando began. "No, I know he wouldn't intentionally, but could he?"

"Orlando, you are far stronger than he could ever dream of being, and his magic won't work on you, so even if he tried to hurt you, you could stop him. You could get away from him. He's not the salaud who made you. You're doing yourself and him a disservice by letting any of those doubts linger in your mind."

Orlando nodded. "Rationally, I know that. It's just not as easy as it should be to get rid of them. Alain is the only lover I've ever had. My only other experience was with Thurloe's rapes. Not exactly conducive to trusting myself to someone else."

So that was the problem, Sebastien realized. "Some men never bottom," he pointed out. "Straight men, for example, but even some gay men never bottom, and not because they've had some terrible experience that keeps them from it. It just doesn't appeal to everyone."

"But the idea of me bottoming appeals to Alain," Orlando explained softly, "and I feel like I'm fighting myself by not giving him what he wants."

"Ah," Sebastien nodded, "yes, I can see that being a problem. Your vampire nature and the Aveu de Sang are urging you to indulge his every whim, while your experience is telling you to fear it. Have you told him this?"

"Not in so many words," Orlando admitted.

"At the risk of sharing secrets that aren't mine to share, Thierry has some of your same fears—without the same reasons," Sebastien revealed. "If Alain has any finesse, he won't just pounce on you and fuck you through the mattress. He'll take his time, preparing you not just the time he actually takes you, but for some days, or even weeks, before that, so that your body gets used to his attentions, so you can learn to relax and enjoy his touch. And then when you're ready, you can take the final step. And if you find it really isn't for you, even with a considerate lover rather than a rapist, tell him. I don't really see him being the kind to pressure you into something you aren't comfortable with. The Aveu de Sang makes you want to indulge him, but you're in a unique situation—and you have to consider your needs too."

The phone rang just then, interrupting their conversation.

"Âllo?" Sebastien answered.

"Sebastien, it's Alain. I know Thierry's still sick, but we need both of you to come to Milice headquarters as quickly as you can. Something's come up. Tell Orlando I'll meet him there instead of at home." Before Sebastien could ask for any more information, Alain had hung up.

Eyebrows raised in surprise, he turned back to Orlando. "We've been summoned, all three of us."

Chapter 31

"WHAT'S GOING on?" Raymond asked as he and Jean walked into Marcel's office. "You said it was urgent."

"Serrier is going after the vampires," Marcel replied. "Or rather, he's planned an attack at place Pigalle. The only reason I can see for him to do that would be to target vampires."

"When?" Jean demanded tightly, mind already racing as he tried to figure out how quickly he could get word to his people to stay inside, away from the clubs and businesses that usually drew them.

"My informant said tonight at ten," Marcel answered evenly. "That doesn't give us a lot of time, unfortunately."

"It's better than no warning at all," Raymond pointed out. "At least we'll be there to counter whatever mischief he intends."

"I fear it's far more than just mischief," Marcel warned. "He's got to realize by now that our increasing victories are thanks to the alliance and the assistance of the vampires. I fully expect our patrols to be sprayed with holy water tonight—and if he bought that, then I imagine we'll run into every other cliché for weakening or controlling vampires, too."

"Fortunately, most of them won't actually hurt us, but that doesn't mean we're completely impervious. He knows we're vulnerable to fire—and the advantage of that is he can hurt anyone with it, not just us," Jean mused aloud. "Do we need to warn the fire department?"

"Their trucks can't do anything against magical fire," Raymond said with a shake of his head. "We'll just have to counter it ourselves. We need to think about what he's going to throw at us based on what he surely believes about vampires, given our own ignorance before the alliance began." As he spoke, he winked at Jean, thinking of the rosary-turned-répère the vampire surely had tucked in his pocket. "I can see him pelting us with garlic cloves, too. That won't hurt anyone, except for maybe a few bruises, but that doesn't mean all his stereotypes will be so generally harmless."

"Garlic, holy water, crucifixes, wooden stakes through the heart, decapitation, invisible in mirrors—although that wouldn't matter to him since it doesn't hurt us, even in old legends," Jean enumerated. "The wooden stake would hurt, but we'd survive if it didn't keep us out until the sun rose. Decapitation is the only one that would, in and of itself, destroy us."

"I have a hard time imagining him creating a spell that would have decapitation as its primary objective," Raymond replied drolly. "Serrier might be known for his cruelty and the pure power of his magic, but he isn't one to create new spells. He doesn't have the patience or the knowledge to do it right."

"Does anyone who follows him?" Marcel asked seriously. "Jean's right that being prepared to counter what he's likely to throw our way is our best defense."

Raymond considered the question for a moment. "Simon Aguirand, maybe," he allowed finally, "but only with enough time and quite a bit of experimentation. I don't know that the few days since we announced the alliance are really enough for him to have mastered something new, particularly not if he was trying for more than one new spell."

"So what would he have focused on?" Marcel mused aloud.

"Fire," Raymond replied immediately. "It would be a variation on an old, but existing spell for starting fires for cooking or heat, and he heard from Jean directly that it was a true weakness of vampires. Beyond that, anything like garlic or crucifixes, or even holy water, that could be thrown is certainly an option since the same spell would launch anything into the air."

A knock on the door interrupted them. "Come in," Marcel called.

Alain walked determinedly through the door. "I talked to Thierry. They're on their way, but they're out in Versailles, so it'll be a few minutes before they can get here."

"Where's Orlando?" Jean asked sharply, the thought of Serrier targeting vampires making him even more protective of his friend than usual.

"With them. He went out to talk to Sebastien. He's coming in now too," Alain replied. "I think they'll be all right. Serrier isn't going to expect to find vampires in the daylight."

"He is going to expect to find them tonight, though," Jean grimaced. "We've got to keep as many of them as possible inside or out of the quartier altogether. Have you called Angélique to warn her? She may want to close tonight so her employees aren't caught in the middle of it. Sang Froid is right off place Pigalle."

"Have you considered that this could be a ploy like the attack at the Tour Eiffel, to draw our forces in one direction while they attack somewhere else?" Alain asked seriously. "It wouldn't be the first time, obviously."

"We can't afford to risk it being a ploy," Jean insisted. "Sure, some spells don't work on us, but others will. If they're caught off guard, the vampires will be easy prey for Serrier's wizards. You're asking me to risk my people—not the ones actively in the alliance, but the ones who didn't come, couldn't come, or didn't find partners. The ones with no defense against whatever Serrier thinks to do tonight. I can't do that. I can't put them unknowingly in the line of fire with nothing to protect them."

"Nor do we expect you to," Marcel interrupted. "That's why I called Thierry back in off medical leave, why Alain's here, why you and Raymond were the first I notified, why Adèle should be here momentarily. I'm calling in every patrol tonight. I can't commit them all to Montmartre just in case it is a ploy, but since he actually did attack the Tour Eiffel the last time, I fully intend to deploy as many people as I can to place Pigalle and the surrounding areas. We'll hold back one patrol in the event of another attack elsewhere, but I won't leave the vampires unprotected. This alliance goes both ways. The vampires are fighting to help us, which means we'll fight to help them. I meant what I said at the press conference to announce the alliance when I told the reporters I considered all magical creatures under the purview of the Milice. The other races have chosen not to be involved, and that is their choice to make, but I won't tolerate a direct threat to anyone because of their involvement with the Milice. So, Alain, Raymond, tell me how we're going to keep Serrier from doing any damage tonight."

"Montmartre," Alain said to the map behind Marcel's desk. Obediently, it focused in on that section of the city. "Where, besides place Pigalle, would the most vampires be on a typical night?" he asked Jean.

Jean rose from his seat to examine the map. "There are clubs and businesses all up and down boulevard de Clichy and boulevard Rochechouart and up toward the place des Abbesses. There are even a few as close to Sacré-Cœur as rue Chappe and rue Gabrielle. And there are vampires residing throughout the entire district."

"Our intelligence specifically named place Pigalle, right?" Alain verified with a glance toward Marcel.

"Correct," the general replied, "but that doesn't mean they're going to limit their attack to that. Just that they intend to strike there."

Alain nodded. "I know, but it gives us somewhere to start. If they intend to attack place Pigalle, then we need to have a strong enough force there to counter them, hopefully to keep them from spreading out beyond there."

"What if they intend to converge there rather than arriving there?" Raymond questioned. "Serrier has used that tactic before, sending a few wizards in at a time and having them all converge on one location. If they do that, they could still inflict quite a bit of damage on innocent bystanders before they get to where we are."

Alain frowned and looked at his watch. "This is why we need Thierry. He's so much better at this than I am."

"He'll be here as soon as may be," Marcel replied. "You said yourself you told him it was urgent. We have a little time. It's not even dark yet, and if Serrier truly is targeting the vampires, it gains him nothing to start a battle at this hour."

"It occurs to me that we're throwing an incredible amount of resources into this defense—and rightly so if the threat is real—on the uncorroborated word of a relatively lowly placed wizard," Raymond observed. "Are we making a mistake here?"

Marcel shrugged. "He hasn't given us unreliable information yet," he pointed out. "The Tour Eiffel battle may have been a feint to draw our attention from the attack at the Palais de Justice, but it was a real attack nonetheless—and the mines they planted at its base would have brought it down if we hadn't stopped them. We'll make sure we have a patrol here in case it is a decoy attack, but we can't afford to hope it's just an attempt on Serrier's part to draw us out."

Another knock sounded at the door. Alain opened it, relieved to see Orlando, Thierry, and Sebastien on the other side. He smiled at his best friend and Sebastien, then turned to study Orlando's face. He did not know what had been so important that Orlando felt the need to go all the way out to Versailles to talk with the other vampire, but whatever it had been, it seemed the conversation had eased Orlando's concerns. His face was serene as he met Alain's eyes, a hint of promise in the dark gaze. Alain felt himself reacting to his lover's expression, his cock hardening as he wondered what Orlando had in store for them.

"So what's going on?" Thierry asked, seeing the map of Montmartre on the wall behind Marcel and the serious expressions on the faces around the room. "It's obviously something big."

Marcel quickly brought the new arrivals up to speed.

Thierry frowned and studied the map. "If I were planning this, I wouldn't arrive at place Pigalle even if that was my destination. Too open."

"Where would you come in?" Jean asked curiously, wondering if Thierry had the grasp of strategy to be a competent player of le jeu des Cours.

"Here and here and here and here," Thierry said, pointing to four small squares north of place Pigalle. "There's enough room for more than one wizard to arrive at a time so they aren't vulnerable to instant attack, but out of the way enough that they wouldn't be immediately noticed by someone trying to defend my main target. And if, as you suggest, the main target is the vampires themselves, then this spreads them out to make a more effective net."

"Does the Milice have enough patrols to put one in each of those locations?" Sebastien inquired. "That way, wherever Serrier does attack, we're ready."

"I wouldn't do that either," Thierry replied immediately. "If we're that concentrated, we risk alerting him to our presence. Better to spread ourselves out throughout the district so that wherever they arrive, we're ready for them. We can put higher numbers in place Pigalle, place des Abbesses and place du Tertre so that we have a greater chance of catching them as they arrive, but we don't want to count on that. We need to be ready to protect as much of the area as possible."

"I'll take my patrol to place Pigalle," Alain offered. "We know he's coming there eventually, and we'll be ready for him when he gets there. It's also where there will be the most vampires, isn't that what you said, Jean?"

Jean nodded.

"Good," Thierry said, making a note on the map. "I can split my patrol between place des Abbesses and the surrounding streets. We'll send Adèle's patrol to the place du Tertre and south from there, and then scatter another three patrols through the smaller places and streets."

"I don't think so," Alain interrupted, "or have you forgotten that you're on medical leave?"

"Not to mention that you're still sick," Sebastien added disapprovingly. "You've hardly been able to get out of bed in three days."

"I'm out of bed now," Thierry replied, voice hard. "And having a cold hardly keeps me from doing magic. We need every wizard we can spare and I'm still the best strategist the Milice has. If things go sideways during the fight, you'll need me there."

"Not at the risk of your magic," Alain protested.

"We all risk our lives every time we fight," Thierry reminded him. "The only reason I wasn't back on active duty as soon as the wild magic was dealt with is this damn cold. It's annoying, but it's not enough to keep me from fighting tonight."

"Will you let a medic look you over?" Marcel intervened.

Thierry nodded.

"Will you accept a medic's conclusions, Alain?" Marcel pressed.

Alain frowned, but nodded. If the medic gave Thierry a clean bill of health, there was really nothing more he could say since, honestly, he would rather have his friend fighting at his side.

"Then let's get you to the infirmary."

"IS everything all right?" Alain asked Orlando when they reached his and Thierry's office.

Orlando nodded, pulling Alain into his arms immediately and kissing him hungrily.

"Thierry and Sebastien will be here in a few minutes," Alain protested weakly.

"Then I guess I shouldn't strip you naked and make love to you, should I?" Orlando teased, his lips skating across Alain's neck. "I'll just have to settle for taking the edge off now and making love to you properly when we get home tonight."

Alain's entire body clenched as lust flooded through him. He had no idea what had gotten into Orlando, but this was yet another new side to his lover. He tilted his head back, offering his neck as he had offered his heart. Immediately, Orlando's fangs found the brand beneath his ear and drove deep, his hands flying over Alain's clothed form, caressing all the wizard's sensitive places through the fabric.

Alain's head spun at the dual assault of Orlando's fangs in his neck and his hands on his body. Never before had the vampire been so bold in touching him as he fed. Could it mean he had finally set aside his reservations? Alain's knees went weak at the thought and he grabbed at Orlando to keep from falling.

Sensing his instability, Orlando's hands slid lower, closing over the globes of his buttocks, steadying him as he backed them toward the desk so Alain would have something to lean against. Alain collapsed against it gratefully, his head tipping back even further as he rubbed eagerly against Orlando's hip.

Hands free again now that Alain was no longer in danger of falling, Orlando ran one hand up his lover's back and into his hair, fingers playing with the short strands, while his other worked open the wizard's trousers, slipping beneath the waistband of his boxers to encircle the hard shaft. Alain's long, low moan was as arousing to Orlando as the taste of lust and love in his blood. Determined to give his lover this much at least before they had to fight, Orlando tightened his grip and stroked with more vigor as he drew deeply on the wizard's neck.

"Orlando," Alain whispered, his voice praise and plea in one. Orlando almost lifted his head, but he had promised Alain that he would bite him the next time they made love. This was not exactly how he had envisioned it, but that did not matter. He intended to keep his promise now—and again later when they had the time and privacy to explore the new dynamic fully. He pulled Alain more tightly against him, the hand that had been playing with the wizard's hair sliding down his back and inside his loosened pants. He was tempted to turn Alain around and drive into him hard and fast now, but they could be interrupted at any moment. Granted, it would be Thierry and Sebastien, who would certainly understand and probably even approve, but he did not want to be interrupted midthrust any more than he wanted to be interrupted with his fangs buried in his Avoué's neck. He contented himself with squeezing one firm cheek, then the other, his fingers dragging along the crevice between them so that Alain could not misinterpret the fact that he had finally set aside his fears of combining feeding and sex.

Alain bucked forward when he felt the direction of Orlando's wandering hand. He wanted to reciprocate the caresses he was receiving, slip his hand inside Orlando's jeans and stroke him as well—but this was new territory and he dared not trespass, not when they would not have time to deal with any potential misunderstandings before the battle preparations began. The last thing he wanted was to go into battle with angry recriminations between them.

His fingers dug into Orlando's shoulders as he climaxed with a long, drawn-out shudder. To his surprise, he felt Orlando tense against him and then suddenly go lax as well. The fangs in his neck drove deeper for a moment, but that only increased the sense of connection Alain felt. He tangled one hand in Orlando's dark hair, holding his head in place for a moment, silently assuring his lover that even the deeper penetration was welcome.

"Let us know when we can come in," Thierry's laughing voice teased through the door.

Alain jerked in surprise at the sound. He had been so caught up in what Orlando was doing that he had not even felt Thierry's approach. Slowly, Orlando lifted his head and met Alain's eyes, kissing his lips tenderly. "We'll talk when we get home tonight," he promised, seeing the question in his lover's eyes. "For now, we have a battle to fight."

"I love you," Alain said softly, caressing Orlando's cheek with the tip of one finger before beginning to straighten his clothes.

"I love you, too," Orlando replied with a tender smile. He waited until Alain had finished righting himself and casting a quick cleaning spell, then opened the door to let Thierry and Sebastien in.

Chapter 32

JUST BEFORE dusk, the Milice patrols began moving into position, Thierry having been cleared for duty again after the medic's exam. He moved back and forth constantly between the various squares, making sure everyone was situated according to plan. Alain had everything under control in place Pigalle, within sight of the Moulin Rouge. Adèle's patrol had secured the place du Tertre and surrounding streets. Raymond and Jean wandered the streets on the lookout for vampires, warning them to get inside and stay inside until tomorrow night. A light mist hazed the dimly lit, narrow streets, bringing a frown to Thierry's face as he considered the potential complications posed by the weather. If the fog deepened, it could make it harder to distinguish friend from foe.

One by one, Jean went into the vampire-run businesses on place Pigalle and places des Abbesses, explaining to the horrified owners what was likely to happen a few hours hence.

"So what do you want us to do?" Laetitia Bastian asked immediately.

"Close for the night," Jean told her. "I know it's lost revenue, but that's better than damage from a wizard attack and dead or injured customers because they came here thinking it would be safe."

Laetitia frowned. "You shouldn't have brought this war here. You've endangered us all." As she spoke, she began lowering the shutters on the café windows.

"Think what you want of me," Jean replied. "When this is over and we have the protection of the law for the first time ever, you won't even remember one night of danger."

She glared at him but locked the door, hanging a closed sign on it before pointedly waiting for him to leave so she could shut it behind him.

Fortunately for his patience, most of the other vampires required very little persuasion to shut their doors for the night to avoid presenting easy targets to the dark wizards. Jean did not think Serrier had done enough research into the habits of the Cour to know which businesses to attack without some indication of the intended patrons. Other than Sang Froid, a closed business should be of no interest to the dark wizards—and with Alain and his patrol all around place Pigalle, Sang Froid was as protected as it could be.

They kept an eye out for dark wizards who might have been sent ahead to secure insertion points for the full patrol, but they did not see anything suspicious. The Milice wizards did their best to blend in with the local inhabitants returning home for the evening, stopping at the boulangerie to buy bread or at the café for a glass of wine before going home.

The rush hour crowds thinned as the hour grew later, leaving only the Milice operatives wandering the streets. Finally, the hour for the attack neared and Thierry began passing the word for the wizards to conceal their presence. One by one, they pulled back into shadowed doorways or dark alleys, until only a few wizards and vampires remained visible, no apparent threat to anyone. He had just stepped into his own position to wait when he saw Mireille and Caroline hurrying into the square. Their faces were set, at odds with the dresses they wore. He moved back into sight to intercept them.

"Did Marcel change Milice dress code without telling anyone?" he joked. "I'm not sure I have a dress fine enough to match yours."

Caroline flipped him off, a smile threatening despite the seriousness of the situation. "We were off duty, on our way out for the evening, when we heard about the attack. There wasn't time to change if we wanted to get here in time to be of any help."

"You didn't have to come," Thierry began.

"Yes, we did," Mireille interrupted. "He's targeting vampires. Uninvolved vampires. If vampires don't help defend them, what good is the alliance?"

Thierry nodded. "Your patrol isn't here—Marcel kept them back in fear of another attack elsewhere—so you can stick with mine or you can head down to Alain in place Pigalle. We've got about even numbers in both locations."

"Then we may as well stay here," Caroline said. "It's getting close to ten and we're a little less inconspicuous than usual."

"Over there, then," he directed. "In front of the café. If you stand close enough together, you'll look like a couple out for the evening, pausing for a private moment in the shadows."

Mireille and Caroline nodded and crossed the square quickly, adopting the pose of lovers in a clinch as they waited for the battle to begin.

A few minutes before ten, Eric and Vincent arrived at place d'Anvers. They came quietly out of the subway, muffled in heavy coats and thick scarves to conceal their identities. If they were more bundled up than the average commuter, no one gave them a second glance, for the wind was chilly and the night damp. The two men walked deliberately down boulevard Rochechouart with the unassuming confidence of people who have every right to be where they are. They made it as far as the rue des Martyrs before someone called out to them, warning them to turn back or hurry home, depending on their destination.

"Is there a problem?" Eric asked, his voice muffled by the scarf around his face.

"Not yet," the wizard replied, "but there could be at any moment. We don't want innocent bystanders caught in the cross fire."

Eric and Vincent nodded. "Thanks for the warning," Vincent offered warmly. "We live just around the corner on rue Houdon. We'll get there and inside as quickly as we can."

The wizard motioned them through, watching until they turned up rue Houdon as they had said. He did not see them pull back into a building and cast an invisibility spell over themselves so they could watch the battle unseen as they waited for the perfect opportunity to carry out their part of the plan.

The sound of fighting rang out suddenly as dark wizards streamed onto the parvis du Sacré-Cœur and down rue Chappe, engaging the Milice wizards they met in a furious exchange of spells. Raymond grinned at their ignorance when floods of water washed over them, soaking them to the skin and leaving the streets slick in their wake, but otherwise doing no damage. "Seems Serrier's even more gullible where old legends are concerned than the Milice is," he joked to Jean before turning his attention to meeting their attackers head-on.

Jean shook his head and backed into a doorway until the nearest dark wizard ran past. He snagged the man's jacket, spinning him around so he could see his attacker's face before snapping his neck and dropping him to the ground. These were not simply enemy combatants anymore. They intended to attack his people—his defenseless people—using fair methods and foul. He had no qualms about dropping them where they stood. Vaulting into the air, he caught the edge of a wrought iron balcony, waiting for another opportunity. When the flood of dark wizards slowed beneath Raymond's onslaught, Jean saw his chance, jumping with acrobatic grace into the middle of the fray and taking out three more dark wizards before jumping away again

In place Pigalle, Alain stepped out of the shadows. "Hold your position," he ordered his patrol. "We know they're coming here. Adèle and Thierry will provide backup to the north."

Almost before he was done speaking, more dark wizards arrived from the south, pouring into the square from rue Frochot and rue Jean-Baptiste Pigalle. Alain turned to confront them, Orlando stepping to his side, ready to meet whatever threat came their way. He knew they were the bait, out in the open that way. His lover's stature would draw them in and then the rest of the patrol would close the door behind them, trapping the dark wizards in the square and forcing them to fight.

The spells began almost immediately, soaking them in holy water as the dark wizards had done to the north. Alain ducked behind the bushes in the center of the square, pulling Orlando with him as the rest of his patrol took up the fight, countering the more dangerous spells that followed. "Give them a minute to draw attention away from us and we'll rejoin the fight," he promised when he saw the scowl on Orlando's face.

Seeing the wisdom of that course of action, Orlando nodded and waited as patiently as he could while Lt. Fouquet and the other members of Alain's patrol engaged the dark wizards in the square. He counted about thirty altogether, slightly greater than Alain's number of twenty wizards, but that did not take into account the vampires who were also scattered around the battle. Nor Angélique and David and a few others who did not belong to any assigned patrol but who had chosen to be here nonetheless. As he watched, David took down a wizard headed straight for Angélique and the entrance to Sang Froid. He could not stop a slight chuckle at the volley of garlic cloves launched in her direction.

In the place des Abbesses and surrounding streets, Thierry listened to the sounds of battle beginning, both to the north and south of his current position. "Which way do you want us to go?" Sebastien asked him urgently, itching for battle. While he did not have Jean's sense of responsibility to the Cour as a whole, he understood the threat Serrier posed to those less aware of it and could not imagine simply sitting back and letting others face it alone.

"Neither," Thierry cautioned, sensing his partner's edginess. "Just because those two groups have come in doesn't mean that's all yet. We'll give them another few minutes and then we'll move."

"You can't just expect us to sit here doing nothing while they fight!"

"We aren't doing 'nothing.' We're doing our job of protecting the businesses here. Once we're sure there isn't a threat here, we'll be free to protect our friends, too," Thierry reminded him.

Before Sebastien could reply, Adèle sprinted into the place des Abbesses. "They're pushing south, down rue Chappe. We can cut them off if we hurry."

At a single gesture from Thierry, half his patrol split off, following Adèle toward the intersection of rue Chappe and rue des Trois Frères. They joined the retreating patrol, Raymond passing off the command to Adèle. "Place des Abbesses is still quiet, as is place du Tertre," she reported quickly, "but I could hear fighting down toward place Pigalle."

One look at Jean's face told Raymond all he needed to know. "Can you handle these goons?" he asked Adèle.

Her smile bordered on cruel. "Just watch me."

Raymond gave her a swift nod. "We're going south. They're all yours."

"They'll never know what hit them."

Raymond had no doubt that was true as he heard her order the wizards with her to spread out across the intersection, blocking any forward progress the dark wizards might make. They would find themselves facing a wizarding firing squad if they continued on their current path. Hearing her next order to her partner and some of the other pairs, he knew they would continue on their path, pushed into her trap by the vampires' flanking move.

Back in place des Abbesses, the other half of Thierry's patrol looked to him, waiting for their new orders. "Let's go help Alain."

With a cheer, they followed him down rue des Abbesses to rue Houdon and place Pigalle, bursting into the square to add their numbers to Alain's patrol.

In the darkness, Eric and Vincent frowned, though neither could see the other's expression. The odds had just tipped against them with both Dumont and Magnier in the same place. They would have to be even more careful if they intended to snag a vampire without getting caught themselves. Eric reached for where he knew Vincent to be, finding a hard shoulder and urging his partner to move with him closer to the fight. They moved on silent feet to the edge of the square right by the metro stop. Eric kept his hand on Vincent's arm so he would not lose track of him.

As they watched, Magnier came out from behind the bushes, firing spells as fast as he could shout them. The man at his side, however, carried no wand. "There, with Magnier," Vincent whispered, his lips brushing Eric's ear. "Is that a vampire?"

Eric observed for a moment longer as Alain engaged one of the dark wizards and the dark-haired stranger came up from the side so swiftly they could barely follow, catching his wrist and wrenching it behind his back. "It must be," Eric replied in the same low tone as the blond wizard cast a binding spell at his captured foe. "Why didn't his spell work on both of them, though?" he asked when he observed the vampire walk away from the dark wizard.

"I don't know," Vincent muttered. "We know magic can work on them. We used it on Edouard when we first took him to Pascal."

"We'll just have to hope Magnier somehow tailored his spell," Eric replied. "Otherwise, we're in trouble."

"He's hardly moving from Magnier's side. This isn't going to work if we can't separate them," Vincent warned. "As alert as he is during a battle, he'll sense the spell and stop it."

"We'll just have to wait for an opening," Eric decided. "They can't stay that close the entire time."

It seemed they were wrong, though, because each time Magnier moved to engage a wizard, the vampire was right beside him, rarely more than arm's length away. "Maybe we should target someone else?" Vincent asked after several more minutes.

"Who?" Eric whispered. "Every vampire I can identify is just as close to some other wizard. We're not likely to catch Dumont off guard any more than we are Magnier. And I think I saw Payet in the fray. You know we'll never get past him."

"We'll be the ones on the torture block if we come back empty-handed."

Before Eric could reply, a chance spell from Richard Lapeyre hit Magnier in the side, sending him to the ground. Eric and Vincent both tensed, waiting to see if this was their opportunity.

Orlando did not hear the words of the spell that hit Alain, but he saw his lover stumble and fall to his knees. Rage surged through him, as strong as any he had ever felt, stronger even than his anger at his creator. He could see Alain struggling to his feet, Thierry at his side, so he knew his lover would be all right. Orlando's current concern was taking out the man who had dared to attack his wizard.

Lapeyre crowed in triumph when he saw Magnier go down. His spell would not hurt the man permanently, more's the pity, but it would allow him to escape. His sense of victory lasted until he saw a slim, dark figure bearing down on him. He cast an *Abattoire*, watched the spell hit, but his attacker did not even slow. Beginning to panic, Richard opened his mouth to cast a displacement spell, but the words never had a chance to form as hands closed around his throat, cutting off his breath.

"No one hurts my partner," Orlando growled in the dark wizard's ear, snapping his neck in a casual move.

"Now!" Eric shouted, dropping the invisibility shield and casting a binding spell at the vampire, catching him before Lapeyre's body could drop from his grip. Next to him, Vincent also reappeared, a displacement spell following immediately on the heels of Eric's spell. It caught both the vampire and the dead wizard, sending them out of the square and to a safe location. "Let's get the fuck out of here," he added as every head in place Pigalle turned their way.

Eric did not bother to reply, simply casting another displacement spell on himself and Vincent, the sound of Alain's anguished howl following him all the way back.

Chapter 33

ALAIN DRAGGED himself to his feet. "Go after them!" he screamed to Thierry, too unsteady on his feet to do more than sway back and forth.

Thierry glanced between the empty space where Orlando had stood moments before and his obviously injured best friend. He took a step toward Alain, a lifetime's habit of backing up his friend winning over even his concern for anyone in Serrier's hands. "Go after them!" Alain repeated, his balance giving out. He fell to his knees again even as Thierry reached his side. "Please," he begged, tears clumping his lashes from the pain in his side and from the undeniable reality that Orlando was now in the hands of the dark wizards. "I can't do it and I don't trust anyone else."

Thierry shook his head. The precious seconds it had taken him to agree could well be too many already, but he would do what he could. "Keep Sebastien safe."

Alain nodded, collapsing onto the sandy path through the center of the square, wand in hand as he focused on doing as Thierry asked. Thierry sprinted to the spot where they had last seen Orlando, chanting rhythmically as he tried to identify the fading magical signature. He blinked out, giving Alain hope that Orlando would soon be back where he belonged.

The pain in his side had faded to a dull ache, but he knew he needed to get it looked at. Under any other circumstances, he would have already headed back to Milice headquarters, but he could not leave. Not now with Orlando missing and Thierry searching for him. He could not do that to his lover or to the other wizards who looked to him for guidance in Thierry's absence. He would simply have to hold out until Thierry and Orlando returned.

"Fire!"

Alain's head spun around as he searched out the source of the call. All along boulevard Clichy, tongues of flame licked at the stone edifices. "Fouquet!" Alain shouted. "Get it out!" His lieutenant nodded and led the patrol toward the building blaze, the entire complement of wizards casting dampening spells to keep the fire from spreading as well as to put out the existing flames.

"Where did Thierry go?" Sebastien demanded, appearing at Alain's side.

"To find Orlando, I hope," Alain replied, eyes never stilling as he sought more foes. Where before, he had done his best to disarm and contain the dark wizards, now he focused his rage and fear into *Abbatoires*, his voice harsh as he cast spell after spell. "The dark wizards took him," he added when he paused again to catch his breath, "and I'm hurt too badly to go after him."

"Then what are you still doing here?" Sebastien scolded. "Get back to the infirmary."

Alain shook his head, though the increasing throbbing in his side told him Sebastien's advice was wise. "Not until I know Orlando's safe. I can direct the battle from here."

Sebastien frowned as all around the square, wizards began disappearing, shooting bursts of magical fire as they did.

"Merde!" Alain cursed. Bodies littered the ground, dead, wounded, or bound. "Raymond!" he shouted. "Where's Adèle?"

"North of here, rue Chappe."

"We've got to get these fires out or it won't matter that we won the battle."

Raymond nodded. "I'll get them down here. Keep the center of the place clear so we have a spot to arrive." He blinked out before Alain could reply.

"Help me up," Alain asked Sebastien. "If the whole patrol arrives at once, I'll be stomped on for sure."

Seconds later, Raymond reappeared with Adèle's patrol in tow. "The fires are already out north of us. We just have to contain these."

And get Orlando back, Alain thought. Adèle's patrol did not wait for his orders, spreading out across the square and down the surrounding streets to help Alain's and Thierry's beleaguered patrols.

"Where's Orlando?" Jean asked, finally arriving at Alain's side. "I lost track of him during the fighting."

Alain bit his lip, struggling to contain the helpless rage that churned inside him. With each minute that passed, the likelihood of Thierry finding and rescuing Orlando decreased. He only prayed he had not lost his best friend as well as his lover.

"Dark wizards took him," Sebastien replied when Alain did not speak. "Thierry's gone after them."

Jean blanched and swayed on his feet. Without even considering that he might be rebuffed, Sebastien reached out to steady the chef de la Cour. "How long has he been missing?" Jean forced himself to say calmly, pushing down the lump of fear in his throat.

"Ten minutes," Alain replied hoarsely.

Thierry reappeared alone before Jean could ask the next question.

Alain's face fell and only Sebastien's supporting arm kept him from tumbling back to the paving stones. "What happened?"

"I followed their first jump," Thierry recounted, "which took me to the parc de la Courneuve, but they didn't cast their next spell from the same spot. I searched the surrounding area to make sure they weren't there hiding, but I couldn't find anything, including any trace of where they cast the next displacement spell."

"Assuming they did," Alain said, voice cracking. "It was Eric and Vincent. With Orlando bound, either one of them could have simply swung him over their shoulder and carried him out of the park."

"We can take a patrol and search a wider area," Thierry offered, though he knew it was probably already too late. If he had acted sooner, perhaps he could have followed them, but his indecision had cost them greatly.

"I'm going with you," Jean insisted.

Thierry nodded. "I expected you would. Alain, did Orlando have his repère with him?"

"I think so," Alain replied, hope lightening his eyes again. "I made him promise to keep it on him at all times, just in case."

"Good. Maybe we can find him that way. Can you get back on your own?"

"I don't think so," Alain replied honestly.

Thierry frowned. "Stubborn fool," he muttered. "Jean, tell Raymond where we're going so he can join us if he wants, or at least not worry if he needs to stay here. Sebastien, round up as many of my patrol as you can find. And you, Alain, are going to let the medics take care of you."

"We need to call in to see where his repère is."

"I'll do that," Thierry promised. He could feel precious time ticking by as he waited for Sebastien and Jean to return. Orlando might have been Alain's lover, not his, but he had grown to like the vampire once he got past his initial reservations. Even if he had not, he would not wish Serrier's brand of torture on anyone—even Serrier himself. He grabbed his phone and called Marcel.

"Chavinier."

Thierry explained the situation quickly.

"He's not on the map," Marcel said, concern lacing his voice.

"Widen the view. Check all of Île-de-France."

"I did. I pulled it all the way back. He's not showing anywhere."

"Putain. Okay, we'll try this the old-fashioned way." He turned to Alain. "Don't panic, but Marcel can't find him on the map. Raymond said Serrier knew about the repères and was trying to find a way to block them. Maybe he finally succeeded."

"And maybe we're too late."

"Stop," Thierry ordered. "The repères for the vampires are tied to the object, not the vampires themselves. Maybe Serrier destroyed the ring. He's done that in the past when he's captured people. Don't give up."

"Close your eyes," Sebastien said before Alain could say anything else. "Quell your panic and concentrate on Orlando."

Alain struggled to do as the vampire requested.

"Can you sense him at all? If he hasn't been destroyed, you should still be able to feel the bond."

"Yes," Alain said slowly.

"Then wherever Serrier's taken him, he's at least still with us. Let the medics take you back to the infirmary. We'll search and hopefully find him."

"Do what Sebastien said," Thierry reiterated. "Trust me to do this."

"I wouldn't trust anyone else."

"Adèle!" Thierry shouted. "Can you take care of things here?"

Adèle turned, long ponytail flipping over her shoulder. She waved for him to go, but before he could, Raymond was at his side. "I want to check out some of Serrier's old hideouts, see if he's taken to using any of them again. I can't take Jean with me, but I'd rather not go alone."

"I'll go," Sebastien volunteered immediately. Thierry frowned, not wanting to let Sebastien out of his sight now that they knew Serrier was hunting vampires.

"I'll keep him safe," Raymond promised before the blond wizard could protest. "I'm not going to fight, just to look. If I see anything worth investigating, I'll go back to base for a patrol, but I'm less likely to trip any lingering wards if I go with just one vampire as backup."

Jean itched to get started, needing to be doing something to help find Orlando, but he understood the concern pushing Thierry. He felt the same concern at the thought of Raymond going off without him. He met Sebastien's gaze steadily. The other vampire stared back before nodding slightly, the silent exchange enough to reassure him that Sebastien would watch Raymond's back even while Raymond protected him.

"We'll be back in an hour," Raymond told Thierry and Jean before taking Sebastien's arm and casting the displacement spell.

"Let's go," Thierry ordered, his patrol winking out.

As soon as Thierry's patrol reappeared in the parc de la Courneuve, he ordered them to spread out, on alert, fanning through the park in search of any sign of Orlando or the dark wizards. As long as it had been since Orlando had been taken, he doubted they would find any magical signatures remaining. Perhaps if they were careful they could find some physical trace to guide them in their search. He wished Alain were well enough to accompany them, on the off chance his bond could guide them in actually sensing Orlando's direction, in addition to knowing Orlando had not been destroyed. As it was, they would do the best they could.

"Thierry!"

The wizard turned, hearing his name. "Look at this," Jean called.

Going to the vampire's side, Thierry examined the sandy ground. "Something heavy was set down here, maybe even dragged a little," Jean said excitedly. "Is there any way to tell if it was the dark wizards?"

Thierry nodded and closed his eyes, chanting lightly, scrying for magical signatures. His stomach churned as he recognized the aura that had once been as familiar to him as Alain's was. "It was them," he agreed. "They were definitely here, but I can't detect any magic to get them out of here."

"Then we search using nonmagical means," Jean declared, eyes scanning the ground as he searched for any sign to show which way they had gone.

Thierry nodded and moved in the opposite direction, but he could see nothing that would indicate which way the wizards had gone. Jean's sharper night vision picked up a trail, but even that petered out quickly when the sandy path changed to stone. Thierry tried scrying again, but he could not distinguish any trace of magic or anything else to indicate where the two wizards had gone or indeed if that was even their trail.

"Fuck, fuck, fuck, fuck," he cursed, sinking to his knees in frustration. He felt like he was letting Alain down by not being able to find Orlando. His best friend had trusted him with this task, and he was coming up empty-handed. He grounded his hands in the earth and let his frustration pour out of him into the ground until the stone glowed with his power, but even with that connection in place, the stone could not tell him what he needed to know. He knew Eric was not tied to the earth to have left a trace in the stones, and if Vincent was, he had not used his magic here. With the connection still in place, though, Thierry stretched his senses as far as he could, sinking deeper and deeper into a trance as he searched for any magical signature, any trace however small, that might give them a direction for continued searching.

A sharp slap across his face drew him back to himself.

He glared up at Jean. "What the hell was that for?"

"You were swaying like you were about to fall over and you didn't answer me when I called you. I swear, you looked like you were turning to stone. I didn't know how else to bring you back," Jean explained defensively.

"How long was I out?" Thierry asked.

"Fifteen minutes."

Thierry frowned. "Thanks," he said, getting gingerly to his feet, all his joints feeling stiff, almost melded. "That could have gotten dangerous." He walked around slowly for a few moments until the stiffness faded. He was beyond frustrated at not being able to find anything useful, but losing himself in the search would serve no purpose either. If Orlando truly was gone, Alain would need every friend he had left to survive that blow. "I… um… I don't suppose you *have* to tell Sebastien about what just happened, do you?"

"Why wouldn't I?" Jean asked seriously.

"Because he'd probably have a few things to say about unnecessary risks."

Jean regarded Thierry seriously. "You're searching for the closest friend I have," he reminded the wizard. "I'm not likely to consider much unnecessary. Nor am I likely to do anything to make your life more difficult when you're trying to help. If you'd rather I not say anything, I won't, but you should probably tell him yourself, if only so he can watch to keep it from happening again."

"There's no need to worry him. I've been keeping myself in check for over twenty years," Thierry demurred.

Jean arched an eyebrow. “That didn’t help you tonight. He’d rather know a danger facing you than lose you because he wasn’t prepared to counter something. Did you learn anything?”

Thierry shook his head. “Let’s hope Raymond and Sebastien had better luck.”

RAYMOND KICKED a stone against the wall of the empty cellar beneath an unprepossessing apartment building just off the avenue de Stalingrad. It clattered across the floor, rattling a couple of times before settling in a spiderweb-infested corner in silent accusation. He and Sebastien had been in a dozen similar buildings all around the outskirts of Paris, and in every one the situation had been the same.

Deserted.

Whether Serrier or his agents still owned the buildings, Raymond could not say—but he had found no trace of any magic anywhere, nothing to suggest that they continued as even safe houses for Serrier’s wizards, much less as active bases.

“It’s like he’s abandoned every location I knew anything about,” Raymond observed in frustration. “While I see the logic behind that, it makes me wonder where he’s hiding now and how he had the resources to acquire new properties. Even in the banlieues, real estate isn’t cheap. None of the buildings we’ve visited have been occupied by anyone else, so he doesn’t appear to be selling them off. Just leaving them.”

“You didn’t know where his funds came from when you worked with him?” Sebastien asked.

Raymond shook his head. “It didn’t occur to me to ask when I first joined his cause, and later, once I started having my doubts, I kept my mouth shut to avoid drawing attention to myself. Dissent is not a quality he appreciates.”

“You survived,” Sebastien commented.

“Only because Marcel took me in,” Raymond insisted. “On my own, he’d certainly have found me and killed me by now. He’d like to.”

“What’s he doing to Orlando?” Sebastien felt compelled to ask.

Raymond frowned. “Don’t ask.”

Sebastien caught the wizard’s arm and pulled him so they were facing each other. “What’s he doing to Orlando?”

Raymond’s face hardened as he remembered the way Serrier had dealt with prisoners and traitors in the past. “Right now, he’s asking questions, trying to see if Orlando can be persuaded to change sides, or at least to give up what he knows. When that doesn’t work, he’ll probably use him as a test subject. He’s got to be frustrated that certain spells don’t work on vampires, so he’ll want to know which ones do. He won’t start with anything that would kill a mortal since he’ll want to get as much information out of the experiment as possible. He’ll start with other spells—spells that cause pain, bleeding, that sort of thing—so he can find the vampires' weaknesses. And when he's done with that, he'll either start in on the ones that should kill or he'll turn him over to one of his henchmen who has a taste for torture."

Sebastien shuddered. "We've got to get him out of there, because he's got an additional weakness the rest of us don't. He can't feed to recover between bouts of torture, like the rest of us could. Anyone's blood besides Alain's will make him worse, not better."

Raymond snorted in frustration. "I don't know what else to do besides what I'm already doing. I've searched every foxhole I know of and a few that were just rumors, and there's nothing here to give me the slightest clue where they are now."

"What about the two wizards who took him?" Sebastien suggested. "They have homes somewhere. Can we stake them out, try to follow them when they leave?"

"We can try," Raymond replied, "but that assumes they arrive and leave on foot rather than magically. Their residences will be warded against intruders, so we'd have to watch from outside, but we might see something useful. I'll suggest it to Marcel when we get back to base, if Thierry hasn't had any more luck than we have."

Chapter 34

HAVING CRISSCROSSED their way around Paris, making sure to run at least a block between each arrival and departure point, Eric and Vincent finally arrived back in St. Denis at Serrier's current headquarters. Their hostage glared at them as he had since they first grabbed him in the parc de la Courneuve, Eric throwing him over his shoulder in a fireman's hold as he and Vincent sprinted out of the park and onto the avenue de Stalingrad. Eric had considered running for the old safehouse he knew was nearby, but he had seen Payet at the battle, and he had known about that location. Instead, they had disappeared from the middle of the street, trusting it would take long enough for the Milice forces to get there that their magical signatures would have dissipated, even if anyone could pinpoint where they had disappeared from.

Entering the building, they wended their way through the winding corridors until they reached Serrier's office. "It's good to see I still have some followers capable of carrying out orders," the bearded wizard drawled when he saw the burden his two lieutenants carried. "Was he a bystander?"

"No," Eric replied. "He was fighting at Magnier's side. He killed Lapeyre just before we took him."

"Oh, good," Serrier replied. "Then I won't have any qualms about using him to test spells. Release his senses from the binding spell. I want to talk to him."

Vincent undid a portion of the spell, making sure the vampire's body was still immobilized. He had seen the man fight, snapping Lapeyre's neck like it was a twig. Until they knew how to counteract that strength magically, he would not trust the vampire loose. He could kill them all before they managed to stop him.

"Welcome," Serrier said before the vampire could speak. "You'll forgive the bindings, but until we can be sure you won't attack us, I'm afraid they'll have to stay in place. I'm Pascal Serrier. And you are?"

"The last mistake you'll ever make," Orlando replied with a bravado he did not truly feel. He knew Alain would tear the city apart searching for him, but he did not know how long that would take. He just had to hold out long enough for his lover to find him.

"Such boastful words from someone so helpless," Serrier drawled, backhanding the vampire viciously. The ring on his middle finger tore into Orlando's cheek, leaving a bloody gouge.

Orlando glared at the dark wizard. "You'll have to do better than that if you plan on intimidating me. You have no idea the power you've unleashed against you by taking me prisoner. Chavinier's ire is nothing compared to what the Cour will do to you for this."

Serrier's laughter had the slightly maniacal twist of a true madman, sending a chill through Orlando. He had heard such laughter once before in his life, from the bastard who had changed him just before he drained Orlando dry. Reminding himself that he had survived that and that he could survive this—for it would surely be of much shorter duration than his time with his maker—he snorted derisively. "There's still time to let me go. My cheek will heal in a matter of hours and the Cour will be none the wiser, but if you continue, they'll know for sure and there will be no respite."

The laughter increased. "They'll have to find me first," Serrier retorted, "and they haven't managed to do that yet, even with that traitor Payet helping them."

Thinking of an early conversation with Sebastien about how the Aveu de Sang had allowed him to sense his Avoué, Orlando's smile deepened. "That was before the vampires joined the war. The Milice has resources now that you can't begin to imagine."

Serrier frowned. "What resources?"

"If you think I'm simply going to tell you, you're even more deluded than I thought," Orlando retorted.

Before Serrier could react, the door opened and another wizard came in with two bound wizards in tow. "The spies, as you ordered," Simon said.

"You might not tell me what I want to know right away," Serrier commented to Orlando, "but maybe one of them will. Or maybe you'll decide you'd rather not go through what they do for betraying me."

"I haven't done anything except what you ordered me to do," Monique protested immediately. "And I've already paid for failing to infiltrate the Milice. Why am I here again?"

"Because I ordered you to be here," Serrier replied, a flick of his wand sending a spell straight into her stomach. She bent double, writhing on the floor as the sensation of her entrails twisting inside her increased rapidly. "Or did you forget the promises you made?"

"Unquestioning loyalty and obedience," she said through gritted teeth. "I'm here, aren't I?"

Serrier released the spell. "You're here, but you are asking questions."

Next to her, Dominique trembled, knowing he was next. Sweat broke out on his face as his eyes darted around the room, searching for an escape, but of course, there was none.

"What about you, Dominique?" Serrier demanded. "Do you have any excuses to offer?"

"I don't know what I'm accused of to try to defend myself," Dominique answered in a trembling voice. "But I submit to whatever judgment you've passed on me."

"Very wise," Serrier agreed, his spell sending spikes of pain up and down the young man's limbs. He fell to the ground gasping.

"Which one of you warned Chavinier about the attack tonight?" the dark man demanded. "You're the only two who have had contact with him since the alliance formed and they started anticipating our every attack. Who told him?"

Struggling to her feet again, Monique remained impassively silent, though she knew it would be only moments before Serrier turned back to her. Her stomach still roiled even though the spell had released her. The pain would take hours, if not days, to fade, even if Serrier did not cast another spell. If he continued…. She preferred not to dwell on that thought.

Her respite was far too short, though. As Dominique's gasps and whimpers grew louder, Serrier turned on her, the feeling of fire licking along her skin. Her eyes could see that nothing was touching her skin, but her mind registered the searing pain as if she were being burned alive. Her screams pierced the silence of the room.

"I did it," Dominique gasped as he watched Monique fall to her knees screaming. He was a walking dead man, regardless of what he said or did at this point, but he could take the blame and hope she would be spared. If she was also Marcel's spy, then the work of defeating Serrier would continue, and even if she was not, pricking Serrier's temper would hopefully hasten his own demise. "I told him everything."

"*Abbattez*!"

The young wizard died instantly.

"Why did you kill him?" Simon asked. "You could have questioned him."

Serrier shrugged. "I'll learn far more from our newest acquisition than that boy could possibly know, and Claude is still playing with the woman so he doesn't need a new toy."

"What about Monique?" Eric ventured to ask, her screams having faded to nothing as she hovered near unconsciousness.

Serrier leaned back against his desk, watching her. "I suppose she's not involved."

"There's nothing to suggest she is," Eric agreed.

"Very well." He ended the spell. "Get her out of here."

Eric bent to pick her up, but Serrier stopped him. "We're not done here. Send her home. She'll recover eventually."

Eric met Vincent's eyes and frowned, but he did as he was told, his spell sending the injured woman to her apartment. He hoped she had someone waiting to take care of her and that he had not made matters worse by displacing her magically. Things would be far worse for both of them if he disobeyed orders.

Orlando watched the entire proceeding in silence. He had known Serrier had a sadistic streak, but he had not realized how deeply it ran. He quailed silently at the thought of that magic being visited on him, but he refused to let it show. The *Abbatoire* could not hurt him, and the rest was just pain. The woman's skin had not been damaged by the fire spell—so while she was clearly in terrible pain, Orlando knew it was all illusory. It could hurt him, but not destroy him. All he had to do was hold out until Alain and Jean came for him as he knew they would, given enough time.

"Would you like to reconsider your cooperation?" Serrier asked the vampire.

Orlando sneered. "To what end? I know your kind. You don't care whether I tell you what you want to know. You'll do what you want no matter what I say. And you'd use whatever I told you to go after my friends."

Serrier shrugged. "Your choice," he declared. "Vincent, take him to a cell while we decide how best to deal with him."

Vincent hoisted the vampire to his shoulder and had started toward the door when Serrier cast one final spell in their direction, making Orlando's back arch even through the binding spell as a searing wave of pain hit him. His fangs pierced his lip as he bit back his scream by force of will alone.

"He'll break," Serrier told Eric confidently. "It may take a few days, but we'll find his limits eventually. Even if all we do is learn what works on vampires, we'll have made progress. And without the spy, Chavinier won't be anticipating our every move anymore. We'll turn the tide back yet. You'll see."

Looking at the dead boy on the floor and thinking of Monique alone in her apartment, Eric wondered whether that was a good thing. His conversation with Vincent about getting out came back to him, and he started to think maybe the other man was right. If only there was a way….

"I WANT to keep you for observation at least until morning."

Alain made himself nod at the medic, giving his nominal assent, though he knew he would sneak out as soon as the man's back was turned. He could not sit down here doing nothing while Orlando was missing. It was simply not in his nature. He could not go after him himself—he had finally admitted that much to himself—but neither would he sit idly by. He had to do something.

Closing his eyes, he lifted his hand to his neck to cover the brand, using that outward sign of their promises as a way to feel closer to his lover. He was more thankful now than ever that he had agreed to bear Orlando's mark, to have this connection to his lover. He focused on that bond, trying to read anything he could in the tenuous connection. Mostly, he just felt confusion. He hoped that meant Orlando was still under the influence of the binding spell and so did not know what was going on around him. If that was the case, when he was released perhaps Alain would be able to learn something useful. If it was his own confusion he sensed, not Orlando's, then he would only be able to assure himself of his lover's continued existence.

He chose to believe the confusion was Orlando's, because to do otherwise was to give up hope. He had lost too many people since this cursed war began to face the possibility of losing another. Orlando had to be all right, had to be safe. His mind simply could not deal with any other possibility. Henri's vacant eyes came back to haunt him, reminding him of how incredibly fleeting life could be. Orlando had lived far longer than any mortal man, but he had barely scratched the surface for a vampire. To have that existence cut short now, when he was finally learning to appreciate all that the world had to offer, seemed too cruel to be conceivable, yet Alain knew just how cruel fate could be. He had lost a child already, had seen others cut down between one heartbeat and the next, had delivered that blow himself on more than one occasion. He could not accept, though, that Orlando would be next. He simply could not.

Tears threatened again, but he bit them back. Now was not the time to descend into hopelessness. Orlando had only been missing a few hours and Alain could still sense him, so he was still relatively safe. Now was the time for action. He would feel better once he was doing something, anything, in the effort to get Orlando back.

He closed his eyes, remembering the hot, fast feeding before they had gone into battle, the way Orlando's fangs had claimed him, the way his hands had worked in concert with them to bring him release. He choked back a sob as he realized how close they had come to making love. He wished now that they had, that he had taken the time to put a giant Do Not Disturb sign on the door, propriety be damned, and turned the couch into a bed where they could have loved each other properly. He could not turn back time and make that dream a reality, but he did console himself with the thought that Orlando had fed just tonight, giving them a few days' grace before his hunger weakened him dangerously. Assuming Serrier would want to keep him alive to experiment before destroying him, that gave them some time to keep searching.

And when they found him, he would spend the rest of his life making good on his promises. He whispered a prayer of thanksgiving that he had told Orlando that he loved him yet again right before they went into battle. If the worst happened, he would have the consolation, small though it was, of knowing the last words he said to his lover were words of love.

Hearing the medic leave the infirmary, Alain pulled himself painfully to his feet. He retrieved his wand from the cabinet next to the bed and did his best to move out of the room quietly, heading toward the Salle des Cartes. He doubted the view had changed since Marcel had checked, but he needed to see for himself. Slowly, he made his way down the hall to the situation room, wishing there were a spell he could cast to undo his injuries as easily as they had been inflicted on him. If there were, he knew the medic would have used it, but that did not stop him from wishing.

As he had expected, Orlando's name was still missing from the map. Compulsively, he ordered the view on the locator map to change, widening and narrowing the view in the vain hope that his lover's repère would suddenly reappear. Other names appeared and disappeared as patrols searched and others worked at place Pigalle, and still others walked their beats to protect the rest of the city, but Orlando's name was conspicuously absent.

Guilt assailed him as he waited, recriminations for not being fast enough to block the spell, for not stopping Orlando from going after the wizard who cast it, for not realizing it was a trap. He should have known better, should have warned Orlando not to leave his side, no matter the provocation, but he had not said the words. He clung to the reassurance that he could still feel his lover, however faintly, through their magical bond, but the sensation was directionless, giving him no idea where to begin searching.

Then a different sensation came through the bond and Alain fell to his knees, the fulfillment of his worst nightmare.

"What's wrong?" Marcel asked immediately, coming to Alain's side.

"They're hurting him," Alain spat, struggling to his feet again. "The bastards. Why didn't they take me?"

Marcel frowned. He understood Alain's guilt, but if his best captain was hobbled by grief and the sensation of Orlando's pain, that would make functioning until they could rescue the vampire even more difficult. "Can you block the feelings of the bond?" he asked seriously.

"Why would I do that?" Alain cried, face angry. "I let him down. The least I can do is take some of his suffering now."

"You don't know that it helps him at all," Marcel reminded him, "and even if it does, unless the sensation can help you find him, it doesn't do the rest of us any good. I need you fit for duty, which you're not, despite your trip to the infirmary, and I need you focused, which you won't be as long as you're feeling his pain. Can you block the bond?"

Alain frowned, but closed his eyes and concentrated on sending his love through the bond to Orlando. He did not know if his vampire could sense him the same way, but if he could, he did not want his lover to think he had abandoned him if he successfully blocked the bond. It was bad enough already that Serrier had started his torture. Physically, Orlando could survive and recover from that as long as Alain's blood and magic held out, but the wizard feared what it would do to his lover's psyche and the progress they had made in overcoming his past. Even if they rescued Orlando, would he still be the same man Alain had fallen in love with? Or would he be some shadow of himself, broken by Serrier's cruelty so badly that not even Alain's love could put him back together again? Silently, Alain vowed to do whatever it took, to give Orlando whatever space he needed to heal, just as long as he did not give up.

If Orlando could feel him the way he could sense the vampire, he imagined that connection was his lover's lifeline at the moment. To deliberately, consciously take that away seemed beyond cruel, and even the thought that his own concentration could be affected by the bond was not enough to convince him this was the right course of action. He would try it because Marcel had ordered him to do so, but any time he was not actively on duty, he would undo the block, assuming he succeeded in creating it, so that Orlando would not think he had been completely abandoned. Concentrating, he tried to project an explanation of what he was doing along with his love and the promise that he would never stop searching for his lover along their connection. He had no idea whether Orlando would feel any of his emotions or understand it if he did, but he had to try. He had to let his lover know he was not alone.

Slowly, hating himself for doing as Marcel ordered, he built a mental block, reconstructing the shields he had used to hold off the wild magic, until he lost track of Orlando. Head bowed, sickened to the depths of his being at his success, he closed his eyes. "It worked."

"I'm sorry," Marcel said softly. "I'm sorry this happened. I'm sorry you can feel his pain. I'm sorry I have to ask you not to feel it. I'd trade places with him in a heartbeat if I could—but Serrier doesn't negotiate, as you well know."

"Can you contact any of your sources?" Alain asked softly. "Maybe someone can tell us where to find him. I'm not asking you to risk a patrol. I'll go after him alone. I just need to know where to look."

"You'll do no such thing," Marcel retorted immediately. "If we can find out where he is, we'll send a large enough force to make sure we bring him—and you—home safely while taking out as many of Serrier's people as we can. I won't send you on a suicide mission. As for my sources, mostly they contact me so I don't put them at risk by contacting them at an inopportune moment, but I'll see what I can learn."

"Thank you. I know you don't have to expend Milice resources on Orlando."

"That's bullshit," Marcel insisted. "Orlando is one of our allies, even without his connection to you. I'd never leave one of my people in Serrier's hands if I could help it. I've just never managed to be in time before. He's usually killed them before I even realize they're taken."

"Not helping," Alain joked darkly.

"He's alive," Marcel reminded his friend. "As long as he's alive, there's hope."

Chapter 35

CAROLINE STARED blindly at the remnants of what had been her favorite dress, the red silk tattered and stained from the fight and its aftermath. Mireille's gold dress, the one they had bought together, had fared little better. She had given them no thought when they had decided to abandon their plans for the evening and join their comrades for battle, and in truth it would not have mattered if she had, for there had been no time to come back and change. It seemed such a banal worry in comparison to everything that had happened in the last few hours, but it was the one loss her mind could take in. This was concrete, a visible destruction, but also reparable. A trip to any of the nearby boutiques would replace it and put this one portion of her life back in place again. She feared the rest would not be so simple to fix.

Her eyes drifted to Mireille, standing motionlessly by the window where she had drifted as soon as they returned home. The vampire's eyes were vacant, her thoughts so clearly troubled. Slipping off the ruined dress and pulling a loose robe around her shoulders, she went to Mireille's side, encircling her shoulders tenderly.

Mireille leaned back against her immediately, drawing strength and comfort from the undemanding embrace. She made no move to leave her place by the window, though, nor to clean up from the battle or prepare for bed. Caroline frowned slightly. "Come with me."

Listlessly, Mireille let herself be led, the horror of the evening still haunting her. Despite the fight at the gare the morning the alliance formed, despite the patrols and the time in La Réunion, even despite the battle at Sainte-Chapelle, she had not really understood just how… vicious… war could be until now. Bodies had littered the ground when the battle ended, broken and bloodied, many of them dead or dying. The sight had shocked her to her core, leaving her feeling cold and hollow. She knew the war was claiming lives; she had consoled a fellow vampire through the loss of his partner not that long ago. That had not prepared her for this night's carnage. Fortunately, Caroline had survived relatively unscathed, but she still mourned the lives lost, even the dark wizards. She shuddered again as she followed her partner into the bathroom, thinking not of the dead, but of Orlando, taken in battle.

"You can't take their deaths on yourself," Caroline murmured as she lifted Mireille's red hair and pushed it forward over her shoulder so she could nuzzle tenderly at the vampire's nape. Reaching around, she slid her hands across the bodice of the dress her partner wore, resting her hands on the flat stomach. "Everyone there tonight understood the chances we all took."

"I didn't," Mireille whispered hoarsely, turning in Caroline's arms. "All those deaths… all those unnecessary deaths."

Caroline tightened her embrace. "I know," she consoled, stroking Mireille's hair. "It's a waste, an inexcusable waste, but Serrier hasn't given us any choice. And yes, before you ask, Marcel tried every diplomatic avenue he could think of when this all began. Nobody wanted it to come to this, but now that it has, we have to do our best to survive and triumph. If we don't, there won't be any future for any of us anyway." Her hands slid up Mireille's back, pulling down the zipper on the ruined dress. "Come on, let's get cleaned up, and then we'll figure out something to do to take our minds off it."

"It doesn't bother you?" Mireille asked, stepping back enough to help Caroline undress her. She opened the taps and stepped into the tub, letting the water slosh around her feet and ankles. Behind her, she could hear Caroline undressing, too, and turned to watch, unable to stop the quickening of her pulse as she watched the ivory skin come into view.

Letting her robe fall to the floor, Caroline joined Mireille in the tub, pulling her distressed vampire into comforting arms as she sat down in the rising water. "Yes, it bothers me, but I learned a long time ago that I can't let that interfere with the rest of my life," she explained. "If I do, if I let what happens out there define who I am in here"—she gestured to the room around her before touching her heart—"then Serrier has already won. We *survived* tonight. We should concentrate on that fact."

"I don't know how," Mireille admitted mournfully.

"Close your eyes and lean on me," Caroline suggested. "Let me take care of you."

Mireille did as Caroline directed, leaning back against her smooth shoulder, trying to relax into the feel of familiar hands on her skin. She was not surprised to feel the rough nap of a washcloth moving across her body, nor the hot prickle of water as Caroline rinsed away the soap and blood and grime. Then Caroline's hands touched her face, spreading a thick cream over her features. "What?" she asked, starting to open her eyes and sit up.

"Keep your eyes closed," Caroline warned. "You don't want this to get in them."

"What is it?" Mireille inquired.

"Just let me pamper you," Caroline replied evasively. "You know I'm not going to do anything that might hurt you."

Mireille did know that, so she subsided against her lover again and let herself be pampered. As her body relaxed, lulled by the hot water and Caroline's tender touch, her mind began to settle as well, the horror of the night fading slowly. She doubted she would ever forget, but as long as she could keep the memories at bay, she could continue to function. She hoped.

Caroline let the thick cream do its work, soothing Mireille's skin and relaxing her body. She could almost feel the tension leaving the vampire's body.

She smiled softly, pleased she could bring such peace to her lover. She only hoped someone was with Alain, offering him such comfort as could be found with his partner missing. She had thought about suggesting to Mireille that they go to him and offer what aid they could, as they had after Laurent was killed, but one look at her partner's wan face had changed her mind. Mireille looked one step away from dissolving into tears, and that would not help Alain or them. She had seen Thierry return. He would take care of his friend. She had to take care of her partner first.

It might have been different if Thierry or Raymond had found any leads worth pursuing, but both men had come back empty-handed. Alain's anguished wail had echoed through the Salle des Cartes and down the long corridors, which were filled with people wanting to help. Unfortunately, there was nothing any of them could do at the moment. Marcel had encouraged the hope that one of the captured dark wizards would reveal pertinent information during interrogation, which had already started when Caroline and Mireille left, but Caroline did not feel they could wait to see if that effort bore any fruit. Mireille was swaying on her feet. She needed to escape from the carnage, from everything that would remind her of all they had seen that night.

"He targeted the vampires tonight, didn't he?" Mireille asked, thinking of the bodies on the ground, some of them vampires she knew, all animation gone from their forms.

"I think he must have," Caroline agreed. "He knows about the alliance now and he's got to be searching for ways to counter it. Intimidation is one of his favorite tactics, and after tonight, the vampires who aren't involved know what he's capable of. Some of them may well join the alliance, but he's the type to hope that others will pressure Jean to abandon it so they won't be targets anymore."

"He doesn't know Jean very well if he thinks that'll work," Mireille laughed softly. "The more pressure he tries to apply, the more determined Jean will be to bring him down. And the vampires aren't likely to join Serrier now after he's attacked them."

"I doubt he wants them to fight for him," Caroline explained. "My guess would be he wants them out of the war entirely. We just have to hope he doesn't learn anything crucial from Orlando."

"I don't think he will," Mireille replied. "Telling him anything would endanger Alain, and it goes against a vampire's fundamental nature to do something that would hurt those who are special to us. The fact that they're Avoués only makes that instinct stronger."

"THERE'S something so wrong about that picture," Sebastien murmured softly as he stood with Thierry on the threshold of the wizard's guest room. Alain was asleep on the bed, knocked out by Thierry's spell so he could get enough rest to function tomorrow. Alain had protested vociferously, insisting he needed to stay and help with the interrogations in case any of the captured wizards had information about Orlando's whereabouts, but Thierry had been adamant: either return to the infirmary or let Thierry put him to sleep. Alain had eventually settled for sleeping at Thierry's house, where he had some chance of being informed and involved if any new information came to light. After his stunt of sneaking out of the infirmary, the medics would hardly leave him unattended again. "He shouldn't be here alone."

Thierry nodded. He ached with Alain's loss, though he knew his emotions bore no comparison to the debilitating power of what Alain was feeling. He had watched his friend fold in on himself as first Thierry's patrol and then Raymond and Sebastien had returned empty-handed. The light that had come back into his eyes the last few weeks faded again, all color leaving his face as he struggled to assimilate the hole in his life where Orlando had been so vibrantly up until a few hours earlier. A sharp look from Thierry and a quiet order from Marcel had cleared the Salle des Cartes of everyone but the inner circle.

As Thierry approached Alain cautiously, his magic had started sparking in the air, accompanied by a long, keening moan. The sound haunted Thierry still, the grief and despair so palpable it seemed a living force in the room. Jean had turned away, Raymond at his side, unable to watch Alain's collapse. If the concerned look on Raymond's face was any indication, Jean was probably fighting a collapse of his own at Orlando's capture. Thierry knew there was nothing sexual between the two vampires, but he likened their relationship to his friendship with Alain. He could only imagine what Jean had to be suffering knowing Orlando was in Serrier's clutches.

He had gone to Alain's side, the only one who dared, wrapping his arms around his best friend, letting his natural connection to the earth ground Alain's magic. Alain had turned against him with a shuddering sob, tears clumping his eyelashes. "They're hurting him," Alain had whispered in an aching voice. "Serrier's already started and I can't do anything to stop it. I know he's alive, but I can't feel where he is. Just that he's hurting."

The last time Thierry had felt so helpless, he had stood at Alain's side over Henri's dead body. He prayed they would not have another body to bury soon. He was not sure Alain would survive such a terrible loss a second time.

"Take him home," Marcel had directed, coming to their side, hand resting paternally on Alain's shoulder, but Alain had refused, saying he would not go home without Orlando. His exhaustion was obvious, though, which had prompted Thierry to suggest going to his house instead.

"You have to rest," he had insisted, "or you won't be well enough to help Orlando when we do find out where he is."

Alain had resisted a little longer, but his fatigue had forced him finally to give in.

Looking away from his sleeping friend, Thierry sought Sebastien, still at his side. "Am I a terrible friend for being glad it wasn't you?"

Sebastien shook his head. "I don't think so. You're only human, and it's natural not to want to suffer. Will he sleep through the night?"

"I hope so," Thierry replied. "I hit him hard enough with the spell, but Alain's powerful, and so is his grief. If he throws off the spell, we'll hear him, though."

"You should rest as well," Sebastien urged. "You're barely over being sick, and you used a lot of energy tonight."

Thierry did not reply, closing the door to the guest room and walking with Sebastien back to the bedroom they now shared. Without speaking, he stripped off his dirty clothes, tossing them in the general direction of the hamper. He wanted a shower, but that would wait. He wanted other things more, Orlando's capture reminding him they were fighting a war and that tomorrow was not promised to any of them. Sebastien had delayed long enough. It was time.

Turning back to his lover, he beckoned for Sebastien to join him.

Immediately, Sebastien shook his head. "We can't. You're still sick."

"Stop," Thierry ordered firmly. "I know what you said, what promises you made, and you've kept them, Sebastien. We don't know what tomorrow will bring, whether we'll have another night together, and I don't want to waste any more time. If you'd been the one taken tonight, I could have lost you without ever having you. Please. Make love to me."

Sebastien could not resist that quiet plea. Nodding, he shed his clothes, coming to Thierry's side in all his naked glory, their lips meeting in a soft kiss, each of them aware of the man sleeping in the next room. Their touches stayed light as their hands explored now familiar territory, but the knowledge that nothing held them back this time lent an unprecedented edge to even the simplest of caresses.

Taking charge, Sebastien turned Thierry toward the bed, lowering him down onto it gently despite the wizard's larger frame. He nuzzled Thierry's neck as he fitted their bodies together, his weight pressing his lover into the mattress. Silently, he reached into the nightstand for the tube of gel he had bought after the debacle with the lavender hand cream. He had not expected to need it so soon, but now he was glad he had gone out while Thierry was sleeping the day before.

"I'm not sure I have the patience for a lot of foreplay," he admitted, "but I don't want to hurt you. I want to do this right, but I'm not sure I can wait."

Thierry shrugged. "It's only pain."

"Pain you shouldn't have to feel," Sebastien insisted, slicking his fingers with lube. He sought the tight entrance, gratified when it gave easily beneath his probing fingers.

Thierry gasped as he always did at that first feeling of Sebastien inside him. The fact that it was just his fingers was irrelevant. His lover was inside him. He spread his legs a little wider, tilting his hips up in silent invitation.

The eager, trusting gesture moved Sebastien more than he would have thought possible. His eyes closed as his fangs dropped. He leaned forward and took

Thierry's mouth, more possessively this time, pouring all his fear for Orlando, relief at Thierry's safety, and frustration at his inability to help Alain into the kiss.

Thierry responded instantly, his hands cradling Sebastien's head, fingers in his long hair, eager for this proof that they were alive and together despite the war that would tear them apart if it could.

"Do you trust me?" Sebastien asked suddenly, lifting his head.

"You know I do."

"Then give me your neck."

Thierry's head fell back before he could even think to respond, his bite-ridden skin an invitation and testament in one. Sebastien's lips moved across the mottled flesh, finding a still smooth place and licking there for a moment before his fangs drove deep.

The hot splash of blood across Sebastien's tongue sent his senses spinning. Hoping Thierry would stay focused on that contact, he slicked his cock and lined it up with the barely stretched hole. He knew he was rushing, but he could not wait any longer. He needed to be joined with his wizard in every way possible.

Carefully, he seated the head of his cock within the snug portal, then lifted his head, waiting for Thierry's eyes to open so he could see they were pain free before he continued. Slowly, the heavy lids lifted, revealing the sea green gaze dark with lust. "Feel me," he urged, sliding home incrementally.

Thierry gasped, but not in pain. The sense of connection was so strong it stole his breath. He grabbed at Sebastien's shoulders, his anchor on this sea of unexpected emotion. He had the stray thought that Alain was right. It still felt a little odd, but so incredibly intimate that he knew he would crave it again as soon as they were done.

He rocked his hips up against Sebastien's, encouraging his lover to move against him, within him. The vampire did not hesitate, setting up a steady, rolling rhythm that left Thierry gasping and quivering. He returned to Thierry's mouth, kissing him hungrily.

Thierry moaned into the kiss, responding eagerly. With each thrust, he could feel his body opening, his heart unfurling, as he placed himself completely in the vampire's tender care. Only one thing was missing.

Breaking the kiss, he guided Sebastien's head back to his neck. "Bite me," he pleaded. "Join us in every way possible."

Sebastien's fangs sank indiscriminately into Thierry's neck, driving deep as he shunted his cock in and out of the welcoming iris. He could taste Thierry's emotions, all the worry he felt for Alain underlying the more immediate passion, and underneath it all, the first glimmers of another, more tender emotion. His eyes closed as he recognized the flavor and knew himself well and truly caught. His fingers sought Thierry's, twining them together as he made love to his partner, his wizard. Thibaut had told him to find love again. He thought perhaps he finally had.

Chapter 36

ANTONIO TRUDGED along the banks of the Seine, kicking pebbles viciously, his helpless frustration eating at him. If he had known a way to contact Monique, he would have done it in the hopes of pressuring her into telling him what the captured dark wizards did not know. Somewhere in the city—he prayed they were still in the city—Orlando was being held prisoner. He did not know the young vampire well, but that did not even matter. The Cours held one law inviolable: hurting a vampire—any vampire—was punishable by death.

He could feel dawn threatening, though the low-hanging clouds and mist from the river would provide a few minutes' protection if necessary. The sky was still dark on the horizon, though, so he did not hurry yet, not wanting to draw the attention of those out already to start their day. He drew enough attention as it was.

Pausing at the entrance to the little park where he had sat with Monique a few nights earlier, he thought about going down there on the off chance she was there again, but the clouds would not hold back daylight forever and her magic had worn off during the night. He had felt its loss like a tangible thing, the sudden feeling of nakedness inexplicable given his fully clothed state, except for Sebastien's and Orlando's descriptions of feeling wrapped in a blanket or a long coat.

She had not been at the battle tonight—at least not that he had seen—but he did not know if that reassured him or not. It made him wonder what she was doing if not fighting. He hoped she was well. Alain could sense that Orlando was not, but they shared an Aveu de Sang. None of the other pairs had mentioned a sensitivity to each other's emotions, and he dared not ask. As far as the Milice knew, he was still unmatched. He could hardly tell them otherwise, given who his partner was.

He spat again, probably the hundredth time he had done so, trying to get the taste of dark magic and hatred out of his mouth, but nothing seemed to help. Hunting would, but he had lost his taste for other blood. Tonight he would have no choice, though, unless he chose starvation. As romantically dashing as that sounded, he was too practical to consider it, and he doubted Monique would thank him for it even if she knew. He did not have time now, so he would wait out the day and hunt when the sun once again hid its face. Then he would go back to doing his part to end Serrier's tyranny so perhaps his partner could be free once and for all.

And if that never happened, he would still have the satisfaction of having brought down a would-be dictator who would have made his existence—his kind's existence—a living hell.

He stepped from the dock onto the deck of his houseboat, freezing immediately with the realization he was not alone. "Who's there?"

"Tell me why I shouldn't kill you."

Her voice made his nerves leap, but he could not afford to have her cast a spell on him because he could not explain why none of her magic worked. "Because I'm already dead?" he suggested facetiously. "Or maybe because I haven't done anything to merit your anger?"

Monique let her pointed wand drop toward the ground, in too much pain to summon the anger to cast an *Abbatoire*—or any other spell, for that matter. Her entire body hurt, though there were no marks on her anywhere. The last time she had found Antonio, in pain then as well though not this badly, she had felt better after he fed from her. The pain was far worse this time. Anything that might help her recover faster was definitely welcome.

"What are you doing here?" Antonio asked, not unkindly, when Monique did not answer his question. All rigidity left her posture as he stood there watching. He wanted to pull her into his arms and tell her he would take care of whatever was bothering her. He held back for two reasons, though. First, he did not think she would appreciate the gesture. Secondly, he was not sure he could actually make that offer, for many of the things that might be bothering her were beyond his control to fix.

"Serrier killed a spy tonight," she told him quietly. "If the kid had been a little less noble or a little more thick-skinned, I might well be dead, too. He suspected us both because we were the only two wizards he knew of who'd been in contact with any of the Milice and weren't either in prison or dead." She rose shakily to her feet. "I needed a safe place to sleep, to recover, in case he changed his mind about my fate. I didn't know where else to come."

"He hurt you again, didn't he?" Antonio demanded, reaching for her without even considering he might be rebuffed. "Come below. You can rest there."

Monique nodded, unbelievably grateful at his kindness. She let him guide her down the stairs and into a dark cabin, the windows veiled behind heavy curtains. "I can't take your bed," she protested as soon as she realized where she was.

"It's the only one on the boat," Antonio informed her, "and you said you needed to rest and recover. That won't happen if you're twisted into some uncomfortable configuration in one of the chairs in the living room. I won't bite unless you want me to."

Monique sat down slowly on the bed, bending to remove her boots, but the pain in her stomach made that task impossible.

"Stop," Antonio ordered, seeing the wince and the sudden cessation of movement. "Lie back. I'll get your boots off."

Monique did as instructed, lowering herself painfully to the mattress. He knelt at her feet, carefully unlacing the tight boots, easing them from her swollen feet and lifting her limbs onto the bed with trailing fingers that could have been a caress.

"Why do you take such good care of me?" she asked softly. "I've been a thorn in your side from the moment you met me."

Antonio shrugged. "I like the way you taste," he replied honestly, "though I do wish everything didn't have the taint of dark magic overlaying it. But even with that, I like the way you taste. Somehow you have a sweetness most of the dark wizards don't."

"Tasted a lot of wizards, have you?" she joked.

"Every one who's been captured since the alliance began," Antonio admitted. "That's my job. I help with the interrogations, to see if they're telling the truth when they answer questions. I know exactly what dark magic tastes like, which is why it's so odd that you don't taste the same way."

"I don't know why it should be different," Monique replied. "Maybe I don't take delight in some of the crueler spells the way Claude does, but I've done my share of nasty things in the past two years. Don't make me some kind of saint, because I'm not."

"I know that," Antonio assured her. "I can taste the dark magic in your blood the same way I can in theirs. The difference is that it doesn't define you the way it defines them, at least not for me."

"So what does define me in your eyes?" she asked curiously.

"There's a sweetness beneath the taste of magic," Antonio explained. "Don't scoff. I'm not a neophyte. I'm centuries old and I know what I'm tasting. Despite what you've done, you aren't defined by it the way most of the dark wizards I've interrogated are."

"You shouldn't tell me things like that," Monique said softly. The feeling of his hand on her ankle, where he had left it after he removed her boots, sent a feminine thrill through her that had everything to do with the feelings he aroused in her and nothing at all to do with the revenge she knew she should take for her fall from grace and for his part in Serrier's ever more frequent defeats.

"Like what?" Antonio pressed, his fingers stroking rhythmically over smooth skin. "That you taste sweet or that I've interrogated other wizards?"

"Either," Monique whispered hoarsely. "Both."

"Why not?" Antonio asked, his hand sliding beneath the hem of her pants leg, finding a rounded calf and kneading the muscle slowly. "There are things I can't tell you, but I don't want there to be lies between us. There's enough between us as it is without you distrusting what I do say."

Monique's eyes closed, her skin tingling at the unexpected caress. She wanted to trust him, but how could she when his allegiance was to the antiquated system that had allowed the kind of repression her family had suffered? The fact that it was a system that preached equality only made it worse when she and her brothers were labeled discipline problems and expelled from school simply because they were still learning to control their magic, or when the police overlooked “accidents” on their family property or blamed the malicious damage on the adolescent wizards themselves.

“Monique?” Antonio prompted when she did not reply.

“I want to trust you,” she admitted softly, “but it’s been so long since anyone’s been worthy of true trust that I’m afraid I’ve forgotten how.”

Antonio shook his head sadly. “I don’t know what I can say to convince you, but maybe it’s better that I don’t anyway. You’d trust me less if I did.”

Monique smiled sadly, eyes opening to meet his dark gaze. “I think you’re right.” She took a deep breath, wincing painfully as it pulled at sore muscles. “I… need a favor, if it won’t be an imposition.”

“I won’t know until you ask,” Antonio answered honestly, not willing to make offers he might not be able to carry through on, “but I’m willing to listen.”

“Last time we met and you fed from me,” Monique explained haltingly, “it helped ease the pain I was feeling. I’m in far worse pain this time and the usual spells aren’t helping. Will you feed from me again?”

Antonio’s fingers dug into her leg, surprising a gasp from her. He released her limb instantly, trailing an apologetic caress over the tense muscle. “Sorry,” he apologized instantly. “Even after all these years, I forget my own strength sometimes.” He caught her hand and lifted it to his lips, brushing them over her knuckles. “I would like nothing more, but only if you’re sure it will help.”

“I’m not sure of anything at the moment,” Monique replied, her voice weaker now that she had admitted to her pain, “but it helped last time. I don’t think I can feel any worse than I do now, so even if it doesn’t help, it can’t hurt.”

Antonio nodded. “Where does it hurt the worst?” he asked, his hand stroking mindlessly up her leg as if seeking the source of her discomfort.

“The spell he used makes it feel like your stomach is twisting its way out of your belly,” she replied, melting beneath the tender caress. Just the touch of his hand was enough to take the edge off her pain, or at least provide sufficient distraction.

Instinctively, Antonio’s hands went to the edge of the sweater she wore, starting to lift the hem. He paused before he had lifted it more than a centimeter, waiting for her permission. A quick nod of her head gave it, and he gently folded the garment back, careful to leave her bra fully hidden, though he had seen her completely naked once before. He lowered his head to the smooth planes of her belly, trailing his lips over the soft skin until he felt her pulse. He licked thoroughly at the spot until he was convinced his saliva would keep his fangs from worsening the pain she already felt.

Monique shifted restlessly on the bunk, the feel of his lips against her skin enough to chase the pain already. A thrill ran through her as she realized she would not have to heal these marks with magic to keep them from being visible. She could leave them as a reminder until they healed on their own.

Antonio's fangs drove deep, knowing he would need their full length to reach her vein here on her stomach where the blood did not run so close to the surface. She gasped lightly, but her fingers tangled in his hair, keeping him from pulling back to check on her. He sucked hard, drawing blood to the surface, immediately tasting the taint of foreign magic in her blood. Anger flashed hot and fast through him at the anguish he could taste, masking the sweetness of her blood. He worked his fangs deeper still, trying to draw out the evil still poisoning her system. He did not even consider that it might infect him as well. His only concern was her well-being, and the dark magic threatened that in a way he could not accept.

The immediate easing of the pain stole Monique's breath, and with its absence, other feelings surged to the fore: his lips against her skin, his tongue licking around his fangs, his fangs within her flesh. She squirmed on the bed as desire caught her off guard.

"Easy," Antonio soothed immediately, breaking the contact enough to speak. "Am I hurting you?"

"Not at all," she purred. "It feels better already."

"Good. Then relax and let me take care of you, because I can still taste its taint." Nor had he drunk anywhere near his fill of her intoxicating blood, but he was not sure it was wise to admit that.

Monique subsided onto the bed, consciously holding herself still so Antonio would not stop again. He had fed from her twice before, taken her to bed once, but somehow this was different. She was lying in his bed this time, not some anonymous cot in the basement of Milice headquarters, a spy on trial, though she had known it not. He had brought her here knowing what she was. She had come knowing what he was, for this very purpose, not to serve some end of Serrier's, but to find the comfort his bite could bring her.

She had not counted on the desire it awoke within her.

Antonio tasted the sudden rise of passion in her blood and knew he should draw back before he became so lost in that flavor that he forgot why he was feeding from her, but he could still taste the pain as well, though somewhat lessened. He would simply have to practice self-control, his instincts preventing him from withdrawing while she still suffered.

Monique's hands moved restlessly over the sheets as she debated whether to act on the emotions his feeding aroused. She wanted him, but there was so much unresolved between them that she feared to take that step. She was trapped in a hell of her own making and she did not know how to escape. Not even for this.

Gently, Antonio captured Monique's hands in his, twining their fingers together carefully, stilling the agitated movements. Sensing the pain fading, he lifted his head and met her eyes. "There's no one here but you and me. For the next few hours, the world outside this room doesn't exist. Tell me what you want."

Monique knew how dangerous that idea was, for the world outside could never truly go away, but the idea of ignoring it for a few, precious hours was tempting. Her eyes closed as she considered how to answer him. If nothing stood between them, what would she want? "He'll kill me if he finds out I came here."

"Then don't go back," Antonio requested, the thought of her lying dead, taken down by some spell, even if it was painless, tearing at his heart. "Stay with me. I'll keep you safe."

Monique shook her head. "You can't stand alone against everything he'd send against me if he thought I'd defected."

"The Milice could."

"I don't have anything to offer them," Monique protested, "no reason for them to offer that protection when I've already tried to spy on them once and failed. They'd never believe I was sincere this time, and I don't want you to risk losing their protection because of me."

"I know what would get you their protection," Antonio admitted slowly.

"What?"

"Serrier captured a vampire tonight. If you could tell us where he is, I know Marcel would take you in."

"He was in Serrier's lair in St Denis, but he could be anywhere by now," Monique replied immediately. "He rarely keeps his captives in the same place for long so they're harder to find. I could go back, see if I can find out where he is now…."

Antonio wanted to refuse, to lock the door and refuse to let her leave unless it was to take her to Marcel, but he knew she was right. If the Milice showed up and Orlando was not there, it would only make matters worse by revealing the depth of his importance in their eyes. "Not yet," he pleaded. "Rest a little, recover your strength before you face him again, in case you have to fight to get away." *Stay with me a little longer.*

Monique did not tell him it would make no difference, that if Serrier decided to kill her, nothing would stop him. She understood the tone of his voice, the silent need. Nodding her head, she relaxed a little onto the bed. Antonio released one of her hands, his palm spreading warmly over her still-bare stomach, fingers feathering over the bite marks his fangs had left.

Her hand covered his lightly, not stopping the caress but not encouraging it either. His eyes darted to her face, to the closed eyes and the dark circles staining the skin beneath them. Setting aside any plan of a more sexual conquest, he toed off his shoes and stood, lifting her into his arms gently to pull down the covers. Her eyes flew open, but he soothed her immediately. "You need to sleep," he insisted. "You'll be safe here until nightfall and then we can decide what to do next. Just let me hold you."

She nodded, the request stealing her breath in its tenderness. She lifted the sheet to invite him to join her, but he shook his head, settling the sheet gently over her, then lying down on top of it. One arm slid beneath her shoulders, rolling her against his side, while the other circled her from the other side, holding her securely in place. He pressed a tender kiss to the top of her head. “Sleep now.”

Monique nodded again, though she expected to find it hard to drift off in the unfamiliar bed, with arms around her, but within seconds her body had relaxed into slumber. “Sleep,” Antonio whispered again, eyes fixed on her face as she slept. He did not ever want to move again.

Chapter 37

SEBASTIEN LAY silent and still at Thierry's side, his arms encircling his wizard's larger form as if he could somehow provide a layer of protection from the outside world, guaranteeing the peacefulness of the few short hours of sleep his lover would allow himself before dragging himself out of bed and back to the undeniably necessary, painful, painstaking work of finding and rescuing Orlando. A part of him suffered the terrors of the damned at what that work would eventually entail, but his heart went out to the other wizard in the house, sleeping for the moment in the guest room where Sebastien had first slept when he arrived at Thierry's villa. The loss of his own Avoué had been to a natural, expected, even desired death—for Thibaut had been ancient for the time, infirm and weary of living—but it had not made the loss any less debilitating. To have that partner, that lover, stolen from him unexpectedly, cruelly, and so soon after their bond was formed was a torture Sebastien could not truly begin to comprehend. More than anyone else in the Milice, though, he could empathize, for he knew the power of the bond Alain was feeling.

Therefore, when he heard a muffled sob, he shifted carefully, not even thinking of waking Thierry, and slid from the bed, searching in the dark for a clean shirt and pants, hoping his lover would sleep a little bit longer.

"What's wrong?"

Silently cursing his too-slow departure, Sebastien returned to Thierry's side. "I hear Alain. I'm just going to check on him."

"I'll do it," Thierry insisted, starting to get up. "He's my responsibility."

Sebastien chuckled. "I think we've moved beyond 'mine' and 'yours,' but even if we hadn't, I know what he's feeling. I lost my Avoué, too. Just let me try?"

Thierry nodded his assent slowly, though he rose as well and followed Sebastien down the hall, not willing to abdicate all responsibility in the matter. He stayed carefully outside the room when the vampire went inside, however sure he was that both men knew he was there.

As Sebastien had feared, Alain lay on the bed curled tightly around himself, his knees pulled so snugly against his chest that he seemed one mound of flesh instead of a man with distinct appendages.

"Alain?"

The wizard did not move, nor even acknowledge having heard his name. In the hallway, Thierry ached for his friend, wanting to go inside the room and comfort him, but he had agreed to let Sebastien do this.

"You know he's not gone," Thierry heard Sebastien say. "You can feel him still. My Avoué used to take great pleasure in catching me off guard. He'd be out during the day, going about his business while I was trapped at home inside. I'd be trying to rest when I'd suddenly get hit by this jolt of emotion, sometimes amusement, but usually love. He'd just swamp me with it so that I ached for him, pacing the floor in front of the door until it was either dark and I could go to him or until he got home and I could pounce."

The comment elicited a surprised chuckle from Thierry's mouth, one he heard echoed in the bedroom, though the sound was as pained as amused. "I don't know how that's going to help him now."

"You don't think he needs to know that you love him, now more than ever?" Sebastien asked softly. "You don't think he needs to know how much you miss him? If ever he needed to feel those things, it's now."

"I'm afraid," Alain admitted at a whisper. "Marcel ordered me to block the bond when they started hurting him so I could function without his pain in my head. I tried to let him know what I was doing, that it didn't mean I'd abandoned him, but I'm afraid to let it down now and feel anger coming back instead of love."

"First of all, you don't know that because you blocked his emotions, you also blocked yours. For all you know, he could be feeling exactly how badly you're hurting right now," Sebastien declared. "And even if he can't, maybe he did understand you and is waiting patiently for your next free moment to feel your reassurance. And if he is angry, wouldn't you rather know he was angry and alive than not know at all?"

"Where's Thierry?"

Alain's voice was so plaintive that Thierry stepped into the room without considering it would reveal his eavesdropping. Neither man seemed to care, though, Sebastien scooting back on the edge of the bed to make room for Thierry between himself and Alain. "I'm right here," he said immediately, hand resting lightly on his friend's shoulder. He imagined he would hear from Sebastien later, but honestly, where else could he have been, knowing his best friend was suffering this way?

"Did you hear?"

"Enough," Thierry replied, not quite ready to admit he had listened to the entire conversation. "I don't think Orlando could hate you, no matter what you did," he continued, addressing what he knew was the true concern behind Alain's question, "but if I'm wrong, we'll just have to figure out how to win him back."

"His need for your blood will keep him coming back," Sebastien added, "and he'll taste the truth every time he feeds. He might try to resist at first, although I'd truly be surprised if he did, but he'll come around. Vampires don't stay mad over misunderstandings for long, especially ones with Avoués. We can't."

"I'm not sure this counts as a misunderstanding," Alain replied sadly, "but I suppose there's only one way to find out. What time is it?"

"Not yet dawn," Sebastien replied. He could not see a clock from where he was sitting, but he did not need a timepiece to tell him the position of the sun in the sky. "You can rest a while longer."

Alain shook his head. "I've wasted too much time already. I need to be up, to be doing something…."

"Then start by seeing how Orlando is," Sebastien instructed. "That will let you know where to start."

"Do you want us to stay?" Thierry asked immediately, not wanting to infringe on Alain's privacy, but wanting to give the other wizard whatever support he needed.

Alain nodded. "At least until I know…." He did not finish the sentence, not wanting to put his worst fears into words, but if he undid the block and found nothing, he would need Thierry's presence like never before.

Thierry's grip tightened, offering silent encouragement as Alain consciously released the mental shield he had erected last night in the Salle des Cartes. He watched carefully as emotions flickered across his friend's face, waiting tensely, praying he would not see more pain in the hooded blue eyes. When relief flooded the etched features, his smile was almost as large as Alain's.

"He's still there," Alain whispered hoarsely, the mixture of emotions tightening his voice. "He still loves me."

"Of course he does," Sebastien smiled, his voice bittersweet. "He always will."

Something in the odd tone of Sebastien's voice drew Thierry's attention away from Alain and back to his own lover. "You okay now, Alain?" he asked. When his friend nodded, completely lost in his mental communion with Orlando, Thierry rose and took Sebastien's hand. The vampire followed him out of the room with only one backward glance at Alain's momentarily calm face.

When they were alone in the kitchen, Thierry released Sebastien's hand. "Thank you for taking care of him," he said softly. "You knew just what to say to him. I'm not sure I would have."

Sebastien shrugged. "You'd have managed. It wasn't what I said, anyway, it was just the fact that I didn't try to change what he was feeling. I just pointed out a few realities he'd forgotten."

"Or never known. Either way, thank you."

"He's important to you," Sebastien replied as if that was all the explanation necessary. "That makes him important to me."

The words were so similar to Thierry's early thoughts about Orlando. "We had no idea what we were doing when we created this alliance," he mused softly, "but Serrier's wrought a far different revolution than the one he intended. Whether the war ends tomorrow or a year from now or twenty, the world will be a far different place because of what we've done. The bonds are too intense, too personal, and too far-reaching for us to go back to the way things were before." He looked up and met Sebastien's eyes. "When we started this, the equality legislation was a means to an end, at least in my eyes, and I'm sure a lot of the wizards felt the same way. It's personal now. In so many different ways and on so many different levels."

"You know this is more than just the alliance," Sebastien began hesitantly, the tender feelings that had swamped him as they made love rushing back. He had thought Thierry felt the same way, but the talk of the alliance made him wonder if he had misinterpreted.

"Of course it's more than that!" Thierry exclaimed. "I thought that was understood."

Sebastien shrugged a little. "It never hurts to hear it. I've gotten pretty good at reading emotions since I became a vampire, but it's always nice to know I'm interpreting correctly."

Thierry's lips quirked in a smile. "You're interpreting correctly," he declared firmly. Listening for a moment and hearing nothing from the guest room, he tipped his head toward the living room. "I've been so caught up in Alain that I haven't thanked you properly for last night. I'm not usually quite such a selfish lover."

"Your devotion to him is nothing to apologize for," Sebastien protested, though he was not averse to having Thierry's attention to himself again. "He's going to need all the support we can give him until we get Orlando back."

"I know," Thierry agreed, "and I'll do whatever it takes to make sure that's as soon as possible, but that doesn't give me an excuse for neglecting you." Moving into the spacious room, barely illuminated by the waning moon, Thierry sat down on the couch and reached for Sebastien's hand. The vampire settled next to him, moving willingly into his arms. Thierry leaned back, snuggling them comfortably onto the soft cushions. "Not quite as nice as our bed, but if we go back there, I don't trust myself to behave—and with Alain awake…."

Sebastien nodded. "It would be beyond cruel to make him listen to us together," he agreed. "It's enough just to lie here and hold you." He nuzzled Thierry's neck, licking at the bite marks in various stages of healing. "Someone's going to see these and think you've been savaged."

Thierry shook his head. "Ravished, maybe, but definitely not savaged. You take care of me much too well for it to be savage." He ran a hand over Sebastien's hair. "If it really bothers you to see them, I'll get Alain to heal them for me. I've never been good at casting it on myself."

Sebastien debated silently for a moment before replying. "Our relationship is private, or at least it should be, but these marks proclaim a portion of it to anyone who chooses to look. A part of me finds that incredibly satisfying, but it's the caveman side I usually try to overrule. I don't want people looking at you and wondering about you because of the marks."

Thierry grinned. "So bite me somewhere else next time. I know you can get blood from places other than my neck. And then the marks will be just for us."

Sebastien's fangs dropped instantly, the thought of covering Thierry's body with marks enough to have him hard and aching. "You don't want to say things like that if you're not going to follow through on them," he warned, "because I don't have enough self-control for both of us."

Thierry's head tipped back before he even thought about it, his hands pulling open the collar of the robe he had slipped on to follow Sebastien into Alain's room. The sight of the smooth, golden chest tempted Sebastien inordinately. He lowered his head, finding the spot where he could feel Thierry's heart beating strongest. He sucked softly on the skin, then bit down hard, fangs sliding through strong muscle to find blood. The need that washed over him stole his breath. He knew he could not feed deeply, not after last night, but he had to taste Thierry again.

The sound of the toilet flushing broke them apart like guilty teenagers caught necking on the couch. Their faces hot, their eyes met and they both started chuckling. "Definitely not just about the alliance," Thierry said, a smile still on his face. "Alain will want coffee, and we've got to figure out a better way to search for Orlando. You probably know more about the bond that links them than anyone else. Do you have any ideas?"

"A few," Sebastien replied. "I thought about it last night while you were sleeping. We'll talk about it when Alain comes out. After all, I know what my bond with my Avoué allowed, but Alain's a wizard. Thibaut wasn't. There may be even more to their bond than there was to mine."

"Then I'd better get the coffee going. The only thing that would get him out here faster would be Orlando himself. And since I doubt I can pull off that miracle, I'll settle for coffee," he said ruefully, wishing there were some way he could find the other vampire and ease the suffering he knew still lurked beneath the surface of Alain's current calm.

The sound of the coffee grinder reached Alain's ears as he showered, followed quickly by the smell of brewing, but the wizard stayed where he was, letting the hot water run over his shoulders and back. His eyes closed, he leaned his forehead against the cool tiles and drifted on the emotions he could feel through the link with Orlando. To his relief, the pain he had sensed the night before was absent. Whatever Serrier had done, it had been mercifully brief.

The loneliness that came through the link was palpable, but Alain was sure he was projecting just as much. He tried to temper it, not wanting to make Orlando feel any worse, but waking up alone in an empty bed had been almost too much for Alain. Orlando had promised to always be there with him when he awoke. That he had no choice only made it worse somehow, but Alain did not want his lover to feel that pain. He wanted Orlando to know how much he loved him and missed him, how hard he was searching for him.

Concentrating, he summoned the image of the last time they had made love before Orlando's capture, projecting his desperate lust and overwhelming love toward the vampire. He knew, though he tried to bury that awareness, that Serrier would not wait forever to begin whatever nefarious plan he had for Orlando, and he wanted Orlando as strong as he could be when it started. His lover had to hold on, had to survive until they found him. Any other outcome did not even bear considering.

The wave of love and desire that came back to him assured Alain that he had succeeded in letting Orlando know how he felt. He only hoped it was enough to tide him through the hours until they were together again. Alain refused to acknowledge that it might be longer than that. He *would* find Orlando, if he had to tear the entire city stone from stone to do it.

A trickle of fear interrupted their communion. Alain's face tightened as he felt it immediately repressed. He concentrated harder, wishing he could get any kind of impression of surroundings rather than just feelings from Orlando, but all he could identify was Orlando's emotions.

Snapping upright, he shut off the water, drying off quickly and pulling back on the clothes he had worn the night before, perfunctorily cleaned with an absent-minded spell. Following the smell of coffee, he joined Thierry and Sebastien in the kitchen, features set. He had given in to his fear and grief last night, but neither emotion helped Orlando. Pushing them aside, he sat down at the table, accepting the cup of coffee Thierry handed him. He did not waste time with casual greetings. They had work to do.

"We need ideas," he said firmly, "and we need them now."

Chapter 38

EDOUARD PEERED around furtively, but all was quiet in the place Pigalle. The bundle in his arms was awkward, but not heavy, at least not to him. He had considered letting Serrier dispose of it rather than doing it himself, but this was not some random body in his arms, a girl he had found on the streets and finished off simply because he felt like it. No, this was a far more personal choice and he wanted to make sure his message was understood.

The doors to Sang Froid were shut and locked so he slipped through the shadows to the sill. He gave no thought to the body's nakedness, to any of the many injuries it bore. He was responsible for some of them. Others came from the wizard, Blanchet. Edouard did not care for their source, only that seeing them on his consort would cause Bellaiche pain. He had made sure to mark her thoroughly as he fed from her, taking from her by force what the whore had willingly given the chef de la Cour. She had been so relieved to see him at first, thinking a vampire would help her as the wizards had not. Her face had lit up, her eyes coming alive again, until the first bite of his fangs. He had tasted her realization that she had gone from bad to worse, had felt the fear flash through her.

It had made her blood so sweet.

And when he had torn the tattered clothes from her, she grew even sweeter as she understood and then accepted her fate. Oh, she had still fought him as his fangs pierced her tender flesh—breast, thigh, cunt—but she had known it was useless, and that was the sweetest taste of all.

Each fresh jolt of pain, each new sense of violation—Bellaiche was obviously a weakling, not to have used her any more than he had—added to his sense of power, until he was high on it. He had tempered the rate of his feeding to prolong the enjoyment, giving himself the leisure to find his own release repeatedly, in every one of her holes, knowing Bellaiche would see her and guess what had been done to her. He would feel every violation as keenly as if he had been the one beneath Edouard's fangs. And Edouard would be at least partially revenged.

Dumping the body where it would be found by the first person to walk in or out of the door to Sang Froid, Edouard pounded loudly on the wooden portal and then disappeared into the shadows.

JEAN LEAPT to his feet at the sound of the phone, praying wildly that it was Alain calling to say Orlando was safe. That the wizard probably did not even have his number was irrelevant. One of the other vampires could have given it to him. He nearly tore the door to the dumb waiter from its grooves as he shoved it up to get to the telephone. "Âllo?"

"Jean, it's Angélique. You need to come to Sang Froid before the police get here."

"What happened?" he demanded immediately.

"Just come."

Jean frowned when the line went dead and turned to Raymond. "I have to go out. I don't know what Angélique needs, but she was adamant."

"Do you want me to come with you?" Raymond asked, levering himself up onto one elbow. He had only barely made it into bed and had no idea what he had left in the way of reserves, but he would use them and more at Jean's side if the vampire asked.

"No reason for you to," Jean replied with a shake of his head. "You're exhausted. You can answer the phone if it rings. If a call comes about Orlando, I'll be at Sang Froid."

"If I hear anything, I'll let you know right away," Raymond promised. "Call me if you need me to join you for any reason."

"I will," Jean agreed, pulling his jacket back on and heading for the door. He paused on the threshold to the hall and came back to the bed, kissing Raymond sweetly. "Rest while I'm gone. We may need your strength and cunning later, and I don't want you worn out."

"Be careful," Raymond warned as Jean disappeared through the door, heart warmed by the thoughtful kiss. "I'd be lost without you," he added softly, staring at the black brocade canopy and wondering how the vampire had become so central to his life so quickly.

Jean navigated the streets between his apartment and Montmartre with more than his usual speed and stealth. Whatever had happened, it had clearly disturbed Angélique, something that did not happen to the generally unflappable entrepreneur. She had mentioned the police, which worried him. The last thing he needed was another death at the hands of the rogue. They were finally beginning to make progress in swaying public opinion, if Marcel could be believed. To have another death would undermine that, even if they could pin all four deaths on the same vampire.

Arriving at Sang Froid, he found Angélique standing outside, her face grim, her robe pulled tightly around her beneath her coat, occasional shivers wracking her despite the vampires' lessened sensitivity to temperature. "What's going on?" he asked with a frown.

Angélique stepped aside, revealing a blanket-shrouded body. "I was getting ready to rest—it's been a long day—when I heard pounding on the door. I came down to see who was foolish enough to keep me from my bed after the day and night I had, and I found her. I looked, but there wasn't anyone I could see."

Jean sighed. "Did you call the police? We can't just hide a body from them, not when we're asking for legitimacy."

"I wasn't sure you'd want me to," Angélique replied honestly. "Jean, this isn't just another body."

Jean's frown deepened. "What's that supposed to mean?"

Angélique sighed and knelt, glancing up at the chef de la Cour with trepidation. She had known him a long time, but she had absolutely no idea how he would react, and that scared her more than she was willing to admit. Taking a deep breath, her stomach roiling at the combined smells of sex and death, she pulled the blanket away to reveal the face beneath.

Jean's vision grayed and he swayed on his feet as he fought not to lose consciousness and a sudden, vicious desire to retch violently. His knees folded beneath him until he knelt on the damp stone at Angélique's side. "No," he whispered, his hand floating above Karine's immobile features as if the denial could somehow change what he was seeing. "No, this is some trick. It can't be…."

She could not be here, lifeless and cold, on Angélique's doorstep. She was safe in her apartment, done with him, perhaps, but alive and well, snuggled up with a lover who could give her what she needed instead of waiting hopelessly for a vampire who probably would not arrive. She was not here. This was some glamour of Serrier's, some trick of the eye to weaken him, to make him reconsider the alliance. The rogue had not found out about her, had not taken her, used her, killed her….

A sob escaped his throat. Soft arms enclosed him immediately, muffling his cries in a generous bosom. The tears would not fall, but still, Jean cried. For the kind, generous woman Karine had been. For the unfulfilled dreams she would never see come true. For the unfairness of her being taken when her only crime had been to love a man who could not give her what she deserved. For the pointless waste of her life.

Angélique held him as his grief overwhelmed him, tucking the secret of his weakness into her heart to guard with all the others she had sworn to protect. Her hand stroked gently up and down his back as he mourned the woman who lay at their feet. She lost track of the time as they knelt there, but the impending dawn finally roused her. "We should take her inside," she suggested softly. "It's almost dawn and people will be out soon. If you have any hope of seeing to her yourself, this has to stay quiet."

Jean nodded, face sunken but set when he pulled away. "I know who's to blame, and I know who to tell. She deserves a proper rite and burial, not a police morgue and autopsy." His hand trembled as he caressed the cold cheek tenderly. "Will you help me see to her?"

"If that's what you want," Angélique agreed, "or you can leave her with me, if you prefer." She had seen the horrors perpetrated upon the poor, deceased woman. It was bad enough for Jean to know she was dead. He did not need to see what had been done to her first. "You have so much else to worry about right now."

Jean shook his head. "She's dead because of me. The least I can do is honor her the way she deserves."

Angélique nodded and rose to her feet with the supple grace of the harem girl she had once been, stepping back to let Jean lift his charge into his arms. He did so with excruciating care, as if he could somehow make amends for all she had suffered before her death.

Opening the door, Angélique let Jean precede her into the dim parlor, a single lamp illuminating the opulent space. She indicated one of the bedrooms off the central room with a tilt of her head. Detouring to gather some towels, she gave Jean a moment of privacy with his grief. She knew exactly the moment he removed the blanket she had wrapped around Karine's body by the keen of outrage and horror that rose from the other room.

"They did this because of me," he said, his voice breaking on the words when she came back in. "They grabbed her from her home, or off the street, and treated her worse than the meanest animal. And then they killed her. Because of me."

"No," Angélique disagreed softly. "They did it because they're sick bastards with no humanity left, be they wizard or vampire."

"He's crossed a line that can't be regained," Jean declared coldly. "He's *extorris* now."

Angélique's eyes widened. From this moment on, any vampire who had any dealings with Edouard was bound by Cour law to bring him before the Cour for judgment under pain of judgment themselves. "Jean?"

"Serrier couldn't have found out about her without the rogue. Every insult done to her stems from his betrayal."

"She wasn't your consort. You never declared her to the Cour," Angélique reminded him.

"And yet she's dead because of her involvement with me," Jean insisted. "Spread the word. I have a funeral to prepare."

His tone was so final that Angélique did not try to argue anymore. She was not opposed to Jean's decision, in reality—the rogue deserved everything the Cour could do to him and more—but she feared Jean was staking his position on shaky ground given Karine's unofficial status in his life. If she had been his true consort, if she had been a vampire or in some other way acknowledged by the Cour, she would support him without hesitation, for there was no denying the cruelty, the inhumanity of the rogue's actions. Jean was implacable, though, and she would not challenge him over it. She just hoped the rest of the Cour was as understanding. As she withdrew, she decided she would make one phone call before beginning to spread the word among the vampires. No one should have to face that kind of brutality alone.

Alone again, Jean knelt on the bed beside Karine's body. Her hair was filthy, matted with sweat, perhaps even with blood. Tear tracks smeared the grime on her face, giving the once elegant, immaculately groomed woman the appearance of a homeless waif. As his eyes ran over the carnage inflicted upon her, he realized her face was the only unmarked skin on her body. Picking up the wet washcloth Angélique had brought, he wiped her face clean, needing to touch her one last time, to restore her dignity to the best of his ability. Her neck was next, wiping away the blood that had oozed from the bite marks he had not left, the marks that had killed her. "I'm sorry, Kari," he whispered as he tenderly ran the cloth lower, over breasts crisscrossed with knife cuts and torn by savage fangs. His eyes prickled as his breath caught on a sob at how cruelly she had been used. He had been rough, sometimes, but never like this. Had she lived, she would have been scarred terribly, both from the knife and from the bites. He rose to rinse the cloth in the en suite bathroom. She had not deserved this kind of suffering. As if it were not enough that she had been tortured, the knife wounds were not fresh—meaning she had endured days of abuse. While he had been falling in love and seducing Raymond, she had been suffering, undoubtedly believing he would come to her rescue. And he had not even realized she was missing.

This grief bent him almost double as he remembered going by her apartment and seeing the flowers he had left for her still by the door. Had they already taken her before he first brought them to her? He should have known she would not dismiss him that way, should have searched for her that first night. If he had, perhaps she would still be alive. Perhaps Orlando would not be in the hands of the same sadists who had tortured Karine.

Forcing himself to straighten, he finished rinsing the cloth and returned to her side. He started at her feet this time, the skin burned and abraded in places, one of the marks looking decidedly putrid. Cursing steadily under his breath, he washed her legs, each mark on her skin a new cut on his heart as he imagined the pain she must have felt as each was inflicted. The knife wound on her leg ripped at him, but not as much as the punctures on her inner thighs. Face tightening, he forced himself to clean higher, rinsing away blood and a heavy stickiness. "He won't survive the dawn when I get my hands on him," he swore angrily as he realized how completely violated she had been before her death. Execution was too kind a fate for the rogue, but Jean would not dishonor her memory by torturing Edouard as he desired to. Gently, he turned her over, so far beyond horrified that the sight of the whip marks and bites on her back and buttocks only left him numb. He did not have to look to know she had been sodomized as well before the rogue had drained her dry.

Movement at the door caught his attention and he turned, a snarl ready for whomever dared disturb him.

Angélique stepped back, giving the two men their privacy as Raymond ignored Jean's expression and strode to his side, his arms encircling the vampire in a firm yet tender embrace. She watched enviously as Jean trembled, the tension in his body visibly fading as he buried his face in the crook of Raymond's neck, arms slowly coming to encircle the wizard's waist. Angélique pulled the door shut quietly, wishing for a chance to undo the mistakes she had made with David. She needed a pair of strong arms, too.

"What are you doing here?" Jean asked finally, though he made no move to pull away, not even lifting his head.

"Angélique said you needed me," Raymond replied as if that should have been obvious.

"They killed her," the vampire mumbled. "They tortured and raped and killed her." He did lift his head this time, his eyes sparking with dark fire. "I'll see them all dead for this."

Raymond did not know the woman on the bed behind Jean, but he recognized the handiwork, a large part of it anyway. "Blanchet," he said with a moue of disgust. "Not much of a wizard, but one hell of a bastard. I always wondered if he used cruelty as a way to make up for his lack of ability."

"I want him. I want his death."

"It's yours," Raymond promised, though he suspected Alain might vie with Jean for the privilege. "I can finish cleaning her up for you," he offered, having read the pain in Jean's voice and posture.

Jean shook his head. "I have to do this for her. I have to take care of her."

Raymond tightened his embrace, preventing Jean from pulling away. "This isn't your fault. Blanchet tortures because it amuses him. They're trying to hurt you, to weaken you so the alliance fails. That's what last night was about at place Pigalle. That's what this is about. If you want to give her death meaning, don't let them win. Focus on that, not on what they did to her."

"I will," Jean promised, "but only after I see to her. They might torture for the hell of it, but they took her because they knew she was important to me. Not as important as they thought—she didn't know anything that could help them—but because she was my occasional lover, she's dead today. And because I was with you, I didn't worry when she wasn't home. I let it go and she died."

"You don't know that you could have saved her even if you'd realized what happened," Raymond reminded him. "We'd have tried, but it might not have made a difference."

Jean tensed, pulling out of Raymond's arms, eyes blazing. "I went to her after the Piège-Pouvoir, flush with power, and I found flowers I'd left for her earlier still outside her door. I thought that was a rejection so I came to you instead of knocking, demanding an explanation the way I would have done before the alliance, instead of realizing she was missing. While we were fucking around, she was being tortured. She deserved better than that."

Raymond recoiled, the words a slap he had not expected. They had talked early on in the alliance about what the partnerships would do to wizards or vampires who already had relationships, but he had not realized Jean fell into that category. "You never said anything. If I'd known, I'd—"

"Have done exactly what we did," Jean interrupted. "This isn't your fault. It's mine. All you did was give me what I asked for. The last time I saw Karine, we argued. She wanted… more than I could give her. I kept telling her to cut me loose. When I saw the flowers, I thought that's what she'd done. It's what she should have done years ago when she first realized I'd never be able to give her the commitment she wanted. Every time I saw her, I told her again to send me away. She never did. I should've known she never would, but it gave me the excuse I needed to go to you instead of confronting her. I believed the easiest explanation and took what I wanted instead of checking on her." His voice cracked, breaking Raymond's restraint. He pulled Jean back into his arms, holding him tightly.

"Let it go. We'll see to her properly and then we'll bring them down."

Jean turned in Raymond's embrace to contemplate the body on the bed. "Do the spell."

Raymond did as instructed, his magic flowing around the dead woman, cleaning away the dirt and blood, healing the marks, giving her back the dignity that had been stolen from her. Letting Jean go, Raymond drew the coverlet over her, shielding her nudity. "Let's go make her arrangements."

"I don't even know what to do for her," Jean admitted. "She wasn't Catholic—not practicing anyway—and I don't think she'd appreciate a Mass."

Raymond glanced back and forth between the vampire and the dead woman. "She died because of the war between wizards. Would a wizard's rite be acceptable?"

The suggestion surprised Jean, but he found it fitting. "I think it would be the perfect solution."

Chapter 39

THE NOW-FAMILIAR binding spell stole the movement from Orlando's limbs, metal handcuffs pinning his arms behind his back before the spell was released again. "Are you sure that's a good idea, Eric?" the bald wizard, one of the two who had kidnapped him yesterday, asked. Orlando's ears perked up at the familiar name. So this was the wizard who had changed sides, shattering Alain a second time in as many weeks. He knew he ought to hate the big man, but both Thierry and Alain had explained what had led him to that choice. It was not one Orlando agreed with, but he thought now perhaps he could understand.

"Pascal said he didn't want any magic so there wouldn't be any chance of interference with his tests," Eric replied. "The cuffs should hold him. He isn't Superman."

Orlando rattled the cuffs experimentally, but he could not break the chain between them at the angle his hands were bound. He refused to show any fear. He knew the type he was dealing with. They preyed on weakness. They could hurt his body, as they had proved last night, but they could not hurt his mind. Alain was coming for him, so he would endure until his lover arrived. Then they would learn that vampires were no easy mark.

The vampire's quiet dignity impressed Eric, making him wish there was a way out of the scene he was sure would unfold. Serrier had ordered him and Vincent to retrieve their prisoner, deciding it was time to find the vampires' weaknesses. Eric was sure the dark wizard had waited until after dawn for the psychological intimidation—but the vampire did not seem at all concerned, even when they entered a room with shuttered windows.

"Welcome again," Serrier said jovially when the door shut behind them. "I'd shake your hand, but you seem to be a little… occupied."

Behind Serrier, Claude snickered at the joke. The vampire's expression never varied.

"I still don't know your name," Serrier continued.

"No reason why you should," Orlando agreed, refusing to give even that much ground. "I'm not a person to you, just a creature of the night worth as much as the dirt beneath your feet."

"Less," Serrier spat, angry at the challenge. "At least the dirt's good for growing food. All your kind's good for is killing."

Orlando snorted. "That's a bit hypocritical, don't you think? I've never killed my prey in all my years of existence. I know you can't say the same since I watched you kill last night." Perhaps it was a mistake to challenge the other man.

Perhaps he would have been smarter to remain stoically silent, but Orlando could not resist the urge to needle the bearded wizard.

"Enough," Serrier roared. "Claude, where's the supplies I asked for?"

Claude scuttled forward, his arms full. "Right here." He dumped the sundry items on the table.

Orlando had to fight the urge to laugh when he saw what the wizard had gathered: garlic cloves, silver chains, a crucifix, a wooden stake, and a vial of water—holy water, he presumed. "That's how you think to defeat us?" he scoffed. "You're even more stupid than I thought."

"Watch your mouth, vampire," Vincent growled, hoping he could instill enough caution in the bound man to keep him from being killed instantly.

Still shaking with disbelieving laughter, Orlando refrained from making any more comments. Let Serrier learn the hard way if he insisted on pelting Orlando with the various objects. Only the stake could do any damage to him, but even that would not be enough to destroy him. He had been about to make that mistake the first time he met Jean.

"That really would not be the wisest of ideas."

The unfamiliar voice broke through the haze of pain and determination that fogged Orlando's mind. His hand wavered on the stake he held poised above his own heart. After years, decades, at least a century of abuse and torture, he had had enough. He was broken... body, mind, and soul. All that remained was the empty husk, and soon that would be gone, too. He had endured his last beating, his last branding, his last rape. All that remained was to end this hellish existence and hope that his soul, or what was left of it, was not completely damned.

"That particular form of torture only finishes us off if we are left impaled until the sunlight hits us, at which point it is the sun, not the stake, that kills us. There is not any light here to end your torment, or I imagine you would have taken that way out long ago."

Orlando's eyes darted over the unknown vampire who stood in the door to his prison. His shoulder length brown hair was pulled back into an old-fashioned queue, wisps escaping to frame a pale face with the most luminous eyes Orlando had ever seen. The voice, the accent and intonation, suggested a fluency, a familiarity with French that Thurloe could not match, for all his vaunted ways. Slowly, he lowered his hand, though the stake remained clutched tightly in his grip, as a weapon if he needed it and as a way out if the other vampire was here at his maker's behest.

"Who are you?" he asked softly, his voice trembling in fear. "What do you want with me?" Thurloe had never allowed another vampire into his domain, as far as Orlando knew. Certainly, Orlando had never seen another in the near-century he had been at the bastard's mercy.

"My name is Jean. I suppose you could say I am the leader of the vampires in Paris," the tall man replied.

"Paris?" Orlando asked. "We are in Paris?"

"Yes," Jean answered. "Where did you think we were?"

"I don't know," Orlando replied. "I suspected we were in France, because Thurloe made me learn French and because I felt us cross the Channel." The memories of that hellish trip haunted him still. He had been gagged and bound, completely unable to move, then enclosed in a wooden coffin, his maker passing him off as the body of a soldier being returned home for burial. When the old vampire had finally released him, Orlando had been so weak he could barely move. Thurloe had forced blood down his throat to revive him, only one of many forced feedings. "All I know of where I am is this room and...." He could not bring himself to identify the other room, the room where his maker visited countless tortures upon him.

"When did you last feed?" the elder vampire asked.

"He forced me to eat three days ago, maybe four. I lose track of time sometimes. There are no windows in the other room either, the one where he... plays with me."

"Tortures you," Jean interrupted. "Call a spade a spade, my young friend. And rest assured, that stops now. First, we need to let you feed. Then, I will deal with Thurloe."

"Deal with?" Orlando questioned slowly. Jean said he was the leader of the vampires. Did that mean he had come, finally, to see justice done?

"Vampires do not condone the kind of abuse he has clearly put you through. You are a vampire, not a slave. You need not worry about him. He will not harm anyone again when I am through with him," Jean assured the young man. "Come. I will take you somewhere safe where you can feed undisturbed."

Orlando hesitated, torn between the desire to escape and the desire for vengeance. "What will you do to him?"

"Do you really care?" Jean challenged. "You will be free of him, never have to worry about him again."

Orlando considered Jean's words and realized that he did care, not because he wanted to protect Thurloe but because he wanted to make sure the sadistic bastard got what he deserved. "I want to help."

They had seen to Thurloe's execution, and Orlando smiled every time he saw a wooden stake. He shook his head to clear the memory and focused back on Serrier, sure his expression had confused the dark wizard. Or perhaps infuriated him, Orlando amended silently when Serrier shoved him backward, pressing the crucifix hard against his skin. Orlando just looked at it in amusement, for although the points of the hands and feet bit lightly into his skin, it did not burn him the way Serrier clearly expected it to do. "You'll have to do better than that," he laughed.

In the hall outside, the unfamiliar voice and jeering tone caught Monique's attention. She had snuck away from Antonio when he rose to use the bathroom, not wanting to wait to make the attempt at finding the captured vampire. The longer she waited, the more likely she was to lose her nerve, and she knew this was her one chance. At the moment, Antonio was willing to believe her, to speak for her with the Milice leaders, but if he changed his mind she would never be able to escape Serrier's control and would end up dead or in prison for sure. Taking a deep breath to steel her resolve, she opened the door and breezed in as if she had every reason in the world to be there.

"Back already, Monique?" Serrier asked. "Did you not get enough last night?"

"Sorry," she apologized, though her voice conveyed no remorse. "I didn't realize you didn't intend for me to come back."

Something in her expression—the tone of her voice, the way her eyes lingered just a moment on the bound vampire, the slight smile on her lips—must have given her away, she thought later, because as she turned to leave the room a spell burrowed into her spine, sending her to her knees. She did not pause to consider. Wand in hand, she cast a displacement spell, careful to choose a neutral location in case she was followed. The last thing she wanted, especially right now while she was too focused on dealing with the pain to fight effectively, was to lead anyone to Antonio.

"Vincent, go after her," Serrier ordered. "Bring her back if you can—Claude could use a new toy since we won't be done with the vampire for a while. Kill her if you can't."

Vincent kept his expression neutral as he strode to where she had stood and followed her spell.

In a nearby alley, Monique fell to her knees, her legs refusing to support her through the pain and numbness in her back. She knew she needed to get up, to move on in case she was followed, but her body simply would not cooperate. She hoped Antonio was right about the information she now carried, because if he was wrong as to its value to the Milice, she was dead.

"Monique!"

Her head spun at the sound of her name, seeing Vincent walking toward her. Fear gave her the strength to push past the numbness. She rose shakily to her feet and ran desperately for the subway stop, hoping the crowds would disperse her magical signature, making it harder for Vincent to follow her. She could not lead him to Antonio.

Moving helped spread the magic through her system, decreasing the pain she felt in any one place. She jumped down the steps, stumbling a little as she landed, then pressing on as fast as she could. She vaulted the turnstiles to the subway, ignoring the shouts of the RATP employees on duty. Rounding the corner, she dashed down one long corridor, casting the spell to take her elsewhere in the middle of a crowd, a dangerous move if one of them brushed against her as she cast, but it would make it nearly impossible for Vincent to follow.

She took off running again as soon as she was steady on her feet, in case Vincent managed to track her. She jumped another four times, crisscrossing the city before pain and exhaustion wore her down. With one last spell, she arrived on the river bank at the edge of the gangplank. Slowly, she walked down to the deck, leaning heavily on the rail as her strength started to fail. She had taken three steps onto the wooden planks when arms closed around her from behind. She started to struggle, to fight against whomever would take her from the safety Antonio had come to represent, but his voice growled in her ear.

"Where did you go?"

Her eyes widened as she felt the sun on her face. "Get inside!" she cried, trying to turn in his embrace.

Antonio scowled, but picked her up and carried her below. "Where did you go?"

"To find your friend," she answered honestly. "I've burned my bridges now, so I hope you're right about the Milice accepting me. Now explain to me how you were outside."

Antonio brushed aside her concern. "You found Orlando? Where is he?"

"In St. Denis," Monique replied. "I'll take you there, I promise, but I need a moment to recover first."

The pinched tone of her voice finally registered. "Where did he hurt you?"

"My back."

Setting her gently on the bed, he rolled her to her stomach, urging her to fold her knees beneath her, forehead to the covers so her back curved up for him. One hand smoothed her shirt up to reveal pale skin while the other settled on the swell of her hip, stroking soothingly. Carefully, not wanting to pierce anything vital with his fangs, he ran his tongue down the length of her spine, stopping just below her rib cage and biting shallowly. Her sigh of relief was audible as the connection between them began to ease her pain almost immediately.

Antonio fed only lightly, having taken more than his fill that morning, but he could not leave her hurting. They would need her well enough to lead them to Orlando and that meant relieving her pain.

Monique's eyes closed when she felt the slight pinch of his fangs, the immediate diminution of the pain in her spine a welcome surcease. The caressing hand on her hip brought other thoughts to the fore, but she pushed them aside, knowing time was of the essence, particularly since for some reason Antonio did not seem subject to diurnal rhythms as she had believed all vampires were.

Feeling her relax completely, Antonio closed the wounds with a last, tender lick, then raised his head, rolling her onto her side so he could see her face. "Why did you leave this morning?"

"I know Serrier's ways," Monique explained. "I was afraid if I waited too long, your friend wouldn't be where I could find him or wouldn't be in any shape to be rescued. I felt so much better that I just went. We should hurry, though. I'm sure Serrier suspects something, even if he doesn't know exactly what I have planned, because he sent one of his goons after me. Is it truly safe for you to move in sunlight?"

"As long as I've fed from you recently," Antonio replied honestly. "I'll explain everything later, I promise, but if you're right about the urgency, we should get to Milice headquarters now so we can rescue Orlando."

Monique nodded and rose from the bed, straightening her shirt to cover the marks on her back, as well as the ones from that morning on her belly. "If they don't believe me, I want you to kill me. I'd rather go from your fangs than from Serrier's torture."

"Don't talk that way," Antonio protested. "Even if Chavinier doesn't believe you, Jean will. He's desperate enough to rescue Orlando that he'll try anything. And when we're successful, the Milice won't have any choice but to offer you their protection."

Monique hoped he was right.

"ANTONIO?" SEBASTIEN exclaimed when he saw the vampire walk into Milice headquarters. "How are you here?"

"It's complicated," Antonio began, "but that doesn't matter right now. I need to see Marcel and Jean. I have information about where Orlando is."

Sebastien's eyes widened. "Come on. I haven't seen Jean, but Alain will be thrilled to hear it. How did you find him?"

"I didn't," Antonio answered honestly. "My partner did."

"Your partner?" Sebastien parroted.

Antonio nodded, opening the door again and gesturing for Monique to come inside. "My partner."

Sebastien looked back and forth between the vampire and the dark wizard. "This is going to get complicated," he predicted.

"Probably," Antonio admitted, "but she really has changed sides this time."

Sebastien did not comment. Antonio had told the truth last time, even knowing she was his partner, but he did not know how long that would be trusted. The lure of a partner's blood was far stronger than anyone had anticipated.

He took them to Marcel's office, tapping lightly on the door. At the general's call, he opened the door and followed Antonio and Monique inside. Immediately, the two wizards inside drew their wands.

"She's unarmed," Antonio said quickly, pulling Monique protectively behind him. "She came to me with information about Orlando, hoping that would be enough to earn our protection for real this time. I checked. I didn't taste any deceit."

"I think we'll let another vampire make that determination," Marcel said slowly, connecting Antonio's protective attitude and presence after dawn. "We can't afford to risk Orlando or our people if she's found a way to trick you because she's your partner."

Antonio bit back the snarl of protest. He had known they might question his word because of the partnership bond, but it did not stop his instinctive desire to keep her to himself.

"We can't afford to wait until tonight to find another unpaired vampire," Antonio warned them. "Monique told me Serrier moves his prisoners around, and he probably suspects she's betrayed him, so time is of the essence."

"I'll do it," Justin offered with a quick glance at Catherine next to him. He squeezed her hand reassuringly, a silent promise that he was not looking to replace her in any way, only to help a fellow vampire. She squeezed back, then released his hand so Justin could cross the room. She kept her wand trained on the possible turncoat, though, not about to risk her partner's safety until she knew more.

"It's okay," Antonio reassured Monique as the other vampire approached, though he had to fight himself to keep his tone even. He wanted to promise her no other vampire would ever touch her, but he had to retain his rationality, at least until she was vindicated, or he would lose all standing within the alliance. "Just let him bite your wrist for a moment so he can confirm what I already know."

Monique nodded and held out her hand tentatively.

Well aware of his partner's eyes on his back and Antonio's on his face, Justin kept his actions as clinical as possible as he lifted the woman's hand to his lips and bit into the smooth flesh. He could taste the dark magic in her blood like an oily sheen he would never be able to stomach on a regular basis, but he could also sense her desire to leave that world behind and her willingness to tell what she knew. He lifted his head, looking around for the trashcan. Finding it, he spat the blood into it, not wanting any blood but Catherine's nourishing him. "She's telling the truth."

Chapter 40

THEY KNELT on the sand next to the small lake in the center of the bois de Vincennes, wizard and vampire on either side of the cloth-shrouded body. Jean's eyes were closed as he listened to Raymond's quiet chanting. The air around them stirred gently, brought to life by his words, brushing over them, over Karine, as Raymond offered her breath. Water came next, anointing her, cleansing her for her return to the elements. He called fire to dance along her limbs, consuming it, turning her to ash. Raymond wished Thierry was there to perform the final step of the ritual, consigning her ashes to the earth, for he had the least affinity with that element. But he was not, and Jean had not wanted anyone else involved—so Raymond concentrated on the last part of the chant, the soil responding to his call, enfolding the ashes into their embrace: ashes to ashes, dust to dust.

Jean remained quiet as silence fell over the grove, letting nature's peace seep into his soul, settling his grief, calming his loss. His hand brushed across the loam where Karine would rest for eternity, a final, whispered good-bye hovering on his lips. He knelt in silence, head bowed, as he prayed for the repose of her soul.

The ritual finished, Raymond settled into stillness, taking refuge in meditation as he gave Jean the time he needed to find closure. Later, he would offer comfort as best he could, but for the moment, he was not the lover or the partner. He was the priest, his only task to accompany the griever on his journey.

Funereal devotion completed, Jean's thoughts turned to all the times he and Karine had spent together, the nights he had come to her, taking her blood and her body, freely offered but always with the unspoken hope for more than he could give in return. His feelings of guilt returned, more strongly than ever. He had taken what he needed because it was easy and attractive without ever considering what she needed. That he offered each time not to return, the words that had allowed him to justify each visit, now seemed an empty gesture, for he had known—until it suited him to ignore it—that she would never send him away, that she would open her door and her body to him whenever he asked. "I'm sorry, Karine," he murmured. "For not being the man you needed me to be, for not being there when you needed me, but only when I needed you, for not realizing what your devotion would cost you. Rest in peace, my dove."

Raising haunted eyes to meet Raymond's steady gaze, he nodded decisively, rocking to his feet. "Let's go. She's at peace and I can do nothing else for her now. We have to find Orlando before this ritual becomes a necessity once again."

They had just regained the path through the woods when Raymond's phone vibrated in his pocket. "Payet."

"Is Jean with you?"

"Yes. Why?"

"How soon can you get here? We've got a lead on Orlando."

"Hold on." He turned to Jean. "Do you have your repère on you?"

Jean nodded. "We're in the bois de Vincennes," he told Marcel. "Send someone to get Jean and we can be there in a matter of minutes."

"What's going on?" Jean asked when Raymond hung up.

"We're going after Orlando."

"THEY'RE IN the bois de Vincennes," Marcel announced. "Catherine, would you go get Jean so we can get this show on the road?"

She nodded and checked the locator map on the wall, fixing their position in her mind before casting the spell. Moments later, she was back with Jean, Raymond right behind them.

"What's going on?" Raymond asked immediately.

"It seems Serrier's cruelty has finally begun to alienate his followers," Marcel replied, canting his head toward where Monique stood with Antonio hovering protectively at her side. "Monique saw Orlando a few hours ago."

"What are we waiting for?" Jean exclaimed. "Let's go!"

"Thierry and Alain are gathering as many wizards as we can find on short notice. If we go in without sufficient numbers, we won't rescue him and we'll be worse off than we are now," Marcel cautioned. "I know you're worried about him—we all are—but he was unharmed when Monique saw him, and Alain's been checking on him periodically. Yes, we run the risk of Serrier moving him, but it's less of a risk than going in unprepared."

"Has he changed the signature on his wards?" Raymond asked Monique, assuming that Marcel had determined her trustworthiness.

"Not as of this morning," Monique replied honestly. "He trusts to the price on your head to keep you out of where he doesn't want you."

"And he was right, until today," Raymond agreed. "I can bring down his wards," he told Marcel. "It may take a few minutes, and he'll know I'm doing it, but I can get us inside."

"Then we just have to wait for Thierry and Alain to finish assembling a strike force," Marcel replied. "They'll be waiting for us in the Salle des Cartes."

"Let's go, then," Jean urged, his need to see Orlando safe again growing stronger with each passing minute, the memory of the abuse Karine suffered only adding vehemence to his voice.

"Remember," Thierry told the assembled wizards as Marcel, Jean and the others walked into the Salle des Cartes, "this is a rescue mission. Whatever else we do—or don't do—we must get Orlando out. Alain will lead the team searching for him, in the hopes their bond will guide him. The rest of us are there to keep Serrier's forces from impeding them. Once the team rescues Orlando, we'll see how things look. If we can capture or kill Serrier, we will. If their numbers are too great, we'll get out too. We'll have other chances at him, but this is our best chance at rescuing our captured comrade."

Seeing the others come in, he nodded to Jean. "I assume you'll want to go with Alain."

"Yes," Jean confirmed. "If anyone sees the rogue, take him down, but don't destroy him. That honor belongs to the Cour, and I want justice done properly."

Thierry tapped the locator map with his wand and the view changed, bringing up a roughly sketched floorplan. "This is where Serrier was holding Orlando this morning," he explained, pointing out the room where Monique had seen the vampire. "It isn't a holding cell, so we probably won't find him there, but we'll start there anyway since it's his last known location." He traced the quickest route from the entrance to the office. "Alain will lead his team this way. Catherine, you'll take your team down the right side and I'll lead a team down the left side to run interference and check those rooms for Orlando as well."

"What about me?" Raymond asked.

"Alain won't be able to bring Orlando out," Thierry reminded them. "I'm hoping you'll do that when we find him." He did not add that he was trusting Raymond to watch Alain's back and make sure he did not do anything ill-advised. "Of us all, you have the best idea of the way Serrier's mind works. You might see something that'll help you find him, or keep you from triggering a trap."

THEY HAD debated waiting for cover of darkness to attack, but neither Alain nor Jean had been willing to let any more time pass with Orlando in Serrier's hands. They arrived a few at a time in and around l'Université Paris 8, the Vincennes Saint-Denis campus, regrouping around the building on avenue de Stalingrad where Monique had last seen Orlando. The street was unusually quiet for a weekday afternoon, a fact that made Thierry nervous—but they were committed now, even if Serrier had turned Monique's defection into a trap. He trusted the vampires' acuity enough to believe her information was not intentional bait, but he knew better than to underestimate the dark leader.

When everyone was in place, he signaled Raymond, who began the work of taking down the wards surrounding the building. The entire squadron braced for the counterattack, sure Serrier would not simply let Raymond undo his protective shields, but nothing stirred in the building.

Thierry frowned. "Hold your positions," he ordered as Raymond continued to work unimpeded. His suspicions deepened as Raymond lowered his wand and still no attack came. "The building's empty," he muttered to Sebastien next to him. "He figured out we were coming and he's retreated elsewhere."

"We still have to check it out."

"I know," Thierry agreed, "but if we find Orlando here, it'll only be a body."

"Alain would already know if he was gone," Sebastien insisted. "Even with the shields up, he'd feel that loss instantly."

"Move out," Thierry ordered the three groups of wizards, "but be careful. This is too easy. My guess is he's got this place booby trapped from top to bottom."

"Can't we just check to see if the building is empty?" Catherine asked.

"That'll tell us if there are any wizards inside, but it won't tell us about Orlando," Raymond replied from her other side. "The vampires don't have auras our magic can pick up."

"They wouldn't leave him inside alone, would they?"

Raymond shrugged. "Why not? It's the perfect bait to draw us inside—where, as Thierry said, he's probably planted who knows what kind of traps. We'll just have to be careful."

"We're wasting time," Alain growled. "Let's get started."

They spread out as planned, storming the door, then breaking into three groups. They worked their way through the building, alert for anything that could help them find Orlando or harm them in their search.

Catherine's patrol took the right corridor, moving carefully as they checked room after empty room. She could tell it had not been long since people had used this space—the tables had clear spaces in the dust where things had obviously sat until a few hours ago—but nothing remained to give any hint of who they had been or where they had gone.

Pulling the door shut behind her, her shoulder brushed the door jamb and pain suddenly lanced down her arm, leaving it numb. She cursed under her breath, Justin at her side instantly. "Don't touch anything," she ground out between clenched teeth, "without checking it for spells first." She shook her arm, trying to dispel the pain, but it intensified steadily until her fingers felt like someone was pounding nails into them. "Marie," she gasped, knowing the blonde woman had an interest in the healing arts, "can you numb my arm? I don't know what I got hit with, but it's a nasty one."

Marie frowned and ran her wand along Catherine's arm, trying to identify the spell. "How are you still standing?" she asked after a moment. "I can't heal it—you'll need a medic for that—but I think I can block it so it won't spread or get any worse."

"Do it," Catherine agreed. "I'll get it looked at properly when we get back to base."

At her side, Justin fought the urge to insist she return immediately. She took her responsibilities far too seriously to leave now, in the middle of a mission, when a bit of field first aid would be enough to let her keep going. Even so, he would watch her carefully and insist she go back at the first sign of weakness.

On the other side of the building, Thierry's patrol encountered a different set of traps. He saw and disabled the first two, but the third one exploded in his face, sending him reeling back into Sebastien's arms. He started fighting instantly, unable to shake the paranoia from the magic, his mind convinced the arms closing around him belonged not to his lover but to a monster out of his worst nightmares, preparing to rend him limb from limb. The creature's grip was implacable, though.

"Thierry, what is it?" Sebastien demanded immediately when he felt Thierry struggling against him. "It's me, Sebastien. What's wrong? What did the spell do to you?"

At their side, Charlotte cast a revealing spell on the spot where the original spell had been. "It's a fear spell," she told them, though only Sebastien registered the words. "I can try to counter it, at least enough for him to hear what you're saying."

"Do it," Sebastien agreed, his voice tense with worry as Thierry fought him. "Relax, Thierry," he murmured. "I've got you. You're safe now. Just let Charlotte help you."

Charlotte cast a dampening spell, knowing it would not hurt Sebastien but would hopefully help Thierry.

After a moment, his struggles eased, rationality returning as Charlotte's spell took effect. He recognized the voice in his ear, not a monster's growls, but Sebastien's worried tones, the arms holding him intending to comfort, not injure. "You can let me go now," he told Sebastien, his voice approaching its normal tone.

Sebastien's arms tightened for a moment, a silent embrace and reassurance, before releasing his lover. He wanted to kiss him, but this was neither the time nor the place.

Alain led his patrol down the central hallway, looking for the room where Monique had last seen Orlando. He reminded himself to be cautious, to check for traps, but the need to rush, to find his lover, overruled his good sense and he ran headlong down the hall. He knew the minute he tripped the spell that he had done it—but by the time he realized it, the gas had surrounded him, befuddling his senses.

He recoiled several steps, shaking his head as he fought the hallucinogen. The sound of his name drew his attention. "Orlando?" he called, turning toward the sound. "Where are you?"

"Alain!" Raymond called sharply, realizing the other wizard had gotten caught by the hallucinatory vapor. "You triggered one of Serrier's traps. Come back with us."

The words did not even penetrate the haze in Alain's mind. He knew only that Orlando was somewhere nearby, calling for help.

Raymond cursed softly, sure Serrier would have mined the hallway to maximum effect. "He's going to get himself killed," he muttered to Jean. "We've got to stop him."

He cast a spell to disperse the gas before they followed Alain down the hall. The magic did not seem to have reached him, though, because he continued to shout Orlando's name, following the voice in his head with no regard for anything but his absent lover.

"Merde!" Raymond cursed as he watched the wizard blunder into one spell after another, pain contorting his body, tearing screams from his throat as he continued forward, forcing his body to cooperate in his desperation to find Orlando.

Deciding this had gone on long enough, Jean stopped him by the simple expedient of tackling him to the floor. Alain struggled. "What are you doing?" he demanded. "Why won't you let me go to him? Orlando's hurt. Can't you hear him calling for me? Or have you switched sides suddenly? You've betrayed him. You've betrayed all of us!"

"Snap out of it," Jean ordered, catching Alain's chin in an implacable grip and forcing the blue eyes to focus on him, to see him. "I want to find him as badly as you do, but he's not here."

Alain's face fell as his senses cleared, the ring of authority in Jean's voice penetrating the lingering haze. "I could hear him. He was begging me to save him."

"I know," Jean replied. "And we will. Somehow we will, but he isn't here."

Alain nodded, heart pounding with desperation and disappointment as he realized what had happened. "You can let me up now. I won't do anything stupid, but we have to finish checking the rooms. Even if he isn't here, we might find something, anything to give us an idea where he is."

Jean did not hold out any realistic hope in that regard, but they could not afford to miss any lead, however small. Rising to his feet, he offered Alain his hand.

They checked three more rooms before they met up with the other patrols at the other end of the warren of chambers. Alain walked into the last one, little more than a tiny closet, and knew. Orlando had been here. He sank slowly to his knees, façade of self-control shattering at realizing how close they had come without succeeding.

At the door, Thierry took in the sight before him and backed out, using his body to block the view inside. He pulled the door shut and turned to the other wizards. "Catherine, take your patrol and go back to base. Tell Marcel we didn't find anything useful and see if the defector knows anywhere else we can look. Charlotte, take my patrol and Alain's and secure the building. If Serrier comes back, we don't want this space to be accessible to him."

The two women nodded and followed his orders. "I don't know how long he's going to be able to do this," Thierry said to Sebastien, Raymond and Jean when the others were gone. "I'm worried about his sanity."

Sebastien nodded his head in agreement. "All we can do is keep his spirits up and remind him that he knows Orlando is still here."

Thierry frowned. "That doesn't seem to be enough."

Inside the room, Alain dropped the mental shields he had erected while they were preparing for battle, letting the connection with Orlando slam back into place, filling him with the vampire's love and faith. He bit back a sob at the latter, their current failure making him question Orlando's unwavering belief that Alain would rescue him. The wizard would certainly keep trying, but he did not know what else to do.

Some of his frustration must have carried through the bond because a new wave of love and reassurance came back to him, warming him, restoring his equilibrium. He could not sense any pain, so at the very least, Monique's defection and Serrier's subsequent relocation had bought Orlando some time in that respect, but Alain was painfully aware of the passing hours and the fact that Orlando would have to feed again before long. He had warned his lover when they first realized the extent of the Aveu de Sang that it was a dangerous choice in time of war, but Orlando had brushed aside those concerns. A part of Alain wished he had been more insistent then, if only so Orlando would have a better chance of survival now. From what little Orlando had said of his previous captivity, Alain guessed that feeding allowed him to heal from his injuries enough to recover between bouts of torture. That had been an option when Thurloe had him, but now Orlando had no choice. He could feed from Alain or not at all.

"I'm sorry," he whispered. "I've condemned you."

THE WAVE of negativity that swamped Orlando surprised him, but he pushed it aside. He understood Alain's fear. If their positions were reversed, he would have been frantic as well, but Orlando had more faith than that. For the moment, he was unharmed, amused even at the pathetic attempts to weaken him. Serrier had so clearly bought into the same stereotypes vampires had fought for centuries. Fortunately, the legends and old wives' tales could do nothing to harm him.

He was not so naïve that he expected Serrier to stop with that—the dark wizard wanted to win this war and to do that he had to neutralize the vampires—but even then, the worst Serrier could do to him was destroy him. Anything else would be nothing more than his maker had done, and Orlando knew he could survive that again if he had to. He clung to Sebastien's assurance that given enough time, he would be able to go as long as a couple of weeks without feeding. He doubted their Aveu de Sang was old enough to support that much time apart yet, but he had fed less than twenty-four hours ago and was not feeling even the first stirrings of hunger yet. They had time. He was not ready to leave Alain, but if the worst happened, he would go to his rest knowing what it was to love and be loved. Focusing on that, he ran his hand over his chest, sending pulse after pulse of love and desire in Alain's direction. He needed his lover determined, not defeated. Slowly, he felt Alain's frustration give way beneath the force of Orlando's emotions. A smile grew on the vampire's face as he imagined everything they would do to each other when they were finally reunited. He did not try to temper his body's reaction or his mind's, consciously sharing as much of his thoughts and emotions with Alain as he could. He only hoped it was enough.

Don't miss the epic finale:

Reparation in Blood

Sequel to *Conflict in Blood*
Partnership in Blood: Volume Four

By Ariel Tachna

The war is at a fever pitch with both sides stretched to the limit, when the dark wizards score a shocking victory and capture Orlando St. Clair. Haggard with worry and grief at the separation from his lover, Alain fears that even if they find Orlando, the vampire's heart and mind may be far too broken to save.

Knowing the Alliance teeters on the brink, Christophe Lombard, the oldest, most powerful vampire in Paris, leaves his self-imposed seclusion to join the fight. Alain's lost friend Eric Simonet, who betrayed him to join the dark wizards, is faced with a choice between revenge and redemption. And Jean, enraged by Orlando's capture, faces the most agonizing decision in his unlife as the final battle looms: Will their actions lead to the shattering of the Alliance or the salvation of the world?

Chapter 1

THIERRY FROWNED as he sat at the kitchen table watching Alain. It had not even been twenty-four hours since Orlando was captured and already his best friend looked haggard, physical and emotional exhaustion wreaking havoc on him. Thierry feared what would happen if those hours stretched into days. He was even more afraid of them stretching into weeks—weeks Orlando did not have, since he could only feed from Alain.

His mind raced with possibilities for finding the missing vampire. Night patrols were searching every location Monique Leclerc, the defector wizard, could identify as a place Serrier had used in the hopes of catching a break and finding Orlando that way, but she had been very honest about the fact that the dark leader deliberately kept his forces fragmented so that anyone captured could only reveal a portion of his plans and hideouts. Thierry was not completely sure how he felt about placing so much importance on her information, but it was the best lead they had at the moment since the wizards they captured during the battle at place Pigalle either knew nothing of value or feared Serrier's retribution should they talk more than they feared going to jail. Thierry was not sure he blamed them. With the exception of Raymond, every wizard who had talked in exchange for a lighter sentence had met a nasty end in prison, despite the best efforts of the wardens.

He watched helplessly as Alain pushed the chair back, the legs scraping harshly across the white tiles on the kitchen floor. His face contorted, he began pacing, a caged lion with no way to escape the confines of its cell. "You're going to wear yourself out and then you'll be no good to Orlando when we do find him," Thierry scolded, though he knew his admonishment would meet with scorn.

He was right.

"Like you'd be sitting here calmly if Sebastien were the one in their hands," Alain snarled.

"No, I wouldn't be," Thierry agreed, "and you'd be sitting where I am, reminding me to take care of myself."

"I should be out searching for him," Alain protested. "I have the best chance of sensing him if they've got him hidden!"

"Maybe," Thierry allowed, "but you can't go with every patrol—that would take too long. It's faster to let them do their jobs while you rest. We aren't sending inexperienced people into the sites. They know Serrier's tricks."

Alain shook his head, but Thierry ignored him. "You've barely slept since he was taken, except for the few hours I knocked you out. You can't go on like that and expect to be able to feed Orlando when he *is* rescued." He emphasized the word *is*, absolutely refusing to consider what might happen to both Alain and Orlando if they could not find the vampire in time.

Alain's face crumpled. "You don't understand," he insisted. "He can't feed from anyone else but me, so he's going to be slower to recover from whatever they do to him." He struggled to explain thoughts and feelings that defied rationality. "He's the other half of me, Thierry. It feels like my soul's being torn in two, just being apart from him. And when I can feel him hurting, it's even worse. I can't rest because he can't."

Thierry did not ask how that had happened in less than a month. He did not have to. He had a partner of his own, albeit without the added depth of the brand on Alain's neck. He could not sense Sebastien's emotions the way Alain could sense Orlando's, but he knew he would be just as frantic, just as far beyond reason, if Sebastien were missing instead of simply out on his way to get Alain's clothes from Orlando's apartment.

"I do understand," Thierry replied softly. A slight blush stained his cheeks as he thought about everything that had transpired between Sebastien and himself since their first meeting, culminating in their lovemaking the night before.

The look on Thierry's face was so at odds with his usual demeanor that it roused Alain from his self-absorption. Not even Thierry's blush was enough to supplant Orlando in his thoughts, but Thierry had been his best friend for thirty years. He would not be much of a friend if he could not acknowledge the change in the other man's life, despite the turmoil in his own. "Being with Sebastien seems to agree with you. You look happy again in a way you haven't in a long time."

Thierry's blush deepened. "I knew from watching you and Orlando together that making love with a vampire would be even more amazing than just having one feed from me, but I hadn't even come close to imagining what it felt like to have his fangs in my neck when we…. Sorry," he broke off, seeing the odd look on Alain's face, "too much information."

"It's not that," Alain replied, his voice tight with suppressed emotion. "It's just that we never… Orlando never fed from me while we made love. He was afraid he'd hurt me."

"Merde," Thierry cursed under his breath. "I'm sorry, Alain. I can't seem to say anything right tonight."

"There isn't anything to say," Alain said hoarsely. "He had his reasons and I have to respect that." He turned away, not wanting Thierry to see the depth of his pain, made worse by the accidental comment. He should have known he could not hide from Thierry, though. A comforting hand settled on his shoulder.

"We'll get him back," Thierry promised, "and when we do, you can change his mind."

"That's the worst part," Alain rasped. "I think he *had* changed his mind, but there wasn't time. We got the news of the attack at place Pigalle and spent the evening focused on that. And then he was captured."

"Then in the office before we left, you weren't…?" Thierry began.

"He jerked me off as he fed, but that's hardly making love," Alain explained. "You arrived right at the end."

"I'm sorry. If I'd known, I wouldn't have interrupted," Thierry apologized.

Alain shrugged, but his emotions were raw in his voice. "You couldn't have known, but even if you had, there wasn't time. I wouldn't have wanted to share something that intimate for the first time in the office anyway. I just wish we'd had more time."

"You'll have the time," Thierry promised. "We'll get him back and end this war and you'll have the rest of your life to discover everything about each other. You have to believe that."

"You tell me that, and then you won't let me do anything to find him!" Alain shouted.

"What would you do that we aren't already doing?" Thierry demanded. "Tell me one thing you can do right now that no one else can do just as well and I'll stop hassling you to rest and let you go do it. One thing, Alain."

Alain opened his mouth to reply, only to shut it again, frustration easily visible on his face. "Damn it, Thierry, I can't just sit here and do nothing!"

"You aren't going to sit anywhere," Thierry replied firmly. "As soon as Sebastien gets back, you're going to take a shower, change clothes, and go to sleep, if I have to knock you out myself. On second thought, the shower can wait for tomorrow. You have to sleep or you won't be able to search tomorrow either. Orlando needs you strong, not on the verge of collapse."

"Fuck you," Alain snarled angrily, pulling away from Thierry and stalking toward the door. "I don't know why you think you know what's best for me, but you don't. Not this time. I'm not going to stay here and listen to your platitudes and condescending attitude. If you won't help me find him, then I'll do it on my own."

The words hurt, even knowing the irrationality that motivated them. They hurt enough that Thierry did not react immediately, biting back his own temper as he tried to keep the shouting match from escalating. Alain apparently did not need any input from Thierry to keep the argument going, though.

"Are you jealous?" Alain snapped, turning back when he reached the door. "Is that why you won't help me? Or are you just too interested in dragging Sebastien back into bed when he gets here to give a shit about what they're doing to Orlando?"

"Don't even go there," Thierry growled back, his temper getting the better of him. "You know I busted my balls last night and all day today trying to find him, but I'm exhausted, you're exhausted, and the only reason Sebastien isn't is because he's a vampire. There isn't any more we can do tonight."

"What's going on?" Sebastien asked, walking into the tense situation.

Alain's head turned, his glare transferring to the vampire, but whatever words sprang to his lips never passed them. Thierry hit him in the side with a sleeping spell before they could. Sebastien's quick reflexes kept the unconscious wizard from hitting the floor.

"You should have let him fall," Thierry muttered. "Ungrateful bastard."

Sebastien's eyebrows shot up. "What in the world happened?" he asked again, hefting Alain over his shoulder and starting toward the bedroom. "I've never seen you act that way toward Alain."

"Dump him in bed and I'll tell you," Thierry answered, the sting of Alain's accusations still strong.

Sebastien carried the other wizard into the guest room and settled him on the bed, pulling off his shoes so he could sleep more comfortably. He set down the bag of Alain's things he was carrying where the wizard would see it when he awoke and returned to the kitchen. "Okay, what's going on?"

Thierry sighed. "I haven't a fucking clue. We were talking—of course, he wants to keep searching for Orlando even though he's completely strung out—and then he asked about you… about us. I answered his question honestly because I've never had any secrets from him, and it hit a nerve. And the next thing I know, he's shouting at me, accusing me of keeping him from going after Orlando because I'm jealous of their bond or because I just want to get you in bed again. How can he think that?"

"He doesn't think it," Sebastien insisted. "He isn't thinking at all. He's absolutely out of his mind with worry and fear. Imagine what it would feel like to be forced to sit and watch Serrier torture Alain. You're in the room, but you can't say anything, can't do anything to stop it. All you can do is suffer with him. That's what Alain's going through with Orlando. He can't see it, but he can feel Orlando's pain, and he's helpless. And it's driving him to say and do things he doesn't mean and would never normally do. But he can't stop himself because he's hurting and so he lashes out at the people around him. He knows, on some level, that nothing he does would be enough to break your friendship and so he's letting all the filth inside him out at you."

"It wasn't even the things he said," Thierry mused softly, Sebastien's presence calming him. "It was the hateful way he said them, like he wanted to hurt me."

"He probably did," Sebastien admitted. "In some twisted way, it probably made him feel less alone to know you were miserable too." He took a deep breath and forced himself to remember the darkest days of his life. "When Thibaut died, I was angry at the universe. The cruel irony of the Aveu de Sang is that the Avoué can't be turned because his partner can't drain him or her, but in the first flush of love, I didn't consider that. He was young. I didn't think about what would happen when he was old. So there I was, holding the body of my Avoué, alone for the first time in almost sixty years. Vampires came to hold vigil with me, but I didn't want company. I wanted to be alone to grieve. The anger was eating me up inside so I lashed out at everyone, trying to drive them away. Some of them went, but one woman stayed and let me pour out all that ugliness until I was exhausted and had nothing else to give. I asked her finally why she put up with that, and she told me I had to get it out or go insane with it—and she refused to see another vampire perish from bottled-up grief. I never saw her again after that night. She came to comfort me and left again, taking my pain with her."

"So what will happen now?"

"I don't know," Sebastien admitted. "Alain's the human half of the Aveu de Sang, not the vampire half, and I don't know of any cases where the human lost the vampire rather than the other way around. I'm sure it's happened. I just don't know of any instances. And Orlando isn't lost. Missing, yes, but not lost, at least not yet, so Alain has hope to hold onto. Of course, that could complicate things, even make them worse as his grief wars with that hope. I just don't know."

"Can you think of any other way to find Orlando that we haven't already tried?" Thierry asked instead. "Alain can sense him. Can we use that?"

"Maybe," Sebastien replied. "I could always tell if Thibaut was home when I got there if I'd been out at night, could always tell when he came home even before I heard him moving around. Alain says it isn't directional, but he might be able to narrow down where to search by the strength of the feelings. We'll just have to experiment and see."

"It would be easy enough to create a grid in the city and check each one to see if the feeling got stronger or weaker," Thierry mused aloud. "The more areas we eliminate, the more we'd be able to concentrate our forces."

"And because Alain would have to be involved, it would ease some of his frustration at doing nothing."

"Not to mention giving him a reason not to block the bond the way Marcel wants him to do while he's on duty," Thierry added. "If that helps ease a little of his guilt, maybe he'll be able to focus more clearly on using the bond to tell us something useful in the search."

Sebastien nodded. "You should sleep, too, while he's out. If this morning was any indication, once your spell wears off, he'll be fighting to go again."

Thierry smiled sadly. "I used a stronger spell this time than last night. Hopefully that'll buy us a little more time, but you're right." He offered the vampire his hand. "I can't even imagine what torture he's going through." He shuddered. "I'm not jealous of their bond and I'm not unaware of how much Alain's hurting, but if he'd accused me of being glad it wasn't you, he'd have been right."

Sebastien took the outstretched hand, walking at Thierry's side toward their bedroom. "That's a perfectly normal reaction. I felt the same way when Laurent was killed. I wouldn't wish that pain on anyone, but I was ridiculously thankful it wasn't you."

Crossing the threshold, Thierry pulled the vampire's slighter form against his, holding on. Sebastien returned the embrace, their bodies resting together, each drawing strength and solace from the other's presence. With unspoken agreement, they undressed each other and climbed into bed, lying face to face, arms around each other in silent support until Thierry's eyes finally closed in sleep.

THE WAVE of anger Orlando felt from Alain surprised him. He understood the frustration, the fear, the grief, but this was a new emotion. The vampire felt his fangs begin to elongate, his hackles rising at the thought of someone upsetting his wizard.

He tried to project back calming thoughts, assuring Alain of his relative safety and of the depth of his love, but the emotions did not seem to penetrate. Concern growing, Orlando rose to pace the room. He did not know what had happened to work Alain up into the frenzy that came through their bond, but not being able to go to his lover, to soothe him, was a physical ache in Orlando's chest. Angrily, he rattled the door to his prison cell, but the lock was as secure as the first time he had tried.

As suddenly as the anger had begun, it ended, sending a jolt of panic through Orlando. It took a moment to realize that Alain was asleep. He frowned, the contrast between the vibrancy of the anger and the calm of Alain's sleeping mind striking him as odd, until he remembered that his lover was a wizard, undoubtedly surrounded by other wizards. He would not put it past Thierry or Marcel to put Alain to sleep, if that was what it took to calm him down.

Relaxing a little, he returned to the narrow cot that was the only furniture in the room, the springs poking him through the thin mattress. Still, Orlando thought, it could be worse. He could have nowhere to lie but on the stone floor.

The rattle of a key in the lock drew his attention. He rose to his feet, preferring to face whoever came through the door from a position of relative power. If he had the chance to fight, he intended to take it. The wizards could overpower him with their magic, but physically they were no match for his preternatural strength.

The big wizard, the one who used to be Alain's friend, stood at the door, wand in hand. "You're Eric Simonet, aren't you?" Orlando asked before the wizard could bind him.

The question took Eric completely off guard. "Why do you want to know?" he demanded.

"Alain told me about you," Orlando replied simply. "He misses you."

Eric frowned, not wanting to hear such things. They made his job so much more difficult. Especially now. "That's in the past," he ground out.

"For you, maybe, but not for him."

"You know him well?" Eric asked, remembering that he had seen this vampire fighting at Magnier's side during the battle where he was taken.

Orlando did not answer, unable to force himself to deny it, yet not willing to give the dark wizards any information that might help them.

Eric took the silence as an affirmation. "I have only one regret," he told the vampire. "That he and Thierry hate me now."

"They don't!" Orlando protested. "They would welcome you back with open arms."

"It's too late for that. Serrier's waiting for you."

Don't miss how the story started!

Alliance in Blood

Partnership in Blood: Volume One

By Ariel Tachna

Can a desperate wizard and a bitter, disillusioned vampire find a way to build the partnership that could save their world?

In a world rocked by magical war, vampires are seen by many as less than human, as the stereotypical creatures of the night who prey on others. But as the war intensifies, the wizards know they need an advantage to turn the tide in their favor: the strength and edge the vampires can give them in the battle against the dark wizards who seek to destroy life as they know it.

In a dangerous move and show of good will, the wizards ask the leader of the vampires to meet with them, so that they might plead their cause. One desperate man, Alain Magnier, and one bitter, disillusioned vampire, Orlando St. Clair, meet in Paris, and the fate of the world hangs in the balance of their decision: Will the vampires join the cause and form a partnership with the wizards to win the war?

http://www.dreamspinnerpress.com

Don't miss what happens next in

Covenant in Blood

Sequel to *Alliance in Blood*
Partnership in Blood:
Volume Two

By Ariel Tachna

The wizards and the vampires have forged an alliance based on blood and magic, hoping to turn the tide of the war against the dark wizards. A few wizard-vampire bonds are as successful as Alain Magnier's and Orlando St. Clair's, but some are much less so, leading to arguments, resentment, and outright fights between the allies despite their mutual goals.

Following his best friend Alain's example, Thierry Dumont determinedly forms a partnership with vampire Sebastien Noyer, despite the wizard's discomfort with being so close to a vampire—a man—so soon after his wife's death. But they find that desperation may be the key to forming a covenant that works: Thierry and Sebastien are almost immediately devoted to one another's safety.

With new strength behind it, the Alliance's leaders move to announce its existence to the whole world, hoping to rally support against the dark wizards who threaten to destroy life as they know it. Struggling to find its way in the expanding war, the Alliance discovers that despite its advantages, the partnerships are affecting the balance of magical power in the world, which may be an even bigger threat than the war itself.

A Partnership in Blood novel

Perilous Partnership

By Ariel Tachna

A year after the end of the war that brought them together, Raymond Payet and Jean Bellaiche have found a balance in their relationship: Jean drinks only Raymond's blood; Raymond sleeps only in Jean's bed. The demands of their public roles as president of l'Association Nationale de Sorcellerie and chef de la Cour of the Parisian vampires keep them busy dealing with fallout from the war and the alliance, particularly the not-always-successful partnerships between vampires and wizards.

The foundation of an institute to research and educate wizards and vampires about the implications of the partnership bonds only adds to those responsibilities. When political factions, both vampire and mortal, oppose their leaders' decisions, the stress begins to affect Raymond and Jean's deepening relationship. And when political opposition turns to vandalism and then to violence, they'll have to find a way to reconcile their personal and professional lives before external and internal forces pull them apart.

A Partnership in Blood novel

Reluctant Partnerships

By Ariel Tachna

Thanks to the efforts of Raymond Payet and l'ANS, vampires now have the same legal rights as mortals, and research at l'Institut Marcel Chavinier is focusing on the mysterious partnership bonds between wizards and vampires. But the battle for public opinion rages on. When Detective Adèle Rougier encounters Pascale Auboussu, a shy young woman turned into a vampire against her will, Raymond and Denis Langlois, chef de la Cour nearest the crime, fear a public relations nightmare.

The vampire responsible for Pascale's turning must be brought to justice, but Denis is distracted by an unlikely potential partner—Canadian researcher Martin Delacroix, who is spending a year's sabbatical at l'Institut—and Denis's lingering feelings for his deceased lover prompt him to reject the bond. There's no denying the attraction between them, though, and the allure of companionship is nearly as strong as Denis's grief.

Growing familiarity and yearning for a true mate may induce Adèle and Denis to soften their stances against new partnerships, but Adèle will have to accept a deeper intimacy with Pascale when she has never considered a relationship with a woman, and it will take a near-deadly attack to make Denis admit his most hidden desires. Now he has to hope Martin will be willing to stay.

A Partnership in Blood novel

Lycan Partnership

By Ariel Tachna

By the time the alpha of the Morvan werewolf pack approaches l'Institut Marcel Chavinier for help solving his people's fertility problems, pack numbers have dwindled and the remaining members are desperate. Though the wizards at l'Institut have no experience with werewolves, their lore, or their brand of magic, Raymond agrees to help.

At l'ANS headquarters, Raymond finds Marc Gourlin, a young wizard fascinated with werewolves. Marc agrees to visit the werewolves' home to study their rituals for the source of the problem. But when he arrives, he finds himself distracted by Adenet Silaire, the pack shaman. The attraction between them is powerful, but though Marc suspects he might be Adenet's mate, Adenet rebuffs him. Marc is a man, and Adenet's sense of responsibility will not let him take a male mate when the pack so desperately needs children.

Meanwhile, Jean and Raymond discover the Aveu de Sang allows a vampire's Avoué to calm his inner beast. For Jean and Orlando, this is wonderful news—but it only convinces Thierry how much Sebastien is missing out on because they cannot form an Aveu de Sang. Determined to give his partner everything he can, Thierry sets out to recreate the bond denied them by Sebastien's past.

A Partnership in Blood novel

Partnership Reborn

By Ariel Tachna

All his life, wizard Raphael Tarayaud has dreamed of a vampire—first as a friend, then as a lover. His search for his missing soul mate brings him to the attention of Sebastien Noyer, one of his childhood heroes. While Sebastien isn't his soul mate, he could be the perfect partner for Raphael's best friend Kylian Raffier.

As strange coincidences mount up, Raphael offers his research expertise to try and help Kylian and Sebastien understand what is happening to them, though the more he learns, the less he likes it. But it won't keep him from fighting with everything he has to secure Kylian's future.

When he finally meets Jean Bellaiche, former chef de la Cour and grieving widower, the meeting is disastrous, but Raphael can't let it go. He doesn't stand a chance with Jean—who could compete with the ghost of Raymond Payet?—but nothing can stop him from dreaming.

ARIEL TACHNA lives outside of Houston with her husband, her daughter and son, and their cat. Before moving there, she traveled all over the world, having fallen in love with both France, where she found her husband, and India, where she dreams of retiring someday. She's bilingual with snippets of four other languages to her credit and is as in love with languages as she is with writing.

Visit Ariel at her website: http://www.arieltachna.com or on Facebook: https://www.facebook.com/ArielTachna, or e-mail her at arieltachna@gmail.com.

THE PATH
ARIEL TACHNA

Lang Downs Series

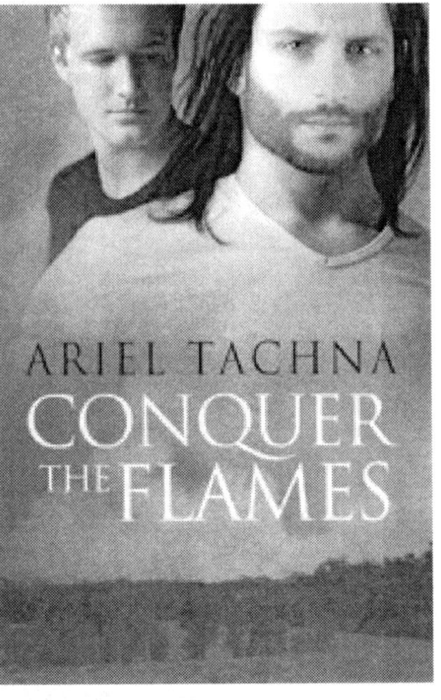

Hot Cargo Series

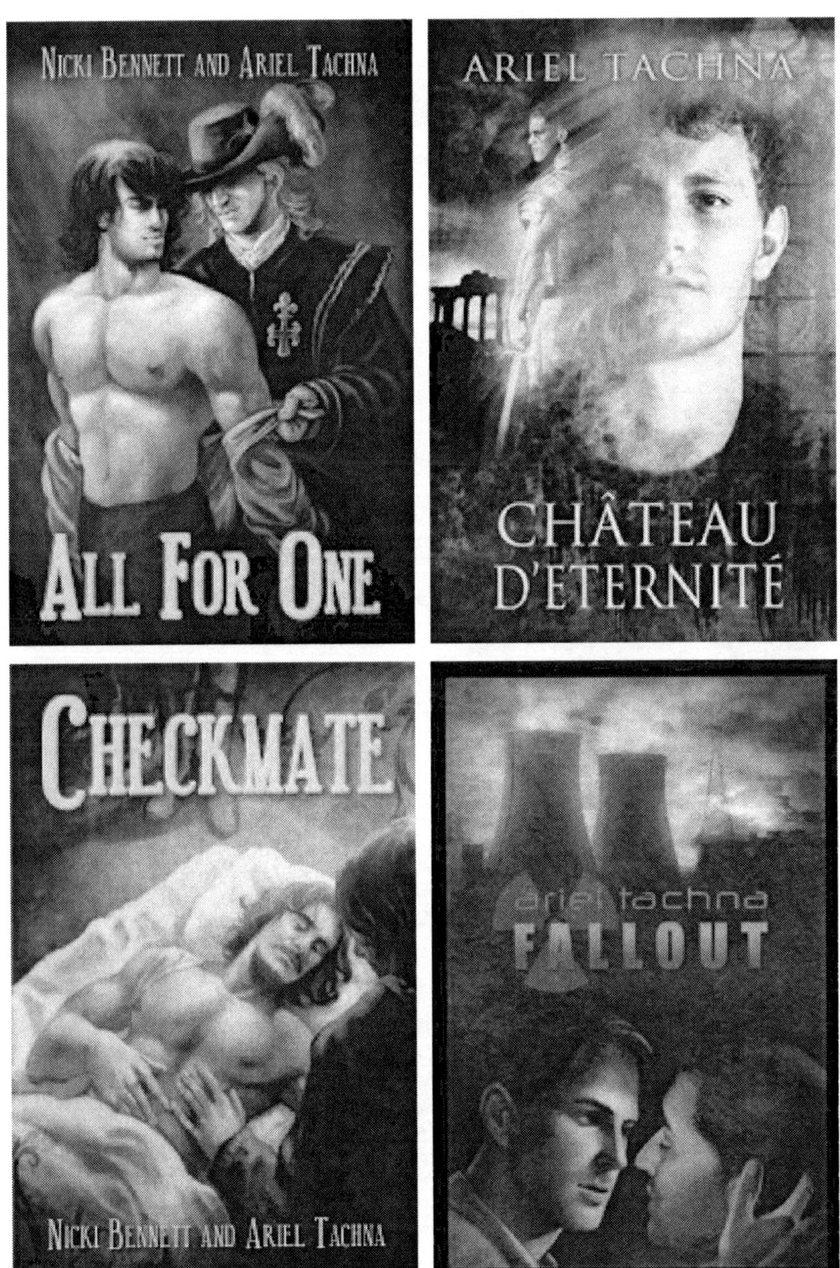
NICKI BENNETT AND ARIEL TACHNA
ALL FOR ONE
ARIEL TACHNA
CHÂTEAU
D'ETERNITÉ
CHECKMATE
NICKI BENNETT AND ARIEL TACHNA
ariel tachna
FALLOUT

HER TWO DADS
ARIEL TACHNA

ARIEL TACHNA
the Inventor's Companion

the Matelot
Ariel Tachna

Once in a LIFETIME
ARIEL TACHNA

Ariel
Tachna
OUT OF
THE FIRE
OVER
DRIVE
ARIEL TACHNA
REDISCOVERY
ARIEL TACHNA
A
ROSE
Among the
RUINS
ARIEL TACHNA

TESTAMENT
TO Love
ARIEL TACHNA

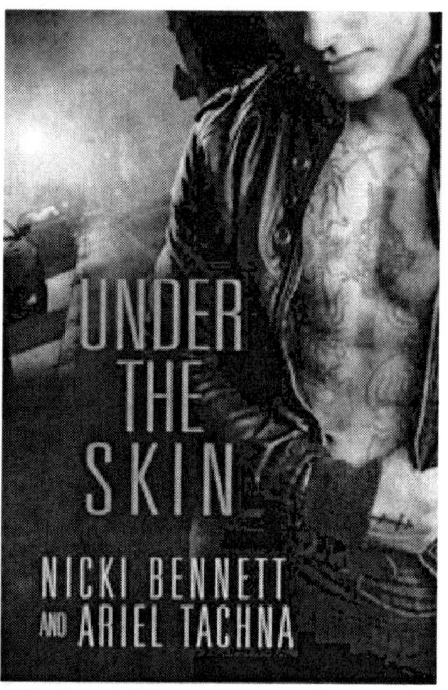
UNDER
THE
SKIN
NICKI BENNETT
AND ARIEL TACHNA

Dreamspinner Press
Fairy Tales:
WHY NILEAS
LOVED
THE SEA
Ariel Tachna

Exploring Limits Series

Exploring Limits Series

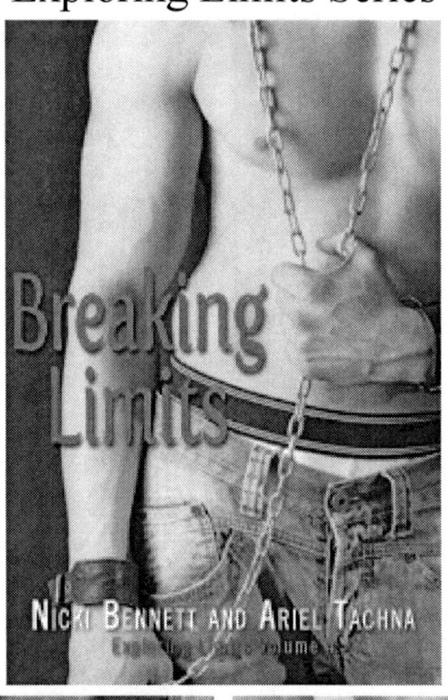

FOR
MORE
OF THE
BEST
GAY
ROMANCE
Dreamspinner Press
DREAMSPINNERPRESS.COM

CPSIA information can be obtained
at www.ICGtesting.com
Printed in the USA
FFOW02n1559271014
8322FF